In a previous life Jo Carnegie was deputy editor at *heat* magazine, interviewing stars from George Clooney, Simon Cowell and Justin Timberlake, to Posh 'n' Becks and Cheryl Cole. As well as still interviewing celebs on a freelance basis, she is also a regular contributor on the radio. *Party Games* is Jo's sixth novel.

Log on to www.jocarnegie.co.uk to find out what Jo is up to, and follow her constant stream of consciousness on Twitter @JoCarnegie 1.

PARTY GAMES

Jo Carnegie

CORGI BOOKS

TRANSWORLD PUBLISHERS
61–63 Uxbridge Road, London W5 5SA
A Random House Group Company
www.transworldbooks.co.uk

PARTY GAMES
A CORGI BOOK: 9780552166812

First publication in Great Britain
Corgi edition published 2013

A CIP catalogue record for this book
is available from the British Library.

Addresses for Random House Group Ltd companies outside the UK
can be found at: www.randomhouse.co.uk
The Random House Group Ltd Reg. No. 954009

The Random House Group Limited supports The Forest Stewardship
Council® (FSC®), the leading international forest-certification
organisation. Our books carrying the FSC label are printed on
FSC®-certified paper. FSC is the only forest certification scheme
supported by the leading environmental organisations, including
Greenpeace. Our paper procurement policy can be found
at www.randomhouse.co.uk/environment

Typeset in 11/14pt Palatino by
Kestrel Data, Exeter, Devon.
Printed and bound by
CPI Group (UK) Ltd, Croydon, CR0 4YY.

2 4 6 8 10 9 7 5 3 1

MIX
Paper from
responsible sources
FSC
www.fsc.org   FSC® C016897

To my family

Chapter 1

The pain was starting to kick in. The sun was hot on Catherine's back, the thin running vest sticking to her skin. Arms pumping, she started down the home straight. Beethoven blared out from a passing Land Rover, the clash of classical music disappearing off into the distance.

The pavement became more uneven and busy, forcing her to slow down. It wasn't a hardship. Beeversham High Street wasn't like any she'd known in London, with its wide grass verges and ancient oak trees. Whimsical signs advertised antique shops and galleries, while cafés seduced passers-by with the baking equivalent of an Amsterdam window show: plump cakes with cherries like nipples, silky fingers of sugared shortbread, jammy buns oozing cream. Freshly watered hanging baskets stood out like a mistress's jewels against the yellow stone. The whole place brimmed with an alluring charm.

As she approached the middle of the High Street, Mr Patel was coming out of his shop.

'Catherine!' he cried. 'Your favourite olives are back in!'

Gasping a thank you Catherine put her head down. She shot past the open windows of Bar 47 and the drinkers enjoying a convivial sundowner. At the market square she turned right and started up Lamb Lane.

The steep climb had defeated many a pedestrian and the blood started to roar in Catherine's ears. The almshouses appeared on her left, before the welcome sight of the church came into view, looming down from the top of the hill. Arriving at St Cuthbert's she collapsed over the gate, sucking in deep, restorative breaths.

Her watch showed a personal best. That earnt her a bloody big glass of wine later. As the feel-good endorphins started to surge through her body, she stood up and turned round.

Catherine would never get tired of this view. Valley rolling as far as the eye could see, as if someone had taken a luxurious green rug and shaken it out. The land dived down low and swept up to perilous heights. Nestled in the middle, like a puddle of melting gold, was the market town she now called home.

A periwinkle sky framed the idyllic scene. The month of May had been more like a July, with un-interrupted sunshine and soaring temperatures. Weather forecasters had excitedly predicted an Indian summer. Everyone hoped they were right, for once.

One thing jarred in the genteel landscape. Perched high in the hills, like a predatory eagle about to take flight, stood a gleaming white box of a house. Beau

Rainford's controversial modernist creation, 'Ridings'. An appropriate name, considering how many women Beau was meant to have bedded. He'd caused local uproar when he'd ripped down an old farmhouse to build his abode of sharp angles and lines. There had been mutterings about dodgy planning permission and people being paid off but nothing had ever been proved. Now it looked down on the town, the mirrored windows matching the arrogant disdain of the owner. Beeversham's notorious bad boy was doing nothing to build his bridges.

On the opposite side of the valley, facing Ridings like a reproving older brother, stood Beeversham's most famous landmark. Blaize Castle, or rather the ruins of the castle, were surrounded by shimmering meadows of wild grasses. The place was a mecca for American tourists visiting the area. The remote location made it popular with local kids and amorous couples bent on misbehaving.

Catherine could have stayed where she was all evening, but John would start wondering where she'd got to. She started a leisurely jog back down Lamb Lane. By the time she got back to the High Street, she was so deep in thought about what to have for dinner that she didn't see the black Bentley coming too fast in the opposite direction. It sounded its horn, shattering the peaceful evening and making her leap a foot in the air.

'Jesus!' she yelled, attracting a disapproving look from an old couple walking by with an obese Jack Russell.

As the car swept past she got a glimpse of a stunningly

beautiful woman on the nearside of the back seat. The woman glared at Catherine with feline eyes before the car zoomed off, leaving her in the road like a piece of discarded litter.

Catherine watched the POW 1 number-plate disappear down the street, carrying its famous cargo. Vanessa Powell, one half of Beeversham's celebrity couple. It was fair to say Catherine and Vanessa had history. In fact, Vanessa loathed Catherine. When she'd been editor of the renowned *Soirée* magazine Catherine had run an article on Vanessa that had nearly wrecked the celebrity's reputation.

Seven years on, Catherine still cringed every time she thought about it. It had been the press week from hell when a story had come in about Vanessa Powell, the then model-cum-socialite being paid to appear at an African dictator's birthday party. What's more, she'd apparently made her entrance rising topless out of a six-foot strawberry layer cake. Print deadline looming, Catherine had assumed a vacuous vamp like Vanessa Powell would be desperate for any publicity and had decided to run it.

It had turned out to be completely untrue. Vanessa had never even met the African dictator, let alone had any intimate dealings with layer cakes. Her lawyers had come out swinging, and Valour Publishing had ended up paying substantial damages. Catherine had nearly lost her job over it. The worst thing of all was the grovelling apology she'd been forced to write in her Editor's Letter, describing Vanessa as 'an icon for their generation'.

The women had run into each other at a high-profile

fashion exhibition a few months later, where Vanessa had 'accidentally' emptied her glass of champagne down Catherine's new Armani suit. Conveniently, a bank of photographers had been on hand to capture the whole thing. The gossip pages had dined out on it for weeks.

It was one of life's bitter ironies that they'd ended up living in the same town. Thankfully Catherine was yet to have an encounter with her Ladyship at the mini market. The only time the residents of Beeversham saw the Powells was on TV or in *OK!* magazine, usually gushing about their wonderful marriage. Once the lights and cameras stopped it was like the celebrity couple ceased to exist.

Catherine had a sudden pang of yearning for her old life when she'd been a person of influence, lawsuits and all. *Now I'm more of a desperate housewife.* That thought was replaced by the one playing endlessly in her head at the moment that, despite all her and John's enthusiastic efforts, she still wasn't pregnant.

Crossing the road, she started for home.

Chapter 2

The Bentley continued the journey towards home. The suave man sitting beside Vanessa gave a dismissive sniff. 'Was that Catherine Connor back there?'

'Yes.'

'Has she cut her hair?'

'Why would I notice?'

'Makes her look like a bloke. I always thought she was hiding a cock in there somewhere.'

Vanessa's husband's comment wasn't made entirely out of loyalty. Conrad Powell had hated Catherine ever since a film reviewer in *Soirée* had described his acting as 'more wooden than a Pinocchio convention'. He'd been positively gleeful when the subsequent revelations about Catherine had come out.

He went back to scrolling furiously down his Black-Berry. 'She looked a mess. Little Miss Hotshot isn't so hot now she hasn't got her precious magazine to fall back on, is she?'

Vanessa turned to look at her husband. His matinée-idol looks showed no sign of fading, the smooth complexion helped out by discreet jabs of Botox. Conrad looked every inch the face of 'Valiant Hair Colour For Men (Dark Coffee)', his most successful campaign to date.

'It went well today, didn't it?' she asked.

Conrad glanced up again, giving her a flash of deep chocolate eyes. 'I suppose, if Vitamin Vite is about to take over the world as you say it is. The way the PRs were having orgasms over it, you'd think they'd discovered the cure for bloody cancer.'

She laid a manicured hand on his knee. 'You were fabulous, Conrad.'

'I just fucking hate these things, all those people mooning at you like brainless sheep.'

Vanessa studied her husband's handsome profile. She knew these things were hard for him. When they'd first met Conrad had been the more famous one. A household name as the dashing Dr Debonair on BBC1's hit show *The Saviours*, his big break had come when he'd been cast alongside Colin Firth in the Hollywood remake of *Of Mice and Men*. He had been convinced it was the start of Hollywood stardom. She could still remember the black moment when her husband had discovered his scenes had ended up on the cutting-room floor.

She had urged him to get straight back to work, but long hours on a TV drama didn't cut the mustard with him any more. Conrad rejected 90 per cent of the scripts he was sent, and as the months and then years went past, Vanessa had started to wonder if his Hollywood dream would ever happen. In the meantime she'd devoted herself to transforming them into the biggest husband-and-wife team since the Beckhams. Vanessa was a huge fan of the former Spice Girl. *What would Victoria do?* was often her mantra.

Her hard work had certainly paid off: Brand Powell now reigned supreme. Advertising campaigns, clothing lines, his and her perfumes, (imaginatively called 'Vanessa' and 'Conrad'). There was even talk of their own chat show, although things in the TV world took a frustratingly long time. In the meantime their profile had soared and the money was rolling in, even in these recession-hit times. Conrad might complain but his wife had turned him into a walking and talking aspiration.

He sighed heavily, as if someone had just sounded the death knell for his soul.

'Are you all right?' she asked.

'Bloody wonderful.' He didn't look up.

She turned to gaze out her window at the fields flashing by. Conrad made no secret of the fact that he found the things they did for Brand Powell demeaning. Vanessa was often made to feel it was her fault. But what was the alternative? To sit back and watch their empire dry up around them? *Just like your career?* she thought disloyally. She had worked too damn hard. The thought of going back to nothing made her shiver.

The car purred along Pavilion Heights, the most exclusive road in Beeversham. Billy their chauffeur turned a smooth right into the private road leading to the gates of Tresco House. Moments later the car was pulling up outside the ten-bedroom mansion the Powells called home.

Conrad got out and went round to open his wife's door. Helping her out, he dropped an extravagant kiss on her hand. 'Back at last, *ma chérie*. Thank fuck for that.'

He flashed a wicked grin, looking heart-stoppingly like the old Conrad, before turning and taking off on long legs across the courtyard.

Smiling wryly, Vanessa followed in his wake. A bundle of white fluff shot out the open front door and threw itself at her Louboutins. It was Sukie, the Maltipoo cross; beloved by her and despised by Conrad after it had left a present in his Italian loafers.

'Hello, my angel, did you miss your mummy?' She picked the squirming ball up and pressed her face into soft fur. Mindful of hairs on her dress, she put Sukie back down carefully and went inside.

Vanessa had grown up in a small Ealing terrace with a garden the size of a cotton-wool pad and neighbours crowding in from every direction. She always got a thrill walking into her beautiful renovated manor house. White marble floors stretched the length of the ground floor, while a white staircase swept up into a circular balcony above. Tall, opulent vases of lilies stood on the heavy Moorish side tables she had specially imported in. The look was very LA; exactly what she'd asked the interior designer for.

'Mrs Powell, where shall I put this?' Billy was hovering on the doorstep, an exquisite cake box in his arms.

'In the kitchen please, Billy.' On closer inspection Vanessa could see that some of the flowers in the nearest vase were brown and wilting. Why hadn't Renata put in fresh ones, as she'd requested?

Conrad had already disappeared to the gym to do his stretches; his hamstrings always played up after a long car journey.

'Vanessa.' A statuesque figure in a purple kaftan and Cartier diamonds stood at the top of the stairs. Slowly, dramatically, Dominique Salijan started her descent. Her heavy Samsara perfume engulfed Vanessa in place of a hug.

'You're late,' she said in her heavy accent. 'I was getting worried.'

'The traffic was bad,' Vanessa said apologetically.

'You were the belle of the ball.' It was a statement, not a question.

'Of course.'

Even at fifty-five Dominique had an essence that could turn heads. When Vanessa had been little she'd thought her mother looked like Sophia Loren; certainly Dominique had always felt as remote and beautiful as the famous actress. It was to Dominique that Vanessa owed her high cheekbones and famous caramel-coloured eyes.

Her mother gave her daughter the usual once-over, missing nothing. Automatically Vanessa pulled in her stomach.

'I got Billy to stop off at Patisserie Valley,' she offered. 'I got your favourite, framboise gateau with white chocolate.'

Her mother sighed, as if she'd been disappointed hugely. 'Oh, darling, I wish you hadn't. You know how I'm trying to keep my figure.'

'I thought it would be a nice surprise.'

How stupid of me.

'I would just prefer flowers. You always get me such beautiful flowers.'

The Victoria Beckham dress was starting to chafe at Vanessa's curves. 'Fine.' She sighed. 'I'm going upstairs to get changed.'

'You look tired, put on some eye cream,' her mother instructed. 'I'll be waiting with drinks on the terrace.'

Vanessa peeled off her dress and hung it on the wardrobe door, ready for dry-cleaning. The La Perla bra and knickers were next, dropped into the rose-scented laundry basket. She turned to look at the line of mirrored wardrobes that dominated the master suite. Anyone else would have seen an exotic beauty with a knockout body standing there, cappuccino mane cascading down her back. Vanessa, however, focused on the minutiae. Her mother was right. The slight tautness around her eyes was a sign that Vanessa hadn't drunk enough water today.

She knew not to rise by now, but her mother's comment still rankled. Why couldn't she just approve for once? Vanessa made sure Dominique wanted for nothing. The more she gave, the more critical her mother seemed to become.

She surveyed her reflection in the glass: the sensuous hips and tiny waist, the impressive natural breasts with large, dark nipples. Vanessa had always been limited as a model: her womanly dimensions were more suited to the old-school glamour of a 1950s pin-up, but even so she had made a fortune.

Slipping into her silk dressing gown, Vanessa walked across to the French windows. As with everything

17

in her life the gardens were groomed to perfection. Striped lawns were centred with a regal stone fountain and an elevated mosaic swimming pool looked down from the far end. Their gardener, Paul, was bending down in one of the flowerbeds, his T-shirt rising up to reveal an expanse of pink flesh.

Her mind wandered back to Catherine Connor. Not that Vanessa would ever say so, but she thought Catherine had looked great. She would never want Catherine's figure – muscles were so unfeminine – but her arch-enemy had looked glowing. Retirement in the country clearly suited her. For a moment Vanessa was wantonly jealous of Catherine's life, the freedom she had to do whatever she wanted. *Can you imagine me jogging through town without a scrap of make-up?* Her mother and Conrad would have a blue fit.

In another world a million miles before this one, Vanessa had looked up to Catherine. She'd subscribed to *Soirée* from the age of sixteen. Clever, funny and sophisticated, the magazine was like the older sister she had so desperately wanted. She had thought Catherine was a goddess.

So when *Soirée* had printed that bunch of lies it was as if Catherine had personally punched Vanessa in the stomach. The fallout had been even worse: devastating insinuations that Vanessa was a high-class prostitute. The *Sun*'s front page would be branded in her memory for ever. *BUSTED! Good-Time Girl Vanessa Powell POPS out at party of shame!* To add to the humiliation they'd superimposed Vanessa's head on a *Carry On* picture of a topless Barbara Windsor.

By then she had reinvented herself as a mesmerizing

beauty, but in a heartbeat she was 'Gyppy Jardine' again, the bullied, friendless teenager. Her mother had been chased down the street by reporters and asked what she thought about her daughter being a whore. Vanessa had been subjected to even worse. The one saving grace was that her father hadn't been alive to see it.

Vanessa had come through it, but she still burnt with anger every time she thought about it – the devastating ripple effect Catherine Connor had created. Clever, opinionated Catherine, who saw women like Vanessa as pointless bits of tits and ass. In a funny way, Vanessa had Catherine to thank. Nothing like a public wronging to send a celebrity's career into orbit providing you played it right. Seven years on she was one of the most recognizable women in Britain.

And when it had been Catherine's turn to get dragged through the tabloids, Vanessa had enjoyed every minute.

Chapter 3

Twenty-three-year-old Fleur Blackwater woke alone in her single bed. It felt like she'd only just put her head on the pillow, but the watery sunlight filtering through the curtains signalled another long day ahead.

The digital clock read 5.28 a.m. Two more precious minutes of rest. She looked up at the sagging ceiling and imagined what it would feel like to have a lie-in. For a blissful moment she was transported away to one of those Greek islands in the holiday brochures. Fleur in a pretty kaftan; sitting on a terrace by the sea enjoying fresh coffee and a leisurely breakfast . . .

The drill of the alarm went off, terminating her daydream. All she wanted to do was pull the covers back over her head, but the familiar gnaw of anxiety had already started. Flinging the duvet back, she pulled off the ancient Gap T-shirt that masqueraded as a nightie and went to rummage around for a clean pair of knickers. It didn't take long to get dressed. Greying bra grabbed from the back of the chair, a fraying polo shirt, jeans that smelt the least offensive close up. As usual the laundry basket was overflowing. Animals came before people in this house.

Her beauty routine was equally quick. Fleur squinted critically in the mirror above the sink and noticed her freckles had got more pronounced in the sun. She hated her freckles almost as much as she hated her E-cup chest, which had been dropped on her petite frame like some kind of sick joke. Fleur had never understood why all these celebrities wanted to pump themselves up surgically. Her breasts were big and heavy and got in the way of her job. She hid them under baggy tops, wishing one morning she'd wake up to find them magically shrunk.

Tying her long, luxuriant red hair up (her one re-deeming feature) she walked out on to the landing. The farmhouse was quiet, the sound of a faraway cock-erel floating in through an open window.

Her parents' bedroom was two doors down on the right. The one next to it had been unused for years. Claire, Fleur's older sister, had escaped as soon as she could and now lived in suburban bliss with her new family in Reading. She came down for a duty visit once a year, itching to get back out of the door as soon as she'd arrived. Fleur didn't really blame her sister: they were hardly the Von Trapps these days. People dealt with grief in different ways.

The kitchen door was still closed, a sign her dad hadn't made it to bed again. Fleur found him slumped on the wooden table, snoring raggedly. A bottle of cheap whisky had been seen off, the empty glass perched precariously in Robert Blackwater's calloused hand.

The chair her mum had always sat in was pulled out, as if Robert had passed out mid-conversation with a ghost.

Fleur went over. 'Dad.' She put her hand on his shoulder. 'Wake up.'

He twitched and mumbled something. She shook him this time, hard.

'Dad!'

'What's that?' He blinked bloodshot eyes open. 'What's going on?'

'You fell asleep at the table again.'

'I must have dropped off. All this bloody extra paperwork they keep giving us.'

The pile of unpaid bills still lay untouched on the dresser. She bit her lip.

Robert Blackwater got up stiffly, avoiding eye contact with his daughter. He went over to the sink and poured out a glass of water.

'Why don't you go and have a shower?' she suggested. 'I'll make a start on breakfast.'

Her dad still had his back to her. 'Don't baby me, girl.'

The smell of stale alcohol was making her queasy. Fleur had to get out of the messy room and its unhappy memories. 'I'll go and see to the cows, then.'

He didn't answer. After making a run for it, Fleur stood outside in the clean morning air for a moment, gulping it down as if coming up for breath. A minute later the Suzuki quad bike was zooming out of the yard, their two English sheepdogs clinging to the back for dear life.

Desperate to put distance between herself and the farmhouse, she rattled up the track to the top field.

22

Tinker and Bess had jumped off even before she'd come to a stop, bounding off further up the hill. She stood up on the bike and looked down on her fields. In the nearest, new calves were wobbling round on twiggy legs, following their mothers. The adjoining field held the April spring lambs, little white clouds moving across the expanse of green.

Predominantly a beef and lamb business, Blackwater Farm supplied meat to supermarkets and businesses across the south west of England. May was calving month, and Fleur was flat out looking after expectant mothers and newborns.

It was back-breaking work in a tough climate. The farming industry was on its knees and every month they heard about someone else going bankrupt. They had let all their workers go now apart from a local lad, Ben, who came in to help out. Every day it felt like they were only just keeping their heads above water. Sometimes Fleur would wake bolt upright in bed at night, her chest hammering so hard she was convinced she was having a heart attack.

It didn't help that she had taken on the lion's share of the work so that her dad could concentrate on the administrative side. They both knew it was an excuse. Robert Blackwater was no longer fit enough for hard physical labour.

She gazed angrily down the valley. Why couldn't she have said something to him just now? Even if it had resulted in a screaming match, at least things would be out in the open. Instead of the two of them going on, pretending everything was OK. *You're a coward, Fleur* ...

The gnawing, pounding sensation started in her

chest again. Fleur tried a breathing exercise from the meditation book she'd bought, but it didn't work. Instead, she trained her eyes on on the huge, gleaming white building. That unwanted house had become a physical manifestation to project all her emotions on.

Fleur had learnt a long time ago to bottle things up. But the day she had found out that her dad had sold a hundred acres of the farm to some bloke called Beau Rainford, she had gone mad. Racing over there, she had found Beau already organizing a team of builders to tear her grandparents' empty old house down to build his own. She had accused Beau of taking advantage of her father. He'd treated the whole thing as a big joke, telling Fleur he'd done them a *favour*. Unable to watch the place she'd spent half her childhood in being demolished, she had stormed out, embarrassingly throwing a clod of earth at Beau's windscreen that totally missed.

The galling thing was that the money had helped: buying a desperately needed new barn and the animals' food and upkeep for the last two years. It still didn't make up for the fact that she had to look at that house every day and endure Beau's helicopter swooping overhead, frightening the livestock. He was an arrogant rich arsehole who had no respect for the countryside or the business the Blackwaters had built up. For the first time, she knew what it was like to really hate someone.

Chapter 4

The text message alert woke Catherine with a start. It was John. *'At Paddington on the 4.15. See you soon. X'*

She typed in a kiss back and put the phone down. A nasty dry taste lurked in her throat and she looked guiltily at the empty bottle of rosé, a leftover from last night's dinner. Still, Catherine reasoned, rolling off the sunlounger, it wasn't like she had back-to-back meetings all afternoon.

Putting her bikini top back on, she padded inside. The cool flagstone floor was a wonderful respite from the heat of the day. The once-dark basement had been transformed into a light-filled kitchen with brushed-aluminium worktops and a sliding glass wall that opened out into the garden.

She leant on the central island with a glass of water and idly perused her reflection in the window. Last month, in a moment of impetuousness, Catherine had gone to see her old stylist in London and had her shoulder-length brown hair chopped off. Now it curled softly round her long neck and temples, giving her a more impish look. John absolutely loved it. Catherine, who thought it made her nose look big, still wasn't sure.

For someone who'd worked in the fashion industry, she had always had a surprisingly functional attitude to her appearance. She knew her strengths: slim, good legs, intelligent blue eyes and a nice smile. She didn't lose much sleep over the fact that her jaw was too strong or that her boobs were never going to give Katie Price's a run for their money. Catherine would far rather look in the mirror and see an inquisitive face full of character than a perfect blank canvas. *Like Vanessa Powell*, she thought rather uncharitably.

Draining her glass of water, she went back outside. It was hard to believe this beautiful oasis had once been a jungle. The gloomy ivy had gone and had been replaced by scented wisteria that clung delicately to the yellow brick. John had cut down the rotting apple tree at the bottom of the garden and put up a beautiful summerhouse. The triffid-like rhubarb patch had been hauled up and was now a herb garden that threw out wafts of basil, mint and coriander. Catherine, who'd never even managed to keep a tomato plant alive, had watched John's miracle-working with wonder.

Catherine gazed round the sun-filled garden. She still couldn't quite believe she'd ended up in the country. A self-confessed urbanite, the grimy London streets and honking traffic were Catherine's wildlife and birdsong. As editor of the famed *Soirée*, she'd blazed a trail through the world of women's glossies, campaigning for bigger issues than just celebrity and fashion. Soirée Sponsors, the charity she'd started for under-privileged teenagers in the capital, had received much praise and was still going from strength to strength.

Catherine knew the magazine industry could be cut-throat, but she had no idea just how cut-throat until a rival editor called Isabella Montgomery had revealed her real identity. How the feted editor Catherine Connor was actually Cathy Fincham, daughter of the infamous 1970s 'Crimson Killer' Annie Fincham.

Annie Fincham, a name that until a few years ago had evoked images of a cold-blooded calculating murderer. A single mother from a tough estate in Newcastle, she had been found guilty of the manslaughter of her live-in boyfriend. The Crimson Killer case had been huge (so called because of Annie's red lipstick that was allegedly found smeared all over the dead man's face). Society back then had been prejudiced against single mothers, especially young, beautiful single mothers who were suspiciously close to their teenage daughters. Neighbours and even Annie's own mother blackened her name.

Speculation was rife about what had happened in the house that night, but Annie had pleaded guilty as charged. Even with her mother in prison, fifteen-year-old Cathy Fincham had become the victim of a witch-hunt, with many, including a corrupt senior police officer who'd sold his story, insisting she had colluded in the murder. When she subsequently ran away from home and vanished into thin air, her persecutors took it as a sign of her guilt. Three decades on, the conspiracy theories still raged.

Catherine still remembered the terrible moment

she'd been exposed with clarity. From reporting the news, she *was* the news. But Catherine was a survivor, and this time, she was determined to stand up and tell the truth. How her mother had been the victim of domestic violence. How she, Cathy, had pushed Ray Barnard down the stairs that terrible night to stop him from strangling her mother and how Annie Fincham had gone to jail to protect her daughter. How Annie had tragically hung herself fifty-four days into her sentence, convinced her daughter would be better off without her.

This time the public had been united in sympathy. No police charges were brought against Catherine. Isabella Montgomery had suffered her own spectacular downfall and Catherine went on to write the best-selling *Cathy: My Story*, donating all proceeds to Refuge. As a result, her mother had been posthumously acquitted.

She had been vindicated but it had taken its toll. Two weeks after the book came out, she had collapsed at home in the kitchen and been unable to get out of bed for a month. Her doctor had diagnosed acute exhaustion and ordered serious time out. Watching his wife go through everything, John had wholeheartedly agreed.

When he'd suggested driving out to the Cotswolds town of Beeversham to see a house he'd heard about, Catherine had expected to hate the place. *Beeversham,* she had scoffed, *Are you kidding me?* Instead, she'd fallen in love with the dilapidated Georgian house they'd gone on to do up. She had dreaded being the focus of town gossip, but she found the locals to be friendly and surprisingly non-judgemental. Catherine and John had been allowed to melt into country life, enjoying rounds of raucous afternoon barbecues and lively dinner parties.

John had sold his successful construction company just before they'd moved to the country, but he still consulted on a few projects and often had to go up to London in the week. When he was gone Catherine met people for coffee and had long lunches in sunny back gardens. For the first time in her life, she had real friends.

Even after a year she found it weird being a lady of leisure, especially on these lazy sunny mid-week days when the rest of the world were at work. Her mobile, which at one time had buzzed every minute, was lying silent on the ground. There were no exclusives to chase, no problems to solve. No one needed her. People kept telling her how relaxed she looked. Privately Catherine thought she was so relaxed she was in danger of slipping into a coma.

She lay back on the lounger and gazed up into the endless blue sky. The sun was like a soporific blanket thrown over her skin. *Is this it?* she wondered. At the age of thirty-nine, had her chance to make a difference in the world slipped by?

Chapter 5

Country life may have been quieter than London, but it still had its fair share of intrigue. Blaize Castle was at the centre of a huge planning scandal after property developers had snapped up the site and applied for permission to build a theme park, ironically called Ye Olde Worlde. The inhabitants of Beeversham were up in arms at the threat of having the Cotswolds equivalent of Disneyland in their backyard. Controversy was already raging about the vast swathes of green belt under threat from the new planning laws. The Beeversham situation had inflamed an already explosive situation.

The residents had quickly formed an action group: Say No to Olde Worlde (aka SNOW) to fight the proposal. As Catherine and John walked up to the town hall that evening for the first meeting people were pouring in. A pudgy blonde woman with corned-beef arms stood outside bellowing into her mobile. Amanda Belcher, the bossy owner of Wedding Belles.

'When will the fabric arrive then? I can hardly ask them to postpone the wedding!'

The chatter dimmed momentarily as Catherine and John strolled in. Catherine wasn't sure if it was because people had *Cathy: My Story* on their bookshelves, or more the fact that she was with a six-foot-four gladiator of a man with green eyes and hair the colour of coal dust.

A plump, brown-haired woman was standing behind a table festooned with SNOW literature. Her large, rather anxious eyes lit up when she saw them.

'My lovelies!'

'Ginny.' Catherine went up and gave her a hug, inhaling the familiar scent of Anaïs Anaïs. Ginny was married to Felix Chamberlain, the much-respected Chairman of Beeversham's Conservative Association. Felix was quite devoted to his wife, a legendary cook and homemaker, although it was just the two of them now their children had left home. The couple were an institution in the town.

'Chaps!' Felix came striding towards them, his thick silver hair making him look more like a benevolent badger than ever. He shook John's hand and kissed Catherine on both cheeks.

'Delighted you could make it.' Felix was also the head of the SNOW committee. He'd been the obvious choice. 'We've got the proposed drawings from Sykes Holdings on the wall. Wouldn't mind getting your opinion, John.' Felix looked to his wife. 'Darling, are you all right to man the fort? Ginny's been quite wonderful,' he told the other two. 'Whizzing up leaflets and all sorts on the computer.'

The two men walked off, John head and shoulders above everyone else. Ginny looked enviously at

Catherine's sleek brown arms. 'You've got the most wonderful colour on you. The moment I step outside I go all pink and blotchy.'

'I've been sunbathing in the garden all afternoon,' Catherine confessed. 'It's horribly lazy.'

A vast bulk barged into her and nearly sent her flying. Jonty Fortescue-Wellington, drunk as usual, walrus stomach gaping out of the bottom of his shirt. The Conservative MP for Beeversham, Jonty was terrible at his job and a raging alcoholic. His bloodhound eyes fastened on Catherine's legs. 'Where's the plonk, Ginny?'

'I'm afraid it's just tea or orange juice, Jonty,' she said firmly.

A gust of sandalwood heralded the arrival of Tristan Jago. Tall, rakish and energetic, Tristan was the big name in Beeversham's Labour Party. Half Jonty's age and weight, Tristan was chomping at the bit for the MP's job. Jonty wasn't putting up much of a fight.

'Missed you at Lavenham's WI meeting last night, Jonty. The plight of our hedgerow robins not important enough for you?'

'I was sitting in Parliament,' Jonty slurred pompously. 'Shipping reforms.'

Tristan's eyes gleamed behind his trendy black-rimmed spectacles. 'Really? I thought that was last week.'

'Jonty, let me find you a seat.' Ginny came round the table and ushered him to the back before he caused any trouble.

Catherine went to find a place herself. Felix was standing at the front, a reassuring figure in jaunty mustard slacks.

'Evening, everybody. Thanks so much for coming along on this wonderful spring evening. I know you're all keen to know what's been happening, so let's get started.'

John came to sit down beside Catherine. 'What do you make of the plans?' she whispered.

'The bloke's got balls if nothing else. It looks like a bloody monster.'

'I'll give you a brief history of Ye Olde Worlde,' Felix continued. 'I'm sure you've read all about it in the newspapers.'

It made for grim listening. A chain of theme parks across the USA, Ye Olde Worlde was a mawkish, whimsical interpretation of British culture. For eighty dollars per head, customers could experience delights such as the Oxford University Terror Plunge (a bare-knuckle ride through the dreaming spires) and the Loch Ness Log Flume. There was even a waxwork museum dedicated entirely to the Middletons, reportedly featuring a statue of Pippa M's bottom. It was a billion-dollar brand and a property developer called Sid Sykes had bought up the first UK franchise.

Tristan Jago's hand shot up. 'Sykes is claiming Ye Olde Worlde will create hundreds of new jobs. Three million people are out of work under this Conservative government, the highest level for three decades. Since your lot got us in the mess in the first place, why aren't you creating more jobs?'

'Ye Olde Worlde would also ruin any existing tourism in the area, Tristan,' Felix said patiently. 'I can't imagine who'd want to come and visit a national heritage site with a theme park looming in the background. Not to mention the disastrous effect it would have on the High Street.'

Mr Patel wasn't quite as diplomatic. 'Oh, be quiet, you silly man!' he cried. 'What's going to happen in a few years' time when you want your gluten-free banana flapjacks and I've gone out of business?'

Realizing he'd misjudged the mood horribly, Tristan sat down. But moments later his hand was back in the air like a jack-in-the-box.

'I'd like to know what our own MP has to say about all this,' he said piously. 'Surely as our representative in Parliament, he should be campaigning for stricter planning rules in rural areas?'

Everyone turned round to look at Jonty. He tucked a hip flask back in his pocket. 'What's that?'

Felix gave a pained smile. 'Tristan, as I'm sure you're aware, planning issues generally come under the county council's remit, not central government's.'

'Fat lot of help they're being,' someone grumbled.

'The county councillors are reasonable people,' Felix said. 'I'm sure they think Ye Olde Worlde is just as much of a bad idea as the rest of us, but they have to go through the proper procedures.'

They all started to feel a lot better. If anyone knew what they were talking about, it was Felix.

There was a slithering noise and a loud thump. Jonty Fortescue-Wellington had passed out and fallen off his chair. Ginny rushed over with a glass of water. 'All right everyone, nothing to see here!'

'Anyone fancy the pub?' someone asked.

*

After a quick drink at Bar 47 Catherine and John headed home. As they crossed the road he put his arm round his wife's shoulders. Catherine snuggled into his chest. At five foot nine she was hardly a short-arse, but her husband still dwarfed her.

A couple were walking down the street towards them. Catherine watched the woman's eyes fasten on John. Her gaze moved over him like a tourist taking in a vast, magnificent view.

'You totally just got checked out then,' Catherine said afterwards.

'By who?'

'The woman who just passed with the huge knockers! Don't say you didn't notice.'

John grinned down at his wife. 'I've only got eyes for you, my love.'

'Liar,' she scoffed. He gave her a wink. They continued down the street in a companionable silence. 'Do you think Ye Olde Worlde will get the go-ahead?' she asked.

Her husband hadn't said much. 'These things look clear-cut, but you never can tell. From what I've heard, Sykes is a slippery bugger.'

'What if it *did* create more jobs though?' She played devil's advocate. 'Wouldn't that outweigh the negatives?'

'You mean at the risk of taking others down, like Felix said?' John gave her a squeeze. 'I'd keep those thoughts to yourself if I were you.'

The Crescent was a handsome curve of Georgian houses just off the top of the High Street. Catherine and John were at No. 4, halfway along.

She got her keys out and opened the front door. The hallway was in darkness. She went to switch on the light, but his hand curled over hers.

'Leave it,' he said softly.

He pushed her against the wall. They stood there for a moment framed in the half-light from the porch. Catherine lifted her hand to trace the six o'clock shadow on the strong chin, the nose broken years ago playing rugby. The lines on her husband's face were as familiar to her as her own.

His hand slipped up inside Catherine's T-shirt to caress the warm flesh of her stomach. A moment later her top was off, dropped on the floor beside him. Underneath, Catherine's breasts were encased in the simplest of nude bras. She'd never been one for pomp and ceremony when it came to underwear.

As John bent his head to nuzzle her cleavage she felt herself grow warm. She reached for the buttons of John's shirt and popped them open one by one, running her hands across the vast pectorals sprinkled with dark hair.

He pulled her bra up to expose her breasts, fingering a hard, dark nipple. 'You still do it for me, Cath.'

'I should hope so,' she told him, wriggling out of her skinny jeans.

He smiled and lifted her up on to the sideboard. She felt the cold ceramic of the car keys bowl pressing against her right buttock. They started to kiss, slowly at first, but then it intensified until their lips were jammed together, tongues moving in and out of each other's mouths. It had been a while since they'd kissed so deeply and she felt aroused by the slightly frantic messiness, as if they were two schoolkids getting it on for the first time.

She heard the clink of metal as he undid his belt buckle. She leant back against the wall and pulled the fabric of her knickers aside. John started slowly at first, getting her used to him again, but as they found their rhythm, he gripped Catherine's hips and started driving harder. She arched her back, taking him in, giving him everything . . .

They both came at the same time, slippery with a sheen of sweat. 'Still got it,' John gasped.

'Still got it,' Catherine gasped back.

He sank his head on her shoulder and Catherine wrapped her legs and arms round him, floating on her own cloud of euphoric bliss. In the darkness their breathing eventually subsided. John stood up, and pushed a tendril of hair off her forehead.

'I don't know about you, but I'm in need of a drink.'

'Round two afterwards?'

He grinned. 'If my knees hold up.'

Arms around each other, they stumbled towards the stairs, Catherine wondering if her husband was thinking the same as her. Was this the one that had struck lucky?

Chapter 6

It was hard to believe that Felix and Beau Rainford were related. Felix was fifty-seven, Beau twenty-four years younger. The two shared the same mother and piercing blue eyes, but the similarities stopped there. While Felix was charm personified and had time for anyone, Beau had a reputation for breathtaking rudeness and arrogance. As much as Felix maintained the equilibrium, it seemed Beau did everything he could to upset it.

The two men's backgrounds were also worlds apart. Felix was a grammar school boy made good, the son of a bank manager and a local farmer's daughter. Sally Chamberlain was only nineteen when she'd married twenty-nine-year-old Trevor Chamberlain and their only son, Felix, had soon followed. The Chamberlains had lived in a cottage on the outskirts of Beeversham and seemed the perfect family. Everyone had been stunned when Sally met American racing driver and real-estate heir Doug Rainford at a local polo tournament and ran off with him afterwards.

At the time Felix had been in his second year at university. Despite his mother running off and Trevor Chamberlain dropping dead from a heart attack six months later, Felix had emerged with a 2:1 in Law and the wonderful Ginny on his arm. They had returned to Beeversham to settle and Felix started his own solicitor's practice, Chamberlains & Co., on the High Street. Property disputes, wills, conveyancing, Chamberlains were the one-stop shop for everything. 'Get Felix to do it' was the most overused phrase in town, because everyone knew he would.

Beau's upbringing was straight out of the pages of *Tatler*. Born to Sally and Doug Rainford four years after she'd left Felix's father, Beau spent his early years travelling the world on the Formula One circuit with his parents. Doug Rainford partied as hard as he drove and at age eight, Beau was sent to Gordonstoun school to board. Tragedy struck the Rainfords' charmed lives a year later when Sally was diagnosed with a terminal brain tumour.

Just eight weeks later, Sally had died. Not long after that, a devastated Doug Rainford had checked himself into rehab in Arizona. Despite the humiliation of his mother leaving, blood had been thicker than water for Felix. He and Ginny became Beau's legal guardians, but it had been a tempestuous relationship, with a teenage Beau wreaking havoc round Beeversham when he came back for the holidays. When he had turned eighteen he had got his hands on the Rainford inheritance and gone off into the world without a backward glance.

Despite a complete lack of scholarly discipline, Beau

had somehow managed to sail through his A levels and, to the astonishment of everyone, had landed a place at Cambridge to read Classics. There he had managed to last a whole year before setting fire to a punt on the River Cam and causing a near-death collision under the Bridge of Sighs with a boat of terrified Japanese tourists. The exasperated head of his college did not buy Beau's excuse that he'd been recreating a traditional Hindu funeral pyre to mourn the death of his pet gerbil, Afro, and kicked him out.

From then on Beau devoted himself to a party lifestyle and caroused his way round the world. Men wanted to be him or be with him, while women openly surrendered to the taut, strutting body and famous cobalt gaze. In his early twenties he surprised everyone by hooking up with Lindsay St John, a buxom fifty-three-year-old rich widow. The relationship had lasted a whole two years before Beau was back on the scene, more badly behaved than ever. The society pages had breathed a sigh of relief and celebrated the return of this outrageous blond playboy who acted like he was king of the world.

Somewhere in between Beau started up a chalet company, selling it for millions a few years later. But it was the British property market where he came into his own, snapping up ailing stately homes and old buildings for renovation. He quickly acquired a ruthless reputation, swooping in to make desperate owners offers they couldn't refuse. His business ethics may have been questionable, but his profits were not. His property company, Beau Rainford Real Estate, or BRR, was one of the most successful in the UK.

When word first spread that he'd bought a place in the Cotswolds the Gloucestershire set had gone into meltdown. At first Felix had turned a blind eye to all the loud parties and Beau's vintage Mustang roaring down the High Street at three times the speed limit. He had kept a tactful silence over Ridings when most other people were up in arms. But when Beau had turned up at Felix's fifty-fifth birthday party two years ago, drunk, and tried to pick a fight with his brother in front of a hundred guests including a visiting dignitary and a lord, Felix had put his foot down. There had been a furious exchange of words in the summerhouse at the bottom of the garden and the two hadn't spoken since.

The Amanda Belcher brigade saw Beau as the devil's spawn, out to impregnate their daughters and destroy their idyllic town. Beeversham's serving staff adored him because of his generous tipping, while the schoolkids worshipped him because he bought them fags and booze from the off-licence. Blond, beautiful, controversial and compelling, no other person had ever divided so much opinion. Love him or loathe him, since he'd moved back Beau had certainly livened things up.

He was the hot topic of conversation when Catherine walked into Mr Patel's at lunchtime. Amanda Belcher was at the counter, deep in conversation with a woman in a tailored floral sundress. Glamorously statuesque, Mrs Patel owned Soraya, Beeversham's exclusive boutique shop.

'. . . And apparently the place just reeked of sex!' Amanda declared.

Mrs Patel gave Catherine a relieved smile.

'Catherine!' Amanda summoned her over. 'I was just telling Ursula here what that depraved sex addict has been up to now.'

'Oh, right,' Catherine said mildly.

'Nicola – who does the flowers in my shop – her sister Karen's neighbour Angela got asked to do some cleaning for Beau last week. So she went up to Ridings, expecting nothing more than pushing the Hoover round . . .'

Amanda paused for effect. 'When she drove in, the swimming pool was seething with naked people. Playing water polo!' Amanda's froglike eyes bulged. 'They had a net up and everything.'

Catherine raised an amused eyebrow. 'Can you believe it!'

'Well, Nicola said Karen said Angela had told her she'd turned round and driven straight back out again. When she got home she only found a used condom stuck to the front passenger wheel!'

'You just said it was an empty sausage-roll packet,' Mrs Patel said.

Amanda flapped an impatient hand at her. 'Of course it was a condom!'

'I don't really think you should be going round saying such things.'

'I'm just telling you how it is, Ursula! We need to keep our wits about us. Next thing Beau will be trying to ensnare Olympia and your Pritti into his den of lust. Nothing is sacred to that man.'

Poor Mrs Patel went a funny shade of green.

*

Catherine emerged from the shop and turned left down the street. As she passed the door of Butterflies gift shop it was suddenly flung open. A teenage girl in St Gwendolyn's uniform came flying out, straight into her.

'Watch where you're fucking going!' Talia Tudor shrieked.

'Watch where *you're* going!' Catherine retorted. 'And mind your bloody language.'

Talia Tudor gave her the evil eye. 'God, what *is* it with people round here?'

The gift-shop door opened again and a woman rushed out. Lynette Tudor, owner of Butterflies and Talia's mum. Her thin, worn face was etched with stress.

'Talia . . .' she started.

'Fuck off, Mum! Stop getting in my face!'

'You've got your history exam tomorrow!' Lynette wailed. 'Talia, these are your GCSEs!'

'So what?' Talia stormed off, school skirt hoiked up to gynaecological levels. 'Like I'm going to pass them, anyway!'

She walked out into the road without looking, causing a Renault Espace to jam on its brakes. Flipping the driver the finger, Talia stomped off down the street. Bursting into tears, Lynette fled back into the shop. Catherine was left open-mouthed on the pavement. Here she was thinking they'd moved to Beeversham for the quiet life.

Chapter 7

There was one anomaly in Vanessa's well-ordered life: Renata, their Polish housekeeper. She'd been with the family on and off for years and had started off answering the phone at Vanessa's dad's carpet-fitting business.

Small and shrivelled like a Californian raisin, Renata could have been anywhere between seventy and a hundred. She'd rejected the nice pink tunic Vanessa had bought her and instead wore her own uniform of tracksuit bottoms and Disneyland sweatshirts. A pair of 1970s-style NHS glasses dominated her face. The glasses actually *were* from the seventies; Vanessa had once asked her.

Alarmed by the amount of dust Renata missed, Vanessa had offered countless times to buy her a new pair but the offer had always been turned down. Renata was also selectively deaf, especially around Dominique. Vanessa's mum constantly moaned about their useless housekeeper, but Vanessa felt bound by a sense of loyalty. Luckily they also had thirty-pound-an-hour cleaners that came in once a week.

The house was quiet that morning. Conrad was in his study reading a script his agent had sent, 'a sci-fi version of *Downton Abbey*'. Dominique had gone back to bed with one of her headaches. Vanessa found Renata in the den in the basement watching a *Dr Phil* repeat on Sky.

Vanessa hovered in the doorway. 'Renata, I was just wondering why you'd chopped the heads off all these roses.'

'They were bad *kochanie*.'

'Bad?' Vanessa repeated blankly.

'Yes, funny colour. Not like roses should be.'

'They're meant to look like—' Vanessa looked down at the massacred Spring Vintage bouquet. They'd only been delivered from Wild at Heart yesterday.

Renata smiled at her. 'I do right, eh?'

'You do right,' Vanessa sighed. She'd better go straight to her study and order new flowers before her mother noticed.

It was a shame to be inside on such a beautiful day, so Vanessa took the iPad out to the pool. Firing an email off to the MAC people about the packaging for her new lipstick range (the gold was still slightly too flat), she sat back and took a break. Through the rose-tint of her Chanel sunglasses the garden looked spectacular. Paul was walking diligently through the beds at the far end, stopping occasionally to finesse a flower or plant.

There was an almost-human sigh from the other sunbed. Sukie lay on her Versace beach towel, her little body rising and falling in the heat.

'Are you thirsty, my darling?' Vanessa asked. 'I'll get you some water.'

Sukie rolled on her back and started cleaning her bits.

Charming, Vanessa thought, reaching for the suncream. Even though she was blessed with her mother's dark colouring, she was meticulous about sun protection. She was meticulous about everything to do with her appearance: still water served at room temperature and sipped at fifteen-minute intervals, no carbs after 1 p.m., only the occasional glass of champagne. Vanessa had been the dumpy kid at school and it was the power behind her relentless self-control now.

There was a shout from the far end of the garden.

'Vanessa!'

'Up here, Conrad!' she called back.

Her husband came up the lawn, looking very French in navy shorts and a pink Armani shirt. He plonked himself down on the end of her sunbed.

'How was the script?' she asked.

'Fucking atrocious. *Brideshead Revisited* meets *Button Moon*. The writers must be on crack.'

'Sounds quite fun to me,' she joked, getting a death stare in return.

'Don't take the fucking piss.'

'I was—'

Bristling with anger, Conrad sprang up. 'You think it's funny, sitting up here with that mangy mutt as you conjure up our next tacky deal? I'm a talented actor, Vanessa.' He spat the words out at her. 'Do you think I like being wheeled out as your bloody plus one?'

'Of course not, I didn't mean it like that.' Vanessa

46

tried to soothe him. 'Conrad, you're *amazingly* talented, you just need another break . . .'

He looked at her in disdain. 'What the fuck would you know?'

'Where are you going?' she cried.

'Back inside, away from you!'

Dismayed, Vanessa watched him go. She'd committed the cardinal sin of making fun of his career. She hadn't meant it, of course, but Conrad was so touchy these days. He seemed to spend most of his time Googling himself and checking how many new followers he had on Twitter. Everything was Colin Firth's fault, apparently, because he'd 'stolen' Conrad's life. Vanessa was seriously starting to worry her husband was becoming obsessive.

She lifted her hand to inspect the huge wedding ring from Graff. The pink and yellow diamonds twinkled back at her prettily. She recalled the first time they'd met: Conrad had been at the height of his success and intrigued by the self-possessed beauty sitting alone at The Collection bar in Chelsea. He'd come over and complimented Vanessa on her Swarovski earrings, offering his commiserations over the Catherine Connor scandal. Ten years her senior, he was funny, charming and romantic. Vanessa had been swept off her feet. The deal had been sealed with a fairy-tale wedding in the Maldives six months later.

Her father had never got to meet Conrad, but he'd had Dominique on his side from day one with a dazzling array of flowers and perfume. The dashing leading man had arrived in both women's lives just when they had needed him. Of course, Vanessa had seen the financial benefit in marrying Conrad Powell. But she'd also been madly in love with him.

Paul was still hard at work as Vanessa came back down the lawn. 'Paul, there's a branch hanging down from one of the birch trees.' She'd just spotted it. 'Would you mind doing something about it?'

The gardener nodded. 'I'll make it my next job, Mrs Powell.'

She bestowed a gracious smile on him. 'Thank you.'

A familiar cockney drawl floated down the corridor as she went back in. Vanessa frowned. It sounded like their manager, Marty. Did they have a meeting scheduled? It was unlike her to forget. She hoped at least that Renata would be organizing drinks for their guest but there was no sign of her. Annoyed and confused, Vanessa went upstairs to change out of her kimono.

When Vanessa walked into the drawing room twenty minutes later in a flowing Cavalli maxi dress, there was a new energy in the air. Conrad was sprawled in one of the Louis XIV chairs looking a lot happier than when she'd last seen him. 'Darling!' he exclaimed exuberantly. 'There you are!'

Marty jumped up out of his own seat. 'How are you, kid? You look as gorgeous as ever.'

She kissed her manager on both cheeks and glanced between the two men. 'What's going on?'

Conrad had a smile on him like a Cheshire cat. 'Guess what Marty's landed us.'

'What?'

'Go on, guess.'

She wasn't in the mood for guessing games. 'What is it?'

'Only presenting this year's Silver Box Awards!'

'The Silver Box?' she repeated. 'Are you being serious?'

Now this was exciting. Held at the end of August at the Royal Albert Hall, the Silver Box Awards combined the credibility of the BAFTAs with the commercialism of the National Television Awards. Last year seven million people had tuned in to watch it on ITV1. A Silver Box award could send an actor's career into the stratosphere.

Conrad was striding about excitedly. 'Every producer and casting agent in the industry will be there. This is exactly the kind of exposure I need.'

'What about Brand Powell's exposure?' Vanessa asked, but she couldn't stop grinning. 'Conrad, this is amazing news!'

'We need to set up a meeting with the producer and whatnot, but it's pretty much in the bag,' Marty said. '*They* approached me, Vanessa.'

'You hear that?' Conrad shouted. 'I'm back, baby!'

'You haven't landed the Oscar just yet.' Vanessa started thinking rationally. 'I assume you've discussed money?' she asked Marty.

'Yeah, we're talking high-end six figures.'

Now she was getting excited. This was just the thing to take Brand Powell to the next level! She had a vision of floating on to the stage in Oscar de la Renta and airkissing Dame Helen Mirren as she gave her the Lifetime Achievement Award.

Conrad picked Vanessa up in a twirl. 'We'll be the toast of the film industry! Brad and Ange will be begging us for a dinner date!'

It was lovely to see genuine happiness on his face. 'I wouldn't go that far!' she laughed.

'Why not? Reach for the stars.' Conrad put her down on the floor. 'I love you, darling.'

'I love you too. Conrad, I'm sorry about earlier . . .'

He kissed the tip of her nose. 'Don't give it another thought.' Releasing her, he looked round. 'I think champagne's in order. Where's Renata?'

Vanessa's euphoria faded slightly. 'It's fine, I'll get it myself.'

'Don't be stupid, what do we pay her for?'

They all jumped as the door handle suddenly rattled furiously. 'Mrs Powell!' Renata's voice sounded frantic.

Vanessa rushed over and pulled it open. Renata had gone completely grey and was clutching at her chest. *Oh my God*, Vanessa thought. *She's having a heart attack.*

'Renata! Are you all right?'

The housekeeper shook her head. 'Paul, he fall off ladder! I think he dead!'

Paul wasn't dead. Vanessa had flown out to the garden, breaking the heel of one of her Jimmy Choos, to find the young gardener dazed but very much alive. An ambulance was quickly called and at the hospital Paul was diagnosed with concussion and a broken left arm. He would be out of action for at least eight weeks.

Racked with guilt, she immediately arranged for flowers to be sent. If she hadn't sent him up there to see to the branch in the first place, none of this would have happened. On a more practical note, thank God they had insurance.

Conrad, on the other hand, was furious with Renata for spoiling his big moment. 'Couldn't the decrepit old bat see he was breathing?'

'She got confused,' Vanessa told him. 'She's an old woman, don't be too hard on her.'

'She looks like she's about to croak any second. We're not running the Cotswold branch of Dignitas here.'

'Conrad!'

'I'm just saying, darling, it makes me *nervous*. She should be in a nursing home where she can't cause trouble. Your mother agrees with me.'

They were in the living room, both nursing strong G and Ts. Vanessa's nerves were in shreds: she'd sent Renata to have a lie-down. Marty had headed back to London shortly after the ambulance had left.

Conrad drummed his fingernails on the arm of the sofa. 'Anyway, back to business.'

'The Silver Box Awards?'

'What else?' His brown eyes glinted. 'My God, I'm going to have the power to make or break a career, Vanessa! Let them bloody know how it feels to be stuck out in the wilderness for a change.'

'We're only presenting them, not deciding who wins,' she pointed out.

Conrad wasn't listening. 'We're the face of Silver Box, beamed into millions of living rooms all over the country! People aren't going to remember Stephen Fry's nauseating speech about how he owes it all to his dead cat, but how great your tits looked and the magnetism of my screen presence.' He sighed happily. 'I'm going to be batting off the roles afterwards.'

'You're incorrigible,' she smiled.

'No, I'm fucking horny.' The thought of being back up where he belonged had given Conrad a raging hard-on. He put a hand on Vanessa's knee.

'We can't,' she protested, half laughing. 'My mother will be down soon.'

He whipped off a cufflink. 'You'd better get your clothes off quick, then.'

Chapter 8

Fleur was on her way back from Evesham market with Ben. As the lorry pulled up at traffic lights she took the chance to wind the window down discreetly. The smell of cheap aftershave was overpowering.

'It'll be better next time,' Ben said stoically. The price they'd got for the ewes had been disappointing. The supermarket meat buyers were paying less too, even though lamb was making good money elsewhere.

'We said that last week,' she sighed. 'And the week before. Face it, Ben, things are crap.'

He looked uncertain, as if the conversation had suddenly got far deeper than he was comfortable with. The same school year as Fleur, he was the archetypal farmer-in-the-making: sturdy and straw-haired, with solid arms and a permanently sunburnt neck.

She gazed out gloomily through the windscreen. Even when things had been better she'd dreaded going to market. There wasn't much that didn't get round the farming community. Everyone knew Robert Blackwater had hit the bottle since his wife had died of cancer. Fleur saw it in people's faces every time she went.

'How's your dad these days, young Fleur?' they'd enquire.

She would answer brightly, with a big smile. 'He's great, thanks! Farm's keeping him busy.'

There was always a fleeting look of sympathy, followed by a stoic nod. Farmers weren't known for being big talkers, thank God.

As they pulled up outside the farmhouse she could see her dad's truck in the yard. He hadn't gone out shopping then, like he'd promised. Fleur noticed the sheds still hadn't been hosed out. She sighed again; another job to do.

'Are you tired?' Ben asked. 'I can take over from here if you want.'

His thigh was almost touching hers on the seat. 'Actually, would you mind?' Fleur said. 'I should really go and check on the heifers.'

She took the quad bike up the hill, frustration burning in her ears. Why did things always have to get complicated? She and Ben used to have such a simple, safe relationship. Now he turned up to work smelling like he was going out on a Saturday night and kept getting caught looking at Fleur's chest. It was a toss-up out of the pair of them who went redder.

'Men!' Fleur exclaimed. As if she had time for a love life anyway.

As soon as she pulled up at the field it was clear something was very wrong. One of the pregnant cows was lying on her side in the throes of labour. Her calf's head was hanging out the back. It was obvious the mother was in great distress.

'Shit.' Fleur should be able to see the tips of the calf's front feet as well, otherwise there was no way of pulling it out.

There was no time to call Ben. She hurriedly assessed the situation. If she pulled the baby out by its head, she risked breaking its neck. If she did nothing the vet would have to be called out for an emergency caesarean and the calf might die anyway.

The thought of another vet's bill galvanized her into action. Very carefully and slowly, she pushed the calf's head back inside the mother. After a painful struggle she managed to unhook its front legs and straightened them out. Tying a rope round each one, she started to pull. It felt like the tiny limbs could snap at any minute but finally the calf came slithering out in a pile of water and mucus. Fleur gave his navel a spray of iodine and got out of the way. Cows could get very protective of their newborns.

'I do hope you're going to wash your hands before lunch,' a voice drawled.

Fleur whirled round. A couple in evening dress were standing on the other side of the five-bar gate. The woman's sequinned gown glittered incongruously in the sunlight. Fleur clocked the man's familiar blond hair and her stomach dropped.

Beau Rainford rested his arms on the top bar, loose bow tie dangling around his tanned neck. 'Flora, isn't it?'

'It's Fleur, dickhead,' she snapped. Did he really not remember?

Beau's eyes rested on her. They were bright blue and glassy, reminding Fleur of a fathomless lake. His companion was nearly the same height as him and anorexically thin. Judging by their ruffled appearance and their evening dress, neither had been to bed yet.

'Did that cow just shoot its load over you?' Beau enquired. 'I've heard how kinky you country folk can be.'

The girl gave a malicious shriek of laughter. 'Oh, that's *disgusting*!'

Fleur's cheeks burnt with humiliation. 'It's a *she*, you idiot, so I very much doubt it. And she and her calf nearly just died then!'

'They look all right to me,' Beau drawled.

Fleur turned back and was inordinately relieved to see the calf standing on shaky legs, suckling its mother.

'We don't care what you get up to in your spare time,' Beau continued, that maddening grin still stuck on his face. 'Valentina here is very open-minded. Aren't you, darling? Although until about half an hour ago, I didn't realize *how* open-minded.'

The two smirked at each other. 'If you don't mind,' Fleur said scathingly, 'some of us have better things to do.'

'Really? This must be more fun than it looks.' Beau draped his arm round Valentina's shoulders, his hand resting deliberately over one perky breast.

'Piss off, or I'll set the dogs on you.'

Beau yawned, not bothering to cover his mouth. 'You could do with chilling out a bit, darling.'

'And a good shower,' sniped Valentina.

There was the sudden growl of an engine and a black convertible Porsche came up the road and rounded the corner, spraying a trail of dust over Fleur's quad bike.

'Taxi's here,' Beau announced. The über-tanned man behind the steering wheel took his sunglasses off.

'What are you doing out here?' he said to Beau. 'Everyone's back at the house.'

'V and I went for a ramble. I had no idea she was such a keen naturist.'

'I think you mean naturalist, mate.'

'No.' Beau smirked. 'I definitely mean naturist.'

Valentina shook her black mane out. 'Baby, let's get out of here.'

'Too right. Bye, Flora.'

'My name is *Fleur*,' she yelled. 'And get off my bloody land!'

Chapter 9

Catherine leant forward in the bedroom mirror. The crease she'd always had between her eyebrows had nearly disappeared. As someone who'd thrived off adrenalin for the last twenty years, she was still rather unsettled by the serene, beatific image now looking back at her.

She went over to the chest of drawers to pull on a pair of socks. Her side of the bedroom looked like a bomb had gone off, clothes everywhere, empty coffee cups, magazines from *Vogue* to the *New Statesman* stacked up by the bed. Vowing again to be a better homemaker, she did a hasty sweep and picked up the dirty cups to take downstairs. As she went past John's study, the door was ajar. He was deep in concentration behind the MacBook Pro.

Catherine leant against the door frame, enjoying the chance to watch him unobserved for a moment. He was wearing what she called his 'Indiana Jones' glasses, big hand resting delicately on the computer mouse. She could smell the familiar tang of Dunhill, the aftershave John had worn for years.

It was so strange how their lives had come full circle. They'd been childhood sweethearts in Newcastle and had met at secondary school when they were eleven. The hunky, popular rugby captain and the skinny girl teased for wearing charity-shop clothes had been an unlikely pair, but the chemistry had been there from the start. When her mother had been sent to prison, John had been the only one to stick up for Catherine. On her seventeenth birthday, a year after her mum had died, Catherine had fled the North for London. She'd honestly thought she'd never see John again.

She could still recall their chance meeting as if it had happened yesterday. It had been *Soirée*'s annual cocktail party at the Natural History Museum. Catherine had been wearing the latest Chanel and uncharacteristic bright red lipstick. The place had been heaving with London's brightest and most beautiful, but the moment she'd clapped eyes on John, dusty-haired and paint-splattered from the job he'd been working on there, everyone else had melted away.

By her own admission, she'd been a bitch at first. Terrified John would reveal her real identity, Catherine had done everything she could to get rid of him. But he'd been a persistent bugger, gently chipping away until he'd regained her trust. When her worst nightmare *had* come true he had been there, by her side. The day they'd married in a quiet ceremony at Chelsea Registry Office had been the happiest of her life.

'Are you going to stand there or come in?' he said, his eyes still on the screen.

'I'm allowed to perve over my own husband, aren't I?'

He grinned and looked up. 'Come here.'

Putting the coffee cups on the side, she went round to sit on his lap. He ran his hand over her Lycra-clad thigh. 'Off for a run?'

'Yeah. You fancy coming?'

'I'll give it a miss this time. I've got a few more emails to reply to.'

She gazed at the computer. 'It must be nice to have some work to do.'

'Is that the voice of discontent I'm hearing?'

When she didn't answer he put his hand under her chin, making her look at him. 'Hey. What's up?'

'I don't know. It just feels weird sometimes, not having a career any more.'

'You've still got a career,' he reasoned. 'You're just taking some time out.'

'What if I go back and no one wants me?' London already seemed an alien and intimidating place.

'Don't talk rubbish. You're the most talented person I know, Cath. You could get back into any job you wanted.'

She kicked the leg of the table, feeling a bit like a child getting a pep talk.

'This is what you wanted, isn't it?' He tucked a piece of hair behind her ear. 'I haven't pushed you into coming out here?'

'Of course you haven't. I've got you and our beautiful home, and we've made really good friends here.' She took a deep breath. 'I guess . . . I mean, what I'm really trying to say is, well, I thought I'd be pregnant by now.'

There was a long pause. 'That's not the only reason we came here.'

'It was a big reason, John, let's be honest.'

'These things take time, Cath. You have to be patient.'

'I'm bored of being patient. I just don't understand.' She had taken so much folic acid she was starting to rattle. 'I'm forty next year. What if I've left it too late?'

'There's still time. You're in fantastic shape, the doctor said so herself. We've still got every chance, OK?'

'OK,' she replied in a small voice.

'And if nothing happens, we'll cross that bridge when we come to it. OK? I love you, Cath. I'm here with you every step of the way.'

The tenderness in his voice made her want to weep.

'Let me look after you for a while,' he said into her hair. 'I want you to enjoy life.'

'I feel bad not having a job,' she sniffed.

He wiped her nose with his shirt sleeve. 'You don't need a job. We've got plenty of money.'

'Maybe I should join the WI,' she said, trying to joke. 'It would give me something to do.'

'Let's not get ahead of ourselves; I'm not sure the old ladies of Beeversham are ready for your jam-making.' After years of surviving on ready meals for one, Catherine's culinary skills weren't the best.

'Any more of that and I'll threaten to make dinner,' she told him.

They grinned at each other. 'Promise me you're OK?' John asked.

'I'm OK.'

He gave her a kiss and let her stand up. 'I thought we'd eat in the garden tonight. I'll grill the sea bass on the barbecue.'

'Sounds amazing. What would I do without you?'

'Starve, probably. Oh and Cath?'

She stopped at the door. 'Yes?'

His eyes were already back on the screen. 'Your arse looks bloody fantastic in those shorts.'

Chapter 10

That Tuesday was the second SNOW meeting at the town hall. So many people turned out that it was standing room only. An outrageously foxy brunette waved at Catherine from across the room. Mel Cooper-Stanley, owner of Buff Nail Bar on the High Street. Mel was forty-three, with a hard aerobics body that made women half her age green with jealousy. She was also a complete hoot and Catherine's wine-drinking partner.

Catherine went over to sit down between Mel and Amanda Belcher. 'No Mike tonight?' she asked. Mel's husband was a long-haul captain for British Airways and always off in some far-flung location.

'He's got a night stop in Buenos Aires, back tomorrow.' Mel brushed a stray hair off her surgically enhanced chest. Henry Belcher, sitting two down, started having a coughing fit. 'How's things with you, babe?' Mel asked.

'Great, you?'

'Run off my feet at the nail bar!' Mel smiled wickedly. 'Still, can't complain. Keeps me out of trouble.'

Felix cleared his throat at the front of the room. 'Welcome, everyone. I hope you're managing to make the most of this glorious weather. Right, we won't waste any time. As you know, the county council have come back with a date for the first Ye Olde Worlde hearing, Tuesday the fourth of July.'

'About time!' Mr Patel shouted.

'Having been to a few of these meetings I can hopefully give you some idea of what to expect.' Felix gave a smile to the person standing on his left. 'We're also lucky enough to have John here, who's been through quite a few planning applications himself.'

The double doors creaked open. Lynette Tudor flushed puce as everyone turned to look at her. 'Sorry I'm late.' She scurried off to find a seat at the back.

'Poor Lynette,' Catherine said in a low voice. 'She always looks on the verge of a nervous breakdown.'

'So would I if Talia was my daughter,' Amanda whispered sanctimoniously. 'Olympia says she's been out drinking every night this week, instead of revising!'

Catherine watched Lynette drop her handbag on a man's foot by accident and start apologizing profusely. 'Is Talia's dad not in the picture?'

'Rumour has it he's a *younger* man Lynette met on holiday in the Bosphorus Strait!' Amanda whispered excitedly. 'One of these "thanks for the shag" jobbies, never to be seen again.'

Mel tutted. 'What kind of arsehole does that to his own kid?'

This time the mood in the meeting was far more relaxed. Felix was his normal jolly, reassuring self. Most of the women were so busy staring at John's broad shoulders as he explained planning law that they forgot to be worried. Everyone seemed sure that the planning officer would recommend against Ye Olde Worlde. It was only common sense.

Felix was wrapping things up by telling people the best parking options at Gloucester County Council Shire Hall when the lady who ran the fruit and veg shop stuck her hand up.

'Are we any closer to finding out who owns Pear Tree Holdings?'

Everyone sat up. Pear Tree Holdings was the mysterious company which actually owned the land. While Sid Sykes was the public face of the development, Pear Tree remained a silent partner in the background. It was both sinister and maddening, as people had no idea who their puppetmaster was.

The fact that Pear Tree Holdings had registered with Companies House on the Isle of Man, where anonymity was guaranteed to company owners, had fuelled suspicion and paranoia. Mr Patel was convinced al-Qaeda were behind it and proceeds from the theme park would go towards building anti-West nuclear missiles. Donald Trump was another contender. Even more terrifyingly, someone had mooted Kate Moss.

'I'm afraid we're banging our heads against a brick wall,' Felix said. 'Companies House isn't legally obliged to release any information about who owns it.'

'Why can't we get Sykes to tell us?' someone else asked.

John spoke up. 'As long as Pear Tree Holdings is legal – which it is – Sykes is under no obligation to release any details about who he's working with.'

'It's just so frustrating!' Ginny exclaimed. 'If we had a name, we could at least try to appeal to their sense of reason.'

Amanda Belcher stood up. 'I have a new theory. Suppose it's someone closer to home? A lot closer to home,' she added significantly.

Murmurs rippled across the room. Beside his wife, Henry Belcher put his head in his hands.

'What if . . .' Amanda paused, eking out the moment. 'Beau *Rainford* owns Pear Tree Holdings?'

The murmurs turned into a babble. Ginny Chamberlain's shocked voice cut across all of them. 'Oh no! It couldn't possibly be true!'

'Amanda, would you care to elaborate?' Felix asked calmly.

'I'm sorry, Felix, but somebody has to say it!' She looked round, warming to her theme. 'Look at how he's practically razed Blackwater Farm to the ground to build that sex den up there. This is just the kind of thing he'd do.'

Henry put his hand on his wife's arm, but she shook it off. 'It would be just like Beau, buying up Blaize Castle to spite you, Felix! You and this whole town!'

People were talking loudly now, contemplating the idea that Beau Rainford would dare shit on his doorstep like that. For once Felix was lost for words. John stepped forward and restored calm.

'Amanda, have you got any actual basis for this?'

'Well, no,' she blustered. 'But that doesn't mean anything!'

'Yes, it does,' John said evenly.

Amanda, who Catherine suspected had a huge crush on John, went pink at his rebuke. 'I was just saying . . .'

'I know, Amanda, but making groundless accusations isn't going to help anyone. In my experience it's quite likely Pear Tree will be owned by a consortium rather than one individual. They could even be overseas investors.'

'Really?' Henry Belcher said. 'Why do you say that, John?'

John shrugged. 'Ye Olde Worlde is an American franchise. I wouldn't be at all surprised if they wanted to have a hand in the UK market. They know their chances are much better trading under a British name.'

Amanda opened her mouth, but John cut her off. 'We can sit here all night discussing who might own Pear Tree, but it won't get us anywhere. We're better off concentrating on what we do know.'

Tristan Jago, who had been uncharacteristically quiet until now, stuck his hand up. 'I have a question.'

'Yes?' Felix said gratefully.

'I'd like to know what our MP proposes to do about the two pence an hour rise in parking charges at Ratchford Hospital. Isn't it enough these poor people have to contend with the demise of their loved ones, without the government launching yet another attack on the NHS? What next, a stethoscope tax on our hard-working doctors?'

'Oh, give it a rest Tristan,' sighed Felix.

Bar 47 may have looked like a quintessential Cotswold pub from the outside, but the interior had been opened up to make a stunning bar and Italian restaurant.

With a team of young, hot staff run by the flamboyant Vincent, the place was always packed. The food was superb and a plate of the lobster ravioli could send a customer into orgasmic raptures for a week.

While John joined the scrum at the bar Catherine wandered out to the terrace, waving at Vincent, who was charming a table of middle-aged ladies.

The back terrace at Bar 47 had the best view in Beeversham, a panoramic vista that opened up across the valley. The sunset that evening was incredible, swathes of melting red and orange. The craggy ruins of Blaize Castle were framed black against the sky. Catherine couldn't take her eyes off it. The castle had been there as long as the landscape. It was unthinkable to imagine looking out on anything else.

John appeared a few minutes later with a bottle of Pinot Grigio in a metal ice bucket. He poured a glass out and handed it to her.

'Thanks, babe.' She stuck her nose in and contemplatively inhaled honeysuckle and wild grass. 'Do you really think an American company owns Pear Tree?'

'Who knows? I just felt so sorry for Felix I had to say something.'

She looked over to where Amanda was talking animatedly to Ginny. Ginny was nodding and responding, but didn't look her normal cheery self.

'Amanda's oblivious, isn't she?' Catherine asked. 'Poor Ginny.' She watched her husband take a sip of wine. 'Do you think Beau is involved with Pear Tree?'

There was a discreet cough behind them. Felix stood there with a pint of real ale in his hand.

Catherine was mortified. 'Felix, I didn't mean . . .'

He smiled tiredly. 'It's fine, really. I just wanted to come and say thank you to John for stepping in back then.'

'It is very possible a foreign company is behind this, Felix,' John told him.

'Maybe you're right.' Felix looked up at the castle and sighed. 'I might be an old fool, but I don't think even Beau has got the chutzpah for this one. At least I really hope not.'

He looked so defeated. Catherine felt desperately sorry for him. 'I'm sure it will all work out,' she told him.

Felix gave her a resigned smile. 'I hope so.'

The new Michael Bublé album had been tinkling in the background. It was suddenly drowned out by a rhythmic thudding reverberating through the air. Everyone stopped to stare as a red helicopter rose out of the hills. The registration was unmistakable: B–RAIN.

The backdraught from the propellers whipped up napkins and ruffled people's hair. The noise was terrific. Catherine imagined Beau sitting beside his pilot, tanned face carved and unsmiling. She glanced at Felix, but his expression was unreadable. The aircraft hovered over them for a second before swooping away across the valley.

Chapter 11

Vanessa had been in her office all morning. She had the house to herself for once: Conrad had gone to Harley Street for his monthly check-up and Dominique had taken the chance to ride along in the Bentley and go shopping at Harrods. Even Renata was out, visiting her cousin in Cheltenham for the day. The house was blissfully quiet without the constant blast of American chat shows from the TV in the basement.

She fired off another email to her PA and sat back thoughtfully. The meeting with the executive producer and controller of ITV1 had gone extremely well. Vanessa and Conrad had done a script read-through in the producer's office, and although Conrad had lingered a *little* too long on his introduction, they had seemed to like it. A schmoozy lunch at The Ivy had followed, with lots of significant looks and enthusiastic laughing, always a good sign.

Conrad was already practising his speech in front of the mirror, but Vanessa didn't want to get carried away. They hadn't signed the contract yet, as she kept reminding him. It was hard not to be buoyed by his enthusiasm though, and it reminded her why she'd fallen in love with him in the first place.

Her mother wasn't around to chide her about not wearing lipstick, so Vanessa had left her face make-up-free and piled her tawny hair up in a bun. She was wearing a simple cashmere vest and the black DKNY leggings Conrad said made her look like a village hall aerobics instructor.

She felt something lick her bare foot. Sukie was sprawled out under her desk like a fluffy slipper.

'Are you hungry, my darling?' Vanessa asked.

The dog jumped up and started wagging her tail furiously.

'Biscuit?' Vanessa asked.

Sukie did a circle of excitement. 'Come on then, darling!' Vanessa said, geeing her up. 'Biscuits, Sukie, biscuits!'

The hypo-allergenic dog food was kept in the utility room, a huge place the size of most people's kitchens. She bent down with a treat. The dog snatched it out of her hand and trotted out without a backward glance.

Animals were about as loyal as most humans she met, Vanessa thought wryly. They got what they wanted out of you and got the hell out.

She opened the utility door to let in some fresh air and went back into the kitchen. That weekend's *Cotswolds on Sunday* lay on the worktop. Getting herself a glass of San Pellegrino, she sat down to flick through it. Amongst the stories about bus shelters being demolished and a knicker thief on the loose, a headline caught her eye.

'THE PROBLEM WITH PEAR TREE!'

It was an article about the Ye Olde Worlde development. Vanessa read it with more interest: she and Conrad had both been alarmed by the prospect of having a theme park at their back door. She was surprised to see Beau Rainford's name mentioned as a possible investor, although his lawyers had issued a strongly worded statement denying any involvement. There was a grainy shot of Beau in black tie, gazing insolently into the camera. Would Beau do something like that? Vanessa wondered.

Over the years, the Powells and Beau had crossed paths at several parties. Conrad couldn't stand Beau, but Vanessa suspected it was more the fact that Conrad was jealous that someone was better looking than him. She had never been into blonds herself, but Beau was really something. She'd read somewhere that his latest squeeze was the Givenchy model Valentina Volosky.

The emails would be mounting but Vanessa didn't feel like going back to work just yet. Leaving the kitchen, she started to wander through the downstairs. Every room looked like a page in *Homes and Gardens*. The dining room that sat thirty, the fully stocked library no one ever used, the gym wing complete with Swedish sauna and a Pilates reformer machine costing four thousand pounds. Vanessa had never been into cocaine or getting annihilated on alcohol. This place was her drug. Everywhere she looked was success, the best of everything.

For the millionth time she wished her dad were alive to see it. An only child, she had been extremely close to her Armenian father, Raoul. He was the only person who'd been able to soften his wife's sharp edges. Her parents had met when her dad had spotted a beautiful girl standing in the rain at Piccadilly Circus with a small suitcase. 'I just saw this sadness,' he'd tell Vanessa. 'I knew at that moment I wanted to protect her.'

She loved hearing the story, because it showed a vulnerable side of her mother that she had never got to see. Unlike Raoul, who'd regaled the family with tales of his life back home, Dominique had never really talked about her upbringing. She'd been born on the French-speaking island of Réunion, a beautiful but poverty-stricken place in the Indian Ocean. Her parents had been killed in a car crash when she was a baby, and Dominique had been brought up by her strict grandmother. As she got older herself, Vanessa often wondered if the early tragedy in her mother's life had contributed to her inability to reach out to her own daughter.

Dominique had stayed at home to bring up Vanessa, while Raoul Jardine had run his own carpet-fitting business. He'd worked hard to make sure his daughter received the education he'd never had. His proudest achievement had been sending her to Vespers, a re-nowned private school in Holland Park.

It had been the darkest time of Vanessa's life. A dumpy, shy teenager, she had stuck out painfully among her leggy, worldly contemporaries. She was bullied about her rough accent and terraced house, excluded from weekend plans and boy talk. The other mums shunned Dominique at the school gates, jealous and intimidated by her beauty. No matter how hard Vanessa tried to fit in, she was still 'Gippy Jardine', the girl with a moustache whose dad was a lowly carpet fitter.

The miracle intervention had come at eighteen. She discovered Jolene for the first time and then, overnight, her puppy fat had literally melted. Suddenly she had become beautiful. Ten years later, she was richer and prettier than any of those bullies at school. That was why having money was so important. Every pound Vanessa made, she made to show *them*.

A brown speckled bird landed on the lawn, beak stabbing the grass in a hunt for worms. When she'd met Conrad he'd promised to take care of her, but Vanessa felt it was increasingly the other way round now. She ran the house and paid their staff, took the conference calls with PR brands and sponsorship people. If she let herself think about it, the amount of responsibility she had would overwhelm her.

Dominique was another constant worry. Vanessa knew she missed her husband desperately, but Vanessa had lost her father as well. When had anyone sat *her* down to ask if she was OK?

Her eyes suddenly brimmed with tears. She wished so much her dad were here. He'd always known how to make her feel better. He'd be able to stop her mother crying at night in her bedroom, and end the yawning emptiness Vanessa was starting to feel these days, no matter what she'd achieved. Her father would know how to stop her marriage unravelling and turn Conrad back into the man she'd married . . .

She was crying so much she couldn't see. At first she thought she had a false lash in her eye, but then the dark shape outside the window moved again. Her despair was immediately replaced by a new emotion. Fear.

There was a scruffy, wild-eyed man in the garden. And he was looking straight at her.

Vanessa dropped to the floor in a panic. How had he got in? The Porsche was in the garage and there were no cars parked out the front. He must have thought the place was empty and decided to try his chances . . .

She always thought she'd be completely capable in a situation like this, but she found herself frozen with fear. A shadow fell on the white carpet. Oh God, he was outside the window . . .

'My jewellery's upstairs!' she screamed. 'Just take it and get out!' She thought of the story in the papers recently about an actress who'd been held at knifepoint in her own home. Something brushed against her face, making her shriek again. It was Sukie, with one of her ornamental silk cushions in her mouth. Aghast, she watched as the dog trotted into the middle of the room with the cushion and started to grind in an unladylike fashion against it.

'Sukie!' she whispered hysterically, but the dog took no notice.

There was no noise from outside. 'What do you want?' she screamed. Was this unknown assailant getting off seeing her cower like a frightened animal?

Mustering up the courage, Vanessa peeked up from under the windowsill. There was no one there. She got up, shooting fearful glances everywhere. Where had he gone? Was he in the house? An icy fist clenched in the pit of her stomach. She'd left the utility door open.

A man's voice sounded. 'Hello, anyone in?'

She clutched her chest and tried to still her frantic heart. Burglars didn't call out a greeting, did they? Picking up the paperweight from the desk just in case, she crept out into the hall. 'Hello?'

Then Vanessa nearly had her second heart attack of the day. The intruder was standing right there, in her kitchen!

'What do you want?' she demanded hysterically. 'My husband is here, you know!'

He glanced at the paperweight. 'Sorry, I didn't mean to startle you.'

If this *was* a burglar, he was the best-looking one Vanessa had ever seen. A second improbable thought quickly followed. *Of all the days not to put on make-up . . .*

'So shall I ask him about gardening work then?' the stranger asked.

She put the paperweight down on the worktop, within reach for safe measure. 'I'm sorry?'

'I'm here about gardening work,' the man repeated. His voice was mellow, almost musical in its quality. Vanessa couldn't stop staring at him. His face was framed by a halo of thick, black unruly curls that made him look like a fallen cherub. She put him in his late twenties, with the crinkles and laughter lines of someone who spent a lot of time outdoors.

'Has Tamzin sent you?' she asked.

'Who's Tamzin?'

'My PA, she's recruiting for me at the moment.' Her earlier fright had made Vanessa's voice shrill. 'Why didn't you use the intercom?'

'The gates were open.'

'They were? Oh.' She swallowed. 'My husband must have forgotten to shut them when he left.'

He surveyed her with a hint of amusement. 'I thought you said your husband was in?'

'He is. I mean he was. He's, er, gone out.' Vanessa trailed off. He really had the most unusual eyes, a silvery, iridescent colour. She wondered if he might be a Romany gypsy.

The man held his hand out. 'Dylan Goldhawk.'

'Vanessa Powell.' She felt the rough calloused palm against hers and snatched her hand back.

'Are you local?' she asked.

'I've just moved into the area.' He looked at her curiously. She realized her eyes must be red. 'Allergies,' she said curtly. She jumped as Sukie brushed past her ankles and headed straight for Dylan. He bent down and put a tanned hand on the dog's tiny head.

'Hello, mouse. My dog would eat you for breakfast.'

'Her name is Sukie,' Vanessa said pointedly. 'And I do hope you haven't brought your dog on to the premises.'

'Don't worry, he's in the van.' Dylan grinned. He seemed to be in no hurry to go anywhere. She felt completely out of her comfort zone.

'As it happens we are looking for someone on a temporary basis. Do you have any references?'

'Nope.'

'No? So you just turn up at people's houses and offer your services?'

'If you're not happy with what I do don't pay me,' he said simply. 'I've never had any dissatisfied customers before.'

The businesswoman in Vanessa winced. 'You'd better give me your mobile number, then.'

'I don't have one.'

Vanessa slept with her BlackBerry virtually clamped on her ear. 'You don't have a mobile phone?'

Dylan gave an easy grin. 'I've obviously caught you at a bad time. Why don't I come back in a few days when you've had a chance to think about it?'

'You can't just turn up, I could be out!' Had he never heard of a schedule before?

'So I'll leave a message.' He gave her a crooked smile that showed off surprisingly white teeth. 'Nice to meet you, Vanessa.'

'Goodbye, Mr Goldhawk,' she said formally.

'See you, Mrs Powell.'

Moments later he loped past the kitchen windows. Vanessa raced through the house to peek out the drawing room, but he was nowhere to be seen. It was as if he'd magically melted back into the countryside.

She flopped on the sofa, out of sorts. What a peculiar man! Who did that, turned up at people's back doors to try and find work? He definitely had to be some sort of traveller.

'Hopefully we won't be seeing him again,' she told Sukie. An image of Dylan's eyes, a pair of shimmery moons, flashed into her mind.

Chapter 12

From Paisley to Plymouth the weather continued its balmy run. A holiday atmosphere descended over Britain and a Tuesday morning on Brighton beach looked like something out of a Thomas Cook holiday brochure, while office workers abandoned soggy sandwiches eaten at their desks and descended on pub gardens with relish. Parks everywhere teemed with life: rollerbladers, mothers with small children and bikini-clad teenagers absconding from GCSE leave to share bottles of cider and the odd mid-afternoon joint.

Driving back to Beeversham that day in her open-top MG, Catherine was in a great mood. It was one of those spring days where everything was in glorious Technicolor. Engorged verges threatened to burst on to the roads at any moment while apple-green trees were framed perfectly against royal-blue skies.

Flicking through the radio, Catherine came across Katrina and The Waves. Nothing like a bit of cheese on a day like this. Catherine whacked it right up and started singing along tunelessly. 'Woo yeah yeah . . .'

She zoomed down into a tunnel of trees. She'd been thinking a lot about her mum today. Catherine had never known her dad, a travelling salesman who had neglected to tell Annie Fincham he had another family, but Catherine had never felt like she had missed out. There might not have been much money, but she had always felt secure and loved.

She glanced across at the passenger seat. She suddenly had the strangest sensation that her mother was sitting there, her radiant smile and long auburn hair blowing in the breeze. *Cathy, how are you, pet . . .*

As she came back out into the light again Catherine was filled with the most wonderful warmth. Blinking back the tears, she smiled.

I love you, Mam. And I'm doing OK.

John was in the back garden on his iPad. He looked up and greeted her with a smile. 'All right, gorgeous?'

'All right.'

He looked mock hurt. 'I'm not gorgeous?'

'I said you're all right,' Catherine laughed, going round to give him a kiss. She caught the headline. TORIES FACE ABYSS AS SUPPORT CRUMBLES.

'Another MP has just defected to Labour,' he told her.

'God, who'd be a Tory politician at the moment? They're about as popular as a raging case of herpes.'

The house phone started ringing. 'I'll get it,' she said.

It was a cold-caller, trying to sell her a stair lift. Catherine was in such a good mood she patiently endured his waffle, even wishing the man a nice day before putting the phone down. 'I'll start on lunch,' she yelled out the door.

She had spent a fortune at the deli, including a six-pound bottle of organic sparkling apple juice in a pretty glass bottle. An extravagance, but it was an occasion that should be toasted in style.

She emptied out a tray of quails' eggs on to a plate. Normally regular to the hour, her period was a week late. Her breasts were tender and achy and she was off her normal beloved morning cup of coffee. Smells and tastes were sharper and more pungent. She didn't need to do a pregnancy test: her own body was telling her.

Catherine went over to the window, where John was at the table engrossed in his iPad. As she looked at his big, dark head bent over, she felt such a rush of emotion. What would their child inherit from each of them? John's practicality and winning smile, the ability he had to sleep through a gale-force wind? Or her flat feet and stubborn insistence on seeing anything she did through to the bitter end? The thought of him or her with their whole life in front of them: experiences, triumphs, defeats and all made her feel exhilarated and terrified in equal measure.

Picking up the tray, she went to break the news to her husband.

Chapter 13

It was official: Conrad and Vanessa were the hosts of that year's Silver Box Awards.

'My wife and I are delighted to be presenting such a prestigious occasion,' Conrad said in the couple's official statement. 'It's every actor's dream.'

In private he was equally ebullient. 'It might just have been a few lines in someone's office, but we all felt the magic.' His dark eyes glistened. 'I'm seriously expecting an Oscar nomination within two years.'

Vanessa laughed. Conrad shot her a look.

'Don't take the piss,' he said sharply. 'This is a big deal for me.'

'Conrad, I wasn't . . .' God, he was being serious!

At least Dominique could be counted on to side with her son-in-law. 'I'm sure you were wonderful, Conrad. There was never any doubt in my mind you'd get the job.'

'What about me, Mother?' Vanessa asked. 'Are you pleased for me?'

Dominique shot her an odd look. 'Of course I am, Vanessa. It's just that Conrad is the actor in the family.'

Silly me, Vanessa thought. *As if I'm anyone important.*

They were in the dining room, a vast all-white room dominated by a marbled fireplace at the far end. The greasy remains of the starter lay on the Wedgwood plates in front of them. Tonight's pan-fried scallops had not been a great success. To make matters worse, Conrad's wine snobbery was on fire tonight. He'd already sent two perfectly acceptable Burgundies back.

'Vanessa, you're really going to have to do something about Renata's cooking skills,' Dominique said. 'This simply isn't good enough.'

A spark of annoyance flared inside Vanessa. 'I've got an idea; why don't you cook one night?' *And lift a bloody finger for once*, she wanted to add.

Dominique shot her daughter an icy stare across the table. Vanessa picked up her glass. Conrad was too involved in celebrating his success to notice the drop in temperature. 'Ah, the Puligny-Montrachet from the Côte de Beaune,' he exclaimed as Renata shuffled back in with a new bottle. He took it and inspected the label with a flourish. 'And a fantastic year, 2001.'

'Oh, Conrad,' Dominique cooed. 'You are knowledgeable.' She turned her back on Vanessa, making her annoyance clear. 'Tell me about the time you worked with Sir Michael Caine again, Conrad, I do love to hear it.'

As Conrad starting waxing lyrical about his screen presence Vanessa gazed round the imposing dining room. What a beautiful, cold house this was. She found herself thinking again about the mysterious Dylan Goldhawk. It was obvious he wasn't coming back. Vanessa thought of Dylan's kind smile and shimmery eyes and was shocked at how disappointed she felt.

Chapter 14

Fleur and Robert Blackwater sat in silence at the kitchen table. She'd made them up a simple chicken salad, but neither seemed to have much appetite.

'Come on, Dad, eat your greens or you'll never grow,' she said. It was a weak joke, but she was worried about how ill he was looking.

He reached for his glass of beer instead. 'Concentrate on your plate and I'll concentrate on mine.'

A few painful moments dragged past. Mustering up a smile, she tried again.

'I saw Ginny Chamberlain in town earlier. Loads of people are going to the meeting at county hall.'

'Can't say I see the point.'

'Dad, if this theme park goes ahead, it's really going to affect us!'

'We're fighting a losing battle up here anyway.'

'That's not true.'

He laughed unhappily. 'Wish I shared your optimism, lass.'

She wanted to reach across the table and shake him.

She wanted to throw the stupid beer bottle against the wall and tell him she couldn't do this all by herself. Instead she sat there and held her tongue.

The dogs started barking outside, signalling they had visitors. Robert frowned and checked his wristwatch. 'Who's this?' They didn't get many people dropping in these days.

A silver Citroën bumped cautiously into the yard. A man in a smart suit was behind the wheel. From the vehicle's pristine appearance, it was clear the driver wasn't someone who had much to do with farming.

Tinker and Bess were still barking, straining at their chains. The man sat behind the wheel looking nervous.

'He must be lost,' Fleur said. 'I'll go and see.'

'He's not lost.' Robert's ruddy cheeks had drained of colour. 'That's our bank manager.'

Herbert Stanley perched awkwardly on the chair looking like he'd rather be anywhere else. His glossy black briefcase was on the seat next to him.

'Robert, you haven't returned any of my calls.'

Fleur's dad crossed his arms and glowered.

'I've also written several times,' Mr Stanley ventured.

'I haven't got time to go through correspondence!' Robert growled.

An embarrassed silence fell over the room. Fleur studied her dirty fingernails. Why had their bank manager driven out here to see them? Whatever the reason, it couldn't be good.

Eventually she heard Mr Stanley sigh. 'Look, Robert, I've known your family a long time now. I know how difficult things are, but we have to come to some arrangement. I've been prepared to use my discretion on this, but I can only go so far.' He sat up, and got down to business. 'You have to start paying the loan back, Robert.'

Fleur's head snapped up. 'What loan?'

Mr Stanley looked at her uncertainly. 'The loan you've taken out against the farm.'

What loan? 'How much for?' she asked, trying to sound calm.

'With interest, the current amount is,' Mr Stanley shuffled through his paperwork as a formality, 'three hundred thousand and twelve pounds and seventy-nine pence.'

The numbers fluttered meaninglessly in Fleur's ears, coming to settle like a pinball machine. 'Three hundred thousand?' she gasped. 'We haven't got that kind of . . .'

'Be quiet, Fleur!' her dad shouted.

Mr Stanley looked extremely uncomfortable. 'If you don't meet your side of the arrangement, the bank will have no options but to start legal proceedings against you. Or else . . .'

'Or what?' Fleur whispered.

Her dad's voice dropped to an unnerving calm. 'They'll take Blackwater Farm off us, that's what.'

'Dad . . .' Fleur was struggling to find the words. 'How could you take out a loan without *telling* me?'

Father and daughter faced each other across the table. Mr Stanley had talked in financial jargon, but she understood the gist of it. To get the loan her father had had to secure the farm against it. If they couldn't start paying it back, the bank could force them to sell to recoup their money.

'It's none of your concern.'

'Of course it is, Dad! We're meant to be a team!'

'You've got enough on your plate.'

Fleur was trying so hard to stay calm. 'What about the money we got from Beau Rainford?' *I can't believe you went behind my back again*, she wanted to scream at him.

'It's all gone.' Robert saw his daughter's face and gave a derisive laugh. 'Open your eyes, lass, we've been going under for years.'

'I wonder why,' she muttered.

'What did you say?' he said sharply.

She dropped her eyes. 'Nothing.'

They sat there in an awful silence. 'How are we going to pay it back?' Fleur asked. 'Three hundred thousand pounds. It's a huge amount of money!'

'Thank you for pointing that out,' he said tightly. 'We'll find a way.'

'What way? We're struggling as it is.'

'It's not your concern.'

'Don't treat me like a child. I'm not stupid!'

'And I'm your father,' he roared. 'So stop challenging me!'

Tears sprang into her eyes and a look of anguish flashed across Robert Blackwater's face. He got up and walked out, leaving his daughter alone at the table.

Chapter 15

'Thanks so much for seeing me, Felix. I didn't know who else to call.'

Fleur sat nervously on the hard-backed chair and glanced round. Chamberlains & Co. wasn't a big office, with the low roof and uneven floor of an old building. A SNOW poster was tacked up in the front window, while sepia photographs of a bygone Beeversham were framed on the wall.

His secretary's desk was at the front of the office, while Felix's more superior one was down the far end. A photo of Ginny in a summery dress stood next to graduation pictures of a young blond man and woman. The woman had Ginny's sweet smile and Fleur guessed they must be Felix's children.

Felix sat back in his chair. 'Do you want to fill me in on what's been going on?'

She told him what had happened the previous day, omitting the part where her dad had passed out later on drunk in his study. Felix listened and took notes, interrupting Fleur occasionally to clarify something she'd said. At the end he laid his fountain pen down.

'And you say the loan is three hundred thousand pounds.'

'Yes.' Hearing the amount again made Fleur feel sick. 'They can't take the farm off us, can they?' she asked anxiously.

'The general principle is that if you take a loan out, you have to pay it back,' Felix said gently.

'I didn't realize how bad things have got. I should have done something sooner.'

'I would imagine you've got quite enough to worry about, Fleur.'

She was horrified to feel her eyes filling up. He handed her a tissue from the box on the desk. 'Here. I always keep these here for emergencies.'

'I didn't mean to come in and start blubbing,' she sobbed.

'It's all right, Fleur, I'm quite used to it.' He gave her a wink.

She managed a small smile back. 'Couldn't we just sell the farm and buy back what we could afford? It has to be worth five times what our loan is.'

'It's not that simple, I'm afraid. The bank could insist on what's called a "forced sale". The property goes to auction and is usually sold at a fraction of its value.' Felix looked concerned. 'Mr Stanley is saying it's not just the amount you owe, Fleur, it's the unpaid interest as well.'

Fleur's trump card had been snatched away. She felt tears prickle in her eyes again. 'Then I don't know what to do . . .'

'Look, I know Herbert Stanley,' Felix said. 'He's

a reasonable sort of chap. I'll have a word with him and see if they can extend their grace period for a bit longer. At least it would give you a chance to market the property for a decent price.'

It wasn't the solution she wanted, but at least it gave them more time. 'Oh Felix, thank you so much!' Fleur blushed suddenly. 'I'm so sorry. I've got no money to pay for your time.'

'Think of it as a helping hand.'

'I promise I won't let you down.'

'I'm sure you have every intention of being honourable, Fleur. I'll let you know what Mr Stanley says.'

Fleur stepped out into the sunlight, feeling some of the stress had been lifted. Even if she had to work every hour of the day and night and eat baked beans for a year, they'd pay that loan back. Every last penny. In the meantime, she would think of new ways for the farm to make more money. Fleur marched back towards the Land Rover with a new resolution. Whatever the outcome, she wasn't going down without a fight.

Chapter 16

Conrad's study door was closed. Vanessa went in without knocking. 'Conrad, have you seen . . .'

He was on the phone, legs tossed up on the desk. 'Out!' he hissed under his breath. 'As I was saying, Jasmine, I use Valiant Hair Colour for Men because I just love the tone and texture it gives my hair. All of us need a little help now and again, don't we, Jasmine? Although I'm sure your hair is just lovely as it is . . .'

She'd completely forgotten he was doing an interview with *ELLE*. Mouthing an apology, she beat a sharp exit and went down into the den. She found Renata reading the latest James Patterson, holding the book an inch from her nose.

'Have you seen my mother?' Vanessa asked, wondering if such grisly material was suitable for a woman Renata's age.

'Sorry, *kochanie.*'

The trouble with three people living in a house this size was that you never knew where anyone was half the time.

'I'll keep looking.' Renata didn't respond. 'I said, "I'll keep looking,"' Vanessa said more loudly.

'I hear you the first time. Oh! There was a man. Here, the other day. He ask for you.'

'A man?' Vanessa repeated.

Renata put the book down. 'Derek?'

'Dylan?' Vanessa prompted. 'Dylan Goldhawk?'

'Yes, that him.' She giggled girlishly. 'Nice bottom!'

Vanessa was reeling. 'When did he come?'

'Sunday? Monday?'

'It's Thursday today!'

Renata looked philosophical. 'The time, it go so quickly these days. He say something about gardening work? I say to him: "Mrs Powell will work you like slave, but she pay good money." I tell him your mother a bitch but she never come out to garden.'

'Is he coming back?' Vanessa asked impatiently.

'I think he come in the morning.' Renata's tiny eyes gleamed under the heavy glasses. 'He is handsome, *kochanie*, is he not?'

'I really wouldn't know,' Vanessa said primly. 'And next time we have visitors, do try and remember to tell me.'

The next morning Vanessa was in her office by 7 a.m. Nearly two hours had gone by and she was beginning to lose hope. Dylan would have arrived by now if he was coming. Renata had obviously got it wrong.

At that moment, Vanessa nearly choked on her San Pellegrino. Dylan had materialized outside the open window. He was nut-brown and sinewy in a faded blue vest.

'Hello.'

'You're late,' she said brusquely. 'I like my staff to start at eight-thirty prompt.'

He gave an easy smile. 'I'll work late, then.'

'We have schedules in this house, Mr Goldhawk . . .' There she was again, sounding like a nineteenth-century countess! Vanessa took a deep, calming breath. 'Sorry. You just startled me.'

'Where do you want me to start?'

'Start?' she said stupidly.

'The garden?'

'Um . . .' she waved vaguely. 'You could start with tidying the flowerbeds up.'

Dylan gave a heart-melting smile. 'I'll get started, then.'

It was such a beautiful day Vanessa decided to have lunch in the garden. She fixed herself a salad and took a tray into the garden. Dylan was on the far side of the lawn, expertly deadheading a rose.

Arranging herself prettily on the daybed, she started to pick at her food while surreptitiously watching him from under her Chanel shades. He bent down to pick up a handful of grass cuttings, exposing a flash of rib under his vest. He really didn't have a spare inch of fat on him, she thought. Good shoulders, though.

Not that she was looking.

When he came over ten minutes later Vanessa pretended to be engrossed in her BlackBerry. 'Sorry, I was miles away!' She looked at the little red fruits in his hand. 'What are they?'

'Wild strawberries. Try one.'

'Have they been washed?' she asked dubiously.

'They won't kill you.' He smiled and tipped a few into her hand.

She hesitated before picking the reddest one. 'It's gorgeous!' she exclaimed as a sweet intense flavour flooded her mouth.

'Much nicer than anything you'll find in Daylesford Organic.'

'I didn't know we had these in the garden.'

'Nature has a way of infiltrating even the best-kept places.'

Dylan's smile was as light and warm as the day. It was impossible not to smile back. 'So where do you live?' she asked.

'Vanessa!' Conrad stopped dead on the terrace. 'Who the hell is that?'

She flushed at his rudeness. 'This is Dylan, our new gardener. Dylan, this is my husband, Conrad.'

Ignoring Dylan, Conrad turned to Vanessa. 'I've just been on the phone to Marty about the Selfridges launch. The paps are going to be all over it. Have you thought about what you're wearing?'

'The Roland Mouret,' she replied, uncomfortable about having this conversation in front of Dylan.

'Far too Carol Vorderman,' Conrad sniffed. 'Go for the caramel Victoria Beckham with your nude Louboutins. And don't forget to ring Billy so he knows what time to pick us up.'

Giving Dylan's khaki shorts a disgusted look, he swept back indoors. Vanessa smiled awkwardly. 'My husband doesn't mean to be rude, we've just got a big day tomorrow.'

'No worries. What's a pap?'

'A pap? You know, a paparazzi, someone who takes your picture when you're out and about.'

'And this is a good thing?'

'Yes, if you're looking good,' she said, feeling a bit uncomfortable again. 'They'll sell them on to the papers and mags and they'll use them, hopefully in something like a "Best Dressed" feature. It's a way to keep people interested in you without really having to do anything.'

Dylan raised an eyebrow. 'What do you and your husband do then? Run some kind of marketing firm?'

Did he really not recognize her? Vanessa thought he'd just been playing it cool. 'Well, I'm Vanessa Powell and my husband is Conrad Powell.'

Dylan looked blank.

'Now we run a kind of brand, putting our names and faces to things,' she said, suddenly aware of how vacuous it sounded. 'You know, a bit like the Beckhams.'

'So you're a celebrity?' Dylan blinked. 'Sorry, I'm not really good with all that stuff.'

Something in his manner made Vanessa feel embarrassed. Why should Dylan have heard of her?

'Is gardening your main line of work?' she asked.

'Anything outdoors, really.'

'So you're not actually a qualified gardener?'

'Not officially, I guess.' His eyes twinkled. 'Is that a problem?'

'Of course not,' she said quickly. 'You're doing a marvellous job.'

They smiled at each other. 'You still haven't told me where you live,' she said.

'You know Foxglove Woods? I'm in the field behind it at the moment.'

'Oh, right,' she said politely. 'And you live in a caravan?'

'A yurt.'

'Like a giant tent?' The only time she had been in a yurt was a silk one that had served oysters at the Cartier polo one year.

The window above them was suddenly flung open. Conrad lifted his wrist and jabbed at the Rolex. 'I'm not paying you to talk to my wife!'

'Conrad!' Vanessa was mortified.

'I should get back to it,' Dylan said easily. 'See you later.'

Vanessa shot a filthy look up at Conrad. Giving her a *What did I do?* shrug, he slammed the window.

Vanessa was shopping in Selfridges with Victoria Beckham, the two arm in arm as they strolled the womenswear department with the ease of two A-list stars who'd been friends for years. As they reached the Stella McCartney section suddenly the racks of clothes turned into wild, curling hedgerows and long grass sprouted all over the floor tiles. Dylan appeared in front of them like a genie, impossibly sexy in a black Hugo Boss suit.

'Mrs Beckham, can I interest you in our wild strawberry collection? They're really rather good this time of year.'

Vanessa gave a snort of laughter. She could feel Victoria pulling on her arm. She tried to answer but her mouth wouldn't move. All that was coming out was a funny groaning sound.

'Mrs Powell?'

She peeled one eye open. Dylan was standing over her, looking quizzical.

'Sorry,' he said. 'I didn't mean to wake you. I'm off now if that's OK.'

'I must have dropped off!' She struggled to sit up, hoping she didn't have dribble on her chin. 'How much do I owe you?'

'Whatever you think it's worth, I don't set a rate.'

'Can you come back?' she said, quickly taking two fifty-pound notes out of her purse. 'I mean, there's so much more to do.'

'Don't you want to have a look first? Make sure you're happy?'

'I'm sure you're fine. I mean, it's fine.'

'OK, great,' he replied. 'Day after tomorrow suit you?'

'Um, yes, that's fine.'

'I'll see you, then. Enjoy the paps.'

'The paps?' she said stupidly.

'Paps, paparazzi?' he said teasingly. 'Surely you know what they are?'

'Oh yes. Ha ha.'

He gave her his crooked grin. 'See you, Mrs Powell.'

She smiled back. 'Call me Vanessa.'

Chapter 17

Catherine got back in the car and burst into tears. 'I feel so stupid. How can I have been such an idiot?'

In the driver's seat, John looked stricken. 'Cath, you're not stupid. Please don't say that.'

She wasn't pregnant. They had bounded in there like a pair of excitable teenagers, thinking the test would only be a confirmation of what they already knew. Ten minutes later the doctor had gently broken the news. *A phantom pregnancy. The symptoms are quite common.* Catherine had thought the woman was winding her up.

'It felt so *real*.' She buried her face in her hands. How could her own body have tricked her like that?

'Cath.' John put his arms round her. 'The doctor said these things happen. You will get pregnant, I promise.'

'You don't know that.' Catherine started sobbing even harder. 'She didn't have any answers. You saw her face!'

'Cath, we have to keep trying. It will be fine.'

'It's *my* body,' she wept. 'Please don't tell me what it

can and can't do. OK? Just leave it, John, please. Just let me have this . . .'

He sat and held her until she'd stopped crying.

John was all set to cancel his meeting in London, but Catherine made him go. All she wanted was to go home and mope in peace. After dropping him at the station she stopped on the High Street to pick up something for dinner. Things went on. They had to.

As she passed Wedding Belles Amanda was rearranging the skirts on a gargantuan puffball. Catherine put her head down and tried to hurry past, but there was a bang on the glass. Come in! Amanda mouthed at her.

Catherine groaned inwardly. She really couldn't cope with Amanda today. Pushing the door open, she was immediately assaulted by the cloying scent of rose potpourri.

Amanda was wearing a polka-dot pussycat blouse that did nothing for her matronly bosom. 'I'm so pleased to see a friendly face. Anything to take my mind off tomorrow.'

It was the day before the public meeting at county hall. Nervous anticipation had gripped the town.

'Are you all right?' Amanda peered at Catherine. 'You look a bit peaky.'

'I'm just tired.' Catherine gazed round the shop. It was a shrine to neutrals: white walls, cream carpets, cream and white striped curtains. The far side of the room was completely taken up with a rail of dresses. Catherine hadn't seen so many sequins and corsages since the *Soirée* fashion cupboard.

'Wish you could do it all again?' Amanda said.

'Sorry?'

'Get married! The most important day of a woman's life.' Amanda's nose twitched knowingly. 'Still, I'm sure you and John are thinking about the next stage now. You'll want to make him a daddy before too long!'

Don't you dare, Catherine thought. *Or I will get that tiara over there and shove it right up your massive arse.*

'Henry and I were only ever able to have Olympia, but what a blessing she's been.' Amanda smiled obliviously. 'Children give you such a purpose in life, don't they?'

On cue the bell tinkled and Amanda's daughter thundered in. 'OMG, Mum, guess what?'

'Ooh, what?' Amanda cast a delighted look at Catherine. 'Girls' gossip!'

Olympia put her hands on a pair of meaty Belcher hips. 'Talia Tudor has only, like, gone and got a massive dragon tattoo on her lower back! She's put a picture up on Facebook, where she's sprawled all over the bonnet of this bloke's Fiat Punto totally, like, wearing this crop top to show the tattoo off. She is so going to fail her exams and become a prostitute and get AIDS or something.'

'Olympia!'

'All right then, a lap dancer.' Olympia patted her swept-over fringe. 'Anyway, have you got any money on you?'

Back on the street Catherine was actually shaking. What right did Amanda have to ask her such a personal question? No wonder they'd only had one kid, who'd want to sleep with such a monstrous woman? Henry Belcher must have been Rohypnoled when he impregnated her.

Her mobile started ringing. Catherine didn't even have to guess who it was. She stopped outside Butterflies to take the call.

'Hi.'

'Hey,' John sounded concerned, 'I just thought I'd check in and see how you're doing.'

'The same as I was thirty minutes ago.'

'Where are you?' John persevered.

'In town. I just bumped into Amanda Belcher.'

'Ah. And how is she today?'

'She basically asked when we were going to start a family.'

'Bloody Amanda!'

Catherine stared blindly across the road. There was a silence on the other end. 'I know how disappointed you're feeling at the moment, Cath,' John said eventually.

'No, you *don't* know how I'm feeling actually! Unless you can't get pregnant and feel like an absolute bloody idiot as well.'

A passer-by glanced at her. Catherine turned to face the shop window.

'Cath, you're not a failure. You're a wonderful woman and I love you.'

His relentless optimism was starting to grate. 'I've got to go,' she said tightly. 'I'll see you at home.'

She hung up and immediately felt even more miserable about being such a bitch to him. Lynette Tudor came out of her shop, car keys in hand.

'Hi, Lynette,' Catherine sighed.

Lynette looked completely stressed as usual. 'Sorry, I didn't see you there.'

'How are you?' Catherine asked, desperate to redeem herself as a decent human being.

'I've been better. The car's packed up again. One more bill I could do without.'

'John could take a look if you like. He's pretty good with all that stuff.'

'Thanks, but my old banger's beyond saving.' Lynette shook her head. 'I won't be able to go tomorrow now.'

'Why not give Felix a call? He's putting on a minibus to take people.'

'Oh, there's probably not space for me,' Lynette said hurriedly. 'I've left everything to the last moment as normal.'

Catherine was suddenly struck by how good Lynette's bone structure was. If you looked past the perpetual air of angst, she was still really rather beautiful. Catherine wondered what it was like to have the whole town gossiping about the paternity of your daughter and a shop business everyone knew was failing. No wonder Lynette hardly mixed on a social level. 'Come with us, if you like.' Catherine gave a smile. 'You can have the back seat to yourself instead of being squashed in with ten other people.'

'Really? You don't mind?'

'Of course not. We'll pick you up at ten.'

John was coming up from the kitchen as she let herself in. They stood in the hallway looking at each other.

'I'm sorry,' Catherine said simply. 'I don't mean to take it out on you.'

'It's all right.'

'It's not all right, John. It's hard for you as well. It's just that Amanda really hit a raw nerve.'

'That bloody woman.'

They exchanged a smile. 'I know you don't think I understand, but I do,' he told her.

'I know. I'm sorry for being such a nightmare wife.' She held up the shopping bag. 'I'm making fish pie tonight, your favourite. I'm going to try not to burn it and everything.'

Chapter 18

Lynette was running late, so they didn't end up leaving Beeversham until twenty past ten. John put his foot down in the Saab as they zoomed through the lanes, leaving green fields in their wake.

'I'm so sorry,' Lynette apologized for the umpteenth time. 'Talia couldn't find her lucky frog ornament to take to her English exam and she had the whole house turned upside down looking for it.'

'Did she find it?' John asked.

'Yes, after all that.' Lynette stared out the window. 'I suppose I should be grateful she was actually going to an exam.'

The Prime Minister was on Radio 4's *Woman's Hour.* Catherine listened to his caressing, well-modulated tones as he defended the latest cuts in child benefits.

'Jenni Murray's giving your mate quite an ear bashing,' John said.

Catherine rolled her eyes. 'He's not my *mate.*'

'You know the Prime Minister?' Lynette said excitedly. 'He's quite a dish!'

'I met him once at a Women in Media lunch at Downing Street.' Catherine shook her head at her husband. 'There were lots of other people there.'

'Cath gave him quite a roasting,' John told Lynette. 'I think he was a bit scared of her.'

'Don't listen to him, Lynette.'

Lynette looked impressed. 'So you used to be important then?'

Catherine exchanged a look with her husband. 'Yeah,' she said flatly. 'I guess I did.'

Gloucester County Shire Hall was a large yellow building in the centre of Gloucester. As they pulled into the car park quite a crowd was gathering outside. The Beeversham lot were off to the left; Catherine could see Mr and Mrs Patel standing in a circle with the Belchers and Jonty Fortescue-Wellington. A few rural campaigners were there, while a militant-looking group of people sporting purple hair and tie-dye milled round, waving placards saying things like 'TORY SCUMBAGS' and 'CAPITALISM OUT!'

A BBC reporter was doing a live broadcast from the bottom of the steps. Catherine wound her window down as they drove past.

'The Cotswold town of Beeversham will today find out its fate.'

Felix was standing beside the hired minibus wearing a natty green and white SNOW rosette.

'Excuse me, I must go and find a loo.' Lynette rushed off towards a dingy-looking pub on the other side of the road.

'Look who's here,' John said.

They turned to see. Sid Sykes may have been the wrong side of five foot six, but he had the confident swagger of a man who got what he wanted. Dressed in a showy grey suit and pink tie, he had the mahogany skin of a serious sun-worshipper. The soberly dressed men flanking Sykes had 'lawyers' written all over them.

A younger man stood off to the left, talking intently into his phone. He had thick black hair slicked off his face and the same darting eyes as Sykes.

'Who's that?' Catherine asked. 'He kind of looks familiar.'

'Damien Sykes, Sid's son and press officer,' Felix said. 'From what I've seen so far, a very over-confident man indeed.'

'So no one from Pear Tree has bothered to turn up?'

'Doesn't look like it,' John said. 'The mystery continues.'

The sun was a high round ball in the sky as they went in. John was still outside talking to Felix and Catherine found herself at the security check with Mel and Mike Cooper-Stanley. The airline pilot looked as disgustingly brown as always, grizzled in a handsome way.

'You must come round for drinks,' he told Catherine. 'I've just picked up some Venezuelan brandy John would love.'

'You and me can stick to the wine, babes.' Mel took her studded denim jacket off to go through the scanner. The elderly security guard woke up for what was probably the first time in a decade.

The council chamber was further along the corridor,

a large, brightly lit circular room. The town mayor sat behind a big wooden bench, the city coat of arms on the wall behind. He was flanked by a stern-looking man and woman.

The public gallery was at the opposite end and gave a sweeping view of the whole proceedings. Catherine squeezed past Jonty Fortescue-Wellington's huge stomach to sit with Ginny Chamberlain. Ginny was dressed in a green and white striped blouse of the SNOW colours. She gave Catherine's hand a squeeze as she sat down.

Below them the members of the county council were taking their seats. There had to be forty people down there, a much larger number than was normal at public meetings.

Felix had already exchanged pleasantries with a few of the members. Catherine hoped he had some allies down there. Sykes and his gang were already seated and their serene faces were unsettling her. They didn't look remotely concerned; or maybe Sykes had a good poker face.

The mayor, a jolly Weeble in red robes, tapped his microphone.

'I'd like to welcome you all here to discuss the proposal for Ye Olde Worlde Theme Park. There's been a lot of controversy and high feeling over this and I appeal to you all to remain calm during the proceedings. Now, the leader of the council will start. Thank you.'

The man on the mayor's right leant into his own microphone. 'Thank you, Mayor. Fellow councillors and members of the public, we're here today to discuss the plans submitted by Sykes Holdings on March fifteenth this year for a five-hundred-acre theme park on the site of Blaize Castle in Beeversham.'

Sykes exchanged a faint smile with his son. Catherine's unease started to grow.

'The planning inspector has attended a public meeting in Beeversham and, while the residents have strong concerns about the development, he has to make an informed decision based on the local planning policies.' The leader of the council cleared his throat. 'The planning inspector also received an economic assessment from Sykes Holdings about how they feel Ye Olde Worlde would contribute financially to the area.'

'I've heard what kind of work Sykes offers,' someone shouted. 'Slave labour!'

Catherine watched the smile drop off Sykes's face. The leader of the council frowned at the heckler and continued. 'I appreciate the strength of feeling on both sides, but we have to look carefully at all aspects.' He glanced at his notes. 'I have the findings of the planning report here.'

Nerves crackled throughout the room. Beside Catherine, Ginny was tightly hugging her handbag.

'In his report the planning officer has advised against Ye Olde Worlde being built, on the grounds of three criteria.'

A communal 'Yes!' rippled across the public gallery.

The leader of the council spoke louder. 'Environmental blight, insufficient transport structure, and inappropriate scale of development. The planning officer feels the plans submitted by Sykes Holdings are, overall, wholly unsympathetic.'

Catherine was watching Sid Sykes closely. He didn't

look too upset for a man who'd just had his multi-million-pound venture shot down.

There was a rumble outside in the corridors, like the buzzing of an enormous swarm of bees. It grew closer and closer, drowning out the voices in the chamber. The shouts could be heard quite clearly.

'Capitalists out, democrats in! Capitalists OUT, democrats IN!'

Next minute the doors burst open and the protestors from outside came streaming in. Their faces were charged with anger as they brandished placards.

'Tory pigs! You're all in it together!'

The mayor stood up. 'You can't just come storming in here! Order!'

An egg flew across the room and hit the mayor smack on the chest. He looked down at his robes in shock.

'Oh my word!' Ginny gasped. 'Someone do something!'

There was nothing they could do. The amount of protestors seemed to have doubled and the two dozy security guards were completely helpless. More eggs started to rain down on members of the council, covering them with yolk.

One man, dressed in camouflage and dark glasses, seemed to be the ringleader. 'We're all in this together! Freedom for Beeversham!' he shouted.

'We most certainly are not!' Mrs Patel shouted back. People started calling to others to ring the police.

As quickly as they'd barged in, the mob miraculously melted away, leaving a sea of fallen chairs in their wake. The county council looked like they'd been dive-bombed by a flock of rabid seagulls. Even the coat of arms had a gloop of eggy phlegm dripping down it. Everyone was in shock.

'Can we have some order?' the leader of the council cried.

Catherine shook her head. Something wasn't right. The way that mob had come charging in and withdrawn suddenly. It all felt too managed, like they'd been watching a stage performance.

'The Sykes had a hand in this!' she whispered to John.

He frowned. 'What do you mean?'

'I just feel sure of it – there's something strange about this whole thing.'

A woman Catherine had never seen before stood up. 'I'm all for Ye Olde Worlde!' she shouted. 'Two of my kids can't find work for love nor money. If Mr Sykes here says he can create new jobs, how can that be a bad thing? It's you bloody posh types down in Beeversham, you don't want the views from your verandas interrupted!'

Mr Patel jumped up. 'I've got a patio, not a veranda, thank you very much! And I'm worried about my business going under if Mr Sykes gets his way! All of us who have shops are.'

'Boohoo for you!' the woman called out. 'Let's have the boot on the other foot for once.'

'Madam, you are lacking in any manners or grace,' Mr Patel shouted, before being shushed sharply by his wife.

The mood had changed dramatically. People were divisive, angry. The leader of the council was wiping egg yolk off his lapel. He looked furious.

'This isn't good,' John muttered.

In their seats below, the council members were sticky and disgruntled. The leader spoke into his microphone. 'Councillors, we have to vote. Can I please have a show of hands for Ye Olde Worlde.'

In the end it was a split verdict. Twenty voted for the theme park and twenty against. Everyone was stunned. No one had expected it to come to a deadlock.

The leader of the council leant across to confer with the woman on the mayor's left. Everyone else waited anxiously. Eventually he sat back and spoke.

'It is clear we are divided on the issue of whether Sykes Holdings should be granted planning permission for Ye Olde Worlde. Therefore we are giving Mr Sykes ten weeks to go away and revise his plans, taking into account the planning officer's concerns. We will meet again on Wednesday the twenty-eighth of August.'

Giving a wide berth to the waiting reporters, the SNOW committee congregated in the old-man's pub over the road. The place was empty and stank of stale booze and cheap disinfectant. Nicotine-stained curtains were pulled across the windows, shutting out the lovely day. It was an apt place for their gloom.

People kept looking at Felix anxiously. He'd hardly said a word since the verdict. Jonty was being as much use as a chocolate teapot: he had been busy texting since they'd come out, apparently on 'important Parliament business'. Catherine had just seen a massive pair of pendulous breasts flash up on the screen of his iPhone.

It was only when he was halfway down his flat glass

of radioactive-coloured orange juice that Felix finally spoke.

'Chaps, I've let you down. I was so positive the plans would get thrown out. All I can say is sorry.'

'Don't be silly, Felix!' everyone cried. Mel Cooper-Stanley patted his arm.

'Felix, you weren't to know. None of us were.' She shook her head. 'Those protestors didn't help.'

'Professional troublemakers with too much time on their hands,' Mr Patel said crossly. 'They don't care about Beeversham at all.'

Catherine kept quiet. Her hunch about Damien and Sid Sykes having something to do with the protestors suddenly seemed rather silly.

'They haven't actually got planning permission yet,' Mike Cooper-Stanley pointed out. 'From what the report says they've got some pretty big hurdles to get over.'

Everyone looked hopefully at John. 'Mike's right,' he said carefully. 'Let's not worry unless we have to.'

Ginny had a resolute look on her face. 'Darlings, it's not all over yet! We have to stay positive and not give up.' She dived into her voluminous bag and brought out a Purple Ronnie notebook. 'I suggest we have a powwow to think of ways we can keep awareness up. People need to be reminded what a special place Beeversham is.'

'Like a charity luncheon?' Ursula Patel suggested.

'That's a good start. Any more ideas?'

'I could do a girls' night in at the nail bar,' suggested Mel.

'Or a sponsored fun run?' Mr Patel said. 'Catherine

would have to give the rest of us a head start, though.'

There were smiles all round. 'I've got an idea,' she said. 'Instead of lots of little things, why don't we do one big event? That way everyone can get involved.'

'What did you have in mind?' Mrs Patel asked.

'I'm thinking off the top of my head, but I was imagining a town fair. We could call it something like "Beeversham's Big Day Out".'

The others fell on it.

'What a marvellous idea!' Ursula Patel said. 'We could have stalls and a funfair for the children.'

'We definitely need a band,' Mel added. 'Me and Mike love a good boogie.'

'And a champagne bar,' Jonty Fortescue-Wellington said hopefully.

Ginny was writing it all down furiously. 'I could ask Fleur Blackwater to bring some lambs for the children to pet.'

Amanda had the most inspired idea. 'How about getting Vanessa and Conrad Powell to open it?'

'Genius!' Mel exclaimed. Her eyes flashed mischievously. 'Maybe Catherine should be the one to ask them. You know, as her and Vanessa have so much history.'

'What history?' asked Henry Belcher.

'Oh Henry, you know the story!' Amanda nudged Catherine. 'Tell us again, it's hysterical.'

Catherine caught John's eye across the table. The sod was grinning with the rest of them. There was no getting out of it.

Afterwards everyone fell about laughing. 'I don't know why Vanessa got such a bee in her bonnet!' Mel hooted. 'She's flashed her bits enough times for her calendars.'

'Funnily enough, Vanessa didn't see it that way,' Catherine said wryly.

'I don't think much of Conrad Powell,' Mr Patel grumbled. 'The man can't act for toffee.'

'I don't mind going up to the house,' Ginny said. 'It would be so nice if they agreed to it. They have so little to do with the town.'

Catherine knew the Powells wouldn't even scratch their own arses without being offered vast amounts of money, but she couldn't let Ginny get savaged by an off-duty Conrad. 'It's all right, I'll do it. At least Vanessa knows me.' *Hates me, more like.*

'Time is of the essence.' Felix got his pocket diary out. 'How about Saturday the twenty-ninth?'

'Cripes,' Mel gasped. 'That's less than a month away!'

A BBC news headline rolled across the tiny television on the top of the bar. 'SHOCK VERDICT AT COUNTY HALL.'

It had a galvanizing effect. 'Don't get too confident, Mr Sykes,' Ginny declared. 'You've chosen the wrong town to mess with!'

Chapter 19

Fleur didn't know what Felix had said to Mr Stanley, but he was their saviour. The bank agreed to give them until the end of August to start paying back their loan. She felt like a prisoner on death row who'd been granted a last-minute reprieve.

She didn't tell her dad about her visit to Felix. Robert Blackwater was a proud man and she knew he would be angry at her 'peddling' their private business. Instead Fleur had been spending her evenings at the kitchen table writing business plans. Her idea to sell lamb burgers online had been put on hold when she realized how much it would cost to even get a proper website designed. An easier, quicker option was renting out the top fields. It was still a drop in the ocean compared to what they needed, but it was a start. All she could do was keep thinking up ways to bring in more money. If by some miracle she saved the farm, maybe she'd be able to save her dad as well.

Ironically, the farmhouse had never looked prettier that evening, bathed in half-light, as Fleur drove back down the hill. It was only on closer inspection that the peeling paintwork and the perilously sagging roof became obvious.

She parked the quad bike in the yard and hopped off. The redundant window boxes and old plant pots were still a sorry collection outside the back door. Fleur made a vow to go down to the garden centre that week. A bit of colour round the place might cheer her dad up.

As soon as she walked in the kitchen, she knew no amount of pretty foliage was going to help. He was still where she'd left him at lunchtime, slumped in the old armchair by the empty fire. The sandwich she'd made for him lay untouched on the side table, the edges curled up and dry.

Fleur went over and knelt down in front of him. 'Dad,' she said gently. 'I'm home.'

Robert Blackwood struggled back from some far-away memory. *He looks so old,* she thought wretchedly. There was a large stain down the front of the shirt he'd been wearing for three days.

'Come on.' She stood up, desperate to inject some positivity. 'I'll get us something to eat. Why don't you go and freshen up?'

Things didn't improve at dinner. Her dad toyed listlessly with the spag bol she'd made, staring off at a spot on the wall somewhere behind her head.

'So Felix Chamberlain has asked if we can bring a couple of the bottle-fed lambs along to this Big Day Out they're putting on,' she said brightly. 'Sounds like fun, doesn't it?'

There was no response. She gazed up at the ceiling, willing someone to give her the answers.

'You shouldn't have to do all this.'

She looked at him. 'Do what?'

'Clean up my mess. I'm a bloody burden to you, Fleur, that's what I am.'

'I'm not cleaning up your mess, don't be silly.'

'You are.' He fixed her with sad, rheumy eyes. 'You're so like her.'

'Who, Dad?'

'Your mum. You've got the same fighting spirit. I can see it there.' He touched his chin.

Her throat suddenly ached with tears. 'If she was here now, she'd say, "Come on, you two! Let's sort this mess out!"'

'But she's not, lass. She's six feet under.'

'Dad,' Fleur said quietly. Did he not know how cruel he sounded?

He laughed bitterly. 'And a fat lot of good I'm doing you up here.'

It was a relief when dinner ended and Robert Blackwater went into his study and shut the door behind him. Fleur was left to clear up. Afterwards she went to take a long hot bath, but it did nothing to alleviate the horrible, tight feeling round her temples.

The farmhouse was quiet and dark when she came back down in her nightie. There was a sliver of light under the study door but she didn't linger. Padding barefoot down the corridor, she went back into the kitchen.

It had always been a ritual that her mum had made Fleur an Ovaltine before bed. She hadn't drunk the stuff for years, but she was suddenly craving it, the familiarity of an old comfort blanket. She didn't even know if they had any, but like a mirage across a scorching desert, there was a jar at the back of the cupboard. Getting it out, Fleur cradled it against her chest.

'I miss you, Mum,' she whispered. 'I wish you were here.'

The glass jar started to warm up in her hands, as if it were responding. She gripped it harder. 'I'm so worried about Dad. I don't know what to do.'

A half-laugh, half-sob escaped from her throat. 'Look at me, Mum! Talking to a jar of Ovaltine. I've lost it, I'm telling you.'

There was a noise at the window. Fleur nearly had a heart attack. Two faces were looking in from the darkness at her. She dropped the Ovaltine on the counter.

'I've got a gun!' she yelled, praying it would wake her dad from whatever stupor he was in.

The faces didn't move. Her heart sank as she clocked a mocking red mouth and pink shirt. Suddenly, Fleur wished the trespassers *were* burglars. Or even bloody axe murderers.

What the hell was Beau Rainford doing at her back door?

He was lounging on the doorstep, a mocking smile playing on his full red mouth. An old-fashioned tandem bike lay on the ground, the back wheel still spinning.

'Hello,' he said languidly. 'Lovely place you've got here.'

Fleur could smell aftershave and the sharp tang of

alcohol. She recognized the man with Beau as the idiot who'd driven the Porsche over her land.

'What do you want?' she snapped, humiliated at being spied on at such a private moment.

Beau's blue gaze rested on Fleur. She clamped her arms across her chest and desperately wished her nightie wasn't quite so short.

The other man was gazing unashamedly at her legs. 'Can we come in? We've got a proposition for you.'

'No, you bloody can't,' she snapped again and started to pull the door closed.

'Hold on.' Beau put a proprietorial loafer on the step. 'Spencer here is my business partner. We were just sitting up at mine discussing your farmhouse.'

The two men exchanged a smirk. Their eyes were glittery, euphoric. Fleur wondered if they were on something.

'What about our farmhouse?' she demanded.

'We want to buy it off you,' Beau said casually.

'What?'

'Everyone knows farming is over. This place would make a seriously good spa for all the desperate house-wives round here. Spence and I have done quite a few similar projects already, haven't we?'

'Yes, mate. I'm imagining the roof terrace already.'

'We'll give you a tidy amount for this place and turn it into a seriously profitable business.' Beau flicked a bug off his sleeve. 'Add some glamour and excitement to this town. Christ knows it needs it.' He gave Fleur what was clearly meant to be a winning 'seal-the-deal' smile. 'What do you say?'

She was so angry she could barely get her words out.

'What I say is, why don't you fuck off before I take that boot jack over there and ram it up your arse?'

Beau just looked amused, which made Fleur even madder. 'Come off it, darling,' he said. 'Those gingham curtains are hardly an homage to style.'

'This is my home!' Fleur yelled. 'How dare you!'

Across the yard the dogs pulled at their chains. Spencer glanced back at them nervously.

'You might be used to flashing your cash and getting what you want,' Fleur hissed. 'But it's not going to work with me!'

Beau gazed at her steadily. 'It worked last time, didn't it?'

'*You*—' There was an old-fashioned scythe resting by the door, which had been left there since Fleur's dad had used it to trim down the apple trees in the orchard. It wouldn't cut through butter these days, but they didn't know that. She picked it up and raised it menacingly. 'Get out! Now! Or I'll chop those smug heads right off your bodies!'

Spencer took a step backwards. 'Christ, Beau, I think she means it.'

Beau didn't move. 'You haven't even heard our offer.'

'I don't want to hear it! And don't bother coming back, because the answer's still going to be no!'

Slamming the door in his face, Fleur ran out into the hall. She sat on the bottom step of the stairs in the dark and fought the urge to cry.

'How dare he?' she muttered. 'How dare he?'

The study door was still closed. Her dad might as well be dead, she thought bitterly, immediately appalled she could think such a thing.

She waited for ten minutes, until she was sure they'd gone, and went back into the kitchen. That cup of Ovaltine had never been more needed. Fleur looked at the label for instructions, only to realize it was five years past its sell-by date. Throwing the jar across the room she burst into tears.

Chapter 20

'Oh, darling. My darling.'

Conrad gazed into Vanessa's eyes with just the right mix of lust and tenderness. They were both naked in the missionary position on top of the bed, Conrad balanced on strong forearms above Vanessa. Once or twice she'd caught him checking out his flexed biceps in the mirror.

The crisp accent was replaced by an American one. 'Oh yeah. Do you like this, baby?' He started moving faster. She began the countdown in her head. *Ten, nine.*

'Oh baby . . .' *Seven, six.*

'Oh God!' Fast panting. *Five, four.*

'Yes! Yes!' *Three, two.*

'Oh my GOD!' With award-winning emotion, Conrad shot his load and collapsed on top of Vanessa.

'Conrad, I can't breathe,' she complained.

'Neither can I,' he groaned. 'Maybe I won't need to do that extra gym session tonight, after all.'

He rolled off her and lay on his back. 'You didn't come, though?'

'I'm a bit tired,' she lied. Conrad had put on an energetic performance but she'd been strangely dis-associated throughout.

'I'm going for a shower.' He got up, giving his stomach a satisfied pat in the mirror. He paused at the end of the bed and looked at her. 'You've put on a bit, by the way. I'd keep an eye on things, we all know the camera adds ten pounds.'

'You bastard!' she shot back. 'Don't be so rude.'

'Darling, you know I love your curves more than anyone!' He winked. 'Maybe you should take up running like that skinny cow, Catherine Connor.'

He disappeared into the bathroom, leaving her humiliated on the bed. How dare he drop in that comment about Catherine! Vanessa thought about Catherine's long toned limbs and seethed even more.

She got off the bed and went over to the mirror, turning this way and that. Was her bottom looking a bit bigger? Conrad knew exactly which buttons to press.

Jaunty whistling was coming from the bathroom. Vanessa flicked a 'V' at the door.

She turned back and studied her ripe, neglected body. She traced a creamy nipple with her manicured finger, daring herself to mouth the name she'd not been able to stop thinking about during sex with her husband.

Dylan.

The intercom raised Vanessa from a guilty fantasy about sex with Dylan in the shallow end of the pool. She went over and opened the bedroom door. 'Renata!'

There was no answer. The buzzer went again. 'For

God's sake!' Vanessa swore, grabbing her silk robe off the chaise longue. 'All right, I'm coming!' she yelled.

She stomped down the stairs, tying her robe as she went. 'What?' she barked down the intercom.

'Um, is Vanessa there, please?'

'This is she. Who is this?'

'Catherine Connor.'

Vanessa stared at the intercom screen, and the MG at the gate. 'What do you want?'

'Have you got five minutes?'

'I really don't have anything to say to you.' Vanessa regained her composure. 'Are you recording this? I'd think very carefully about making up another bunch of lies again.'

'Of course I'm not recording this!' There was a pause. 'I wanted to ask you a favour,' Catherine said in a more controlled voice.

'You? Ask *me* a favour?'

'Please. It won't take long.'

'It had better not,' snapped Vanessa and hung up. She should have told Catherine where to go, but Vanessa had to admit, she was intrigued. What was the purpose of this little visit? Sweeping upstairs, she went to get dressed.

When she opened the door twenty-five minutes later Catherine was looking suitably pissed off. 'I was beginning to think you'd forgotten about me.'

Vanessa gave her a chilly once-over, making the most of the height advantage from the top step. Catherine would never be a classic beauty, but shorter hair did suit her. Very gamine.

Vanessa would *never* do gamine.

Catherine gave an awkward smile. 'Thanks for seeing me.'

'What do you want?' Vanessa snapped. 'I'm very busy.'

She heard Conrad coming down the stairs. He was at Vanessa's shoulder in a flash. 'What is *she* doing here?'

Vanessa pulled the door to an inch. 'Well?'

Catherine's eyes flickered past her. 'You've probably heard about the plans for Ye Olde Worlde theme park?'

'What about them?' Vanessa asked. Conrad was still hovering behind her in a cloud of freshly applied Hermès.

'Well, we had the public meeting at County Hall on Tuesday.'

'I do watch the local news,' Vanessa interrupted.

Catherine blinked. 'Oh. Well, you'll know all about Sid Sykes getting another chance to put in a new planning application.'

Vanessa hadn't, but she wasn't going to admit it. 'And?'

'The town has decided to put on a "Big Day Out" fundraiser.' Catherine looked like she was having trouble moving her mouth: 'We'd be delighted if you and Conrad would open it.'

'Us? Open a *fete*?'

'It's a bit more than a *fete*,' Catherine said. 'It's raising awareness for an issue that affects us all. Of course, we could always ask Liz Hurley,' she added innocently. 'She doesn't live far from here.'

Bitch. Vanessa gave Catherine a chilly smile. 'We have a fee for public appearances.'

'Twenty grand an hour, plus expenses!' Conrad hissed in her ear.

'I'm afraid we can't pay you,' Catherine said carefully. 'But I'm sure you'll agree it's a wonderful way for the community to pull together.'

Vanessa stood there, considering for a moment. The great Catherine Connor begging at her door. Under any other circumstances she would have laughed in Catherine's face, but Conrad's cruel comments were still fresh in her mind.

'We'd be delighted. I'm sure under these exceptional circumstances our fee can be waived for once.'

She watched Catherine's mouth fall open. Conrad's stage whisper came from sharp left. 'Are you fucking *joking* me?'

'Call my PA with the details,' Vanessa said, finally getting to slam the door in Catherine's face.

Chapter 21

Catherine drove away from the Powells' mansion in a state of shock. She'd never expected to get past the intercom, let alone be granted a doorstep audience with Vanessa Powell in a Cavalli kimono. It had been painful, but nowhere near as painful as Catherine had been expecting.

The celebrity had looked as immaculate as ever, but Catherine had been struck by how girlish, almost vulnerable, Vanessa had looked when she had opened the door. It was like the house had swallowed her up.

Catherine accelerated down Pavilion Heights. Now she thought about it, she was sure there had been another tension in the air. Had the famously perfect couple been in the middle of a row? Catherine didn't care if Vanessa had been about to chop Conrad's head off with an axe. Bloody hell, they'd got the Powells! Amanda Belcher was going to wet her French knickers when she found out.

The sun was climbing high above the valley as she continued back down the hill to her house. The black mood that had descended after finding out she wasn't pregnant was finally starting to ease its grip. In its place was a philosophical resignation. If it wasn't meant to be, so be it. Plenty of women she admired didn't have children. It hadn't stopped them leading happy, full lives. She wasn't going to patronize herself – or them – by thinking otherwise.

It still didn't stop her stomach twisting every time she thought of what she couldn't give her husband.

Her mobile started ringing as she pulled up outside her home. It was a private number.

'Hello?'

'Catherine?' A gravelly Welsh voice. 'So you do get reception out in the wilds?'

She smiled. 'Ha ha, Gywn, very funny. I've missed your dulcet tones.'

Gywn Hughes was Catherine's reporter mate from the nationals. A brilliant journalist, he'd been responsible for some of the biggest news scoops of the last ten years. Catherine had persuaded him to do a piece on Soirée Sponsors and they'd hit it off. Gywn had been one of the main campaigners clearing Catherine's mum's name when the Crimson Killer case had hit the news the second time. On the off-chance she had given him a call about Pear Tree Holdings. If anyone could get to the bottom of things, it was Gywn.

He cut straight to the chase. 'I've been asking round.'

'Shoot.'

'Not much, I'm afraid. The Isle of Man Companies House operate behind one big fat closed door. It's a completely different system to the UK.'

'The company directors are still listed though, aren't they? They could at least tell you who owns it.'

Sirens wailed in the background. Gwyn exhaled down the phone; he was obviously smoking one of his frequent cigarettes.

'They don't know anything. They're literally three old boys who live on the Isle of Man and get paid once a year to rock up and sign the forms to keep Pear Tree going. They could be directors for literally thousands of companies. It's a nice little earner; I might move there when I retire.'

'It sounds so dodgy, Gwyn. I can't believe it's legit.'

'It's completely legit. A lot of the supermarkets do it for tax reasons, plus it's easier when you're buying up vast swathes of land if nobody knows who you are. Especially if it's a controversial development.'

'Like Blaize Castle,' she said grimly.

'I haven't given up yet, Catherine. You know what I'm like once I've got the bit between my teeth.'

'Which is exactly why I came to you.' She rubbed at a grease mark on the steering wheel. 'You haven't heard the name Beau Rainford in any of this, have you?'

'That rich-boy property developer? You think he's behind it?'

'It was just a theory,' she said quickly. 'Forget it.'

'Nah, this is too big even for a character like Beau Rainford. My hunch is it's a big company. Probably a multinational that is being extra-cautious because of all the controversy about building on green-field sites.'

'That's what my husband said.'

'I think he's right.'

Catherine still couldn't put her finger on it, but there was still something definitely off.

'I'll keep plugging away, I must admit you've piqued my interest,' he told her. 'How are things going in the country? Are you a jam-making expert now?'

'Don't joke,' she sighed. 'It's not far off that.'

The reporter gave a throaty laugh. 'I've got a call on the other line; I'll be in touch.'

Chapter 22

Vanessa was on the phone to her PA, Tamzin. A plump blonde twenty-something, Tamzin was something of a godsend. Competent and organized, Conrad's mood swings seemed to wash over her. She'd been with the Powells in London, and Vanessa couldn't bear to let her go when they moved.

'Don't forget Selfridges are still holding on to the new Chanel for you,' she was telling Vanessa.

Dylan was bending over outside. Vanessa craned her neck to get a good look at his bum. 'I'm not sure when I'll be in London next. Could you courier it to me?'

'I don't blame you, home must be a very attractive option at the moment.'

'I'm sorry?' Vanessa's mind raced – what had Tamzin heard?

The girl laughed. 'Given the choice between the beautiful Cotswolds and hot, smelly London I know what I'd prefer!'

*

At midday Vanessa took a tray of drinks out to the terrace. 'Come and sit down!' she called. 'You must be parched.'

Dylan came up the lawn, black curls and bronzed skin making him look like a raffish pirate. There were rings of sweat under the arms of his vest, his dark armpit hair poking out the sides. For some reason Vanessa found it extremely erotic.

'Please, take a seat,' she said nonchalantly, as if taking refreshments with her staggeringly handsome gardener was an everyday occurrence.

Sukie was far more obvious. She'd been out in the garden all morning, watching Dylan in complete adoration. As he sat down, she jumped up and nestled her head in his crotch.

Lucky bitch, Vanessa found herself thinking. The glass she was holding slid through her hand. Dylan leant forward and caught it.

'S-sorry,' she stuttered. 'Iced tea OK?'

'Perfect.'

She wrenched her gaze away from the luminous eyes. 'You said you had a dog, didn't you?' she asked him, pouring him a glass. Her hands were shaking.

'Yup, an Irish wolfhound called Eddie. He's holding the fort for me at home.'

'Does Eddie live in the yurt with you?'

'No, I built him his own one.'

'Your dog's got its own yurt?'

Dylan looked deadly serious. 'Oh yeah. And his own toilet.'

'Really?'

'You bet.'

It took a second for the penny to drop. 'Oh, very funny,' she retorted.

He chuckled. 'I had you there.'

She couldn't help but smile back; there was something so wonderfully easy about him.

'Did you have to get permission to stay places in your yurt?' she asked.

Dylan tickled Sukie's pink belly with his long tanned fingers. 'Sometimes, but Foxglove Woods is a pretty private spot. I can always move on if anyone objects.'

It was such a nomadic life, never knowing where you would be at the end of every day. She couldn't imagine it and said as much to him.

'That's exactly why I like it. I've got the air in my lungs and the sun on my back. That's all I need.'

Vanessa looked down at her jewels, up at her beautiful house. These were the things that mattered. Tangible symbols of your own worth and status. How could he survive on so little?

'What do your parents think about your lifestyle?'

'They're cool.' He tickled Sukie's ear. 'They live on a farm in Andalucía with twenty-five stray cats. No wait, twenty-six. Mum just told me they've taken in another one.'

It was all starting to make sense. 'I've got a brother as well,' he told her. 'If you want the whole family history.'

'What does he do?' She winked. 'Train wolves in the wilds of Alaska?'

'Actually, he's a chartered surveyor who lives in Cambridge.'

Vanessa's face dropped. 'Oh. That was a joke. Not a very good one, sorry.'

He glanced up from stroking Sukie and gave her a smile. His gaze was magnetic. Vanessa felt like her body had dissolved into a million particles that were all racing round and bumping into each other.

'H-how long are you staying?' she asked.

'Not sure yet.' Dylan held her gaze. 'It depends.'

She swallowed. 'On what?'

'What the hell is going on here?' Conrad was standing behind them, Hugo Boss jacket slung over one shoulder. He didn't look very happy.

'Conrad!' she jumped up. 'I wasn't expecting you back until later.'

'Evidently not. What is that fucking hippy wagon doing on our driveway?'

'I let Dylan park outside the house. I didn't think you'd mind.'

'Well, I do. I don't want people thinking we're putting up a load of crusties.' Conrad jerked his hand over the table. 'What's this?'

'I just stopped for lunch,' Vanessa lied. 'Seeing as it was hot, I thought Dylan would like to join me for an iced tea. You know, to say thank you for all his wonderful work,' she added, wondering if that was over-egging the pudding.

Conrad narrowed his eyes at Dylan. 'Thought you'd slack off to chat up my wife, did you?'

'Conrad!'

'Hello? I'm joking! As if you'd be interested in the hired help!' He put a proprietorial arm round Vanessa's shoulders. 'Anyway, chappie, I'm afraid you haven't passed your trial period.'

'What trial period?' she started to say, but Conrad's

135

nails dug warningly into her flesh. Dylan put Sukie down on the floor and got up.

'Sorry, I wasn't aware there was a contract.'

'There isn't!' she protested, earning herself another sharp nail dig. Conrad looked down fondly at her.

'Bless my darling wife; she's never very good at confrontation.' He smiled coldly. 'I, on the other hand, won't stand for sub-standard work.' He fixed Dylan with a condescending stare. 'You've had your chance to shine, chappie, and it hasn't worked out.'

Vanessa watched in horror as he produced his Italian leather wallet and pulled out a slab of twenties. Peeling off two, he threw them down on the table.

'I think that's more than generous. '

Dylan's face was expressionless. 'It's all right, I hadn't done much today.'

'You've worked all morning!' she cried.

'You heard the man, darling.' Conrad pointed towards the side of the house. 'I've spent enough time being good about this, now fuck off,' he told Dylan. 'And take that sorry excuse for a tin can with you.'

Vanessa looked wildly between them. 'Dylan, I . . .'

'It's fine, really.'

Was that a hint of pity in the smile he gave her? Helpless, she watched him walk off. When he was out of sight she wrenched herself out of Conrad's grip.

'You bastard,' she yelled. 'That was totally out of order!'

He was up in her face in a second. 'No, darling, *you're* the one who's out of order. I come back to find my wife offering herself up like some kind of slut with the hired help. Did you think you'd fit in a quick alfresco fuck before I got home?'

'How dare you! Let go, you're hurting me!'

'Don't think I haven't noticed the way you've been throwing yourself at him. Living out our Lady Chatterley fantasy, are we?'

She flushed again. 'I don't know what you mean.'

'I think you do. My God, he must have thought his luck was in. I might have started to get worried if I'd thought you still had a pulse between the legs.'

Releasing Vanessa's arm, he strode back inside the house.

Chapter 23

The hot weather shimmered on. Weather forecasters started to predict the hottest June for decades, while newspapers warned of imminent hosepipe bans. Barbecues overtook Sunday roasts and the British public enjoyed waking up to uninterrupted skies every morning. Even daily headlines about the faltering economy and the next round of public-spending cuts couldn't bring down the general *joie de vivre*.

In Beeversham, however, everyone was very much focused on the Big Day Out. That evening the SNOW committee were meeting at the Cooper-Stanleys' sympathetic new-build in Lavender Close. By the time Catherine and John arrived, the others were already in the back garden being plied with Oyster Bay by the host.

Mel was in the glossy black kitchen, putting the finishing touches to a selection of canapés. She engulfed Catherine in a warm hug that reeked of Trésor. 'How are you, darling?'

'All the better for seeing you.' Catherine looked at the spread before her. 'This is all very impressive.'

'M&S's finest. You know I don't even know how to turn the cooker on. '

Amanda bustled in. 'Mel, do you have a water jug? There's rather a lot of wine going round out there and we need to keep a clear head.' She looked at the wall clock pointedly. 'We should think about starting.'

'I'll take a tray out,' offered Catherine.

'You're a darling. See you in two secs.'

Catherine found Mr Patel in the corridor, mesmerized by a huge professional portrait of Mel, lounging amongst acres of fluffy rug.

'Don't worry, Mr Patel,' Catherine remarked cheerfully. 'I think she's wearing underwear.'

Mr Patel jumped violently. 'Thank goodness for that!' he said, rushing back out.

It was a beautiful summer evening. Wisps of clouds coasted across the red and pink sky as people helped themselves to prawn satay and caught up on the gossip. The Powells opening the Big Day Out was the main topic of conversation. People were very excited at the thought of rubbing shoulders with their resident celebrities.

'I wonder what Vanessa Powell will wear,' Ginny pondered. 'She's so stunning!'

'Conrad Powell is such a dish, and so devoted to her!' declared Amanda. She went in for another mini-tartlet. 'If only the rest of us were so lucky.'

Poor Henry Belcher, who'd forgone a weekend of watching the Ashes to paint the downstairs loo, looked crushed.

'What are we looking like press-wise, Catherine?' Felix asked.

'A bit better, now we've got the Powells on board. Cotswold FM have confirmed they'll be doing a live broadcast, talking to Felix and a few locals etcetera, and the *Cotswolds on Sunday* want to do something too. I said an exclusive interview and shoot with the Powells might be *slightly* unrealistic, but I'm sure we can get a few quotes off them. Oh, and I might have an in with someone at the *Daily Telegraph*. You know how hot they are on green-belt building.'

The others looked impressed. 'I forgot how well connected your wife was,' Ginny told John.

'Hardly,' Catherine sighed. She decided not to tell them about the other papers she'd tried, unsuccessfully. It was scary how quickly even someone like her fell off the radar.

'Where's Jonty, by the way?' Mr Patel asked. 'I saw his name on the email.'

'He's been held up in London and sends his apologies,' Felix told them.

Everyone exchanged a look.

'Never mind, I can fill him in.' Felix smiled decisively. 'That's the press sorted, who's next?'

People weren't having much success. Amanda Belcher had been gazumped on two bands. There was a dearth of children's magicians. The Patels were struggling to fill the food and drink stalls.

'Most people are booked for Chipping Norton's food festival on the same day,' Mr Patel told them gloomily. 'We're going to struggle to get the crowds, even with Conrad and Vanessa.'

'Um, if I could maybe make a tiny suggestion.' Henry

Belcher gave an apologetic smile. 'I wonder if all this tombola stuff is a bit predictable?'

'It's a fete, Henry,' his wife said crossly. 'What else do you expect people to do?'

Henry swallowed nervously. Going against the female rule in his family wasn't something that happened often. Escaping Amanda's fish-eyed stare, he appealed to the rest of the table.

'How about rebranding the whole thing and calling it Beeversham's "Big Charity Game Show"?'

'I'm afraid I don't quite follow, old chap,' Felix said.

'I'm not explaining myself very well,' Henry said sheepishly. 'Something Olympia was watching gave me the idea, one of these reality TV shows that seem very popular these days. Instead of your bog-standard fete, why don't we have a game show theme? People could pay a small fee to enter, which we could donate to a local charity. We could get businesses from the area to donate prizes for the winners.'

He pulled out a sheet of paper from his notes. 'It's only rough, but I've made a few suggestions. The first one is *Big Brother.* I thought we could recreate it in our living room and people could look through the windows and watch. It could go on all day, with people being voted out every hour . . .'

Amanda Belcher looked aghast but Henry bravely ploughed on. 'We could still have a petting corner but perhaps we could commandeer some more animals and put on a mini *I'm a Celebrity . . . Get Me Out of Here!*'

'What on earth is that?' Felix sounded baffled.

'The jungle one, darling,' Ginny told him. 'Go on, Henry, I think this sounds marvellous!'

Henry smiled, encouraged by her reaction. 'I thought we could also have a more straightforward game show like *Who Wants to Be a Millionaire?* or even one of the old classics like *Mr and Mrs.*'

'OMG, amazing!' Mel said. 'We have to have *The X Factor!*'

'Didn't Churchminster village put on a *Churchminster's Got Talent* a few years ago?' Mrs Patel asked. 'I hear it was a big success. We could hire a stage to put in the market square.'

Henry nodded enthusiastically. 'Exactly what I was thinking! I was even wondering if we could do a *Supermarket Sweep* at the mini market. But only if you had old stock to get rid of,' he added hurriedly, seeing Mr Patel's face.

Amanda regained the powers of speech. 'Henry, I don't know what on earth has got into you! This is preposterous! We can't turn Beeversham into a giant TV set for the day.'

Catherine watched Henry's face drop. 'It's a brilliant idea!' she said. 'Henry's right, we need something different to draw people in.'

'I agree,' Mel declared.

'Me too,' said Mike.

John put his hand up. 'I suggest we vote.'

Felix had been looking a bit surprised by the change of events, but he nodded. 'Let's have a show of hands, then. All those in favour of changing it to Beeversham's Big Charity Game Show.'

Everyone's hand went in the air, apart from Amanda

Belcher's. There was a long silence. 'Oh, for heaven's sake,' she said crossly.

Mel gave a hoot of laughter. '*Big Brother*, I love it!'

Over more wine the duties were quickly divvied up. Henry's inspired idea had renewed enthusiasm and everyone had great fun discussing the logistics and whether they really could get a couple of snakes for *I'm a Celebrity . . . Get Me Out of Here!* from a reptile zoo. When Mike Cooper-Stanley bought out the excellent cognac he'd picked up in duty-free that week, even Mrs Patel didn't say no.

Chapter 24

Vanessa side-stepped another cowpat and swore loudly. Her vision of arriving gracefully out of the foliage like an intrepid Joanna Lumley wasn't going according to plan. Instead she was hot, hopelessly lost, and her new silk Etro pants had stains all down them from where she had tripped on a tree root and gone flying.

Despondent, she slumped down on a tree trunk. This whole quest to find Dylan's yurt was madness. The only reason she was here was because Conrad had gone to London and wouldn't know what she was up to. She still felt a chill from their encounter yesterday afternoon. Conrad could be caustic, cruel even, but now she wondered if perhaps he might be even more dangerous. If he ever found out about this little trip she would be in deep trouble.

She'd make one more effort to find Dylan. Trying a new route through the woods this time, she came out on to a large overgrown field. On the far side was a little thicket. He had said he lived beyond the woods.

Feeling encouraged, she set off, picking up the hem of her floaty trousers to avoid more lurking cowpats.

She had nearly reached the thicket when an ominous growl started up inside it. There was a rustling of leaves and suddenly the most enormous dog sprang out of the undergrowth. She saw a flash of wolfish eyes as the animal started running full pelt towards her.

Panic-stricken, Vanessa began to run back in the direction of Foxglove Woods. It was no good, the dog was too fast. She could hear it closing in on her, feel its hot rancid breath on her neck.

'Help!' she screamed. 'Somebody help me!'

Knocking her over with one fell swoop, the dog jumped on her back. 'Help!' she screamed again, blindly whacking it with her Hermès Birkin. 'Somebody please!'

She curled into a ball, trying to protect herself. The dog opened its mouth and she saw the dripping, canine teeth. *Oh God*, she thought. *It's going for my face.*

Next moment she was drenched in a succession of frantic licks.

'Get off me! Urgh!' she shouted, as a smelly tongue licked her teeth. With a Herculean effort she pushed the dog off. Her sunhat was gone, as was one of the heels on her Brian Atwoods.

'Vanessa!' a voice said. 'Are you all right?'

She looked up. Dylan was standing there, silver eyes full of alarm.

'I did shout that he was a big softy but you didn't hear.'

He handed the hat back to her, retrieved from a nearby clump of grass. Her lost heel was lying beside it. She brushed herself down, trying to regain some semblance of elegance. The Hound of the Baskervilles, aka Dylan's Irish wolfhound Eddie, was gambolling round in the background chasing a butterfly.

'I've never seen someone move so fast,' Dylan told her. 'If you ever wanted to give up this celebrity lark you could always carve out a career as an international sprinter.'

They both started to laugh, Vanessa more from sheer nerves than anything else. Dylan was wearing the same white vest as when they'd first met. To anyone else it would be just an identikit old vest, but she remembered the way it clung to his body, the little stain of rust on the front. Every single detail of Dylan had imprinted itself on her brain.

'How come you're here?' he asked curiously.

'I was just out for a walk anyway, and stumbled across this place.'

He glanced at her heels. She went red.

'OK, I came out here to find you,' she confessed. 'Dylan, I wanted to say how sorry I was for the way my husband spoke to you.' She had the impression of grey clouds passing through his eyes, making them impossible to read.

'Since you're here,' he said. 'Would you like to come and see the yurt?'

'Yes.' She smiled. 'I'd like that very much.'

Vanessa had been expecting a rustic shack, not this neat little oasis tucked away from the world. In the middle of the camp were the remnants of a campfire, a director's chair by it. A guitar was propped awkwardly against the chair, as if Dylan had stopped playing suddenly.

To the left of the grassy clearing was the yurt, a medium-sized canvas tent that looked a bit like a circus top. His green camper van was parked nearby and a hammock stretched out between two of the overhanging trees.

'Let me give you the guided tour,' he said. She followed him through the little door into the yurt and was immediately struck by how spacious it felt. And clean. On the floor was a mixture of striped rugs and sheepskins, while a day bed was in the far left, artfully adorned with more striped scatter cushions. There was a low wooden table in the middle of the room, with more cushions to flop down on to. A pair of Moroccan lanterns, not dissimilar to the ones Vanessa had in her own house, were suspended from the roof poles.

'Dylan, it's really lovely.'

'You're surprised. Were you expecting a troglodyte's cave?'

'Of course not!' Her pink cheeks gave her away.

'I'm kidding you.' He gave her one of his lopsided smiles. The yurt suddenly felt awfully close and sticky.

'Shall we continue the grand tour?' she said hurriedly.

The kitchen area was under a canopy outside: a small gas cooker with two hobs and a grill. Pots and pans and cooking utensils hung from hooks. 'I normally cook over the fire in summer,' he explained.

She was fascinated. A wooden cubicle with a large plastic drum suspended above it was apparently a very good shower. It was all well run, but she was dying to ask a question.

'Do you have a loo?'

He laughed. 'Of course. It's over there, through the trees.'

Despite the unsavoury subject matter she was intrigued. 'How does it work?'

'You dig a pit and fill it with wood shavings or leaves or whatever. Then you build a toilet above it, and when you go, you just chuck down another handful of leaves. Masks the smell completely. Then when you pack up, you cover the pit with topsoil and leave it to do its work. Human waste makes brilliant compost.'

Vanessa was transfixed watching his mouth move. He even made effluence sound sexy. She realized he was telling her something. 'Take a seat,' he said.

She sat down in the canvas chair and placed her Hermès at her feet. Eddie came lolloping over, dusty and ragged after a good roll. Her outfit was beyond saving, so she let Eddie rest his big hairy head on her knee. Dylan must think she was a complete drama queen for overreacting earlier.

He came back out of the yurt with two tin mugs. 'Here.'

'What is it?' she asked dubiously.

'Homemade elderflower juice.'

The liquid was cool and deliciously tart. Vanessa sat back, surprisingly contented. On a day like this, surrounded by the beauty of nature, even she could see the benefits of living under canvas. It must be a different story in the depths of winter.

'Don't you freeze to death?'

'Not at all. I've got a wood-burning stove that keeps the yurt pretty toasty.'

'All that cold and mud, though.' She shuddered. 'Urgh.'

'That's exactly why I love it. Living so close to the wind and the rain and the mud; it makes me feel alive. We spend far too much time indoors these days, in our centrally heated houses and air-conditioned cars and offices; we lose touch with the real world around us.'

He pointed at the yurt. 'I can put that up in thirty minutes, less to take it down. Then I'm on to the next place, with no trace I was ever here. I've got control over every aspect of my life. It's the most incredible freedom.'

'But what about earning money? Having responsibilities? Real life isn't that simple, Dylan.'

He fixed her with his huge grey eyes. 'It's as simple as you make it, Vanessa. I've got everything I need right here.'

She thought about what he'd said. Did she have freedom in her own life? There were constant demands to be met. Houses to be run, appearances to keep up, deals to be done. So many people depended on her: Conrad, her mother, Marty, Renata, the rest of their staff. All the sponsors and journalists and paparazzi who wanted something from her.

'You were miles away,' Dylan said, interrupting her train of thought.

'Sorry, I was just thinking.'

He studied her for a moment. 'Tell me a bit more about yourself.'

She laughed. 'Pick up any gossip mag and you'll get an idea.'

He studied her from under long lashes. 'I want to hear about the real you.'

'There's not lots to tell, really. You've seen where I live.' She had done a thousand interviews about her life. She had it down pat, even making the bad bits sound fabulous, but with Dylan everything felt stripped. She didn't want to put a gloss on it.

'What about your upbringing? Before all the fame?'

'We didn't have much money, but I still considered myself privileged,' she said. 'My dad worked hard to send me to one of the best schools in London.'

'He must be really proud of you.'

'He's dead,' Vanessa said flatly.

'I'm sorry, I didn't realize.'

'Why would you?' she asked.

Dylan paused. 'How long ago? If you don't mind me asking.'

'Nine years ago. The day of my nineteeth birthday, actually. He had a massive heart attack.' She stared at her drink. Ironically, her dad had been laying carpets at the new house of one of her biggest bullies from school. She could still remember the disdain the family had showed her and her mother during the inquest.

'God, Vanessa, that's awful.'

'It was pretty shitty, actually. My dad had been the centre of our family. Suddenly he was gone. My mother went into shock and so I had to do everything.'

'What about your friends?' Dylan said.

She gave a bitter laugh. 'I've never had any friends. Still, it taught me you can only rely on one person, and that's yourself.' She pulled at a piece of grass. 'I could have gone to pieces, but what good would that have done? I had my mother to think about. I had to make a living to look after both of us.'

'I'm sorry, Vanessa.'

She smiled tightly. 'What's there to be sorry about? I met my husband, and we have a wonderful life now.'

His eyes rested on her. 'You don't always have to be the strong one,' he told her.

It was so intuitive, so unexpected, that Vanessa felt her eyes fill up. 'I should go.' She stood up abruptly. He got to his feet as well.

'I didn't mean to upset you. Please, don't leave like this.'

She gazed into his eyes. There was a tenderness to them that she hadn't sensed from anyone for such a long time. Without really knowing what she was doing, she stepped forward and kissed him.

For a terrifying moment he didn't respond, but then she felt his lips part and Dylan was kissing her back. His mouth was like the softest velvet. As he put his arms around her she felt herself melting into him. His hot, hard body felt like the most familiar thing she'd ever known. She closed her eyes and drank him in. She started falling, falling.

With a superhuman effort she pulled away. 'I'm s-sorry,' she stuttered. 'I don't know what came over me.'

He still had hold of her. 'Don't be sorry. I'm not.'

'I'm married. You must think I'm a complete floozy.'

'I don't think you're very happy,' he said softly.

Vanessa felt herself welling up again. 'I should go.'

He gazed at her. 'Will you come back?'

'Yes, I promise,' she said, kissing him again. When they eventually drew apart, it was like vapour trails were left hanging in the air between them. Dylan saw her off from the thicket, standing there for as long as she could see him. Vanessa got back to the car in a daze. She'd never felt this way, not even when she'd kissed Conrad after her wedding vows.

There and then she knew she was in trouble.

Chapter 25

Blaize Castle was a picture of serenity as Catherine powered up the hill that evening. Scudding to a stop, she turned round to get her breath back. A sea of meadow rolled before her, wild grasses undulating in the breeze. It was hard to imagine such a heavenly vista being wiped out with steel and wire monstrosities called the Loch Ness Log Flume and the Big Ben Terror Plunge.

She bent down to loosen the laces on her trainers, ready for a leisurely walk back, when out of the stillness came a woman's scream. She looked up. It had come from a meadow beyond the ruined gatehouse. Alarm bells started ringing. It might be beautiful up here, but it was also very remote.

Hesitating for a moment, she walked into the meadow. The grass shimmered and waved at her, hiding its secrets.

'Hello?' She sounded far more confident than she felt, up here alone, without her phone. There was a dark clump of trees on the far side. She was so convinced the cry had come from there that she practically fell over the two bodies lying in her way.

'Fuck a duck!' She clutched at her chest. 'What are you doing here?'

Talia Tudor lifted her bug sunglasses and glowered. 'You scared *us*! What are you doing, creeping round here?'

'I'm not creeping round anywhere,' Catherine retorted, taking in Talia's pornographic bikini and the topless man sprawled next to her. Judging by the tattoos and stubble, he wasn't from St Edward's, the local boys' school.

A plastic bottle of Strongbow stood half-drunk between them, while there was a very fruity smell in the air that definitely wasn't coming from the flowers. 'Shouldn't you be revising?' Catherine said, looking pointedly at the Rizla packet the man was holding.

'What are you, my keeper?' Talia leant back on her elbows and shook out her long hair, showing off her young, nubile body to its full effect. Her companion grinned and went back to rolling up his cigarette.

'What's that, then?' Catherine asked him.

'Good old tobacco, love, you want some?'

She gave the man a withering look and turned back to Talia. 'Does your mum know you're up here?'

'I'm sixteen, not six.' Talia put her sunglasses back on.

Catherine gave up. She could stand here and give a lecture but it wouldn't get them anywhere. Besides, Talia wasn't her daughter. 'Just look after yourself, OK?'

The girl gave a strange smirk. 'You don't have to worry about me.'

Catherine had a leisurely jog back down the hill. The sun was sinking in the sky as she walked into the outskirts of the town. It was the less pretty part of Beeversham, the buildings a mismatch of new-build houses and ugly 1970s bungalows. The Black Bull pub, a grotty establishment popular with underage schoolkids, stood further down on the main road. As Catherine passed it the front door opened and she nearly collided with a fat sweating bulk in pinstripe. Jonty Fortescue-Wellington peered foggily at her chest. 'Fancy coming back to mine for a Johnnie Walker?'

'Not tonight, thanks.'

'Sexy legs,' he slurred, as she neatly side-stepped round him.

By the time she got home the sun had dipped behind the roofline of the Crescent. She reached for the key under the metallic plant pot and opened the front door. Sounds of classical music crashed out from the kitchen.

She kicked off her trainers and wandered down the corridor. A well-run operation was taking place in the kitchen. John was at one of the worktops chopping tarragon, a tea towel over his shoulder. Against his huge physique it looked like a napkin.

She went over and turned down the Bang and Olufsen. 'What's this racket?'

He gave her a long-suffering look. 'Monteverdi's *L'Orfeo*; only one of the greatest Italian operas ever.'

She poured out a glass of filtered water and drained half of it in one.

'I just saw Jonty Fortescue-Wankington in town.'

'Half-cut?'

'Of course. He propositioned me and asked me back to his for a bit of "How's your father".'

'You are joking me.'

'I'm not. Maybe I should have gone along and told him what I thought of him.' Catherine went to grab a few grapes from the fruit bowl. She noticed the parking ticket she'd chucked in there had gone.

'Have you seen that fine I had?'

'I've paid it. I got tired of looking at it.'

'John, that was my ticket,' she protested. 'You shouldn't have paid it.'

'It had been there for a week, Cath.'

'That's why it was in the fruit bowl! To remind me.'

He just arched an eyebrow at her.

'Well, thanks,' she mumbled. 'I'll obviously reimburse you.'

He started chopping again. 'Don't be ridiculous.'

She wandered over to the fridge and opened it. 'Oh. You've been shopping.'

'Yup. I was passing the supermarket on the way home.'

'I was going to go shopping tomorrow,' she said uselessly.

She drifted round the kitchen in her socked feet. Every surface gleamed. Next door in the utility room the washing machine was churning. How did he do it? She'd only been gone an hour!

He heard her sigh. 'What's up?'

'I just feel a bit – I don't know – *redundant*.' She hadn't lifted a finger in weeks. Ever since the pregnancy disappointment he had been treating her with kid gloves.

'I know you're looking out for me,' she said more gently. 'But I'm OK.'

He put his knife down and came over. 'I just worry about you, Cath.'

'You don't have to!' she protested.

'I know I don't.' He put his arms around her. 'It just kills me to think I wasn't there for you all those years.'

'Oh, my darling!' She hugged him back. 'Don't be so silly.'

'I know, I'm an overprotective bugger. Just indulge me.'

They smiled at each other.

'You know, you're going to have to try harder with this kept-woman thing,' he told her.

It hit a raw nerve. 'Don't say things like that!' Catherine snapped. 'It's fucking insulting!'

'Whoa, Cath! Of course I was joking!'

'It wasn't very funny,' she retorted.

'OK.' His eyes widened. 'Sorry. Bad joke.'

The doorbell rang. 'Shall I get that?' sniped Catherine. 'Or does it not fall under my *kept-woman* remit?'

She stomped up the stairs, not knowing why she felt so furious.

Chapter 26

Dylan's arrival had not gone unnoticed by the other female residents of Beeversham. When Catherine hit the High Street the next morning, Amanda Belcher and Mel Cooper-Stanley were deep in discussion outside Wedding Belles.

'Have you heard? We've been invaded by gypsies!' Amanda exclaimed.

Mel rolled her eyes. 'He's not a gypsy.' She turned to Catherine. 'He's living in a yurt near Foxglove Woods, one of these alternative types. He came into Mr Patel's the other day and they got talking. Dylan, I think his name is.'

'You say yes to one and suddenly they're all swarming in!' Amanda's bosom quivered excitedly. 'I did hear he was very attractive, though, all wild hair and dark flashing eyes, like Omar Sharif in *Dr Zhivago*.'

Catherine had an unwanted headache, not made any better by the glaring daylight. Still antsy at John, she'd drunk the best part of a bottle of wine at dinner by herself last night.

Tristan Jago was striding up the street, long legs displayed nicely in a pair of skinny trousers. 'Morning, ladies.'

'Morning,' they all chorused.

He powered past, manbag over his shoulder. 'Do you think Tristan's gay?' Catherine asked. 'I've never seen him with a woman.'

'Heavens, no!' Amanda exclaimed. 'Apparently he's got quite an appetite for other people's wives. Mel, remember that anorexic liberal he brought along to the Scarecrow Festival two years ago? She'd only left her husband the week before!'

'I really wouldn't know,' Mel said.

Over the road Lynette Tudor came out of her shop, looking as stressed as ever.

'Guess what I heard yesterday,' said Amanda. 'Lynette has started doing cleaning work for Beau Rainford. Of course, I sympathize with poor Lynette having to make ends meet in that little shop of hers, but cleaning out Beau Rainford's filthy sex den?' Amanda shuddered. 'I bet he makes her do the dusting topless!'

They watched Lynette hurry off down the street, shoulders hunched round her ears.

Catherine was suddenly transported back two decades as Alannah Myle's 'Black Velvet' filled the air. A familiar low red car pulled up beside them. It was Beau Rainford himself, in his old Mustang. Catherine immediately recognized the rail-thin woman in the passenger seat. Valentina Volosky looked down her nose at Catherine and haughtily tossed her hair back.

Turning down the music, Beau removed his Ray-Bans. The famous blue eyes were ice-cold.

'I've got a bone to pick with you,' he told Amanda. 'A little bird tells me you've been going round casting aspersions on my good name.'

A mottled rash spread up Amanda's neck. 'I don't know what you mean.'

'I think you do.' Beau's face was carved and dangerous. *God, he's good-looking*, Catherine thought. *But you wouldn't want to mess with him.*

'I suggest you keep your nose out of other people's business and concentrate on your own.' Beau glanced at the overdressed window of Wedding Belles. 'You could do something about that hideous display for a start. No wonder marriage rates are in freefall.'

'How dare you, that's a Jane Morgan!' Amanda started to say, but Beau cut her dead.

'It's fucking horrible, that's what it is. What is it with you small-minded parochial types?' He looked pointedly at Amanda's bottom. 'Although that's probably the only thing that *is* small about you.'

Amanda gave a barely audible gasp. The rash spread further up her neck.

'Oi, that's not on,' Catherine told Beau.

Beau's eyes slid on to her for a moment, before he turned his attention to Mel. Suddenly the sunshine was back in his face. 'Hullo, darling, how's tricks?'

'Hullo, Beau,' Mel said quietly.

'That husband of yours looking after you?'

'Can't complain.'

Valentina laid a possessive hand on Beau's knee. He slid the Ray-Bans back on. 'You ladies have a nice day.'

He looked at Amanda as he said it; a threat rather than a well wish. The engine revved and the car sped

160

off, nearly taking out an old man crossing the street.

Mel turned to Amanda. 'Are you all right?'

'Y-yes, of course.' Amanda looked flattened. 'I should get back to work.'

She went inside the shop, tugging her shirt down over her bottom.

'Beau was out of order then,' Mel said. 'Amanda can be a pain, but she didn't deserve that.'

'I wonder who told him?'

They both looked across the road at Butterflies.

Chapter 27

The sky was peacock-blue as Vanessa made her way through Foxglove Woods the next day. Eddie was sitting under a tree, as if he'd known she was coming. Bending down, she stroked his long friendly face. 'Hello, boy. Have you come to escort me?'

The dog led her across the flower-strewn meadow, stopping at the edge of the copse as if to say: *That's my part done.* She watched him bound off across the woods, tail sticking out like a piece of wire. Her wedding ring sparkled accusingly in the sunlight. Guiltily, she took it off and put it in her handbag.

It was dark and cool under the canopy of trees. She trod across the grassy carpet, the smell of wild garlic pungent in the air. As the trees thinned, the grassy clearing came into view. Her stomach lurched. Dylan was sitting by the campfire, topless, mending a piece of yurt canvas. She'd not been able to sleep all night for thinking about him.

She felt a longing as she saw his naked torso for the first time. Her eyes devoured the lean pectorals and small dark nipples, the ribs showing through his sinewy back. He wove the needle through the rough canvas dexterously. She imagined those hands running over her naked skin and shivered.

He glanced up and saw her, his expression blank. Vanessa's heart plummeted. She shouldn't have come. Then she nearly collapsed with relief as his face lit up with the biggest grin.

He was already walking towards her. They stopped a foot apart. In the light his eyes reminded her of iridescent fish scales flashing in a sun-dappled stream.

'Oh, Dylan.' The next thing she was in his arms, kissing him deeply. As he wrapped his arms round her she revelled in the feeling of his taut, sun-warmed flesh.

'I missed you,' he told her.

'I missed you, too. I told Conrad I was going for a spa day at Daylesford.'

He cut her off with a kiss, and the heat exploded between them. Tongues were frantic, hands running over skin and raking through each other's hair. She had never even had a one-night stand in her life, but with Dylan the desire was just overwhelming. All she wanted was him inside her.

His long fingers caressed her shoulders straps. 'Take it off,' she whispered. The Temperley dress fell to the ground in a luxurious puddle. His eyes ran over the swell of breasts under the La Perla bra; the hourglass waist oozing into voluptuous hips.

'God,' he said softly. 'You're so beautiful.'

He ran his hand between her breasts. Vanessa felt a throb between her legs.

'You're shaking,' he said. 'Are you all right?'

'I-I'm shaking because I want you so much.'

His eyes were so huge they filled his face. Pulling down a bra strap, he pushed the lace aside to reveal her breast. As his tongue started to circle her nipple with exquisite lightness she wanted to explode.

His other hand slid down her belly towards her matching G-string. She was sure she'd come if he even touched her between the legs.

'I'll get a blanket.'

'I don't want a blanket!' Vanessa was sick of cold, unsatisfactory sex on Egyptian sheets with a three-hundred-thread count. She wanted to feel the grass scratching against her back, leaves in her hair. Grabbing him round the neck, she pulled him down on top of her. The next moment he was inside her, moving joyously and freely. He felt so wonderful. She didn't know where she started and he ended . . .

He gazed down at her. 'You're so beautiful,' he said again.

Her eyes filled with tears. It had been so long since she'd been made to feel like this. He looked horrified.

'Oh no, what's wrong?'

'Nothing,' she sobbed. 'It's lovely. Keep doing what you're doing.'

Ten minutes later, after the most amazing orgasm she'd ever had, Vanessa collapsed into his arms. He held her tight, stroking her hair until their heartbeats calmed down. She lay on his chest, unable to speak. *I've just had sex with another man.*

All she could think was how happy she felt.

*

Marty's BMW was parked next to the Porsche as Vanessa pulled up outside Tresco House. She'd completely forgotten their manager was coming to dinner. She checked her reflection in the rearview mirror: the face of an adulteress looked back. Grabbing her bag off the seat, she hurried across the courtyard into the house. Sukie trotted into the empty entrance hall, looking quizzical. 'Ssh, cover for Mummy, angel,' Vanessa whispered, willing her to be silent, and rushed upstairs.

Thirty minutes later she appeared on the back terrace, freshly showered and changed, the last traces of Dylan washed off her skin and hair. Conrad was sitting at the table outside with Marty and her mother. An open bottle of Cristal was in an ice bucket on the table.

'There you are,' her mother said. 'I thought I heard you come in.'

'Sorry,' Vanessa said. 'I had to have a shower, you know how the oil gets in your hair.'

'Looking good, kid,' Marty told her. 'That must have been some facial.'

Conrad's dark eyes were boring into her, as though he could tell something was different. Vanessa suddenly went cold. She hadn't put her wedding ring back on. Conrad was bound to notice and know something was up.

'Is that new?' he said, looking at her dress.

She almost collapsed with relief. 'It's last season's Gucci, you were with me when I bought it, remember?'

She sat down beside her mother, and Sukie immediately jumped up on her lap. Vanessa buried her face in the dog's soft fur, hiding her guilty conscience.

'You want a drink, kid?' Marty handed her a glass of Cristal. No doubt he'd brought it with him; Conrad was far too tight to open such good champagne for anyone on his payroll.

Vanessa drained half her glass in one go. The alcohol took the edge off her nerves. An image of Dylan, moving dexterously on top of her, popped up in her mind.

'What inedible monstrosity is Renata dishing up for us tonight?' Conrad asked.

'Coq au vin, I hope,' sighed Vanessa.

Conrad stared at her as if she were mad. 'In this heat?'

'I mean, I think we're having salmon,' Vanessa spluttered.

'Renata,' he bellowed. 'Can you bring out some nibbles?'

The housekeeper stuck her head out of the kitchen window. 'No food. You on diet now, Mr Powell.'

'I'm sure you can rustle up something. What else do we pay you for?' Conrad muttered. 'Vanessa's contribution to Help the Aged,' he told Marty. 'My wife is a firm believer that charity starts at home.'

A few minutes later Renata shuffled out with a bowl. Conrad broke off his monologue. 'What have you got?'

'Root vegetables.'

'Excellent, my favourite!' Conrad scooped up a generous handful of the colourful crisps. 'Anyway, as I was saying, Marty, Daniel Craig only got the James Bond part because . . .'

He stopped mid-sentence and started to choke. A

mouthful of purple and red sprayed all over the table. Vanessa and her mum flattened themselves in their chairs.

'Are you trying to poison me?' Conrad shrieked. He looked closer at the bowl. 'Renata, you moron, this is fucking potpourri!'

Vanessa breathed a sigh of relief as he rushed off to dry-heave in the toilet.

Chapter 28

Britain was now officially hotter than Barbados. Sales of suncream continued to soar as forecasters predicted no break in the run of freakishly good weather.

The rising temperatures were having an extraordinary effect on the British public. That Tuesday there were unprecedented scenes at Downing Street as a group of middle-class mums chained themselves to the gates in protest about cuts to child benefit. The hapless Deputy Prime Minster was sent out for peace talks and got a (homemade) custard pie in his face. The women were eventually cut free and released without charge, but it was a clear sign just how disenchanted people had become.

In Beeversham it was only four days until the Big Charity Game Show. The change of format had been a masterstroke. Well-wishers had donated prizes from cooking lessons at a Michelin-starred restaurant to a day on the set of the latest Benedict Cumberbatch drama. The SNOW committee had been inundated with people wanting to do food stalls from as far afield as London. With the current economic climate it was felt that a champagne tent might be a little out of keeping, so there was a Prosecco one instead, run by the staff from Bar 47.

The stage was being put up in the market square. The local pet shop had been persuaded to loan out twenty rats and a boxful of stick insects for *I'm a Celebrity* . . . Mr Patel had hired a shiny tuxedo for his role as an *X Factor* judge. John had gone up even higher in everyone's opinion by knocking up a couple of beautifully made wooden stall stands from scratch. All proceeds from the ticket sales were going to a local hospice.

Every telegraph pole and gate in the area had been plastered with posters about the event. The *Daily Telegraph* had run a great 'David v. Goliath' article on how Beeversham was fighting back against the might of Ye Olde Worlde. The SNOW committee had done everything they could. It was now a case of praying people turned up.

Bar 47 was buzzing with daytime punters enjoying the super-strength coffee. Catherine found Ginny ensconced on the terrace, texting.

'Hello, darling, I won't be a minute. I'm just sending a text back to Emily.'

'How is she?' Catherine asked as she sat down. She'd never met the Chamberlains' children, who both worked abroad. The family home was plastered with photos of them. Ginny was an enormously proud mother.

'Good, she's applying for a new teaching post in Beijing.' Ginny put her phone back in her handbag. 'I miss them both terribly,' she said, 'but they're having such an adventure. Young people have such exciting opportunities these days.'

'They'd never come back to Beeversham?'

'Heavens, no.' She smiled brightly across the table. 'I love your dress. I wish I had the figure to wear something like that.'

'Don't be silly, you look lovely.'

Despite the age gap the two women were good friends. Ginny was a dreadful worrier, but she was warm and discreet. She was also good fun after a glass of wine.

The waitress came over to take their order. Ginny put her face up to the sun. 'It's lovely to have some time out,' she confessed. 'We're eating, living and sleeping the charity game show at home.'

'Tell me about it. Someone else has asked John to knock up another stall. The garden is covered in wood shavings.'

'The man is a miracle worker! Whatever would we do without him?'

'Yeah,' Catherine said sardonically. 'Saint John the Great.'

Ginny glanced across. 'Is everything OK?'

Catherine picked miserably at a sachet of sugar. 'Oh, I don't know, Ginny. I'm being a real bitch to him at the moment.'

'I'm sure you're not.'

The waitress appeared with their coffees. Catherine waited until they were alone again. 'It's just that he won't let me do anything,' she told Ginny. 'It's driving

170

me mad. I did manage to look after myself for over twenty years before he came back along!'

'John is the protective sort. That's what most men see their role as.'

'There's a difference between protecting and suffocating,' Catherine grumbled.

'Have you told him how you feel?'

'I've tried, but it always seems to come out wrong. What do I say? "Sorry, John, you're just *too* perfect."'

'Aah, no one's perfect, not even our John!'

Catherine stared at the heart on the top of her froth. 'We've been trying, you know, for a baby. I'm healthy, John's healthy, but nothing's happening.'

'You just have to give it time, darling. I'm sure it will work out in the end.'

'That's what John keeps saying.'

'Doesn't make it any easier, though, does it?'

The two exchanged a smile. 'I don't mean to sit here and moan,' Catherine said. 'I'm just having a bit of a wobble.'

'You're perfectly entitled, darling. We all have them.'

There was something in Ginny's voice. Catherine didn't know why she asked the next question. 'Do you see Beau much?'

Ginny gave a sad little smile. 'Not often.'

'Do you think Felix and Beau will ever make up?'

'Felix believes Beau has let him down very badly. He's very black and white about things.' Ginny trailed off. 'It's a difficult situation.'

There was a commotion inside. Jonty was at the counter, complaining loudly about something. They watched him stagger off to a table, nearly taking a waitress out on the way.

'Excuse me for speaking out of turn,' Catherine said. 'But how the hell does Felix put up with Jonty?'

'Felix is very loyal.'

'Why isn't he our MP? Everyone loves him.'

'I think his days of running for MP are behind him. Besides, Felix is very good at being chairman.' Ginny emptied another sachet of sugar into her cappuccino. 'You know, he ran against Jonty once, years ago.'

'No way! And Jonty beat him?'

Ginny suddenly looked terribly anxious. 'You won't tell Felix I told you, will you? I'd hate him to think I'd been talking behind his back.'

'Of course not.'

'Jonty was rather sharp back in the day.' Ginny gave a weak smile. 'I think we're all hoping he'll sort himself out.'

Catherine didn't share her optimism. If Jonty didn't lose his seat to Tristan Jago in the next few years it would be a bloody miracle.

Chapter 29

'Can I get you anything else?'

'I'm fine, thanks.'

The waiter nodded and melted away. It was the fifth time he'd been over in as many minutes. The over-solicitousness was all a bit embarrassing; he didn't look that much older than Fleur.

She watched the couple at the next table gaze gooily at each other, oblivious to their plates of pasta. She turned away and looked round Bar 47's restaurant instead. The lights were dimmed low, candles on each table casting a warm glow over the white walls. The full-length windows at the front had been pulled open, bringing in a warm breeze from the street.

An old lady dining with friends across the room caught her eye again and gave her a sympathetic smile. Fleur gritted her teeth and smiled back. Was she the first person ever to eat out by herself? She started to count the array of vodka bottles behind the bar for something to do, wishing people would stop staring.

'Your lobster ravioli, madam.' The waiter reappeared

back in front of her, holding a large white plate. He placed it down with a flourish.

'Is there anything else you'd like? Some sides perhaps? More bread?'

'I'm fine, really.' She wished he'd go away.

He finally got the message and left her to it. Fleur picked up her cutlery and started to eat. The ravioli was succulent and spicy, dressed in a rich tomato sauce. She tried to concentrate on the flavours, imagining what she'd write if she were a food critic.

The new Adele album was playing gently in the background. A gentle hum of conversation reverberated from other tables. Fleur chased a piece of lobster round her plate and forked it up. Her chewing sounded thunderously loud.

She reached for her wine nonchalantly, as if she dined out alone the whole time. The old lady gave her another stoic smile. Fleur looked back at her plate.

As tasty as it was, the ravioli was taking an awfully long time to get through. Each mouthful seemed to get stuck in her throat. She battled with an ever-growing feeling of self-consciousness.

'You're an independent, modern woman,' she muttered. 'You can do this.'

The girl on the next table exchanged a look with her boyfriend. Great. Not only was Fleur a total friendless loser, but she was now the mad girl who talked to herself.

The plate of food was insurmountable. She put her fork and spoon down. The next moment the waiter was back at her side.

'Is everything all right?'

174

'Lovely.' She looked apologetically at the half-finished food. 'I'm just really full.'

'Would you like to see the dessert list?'

It felt like the whole room was watching her: the couple, the old lady, the waiter behind the bar polishing the glasses.

'Can I just get the bill?' she said.

'No coffee?' he asked.

'I have to go.' She got up so quickly she nearly knocked her chair over. Three minutes later she was back out on the High Street. Her meal had lasted a grand total of thirty-three minutes.

She unlocked the door of the Land Rover and climbed in. Her heart was racing, palms clammy. *Pathetic*, she told herself. You can't even have a bloody meal by yourself.

She sat in the darkness, trying to calm herself down. After a minute or two, she reached across and opened the glovebox. She pulled out the long white envelope.

The interior light was broken, but she could just about see in the glow from a nearby streetlamp. It was a generic pink card with a bunch of flowers on the front. The official message read 'Special wishes on your special day'. Her sister's neat, officious writing was underneath. 'To Fleur, love from Claire, Graham, Olivia and William.'

Fleur sat back. 'Happy birthday,' she told herself sadly.

Chapter 30

An African sky yawned over the valley as Catherine stood in the ensuite that morning, attacking her teeth with the electric toothbrush. They couldn't have wished for a better day for Beeversham's Big Charity Game Show.

John came in with a coffee. 'Where do you want it?'

'Mmm,' she said through a mouthful of toothpaste.

He put it down on the side. 'So I'll see you down-stairs?'

She spat out a mouthful into the sink. 'Perfect. Give me ten minutes.'

Their eyes met in the mirror. Her husband gave her a cautious smile. 'Great. I'll go and lock up.'

He hadn't said anything, but she knew he was keeping his distance. As if he were married to a neurotic house cat who could go wild at any minute.

She didn't blame him. Tetchy, up and down for no good reason, she knew she was acting irrationally. The problem was, she had no idea how to stop it.

*

The SNOW committee met on the terrace of Bar 47 for breakfast. It was already hot enough to feel the sun burning on skin.

'I can't wear a bra, I burnt my nipples sunbathing in the garden yesterday,' Mel was telling Mrs Patel. 'You can't tell, can you?'

Mrs Patel, elegant in a wide-brimmed straw hat, looked at Mel's pneumatic breasts rearing up in the lime-green halterneck.

'No, dear,' she said kindly.

'Let's have a quick run-down,' Felix said. 'How's *Big Brother* looking at Belcher HQ?'

'A bit more furniture arranging in the living room and we're all set,' enthused Henry. Amanda, lost for words for the first time in her life, stared into her orange juice.

Mr Patel had been persuaded to do a *Supermarket Sweep* in the mini market and was looking nearly as nervous as Amanda. On the opposite side of the street *I'm a Celebrity* . . . had been set up on the memorial green.

'We've got six snakes, twenty rats and a box of stick insects on loan from Pete's Pets', Felix informed them. 'And Fleur Blackwater is still coming down with some of her animals for the childen to pet.' He glanced down at his notes. 'What's the latest about the Powells?'

Amanda perked up. 'It's all under control. I've been liaising with their people; Vanessa and Conrad will be here on schedule to open the event.'

Mel and Catherine exchanged looks. Amanda had completely taken over their VIP guests, but Catherine didn't mind. The fewer dealings she had with Vanessa the better.

'I've asked if they want a rider,' Amanda announced.

'They're coming by horseback?' asked a confused Mr Patel.

'A rider, Dilip,' Amanda said patronizingly. 'It's the list of things celebrities want when they do an event.'

'I remember hearing J Lo once asked for a room full of red lilies and diamond-encrusted headphones at the MTVs,' Mel said.

'We're a market town, not the Hollywood Hills,' Felix said firmly. 'We can stretch to a free bottle of champagne, Amanda, but I'm afraid that's about it.'

Vincent, Bar 47's manager, came outside. 'Felix, there's a couple of policemen here to cordon off the high street.'

'Excellent, right on schedule.' He grinned boyishly. 'Let's get this game show on the road.'

It was quickly apparent they had enough booze to sink a battleship. As well as the Prosecco tent, a local vineyard was selling their wine alongside an organic cider stall. There was a row of real ale stands and something called Tipsy Gins.

'They'll be more than tipsy by the end of that lot,' John said.

Catherine smiled. 'I think that's the idea.'

There was also a mountain of food on offer, including an ice-cream stall, a hog roast and a customized old-fashioned van selling organic meatballs.

Ginny Chamberlain was manning the SNOW stall. She was putting out a bundle of leaflets as Catherine and John walked up.

'My lovelies!' She'd put on a straw hat with a striped pink band that matched her cheeks. 'Have you had to avert any major disasters yet?'

'Nope,' John deadpanned. 'But there's still time.'

Ginny came round the stall. 'I'll come with you, I need to find Felix.'

An area had been cordoned off on the memorial green. There was a trestle table with a large glass tank on it, containing three brown snakes. Nearby a man wearing a cap saying Pete's Pets was prodding a cage of comatose rodents.

'I hope we don't get accused of cruelty to animals,' Ginny sighed. 'Oh, hullo, Fleur! How lovely to see you.'

On the other side of the green a petite young woman with startling red hair was leading two lambs down the ramp of a trailer. She looked up, her freckled face transforming into a smile.

'Hullo, Ginny.'

'This is Fleur Blackwater,' Ginny told Catherine and John. 'Fleur and her dad live up at Blackwater Farm.'

'Nice to meet you,' Fleur said.

'You too,' Catherine smiled, thinking what beautiful amber eyes Fleur had. They were huge and wary, like a fox's. 'I see you've brought quite a menagerie.'

'Four lambs, one cow, and I managed to borrow a pair of Gloucester Old Spots off a mate of Dad's.'

The huge pigs were making a fearsome snuffling noise as they burrowed around in straw at the front of the trailer.

'This is Ben,' Fleur said, introducing them to the stocky, pleasant-faced young man with her. 'He's helping me out.'

'Thank you, Ben, it's all very much appreciated,' Ginny said, then turned back to Fleur. 'Your dad didn't fancy it today?'

'He's busy at the farm.'

'Of course,' Ginny said. 'Do send my regards to him, won't you?'

'It's dreadfully sad,' she said in a low voice after they'd walked off. 'Fleur's dad was a very successful farmer, but after his wife died, he's found it hard to cope. Especially with farming the way it is now. Felix does a bit of free legal work for Robert now and again.'

Catherine thought about the determined tilt of Fleur's chin and decided that she was a girl who could hold her own.

By 11 a.m. people were starting to stream into the streets. Catherine saw the woman from the cheese stall lugging a box towards the back of her van, and she went over to help. 'Here, let me.'

'Thanks, love,' the woman said. 'Men are never around when you need them, are they?'

'Can I help?' John came striding over, sunglasses pushed up on his head.

The woman took one look at the green eyes and big biceps and melted.

'Ooh, if you wouldn't mind!'

'Not at all,' John said, lifting the box clean out of Catherine's hands.

'Isn't he wonderful?' the woman sighed as John walked off. 'You're lucky having one like that, I can tell you.'

'Aren't I just?' she said sarcastically. She spotted

a small wooden barrel by the car. 'Does that need moving?'

The woman glanced over. 'That one's really heavy. My husband can move it when he comes back.'

'Leave it to me,' Catherine declared, walking off. She bent to pick up the barrel. It didn't move. As she tried again, a pain shot across her back.

'What have you got in here?' she joked. 'Lead weights?'

'A hundredweight of Double Gloucester. Honestly, love, don't worry. You look like you're about to bust a gut.'

John came back over. 'Here, I'll do that.'

Catherine adopted the stance of a Bulgarian weightlifter. 'I'm fine.' Face purple, she managed to lift the barrel a few inches off the ground.

'Put it down, you'll strain your back.' He went to prise it out of her fingers, but she clung on to it.

'I said I've got this!' she cried. 'Get off!'

'Cath,' he said in a low voice. 'What are you *doing*?'

She ignored him. 'Where do you want this?' she puffed to the woman.

'Er, over there by the stall, please,' the woman replied, sounding rather astonished. She and John watched as Catherine staggered across to the stall with the barrel banging painfully against her shins. Lumping it down defiantly, she turned round.

'What's next?'

'I think that's all, thanks,' the woman said, clearly thinking she was dealing with a nutter. 'Oh look, I can see my husband anyway.'

They walked off, a spasm twingeing painfully across

Catherine's lower back. 'Don't treat me like a child,' she said grumpily. 'I am capable of doing things.'

John looked at her, bent over like an old woman. 'Fine. I just thought you needed help.'

'I'm sick of your help!' she snapped. 'Stop trying to control me!'

'I'm not trying to. *Jesus.*' John shook his head. Shooting his wife an unimpressed look, he walked off.

Chapter 31

By five to twelve the market square was brimming with people, but there was still no sign of the Powells. Catherine kept trying their PA's number but it was going straight to voicemail.

'Celebrities are always late,' she reassured Felix. 'They'll be here soon.'

'I jolly well hope so.' He sighed. 'Otherwise people are going to be sorely disappointed when they only get me.'

John was standing at the other end of the stage with the Cooper-Stanleys. She tried a tentative smile, but he was either ignoring her under the sunglasses or he hadn't seen. *Hell,* she thought glumly. *Am I officially the worst wife in the world?*

A ripple of excitement started that could only be due to the arrival of somebody special. Amanda's bossy voice blasted out over the hordes of people.

'Out of the way, please! We've got a pair of VIPs here, you know.'

Catherine and Felix exchanged a relieved look. The

crowd parted like a sea before them, to reveal Amanda ushering the Powells through. Conrad Powell was tall and dashing in a white linen suit, luxuriant dark hair brushed off his handsome face. Vanessa Powell was tiny and radiant in purple. They stopped to sign a couple of autographs for star-struck fans.

Amanda arrived near to Catherine and Felix just ahead of them. 'One, two,' she said into the walkie-talkie she was holding.

Catherine resisted the urge to burst out laughing. This wasn't Kevin Costner and the bloody *Bodyguard*!

'One can never be too careful about security when there are famous people involved,' Amanda said. 'Henry, do you copy me?' she snapped into the walkie-talkie.

Conrad came up and Amanda put an over-familiar hand on his arm. 'Conrad, this is Felix Chamberlain, head of the SNOW committee. Felix is also our beloved chairman of Beeversham Conservative Association.'

'For my sins,' laughed Felix, putting his hand out. 'It's very nice to meet you, Conrad. We're extremely grateful to you for lending support to our cause.'

Conrad smiled expansively. 'Whatever we can do to help.'

'You know Catherine, don't you?' Amanda trilled. 'She's our very own media powerhouse!'

'The name does ring a bell. Didn't you use to edit *Saga*?'

'*Soirée* actually.' Catherine returned the smile.

Vanessa appeared at her husband's shoulder in a huge pair of Victoria Beckham sunglasses. Her strapless dress was cinched with a crocodile-skin belt, showcasing the va-va-voom curves.

Catherine attempted a placatory smile. The celebrity's face didn't move behind her glasses.

There were two other people with the Powells: a smiley, chubby girl – probably their PA – staggering under the weight of a huge shoulder bag, and an older lady, draped in an extravagant kimono. She was taller and harder in the face than Vanessa, but there was no mistaking the cat-like eyes and remarkable bone structure. She had to be the mother.

'Felix, shouldn't you think about making a start?' Amanda said importantly. 'We don't want to keep our special guests waiting.'

He checked his watch. 'Crumpets, you're right. I'll get up and say a few words, and then I'll welcome Vanessa and Conrad on stage.'

'Super duper,' Conrad drawled.

Felix climbed up on stage and did his bit about Ye Olde Worlde, but most people had their eyes on the Powells. Catherine watched Conrad pose for a picture with a gaggle of grannies, gushing over one old lady's cat brooch and chuckling indulgently with another. *Charm personified*, Catherine thought. *You'd never know he had a reputation for being a complete monster.*

The Powells' PA came up to Catherine after a few minutes. 'Mrs Powell wants to know how long before they're on.'

'I think Felix is about to finish.'

Signing another autograph, Vanessa walked over. 'Tamzin, can you get Conrad's attention?' She gave Catherine a curt smile. 'I'm afraid my husband would sign autographs all day if he could.'

The two women were left together. Vanessa stared

pointedly at the stage, ignoring Catherine. Catherine snuck a sideways look at her, beautiful and remote under the huge sunglasses.

'I expected you to be late,' she joked. 'You'll start to give celebrities a bad name, arriving on time like this.'

'I'm never late,' Vanessa replied coolly. 'I think that's another misconception you have about me.'

The crowd was becoming restless. 'It's the moment you've been waiting for!' Felix announced. 'They're huge stars and we're very lucky to have them here today. Ladies and gentlemen, please give a warm welcome to *Conrad and Vanessa Powell*!'

I'm a Celebrity . . . was well under way. The queasy-looking contestants had already been made to drink a tripe milkshake and eat a pig's snout each. Now one of the red team had a blindfold on and had their hand in the rat cage, rummaging round for a gold star.

The contestant, a man in his mid-thirties in a garish Hawaiian shirt, was making a hell of a racket. 'I hate rats!' he screamed, every time a rodent scampered over his hand. 'Don't let them eat me!'

Fleur had a closer look. 'Aren't those hamsters?' she asked Pete from Pete's Pets.

'Rats are useless in the heat,' he whispered. 'Hamsters are much better, they're mental little fuckers.'

Henry Belcher was meant to be overseeing the event, but he kept being summoned home by a hyperventilating Amanda, worried about *Big Brother* contestants knocking her china over.

'Fleur, do you fancy an ice cream?' Ben asked.

'Yes, please. Mint-choc chip if they've got it.' Fleur

rummaged in her pocket. 'How much do you need?'

'My treat, won't be a minute.'

Fleur watched Ben amble off down the street. It was just nice to be doing something other than worming cattle and mending broken fencing. She felt like she hadn't left the farm for months. She felt guilty thinking it, but it was also a relief to get away from her dad.

'Fleur, would you like some suncream?' Ginny Chamberlain had appeared in her straw hat, brandishing a bottle of factor 30. 'Your nose is going a bit pink, dear,' she said kindly. 'I'm exactly the same, I go like a lobster as soon as I step in the sun.'

'Thanks, Ginny.' Fleur squeezed out a blob of lotion and rubbed it into her skin. She was boiling in her check shirt, but there was no way she'd wear a vest top.

Ben reappeared with two cones that were already starting to melt.

'Can I get you one?' he asked Ginny.

'You're an angel, but my dress is bursting at the seams already.' She rushed off, looking for more sunburn victims.

They ate their ice creams and watched the crowd meander past.

'Why is it . . .' Fleur said through a huge mouthful, '. . . that British men dress so badly in the summer?'

'Search me.'

'Look at those socks and sandals!'

Ben shot her a sideways glance. 'You look really pretty today.' His voice came out all throaty.

They both went violently red. The next moment, a familiar voice cut through the embarrassed silence.

187

'Is this the petting pen? Looks like we've come to the right place, V.'

Fleur whirled round. 'What are *you* doing here?'

Beau was standing on the other side of the pen, blonder and browner than ever. Even worse, he had his vile girlfriend with him. His navy blazer and white trousers looked totally out of place amongst the casually dressed crowd. Valentina was in something floaty and expensive. Her bottom lip jutted out almost as far as her collarbone.

'Just dropped in on our way to Henley,' Beau drawled.

Was she supposed to be impressed? Fleur looked at his tie. 'Like a bit of pink, don't we?'

'It's *cerise* and it's the colour for Beau's club, you idiot,' Valentina sniped. 'The Leander Club is only, like, the most prestigious rowing club in the whole world.'

Fleur went the same colour as the tie. Valentina tugged on Beau's hand. 'Baby, can we get out of here? We're late already, and this place stinks.'

'Won't be a minute, darling. Why don't you have a wander round? I'm sure I saw a tombola stall. Maybe you can win us a nice jar of marmalade.'

'Fuck's sake,' Valentina huffed and stalked off.

Beau looked back at Fleur. 'Can I have a quick word?'

Fleur crossed her arms. 'Go on, then.'

'In private,' he said, looking meaningfully towards Ben.

She went over reluctantly. 'What?' she asked, keeping a good few feet between them.

Beau gave her a winning smile. 'Have you reconsidered my proposition?'

His thick hair gleamed in the bright sun. She took in the arrogant, supercilious tilt of Beau's jaw, the smooth, brown skin no doubt massaged daily with expensive moisturizer. She thought about how he'd humiliated her and the careless way he'd tried to buy the farm like it was a second-hand car. People like Beau might look golden on the outside, but they were rotten underneath.

'I think you've misunderstood me,' she said evenly. 'You might be used to always getting your own way, but unfortunately – no actually, make that *fortunately* – we have no intention of selling. So I suggest you go and find someone else's house to buy, OK?'

The easy charm drained away in an instant. Beau's eyes took on that flat, opaque look Fleur had seen before. Somewhere in the pit of her stomach she felt a twinge of unease.

A spotty young man came bounding up. 'Troy Fletcher from the *Cotswolds on Sunday*. Beau, any chance of a word?'

'Word,' Beau snapped, and strode off without a backward glance.

A crowd had gathered outside the Belchers' house to watch *Big Brother*. Catherine noticed the contestants had given up on a Giant Jenga task and switched on the telly. On one end of the overstuffed Laura Ashley sofa an elderly man in plus fours and a flat cap had snoozed off, mouth wide open. It wasn't exactly scintillating viewing.

Out in the street, Olympia Belcher was throwing a fit after being the first one voted out by the onlookers.

Amanda was consoling her daughter, who'd crammed her bulk into an unflattering playsuit.

'It's not fair, Mummy! I bloody live there!'

'I know, darling, hush now. Shall I buy you an ice cream instead?' Amanda broke off to bang on the living-room window at a contestant. 'That's nineteeth-century Wedgewood! Keep your hands off!'

A gaggle of St Gwendolyn's girls stood nearby. They were all long coltish limbs and bouncy hair, whispering and casting disdainful looks at Olympia's chunky legs. Catherine suddenly felt sorry for Olympia. Teenage girls could be such bitches.

From nowhere the memory reared up. Catherine, eleven years old, surrounded in the changing room by Lynn Elkins and her gang.

'Fishy Fincham! Fishy Fincham! Why *do* you always smell so disgusting?'

'I don't,' Catherine had wept, wincing as someone had viciously yanked her hair.

Lynn had shoved her hard little face in Catherine's. 'You smell like a tramp, Fishy. Look like one, too. Isn't it true you live on the rubbish tip?'

'Yeah!' someone had hissed. 'Your dad's Stig of the Dump!'

'What do you mean? She hasn't *got* a dad!'

Despite the hot day Catherine was shivering violently. She could still smell Lynn's cheap sickly perfume, mixed with the stench of her own fear.

A man next to her gave her a strange look. 'Are you all right?'

'I- I'm fine,' she stuttered, quickly walking off.

Gradually the familiar sounds and sights of the day

started to come back. She stopped to gaze at herself in Mrs Patel's shop window. A together-looking, stylish woman looked back. The gawky, bullied loner was a thing of the past. If Lynn Elkins could see her now: a bestseller under her belt, a beautiful home, a loving husband. She was living the dream, wasn't she?

She watched a young couple walk past, their arms wrapped round each other. Every day that went past, her feelings of restlessness intensified. She felt guilty for reading a novel or having a facial, when everyone else was at work. Her literary agent wanted her to write another book, but she was paralysed by a lack of inspiration. She could walk back into an editing job, but Catherine wasn't sure her heart was in it. For the first time in a long while, she'd lost her confidence.

Who am I meant to be? she despaired. *Wife, mother, career woman?*

At that moment, she had no idea.

Chapter 32

Having to mix with the public never brought out Conrad's good side. 'How many more hands am I expected to shake?' he hissed. 'Once we're out of Wet Wipes I'm done.'

'Mr Powell?' It was another middle-aged lady with a sunburnt face. 'Can I just say how much I admired you in *The Saviours*?'

'Oh, thank you, darling. How nice of you to say so.'

'What are you appearing in next?'

'I couldn't possibly give away any secrets!' Conrad gave the woman a wink. 'Let's just say there are some very exciting things in the pipeline.'

'Maybe you could play Colin Firth's brother in something?' the woman suggested. 'You're very similar.'

Conrad's smile dropped like a boulder off a cliff. 'Yes, well, we'll have to see.' As soon as she had walked off he launched into another rant.

'These fucking people! They think they can say anything. That's it, we're going.'

Tamzin came back over from talking to the press.

'Cotswolds FM wants to do a quick interview.'

'Why don't you just take my soul, and be done with it?' moaned Conrad.

'How about if I go and get us some champagne?' she offered.

Conrad rolled his eyes. 'Oh good *God*. If we have to.'

'You're being very quiet,' Dominique said to her daughter.

'I'm fine, Mother. I'm just enjoying watching everything.'

Vanessa wasn't fine. Under the pristine hair and perfect make-up she was a nervous wreck. Even the sight of Beau Rainford's sleek blond head across the crowd, being mobbed by a gaggle of girls, didn't hold her attention. She hadn't seen Dylan since their passionate lovemaking. Her schedule had made it impossible to get away, and since he didn't have a phone or email, she had had no way of contacting him.

'Vanessa, I'm your biggest fan!' A man with piercings in every orifice was waving a copy of her calendar at her. 'Would you mind signing this for me?'

'Of course not,' she said automatically, taking it off him.

'I'm so excited you're presenting the Silver Box Awards. Do you know what you're wearing?'

'Not yet.'

She handed the calendar back with a smile, but the man wasn't finished yet. 'Can you give me a hint? Will it be a British designer?'

'Oh, I'm sure I'll be sticking close to home.' She laughed, all the time thinking *Dylan Dylan Dylan*.

She had been scanning the crowd since they'd got

here, hanging on to the futile hope that he would have come along to the charity game show. She'd once or twice caught a glimpse of a dark head and grown hot with excitement, but it was never him. The disappointment was crushing.

Conrad was droning in her ear. 'Where's Tamzin with our champagne? Is it not enough I've got to stand out here in this searing heat? I'm seriously about to keel over, my blood pressure's at rock bottom.'

She was about to tell him to shut up, when her stomach lurched. Dylan was outside Bar 47 looking straight at her. He gave her the tiniest of winks. She had to fight to keep the huge smile off her face.

'Conrad wants to go and find Tamzin,' her mother said. 'Are you coming?'

'You go,' she said. 'I'll catch you up in a minute.'

She watched Conrad stomp off, her mother clinging on to his arm for dear life. A woman came up to her, but Vanessa brushed her off with a vague smile. Dylan was still standing across the road, looking more lean and tangle-haired than she'd remembered.

He gave her his lopsided grin. There was a cobbled alleyway leading off the street. She gave a tiny nod as he turned and walked off down it.

The alley was cool and quiet, a stark contrast to the pulse burning between Vanessa's legs. Dylan was leaning against the wall in a faded denim shirt and jeans. Her heart did another backflip. He just got more and more beautiful.

'I can't be long,' she said, removing her sunglasses with trembling fingers. She glanced back the way she'd come again, paranoid someone might have followed her.

He took her by the hand further down the alley and stopped at the back of a walled garden. She let him press her against the dry sandy stone.

'I've missed you,' she told him.

'I've missed you too.'

He started to caress her face. She took the opportunity to drink in every detail of him. His eyelashes were dense and luxurious, flecks of a beautiful violet colour streaking around his irises. God, his eyes were incredible. Up this close, she could see a paper-thin, white scar running through his right eyebrow. The tiny flaw only added to his beauty.

She felt his other hand move to her waist, and then travel down to the hem of her dress. Deftly, he gathered up the silk material to expose a length of Vanessa's bare thigh.

Bursts of music and laughter drifted up from the street. All Vanessa could hear was her own short, hot breaths as Dylan's fingers gently pushed inside her.

'God, that feels so good,' she moaned, circling her hips to match his touch.

His erection was hard against her. Vanessa pulled her knickers across to one side. 'I want you in me.'

He didn't need any encouragement. Putting his hands under her buttocks, he lifted her up and slid inside her.

She could feel her dress snag on the Cotswolds stone, but she didn't care. She didn't care about anything else right now.

It got faster and more frenzied. Vanessa started to

feel that glorious internal build-up. She held on to him more tightly.

Voices floated down the passageway. 'Someone's coming,' he panted.

'Me,' she moaned, as the orgasm shuddered through her body.

The voices were getting closer. He zipped himself up and pulled her skirt down. 'Go,' he whispered. 'I'll walk the other way.'

Still in a post-coital daze, Vanessa smoothed her dress down. He picked up her handbag and gave it to her.

'Do I look all right?' she asked him.

'You always look all right.' Giving her a final kiss, he disappeared back into the myriad of Beeversham's back streets.

I miss you already, she thought.

The voices were just round the corner. Vanessa slid her huge sunglasses back and stood up. The transformation into the self-possessed celebrity was instant. She'd swished past the couple before the woman even had the chance to double-take.

Chapter 33

The day wore on. In the intense heat people were drinking like fishes, and a long queue snaked out of the Prosecco tent. The elderly couple manning the St John Ambulance were quite overwhelmed with the amount of casualties. Another young woman had just collapsed with suspected heatstroke and her friend had passed out, full stop.

Catherine found the Chamberlains and Patels standing outside Butterflies drinking Pimms from plastic glasses.

'I'll get you a drink,' offered Felix.

'Thanks, but I might wait for a while.' Catherine's head was swimming from the giant glass of white wine Mike Cooper-Stanley had just bought her.

Ginny suddenly gave a gasp. 'You'll never guess who's here!'

They all turned to look. Strolling past, as if he didn't have a care in the world, was Sid Sykes in pink Pringle. The two heavies either side of him were clearly there to ward off any confrontations. Damien Sykes was also with them, hair slicked back like a Sicilian gangster, as he talked rapidly into his mobile phone.

Spotting Catherine and the others, Sykes tipped an imaginary hat. The gesture couldn't have been more insolent. 'Afternoon, Felix,' he called in a gravelly smoker's voice. 'Lovely day for it.'

Catherine glanced at Felix. He looked completely furious.

'The cheek of that man!' Mrs Patel cried. 'Turning up here and rubbing our noses in it!'

'Let's not give him another second of our time,' Felix said shortly.

The air was shattered by a loud expletive as Talia Tudor staggered out of the crowd, pie-eyed in towering heels and denim hot pants. 'Get out of my way!' she screeched, stopping to empty the rest of a plastic cider bottle down her throat.

Mr Patel tutted sadly. 'Dear, oh dear.'

Talia lurched forward dangerously, banging into the sign outside her mum's shop.

Ginny took a step forward, but Felix laid a hand on his wife's arm. 'No.' His voice was like steel.

A second later Lynette Tudor came flying out of the shop.

'Talia! What on earth are you doing!'

Talia's eyes rolled into the back of her head. 'I feel sick,' she moaned. 'Muuuum.'

Lynette dragged her daughter into the shop. Catherine and Felix exchanged sympathetic glances.

Inside Butterflies loud yelling started up.

*

In the market square *Who Wants to Be a Millionaire?* was reaching its climax. Travel TV presenter Gideon Armstrong, who lived in the area, had been drafted in as Chris Tarrant. 'Third question: for a million pounds, or in this case four tickets to see the Rolling Stones at the O2 . . .' he boomed into the microphone '. . . Which revered Indian leader was assassinated in Delhi in 1948? A: Mandy. B: Gandhi. C: Andy. D: Pandy.'

The contestant on stage had used up all his other lifelines. 'Phone a friend,' he said.

Gideon made a big show of getting out his mobile and calling up the number the man had given him. He held it close to his microphone. The ringtone echoed round the square.

A man at the front handed his pint to someone and answered his phone. 'Hello?'

'Is that Chris?' asked Gideon.

'Yeah, but there's no need to shout, mate. I'm standing right in front of you.'

'Chris!' Gideon boomed again. 'Which . . .'

He read out the question again. The crowd held their breath. Chris furrowed his brow knowledgeably.

'I know this! It's C. Andy.'

'I'll go with that,' the contestant said. 'Chris is a clever guy, I trust him.'

'Are you sure?' Gideon asked.

'Yup.'

'Final chance. Your answer is C.' Gideon winked at the audience.

'That's right.'

Gideon banged a gong. 'The correct answer is B: Gandhi!'

Everyone screamed with laughter. Gideon pulled out a horrific watercolour and handed it to the disappointed contestant.

'You don't go home empty-handed! The consolation prize is this,' Gideon did a double-take at the painting. 'Er, stunning piece by Cotswold artist Babs Sax.'

The unlucky contestant gazed at the psychotic daubings. 'I suppose it's a good burglar deterrent,' he said gloomily.

The last event of the day was *The X Factor*. Catherine and Mel Cooper-Stanley were judges, along with Dilip Patel and the headmistress of St Gwendolyn's, who was an absolute hoot and had turned up clutching huge G&Ts for them all. At that moment one of her pupils was massacring Celine Dion's 'My Heart Will Go On'.

'Mother of Moses,' the headmistress muttered. 'How much longer *will* this go on?'

They were still killing themselves laughing when Felix announced the next act. 'Next up is MC Killah, who is performing some of his own material today. Jolly good.'

A rotund little man with owlish glasses got up. The incongruous bandana round his head didn't really go with the trainspotter's outfit. He positioned himself in the centre of the stage, head down. The stereo speakers bristled. Everyone stopped talking.

Loud music suddenly blared out, causing several people to spill their drinks. Eyes fixed to the floor, MC Killah started making peculiar noises into his microphone.

'Is he being sick?' Mel asked.

'I think he's trying to beatbox,' whispered Catherine. They were all taken by surprise as MC Killah whirled round and hoiked up his private parts at them.

'Wassup, Beeversham!' he yelled.

Catherine had barely recovered before MC Killah was marching round the stage, shouting into the mike.

'They call me MC Killah
Cos I'll scare you like Thriller
I sting like an elephant
And I'm hung like a bee . . .'

He stopped, looking furious with himself.

'I mean I'm HUNG like an elephant and I STING like a bee
All you hos and bitches out there want to take it off me!'

In the crowd at the front, a group of old ladies were clapping along enthusiastically. 'He's awfully good, isn't he?' shouted one. 'Wonderful rhythm.'

As MC Killah grabbed his crotch in front of a startled little girl, Felix rushed on stage. 'Thank you, Mr Killah,' he said firmly, grabbing the mike.

'I ain't even reached the chorus yet, blud!' MC Killah cried, in an accent that was pure Gloucester. Felix gave the wannabe rapper a withering look and he skulked off, looking mutinous.

Things just about calmed down enough for the judges to decide the winner, a 65-year-old grandmother from Blockley who'd reduced everyone to floods with an astonishing rendition of Adele's 'Someone Like You'.

After the prize-giving, Felix took the microphone

back to address the crowd. 'I think that just about wraps things up with the game shows. On behalf of the Say No to Olde Worlde team and everyone else in Beeversham, I'd like to say a huge thank you to you all for coming down today. We've raised a fantastic amount of money for our hospice, and, hopefully, highlighted our cause and those of other towns and villages facing the same predicament.'

Everyone started clapping. 'Thank you, Felix!' someone shouted. 'We couldn't have done it without you.'

'Hear hear!' called Mike Cooper-Stanley. As the applause died down, one person started up again, a slow, deliberate clap that made people turn and look.

'Hear hear, indeed,' a voice said. 'Three cheers for fabulous Felix.'

It was Beau Rainford, devastatingly handsome in a navy blazer and crisp white shirt. He had an empty champagne flute tucked under his arm and an insolent smile on his beautiful face.

'You really do deserve the accolade. I can't think of another person so devoted to his town.'

'Hell's bells,' Mel murmured. 'Beau could have picked a better moment to get one over Felix.'

'Congratulations, old chap.' Beau raised his empty glass. 'You've really managed to pull this one off.'

Felix didn't miss a beat. 'Well, we've still got lots of things going on here, so all that's left for me to say is thank you again, and enjoy the rest of your day.'

To a smattering of applause he walked offstage.

Slightly sloshed, Catherine and Mel headed back towards Bar 47.

'Did you see Ginny's face?' Catherine asked. 'Poor thing looked mortified.'

Mel neatly side-stepped a drain in her heels. 'I think she's rather torn. For all his faults, Ginny seems to adore him.'

Catherine shot her friend a quizzical glance. 'How do you know him?'

Mel laughed. 'He's brought enough of his girls into the nail bar. Popped in for a drink by himself a few times, as well.'

Catherine wondered if Mike knew about those little soirées, before chastising herself. She was getting as bad as Amanda.

As they passed one of the alleyways they heard raised voices. Ginny and Beau were standing halfway down, in the middle of a heated discussion. Catherine and Mel exchanged a look. 'Oh dear,' Mel said. 'Trouble in the not-so-happy family.'

In the car park of Bar 47 a bunch of mums and dads were grooving to 'Up the Khyber'. Catherine could see their embarrassed kids standing on the sidelines, pretending not to know them. Up at the front, Jonty Fortescue-Wellington was dancing like an out-of-control Weeble, a pint of cider sloshing round in his hand. 'YES!' he roared, as the bearded lead singer launched into a scratchy version of 'Your Sex Is On Fire'. 'Bring it fucking on!'

He staggered past, a streak of white powder clearly visible under his port-drinker's nose.

'OMG,' Mel said. 'Jonty's off his man-boobs!'

Tristan Jago was on the other side of the dance floor,

schmoozing a local business bigwig. Luckily for Jonty, neither seemed to have noticed the Class A smeared across the MP's face.

Mel patted her Louis Vuitton bag. 'I'm gonna pop off for a quick fag. If you bump into Mike . . .'

'I haven't seen you,' Catherine laughed.

She topped up with a pint at the cider stall and decided to stay and watch the band. The four sweating middle-aged men in too-tight rock T-shirts were massacring 'Paint It Black' when a familiar hand dropped on her shoulder.

'Hey.' It was John. He'd caught the sun on his face, making the green eyes even more potent.

'Hey. Look, I'm sorry about earlier.'

'Forget it,' he said simply. 'I have.'

They watched Jonty flailing round the dance floor. He let out an enormous burp and a bit of sick came out, dribbling down his treble chin.

'What a fucking disgrace!' Catherine couldn't stop herself thundering. 'We've all been working our arses off for this, and Jonty has done sod all. I hate it when people don't do their job properly. Jonty should have the backs of the people in this town! You know what, when I was editing I may have made mistakes along the way but I always had my team's back, John. *Always.*'

John prodded her playfully. 'Is someone a bit drunk?'

'What, so now I'm not even allowed a drink any more?'

'Cath, I was joking. Jesus! I don't know whether I'm coming or going with you.'

'Well, guess what, I don't even know myself!' she shot back.

'Look.' He stopped and checked himself. 'I know you're still upset about not being pregnant.'

'Why does this have to be about me getting pregnant? There are other things going on in my life!'

'If I'm doing something wrong,' he said quietly, 'then you'd better tell me.'

The booze made her angry and confused. 'That's just the problem! You don't do anything wrong. It's hard work being married to Mr Bloody Wonderful.'

He looked at her in disbelief. 'Let me get this right. You don't want me to treat you well? You want me to start acting like a complete bastard, Cath, is that it? Be a selfish, egotistical shit who goes out and sleeps with other women?'

It killed her to hear him speak like that, but Catherine just clammed up. How could she tell John that everything he did for her, every act of love and selflessness, only made her feel more inadequate?

Her eyes burnt with helpless tears. 'I'm going to get a drink,' she said.

'Do what you bloody want,' he told her.

The bearded lead singer blew into his microphone. 'We're taking things down a bit, with the legendary Amy Winehouse. This is for all you couples going through a bad patch.' He looked dark. 'Trust me, I know what I'm talking about.'

On stage the opening chords of 'Love is a Losing Game' spluttered out.

Chapter 34

By seven o' clock in the evening, the High Street resembled a Saturday night out in a major city centre. The Prosecco tent had run dry hours ago, so everyone had packed into a heaving Bar 47. Customers were six deep at the bar as they lined up to do flaming sambucas.

Over on the memorial green, the animals were getting restless. 'Shall we call it a day?' Fleur turned to Ben and caught him staring at her boobs for the umpteenth time that day.

'Er, yeah,' he mumbled. 'I'll go and get the lorry.'

She was still red with embarrassment when Pete from Pete's Pets rushed over. 'One of the bloody snakes has escaped!'

'Shit! Is it poisonous?'

'Only if you step on it. Oh, Jesus, I'll never find it.'

There was an almighty whining sound and what sounded like three gunshots. A trail of stars fell down from the sky.

'Which stupid sod is letting off fireworks?' Pete said. 'People could get seriously hurt!'

Fleur had barely recovered before another rocket went up, exploding above them with a massive bang.

'Bloody hell!' she shouted. 'The animals!'

It was too late. Terrified by the noise, the cow bolted straight through the flimsy wooden railings. It thundered up the High Street, closely followed by the pigs and both lambs. The menagerie scattered revellers and stalls in their wake.

'Stop them!' screamed Pete.

The animals started looping the market square, joined by someone's Labrador and a confused drunk man who kept shouting, 'Is this a race, then?'

People were running all over the place in utter panic. 'Somebody do something!' Ginny screamed. 'They're going to kill somebody!'

Catherine came running out of Bar 47 and took off up a side street, not really knowing what she was doing. Charging round a corner, she ran full pelt into a couple. Olympia Belcher was down on her knees, in front of a spotty youth from the boys' school.

'Shit!' Catherine yelled.

Olympia leapt up. 'Shit!' she whimpered. Catherine gaped at her and the Harry Styles lookalike, nonchalantly tucking away his pubescent appendage.

'Don't tell Mummy, she'll seriously kill me!' Olympia pleaded.

Catherine was speechless. 'Olympia,' she started. There was more screaming up ahead.

'Fuck me,' the boy said. 'There's, like, a massive cow heading straight for us!'

They heard the scrape of hooves and wild grunting. Half a ton of prime Cotswolds beef was thundering down the passageway straight for them.

'I am out of here,' the boy said, taking off like a whippet.

'Move it, Olympia!' Catherine shrieked.

'I can't run without my sports bra!'

Catherine grabbed the girl's arm. 'What's worse, a pair of black eyes or being trampled to death?'

Back on the High Street it was bedlam. Two lambs and a pig came flying out of a side passage, hotly pursued by Mr Patel. They took off for another lap round the market square.

'Stop chasing the animals everyone!' Fleur screamed. 'You're frightening them!'

One of the lambs was sniffing round the collapsed cheese stall. She ran over and retrieved it, pushing it quickly into the trailer. Where was Ben?

There was a fresh commotion further up. The organic meatball van was rolling down the street with no one behind the wheel. A young guy was running after it, shouting about the handbrake. It quickly started to gain speed. Fleur watched an elderly gentleman rugby tackle his wife out of the way.

'MOVE!' people shouted, but her feet were glued to the spot. She stared transfixed at the windscreen.

I'm going to die, she thought dazedly.

People were yelling at her, real fear in their voices. At the last moment she snapped out of her trance. The bumper was inches away. It was too late . . .

She suddenly felt herself being pushed out of the road. The van hurtled past with inches to spare, crashing to a halt into a lamp post.

'Are you OK?' a deep voice asked. She stared dumbly

at her rescuer. It was that big dark man from earlier, the one with Catherine Connor.

'That was incredible!' A photographer was waving his camera at them. 'Can I get a pic of the two of you together?'

'Fleur!' A frantic Ginny Chamberlain rushed up. 'Are you all right?'

'I'm fine.' With that, Fleur closed her eyes and quietly fainted.

She came round to a sea of anxious faces and Ginny Chamberlain dabbing her brow with a damp cloth. She was half-carried by John Connor to sit down in the nearest chair. Someone rushed out from Bar 47 with a glass of mineral water and a lime slice bobbing in it, and placed it in her hand.

'I'll go and ring Robert,' she heard Felix say.

'No!' she shouted. 'Don't call my dad!'

Felix and Ginny exchanged a look.

'I'm OK, really,' Fleur said, struggling to sit up.

'My dear, you're shaking like a leaf!' Ginny exclaimed. 'We should really get someone to have a look at you.'

'Why don't we just let Fleur sit here for a few minutes until she feels better?' Felix suggested. He gave her a reassuring wink.

Everything was gradually brought under control. The rest of the animals were caught with the help of the Gloucestershire constabulary and a group of off-duty vets. The young guy running the meatball van was interviewed by a police officer about his dodgy handbrake.

'It's just had its MOT,' he kept saying inconsolably. 'It's never happened before.'

Catherine, who'd been watching her husband being swamped by journalists and women with sunburnt chests for the last fifteen minutes, couldn't help butting in. 'Have you found who let off the fireworks yet?'

'Kids, having high jinks probably,' one of the policemen said sagely. 'We'll hunt the little sods down.'

'What if it wasn't kids?' she asked. 'What if someone let them off deliberately?'

'What are you saying, madam?'

Catherine saw Felix coming over. 'Felix! What if Sid Sykes is behind all this?'

His silver eyebrows shot up. 'Whatever do you mean?'

'It's just a bit strange, isn't it, how he turns up and then all this happens?' She swallowed a wine burp. 'What if he planned all this, to deflect attention from the Charity Game Show? I remember watching a Channel 5 film about something similar once. You know, the one with John Travolta . . .'

The police officer interrupted. 'You're saying, madam, that Sid Sykes let off fireworks to sabotage the event?'

'That's exactly what I'm saying!'

'Madam, have you been drinking?'

'Yes, but I don't see what that's got to do with it.'

'Catherine, that's a very serious allegation to make,' Felix said. 'Sykes is long gone. How on earth can he have had a hand in it?'

'I don't know. I just know there's something fishy about this whole thing! Who has fireworks in June?'

'Have you met Catherine Connor, our famous magazine editor?' Felix asked the policeman.

'Magazine editor, eh? That would explain the wild imagination.'

Peace restored, there was only one thing for it. Most people piled back into Bar 47 to start drinking heavily again.

After reassuring Ginny she was fine to drive home, Fleur said goodbye to Ben. Screams of laughter burst out of the pub while a purple-pink sunset lounged languorously in the sky above.

'Are you sure you're all right?' Ben asked again.

'I told you, I'm fine,' Fleur snapped. She watched his face drop and immediately felt guilty.

'Sorry, Ben. I'm just a bit tired. I'll see you back at the farm.'

The streets were beginning to empty of revellers as she trudged her way back to the Land Rover. As she passed one of the back lanes two respectable-looking men peered out at her from a swirl of smoke.

The fatter one waved a glowing joint at her. 'Fancy a drag, gorgeous? This is some really good shit.'

'No thanks,' Fleur sighed. 'My life's shit enough as it is.'

The old vehicle took three attempts to start. She still felt shaky and probably shouldn't drive in her state, but there was no way she was letting anyone take her home. Her dad's drinking was getting worse. Last night she'd come in from doing the animals to find her dad passed out, half in and half out of the kitchen door.

The Land Rover chugged up the back streets of

Beeversham and headed out towards the darkened fields. With every second Fleur felt like she was leaving civilization to go back to the stale dregs of her life. She was still mortified that she'd fainted in front of all those people. Her worst fear was that they thought she'd been drunk, just like her dad.

She was on the main road home before she remembered the fridge was empty. She was too tired to go back into town. Cereal it was, then, for the third night running.

'Bran Flakes or Weetabix?' she said out loud. 'Sod it, Fleur, why don't you push the boat out and go for the organic granola.'

She rounded the bend, overcome with hysterical laughter at how crap her life was. 'Organic . . . granola,' she spluttered. The smile froze on her face. Up ahead a horribly familiar Ford pickup was in the ditch, headlights still blazing. She jammed her foot on the brake. The Land Rover did a terrifying swerve, but she barely noticed.

'Dad!'

Chapter 35

Her dad's eyes were closed. His face was ghastly with slick red blood. 'Dad!' Fleur wept. 'Oh God!'

She stood up and screamed futilely into the night. 'Someone help me! Please!'

She started running back to the truck. Halfway there she remembered her phone was dead. *Shit shit shit*. What did she do now? She couldn't drive off and leave him.

At that moment, she had never felt more alone and frightened. 'Please, someone drive past!' she cried. As if by a miracle a pair of headlights appeared further up the road, whooshing along at a terrific speed.

She ran into the middle of the road waving frantically. 'STOP!'

She was momentarily blinded by the glare of the headlights. The screech of tyres ripped through the air. A low, wide bonnet came to a stop, inches from her knee, so close she could feel the heat from the engine. How could she nearly get run over twice in one night?

Hysterical, she ran round to the driver's window.

'Please help!' she screamed. 'There's been an accident!'

The window slid down. A pair of brilliant blue eyes glared at her. 'Are you trying to fucking kill both of us?' Beau Rainford exploded.

She gaped in horror. *Not him, of all people!* In vain she searched up the road for another car. 'My dad. H-he's been in an accident . . .'

'Have you called an ambulance?' he demanded, pulling his seat belt off.

'M-my phone's dead,' she stammered, but Beau was already out of the car and taking off on long legs. By the time she caught up he was kneeling close to her dad's face, listening intently.

'Is he alive?' she wailed. 'Oh my God!'

'He's breathing,' Beau said. He spoke to her dad. 'Can you move?'

Robert Blackwater gave a stricken moan.

A red Clio Fleur didn't recognize pulled up behind them. The driver's window slid down. 'Do you want me to call an ambulance?' the woman called.

Fleur froze. The whisky fumes coming off her dad were overpowering. He would be arrested for drink-driving. He might even go to prison. They were going to lose everything.

Helplessly, she waited for Beau to land them in it. They'd played right into his hands.

'We're fine, thank you,' he told the woman calmly. 'The ambulance is on its way.'

It was all a complete blur after that. Somehow Beau had got Robert up and into his car. Fleur had followed the

Mustang back to the farm in her own vehicle, hands frozen on the wheel. Between them, they'd got Robert up the stairs and into his bedroom. Fleur remembered shaking uncontrollably as Beau asked her questions she couldn't answer.

At one point a stranger had turned up, a silver-haired man in an expensive suit and a signet ring like Beau's. He had been introduced as Henry Watson, Beau's private doctor. Diagnosing mild concussion, Henry Watson had expertly stitched up the cut above her dad's eyebrow. 'Complete bed rest for a few days,' he had told Fleur afterwards. 'And you're in shock yourself, take it easy.'

He had handed her his card. She had read the glossy address in glossy lettering and known they'd never be able to afford him.

She came down to the kitchen to find Henry Watson gone and Beau standing by the kettle. He handed her a mug. 'Here, doctor's orders.'

She took a mouthful and winced at the scalding, sugary tea.

'Do you have anything stronger?' he asked.

'We're not big drinkers in this house,' she mumbled.

They stood in silence, Fleur gratefully sipping the hot drink. Beau's face was unreadable, arms crossed as he leant back against the worktop. She looked at the arrogant red mouth, the pinky ring glinting on his little finger. He was the enemy. How could he have just come to their rescue?

The clock ticked thunderously on the wall. She finally dislodged the words that had been stuck in her throat.

'Thank you,' she said gruffly. 'You didn't have to help us.'

'Don't mention it.'

'You're not going to tell the police?'

He shrugged carelessly. 'What do I care what your father gets up to? I can hardly claim a glowing record myself when it comes to traffic offences.'

There was something about the way his eyes were roaming round that made Fleur uncomfortable. She was suddenly ashamed of the mess, the piece of cardboard in the broken windowpane. How pathetic her life must seem to him.

'I'll pay you back, obviously.'

It was like she hadn't spoken. He checked the fat watch on his wrist. In two strides he was across the kitchen and out of the door. Fleur was left there speechless. *So I guess that's goodbye, then.*

She jumped as he suddenly reappeared in the doorway, holding a greasy paper bag.

'Here, it'll need warming up.'

'What is it?'

'Takeaway curry. I hope you haven't got a strong aversion to lamb dansak.'

'I can't take your dinner!'

He held the bag out impatiently. 'It doesn't matter. You look like you need it more than me.'

She took it from him. 'Thank you. That's really nice of you.'

'I'm not always take, take, take,' he told her. Moments later the Mustang was revving up in the yard and he was gone for good.

Chapter 36

With the Silver Box Awards fast approaching, preparations for Conrad's grand comeback were gaining momentum. Tonight he was in London hosting an important industry dinner at his private gentlemen's club. Vanessa didn't ask who was going to the dinner and didn't care. Conrad was far too concerned about whether his new tuxedo really did capture his shoulders perfectly to notice his wife's unusual lack of interest.

It was a hot, still afternoon when even the wild flowers had stopped swaying. A few white clouds hung sleepily in the sky. Vanessa found her mother lying under the huge striped umbrella by the swimming pool. The new *Homes and Gardens* lay untouched on the ground next to her.

'Are you coming to sit with me?' Dominique asked.

'Actually, I thought I'd pop out for a drive.' Vanessa felt a pang. Her mother had looked so alone when she'd walked up.

'Again?'

'I just like the thinking time,' Vanessa lied. 'Who needs to pay for therapy, ha ha!'

Dominique didn't smile. 'I'm really not sure these little excursions are a good idea, Vanessa. What if you break down in the middle of nowhere?'

'I won't break down. You won't mention it to Conrad, will you?' Vanessa added hastily. 'You know how super-protective he is.'

Dominique took her sunglasses off and surveyed her daughter shrewdly. 'Are you all right?'

'What do you mean? Of course I am.'

'You seem very distracted at the moment.'

Vanessa started going red. 'I'm just a bit stressed. There's such a lot to think about, what with the awards and everything.'

She made herself hold her mother's eyes. After what seemed like an age, Dominique broke her gaze.

'Darling, stop picking at your fingernails. It's very ugly.'

Vanessa dropped her hands by her sides. 'Is that it? Can I go?'

'You make it sound like you're the hired help.' Dominique slid her glasses back on. 'I'll see you later.'

An hour later Vanessa was lying in Dylan's arms, their naked bodies entwined. The yak-wool blanket he'd laid down on the ground was far softer than her cashmere. She didn't even mind the occasional pungent waft of animal, ripened by the day's heat.

The wild abandon of their reunion was evident round the camp. Her Bottega Veneta bag was where she'd dumped it. Her Deborah Marquit thong was lying nearby, twisted up like a piece of used tissue. Eddie was snoozing at a discreet distance under the trees, his tail occasionally flapping to swat a fly.

Dylan was breathing peacefully, his tanned chest rising and falling. Extricating herself, she sat up. She gazed round the camp; at the rusty camper van and tiny stove, the washing bowl that doubled up as a sink. All the clothes Dylan owned could fit into one suitcase. Conrad had an entire wardrobe just for his Savile Row shirts.

She looked back down at Dylan. He was on his back with his eyes closed, face up to the sun. He was still refusing to let Vanessa give him severance pay after Conrad had sacked him, but she wasn't sure if it was a pride thing. How could he survive on so little?

'Are you awake?'

He opened one eye. 'Uh-huh.'

'I was just thinking.' She hesitated. 'You know, if you ever needed any money. I mean especially after we had to let you go. I'd be happy to give some to you . . .'

He sat up. 'Is that what you think this is all about?'

'No! I just wanted to say the offer is there if you ever need it.' She knew by the look on his face that she'd got it wrong. 'I'm sorry. I didn't mean to offend you.'

'I don't want your money. Vanessa, look at me.' His silver eyes were serious. 'Whatever you're thinking, that's not what I'm here for.'

Was she relieved? She couldn't deny the thought hadn't crossed her mind. *Rich bitch meets broke guy.*

Now, looking into Dylan's honest face she felt guilty for ever thinking it.

Chapter 37

The Draysborough restaurant near the village of Minchinhampton had been dubbed by critics 'the most romantic place on earth'. Situated next to a babbling brook, the seventeenth-century coaching inn was a masterclass in relaxed elegance. With three Michelin stars, the rich and famous pulled all sorts of strings to jump the queue for a coveted outside table in summer.

There were several well-known faces on the terrace that lunchtime, including a married actor dining with his rumoured mistress. Catherine watched, fascinated, as the actor's hand caressed the woman's thigh under the table. She couldn't be more than nineteen.

The sommelier appeared at their table. 'Your Sauvignon, Monsieur.'

'Thank you.'

'Madame?'

'Just a little, thanks.'

The man disappeared, leaving them to it. 'This place is fantastic,' John told her. 'I daren't ask how you got us in.'

'If I tell you I'll have to kill you,' she joked. In fact, *Soirée* had once done a review on the place. Catherine had rung the owner, begging for a table.

'Is it a special occasion?' he'd asked.

'How about saving my marriage?' she'd said back.

'In that case, you're booked in.'

She watched her husband study the menu. 'What are you going to have?'

'Terrine I think, followed by the Bilbury trout. You?'

'I haven't even looked properly.' She toyed with her wine glass. 'I'm really sorry again about losing it on Saturday.'

'It's fine, you've said sorry.'

'I don't know what's wrong with me,' she said. 'I guess I've been going through a bit of a blue patch and it all got on top of me. Getting pissed didn't help.'

'If you feel like that again just tell me, OK?'

'OK.'

'But you are feeling better?' he asked.

'Yeah!' she said. 'That's why I brought us here. Fresh start and all that.'

'Fresh start.' They clinked glasses. 'I'm really glad we came, Cath,' he told her.

'Me too.'

He sat back in his chair. 'What have you got lined up in the next week?'

'Oh, you know, sunbathing, reading, the usual lady-of-leisure stuff. You?'

'I've got to go to London on Wednesday. You could come with me, there's a fantastic exhibition on at the Tate.'

'Maybe,' she said apathetically.

He gave her a quizzical glance. She looked away, around the beautiful restaurant with its snowy white cloths and exquisite tables. She had a sudden urge to jump up and pull it all apart, bring chaos to the perfect order. *I'm drowning*, she thought desperately.

'Are you all right?' He was looking at her.

'Of course,' she said, except the smile didn't reach her eyes. She knew it and he knew it. They were falling apart by the second and it was all her fault.

'Excuse me.' A pretty young waitress materialized at their table. She looked at John, blushing attractively. 'I hope you don't mind me saying, but I saw your picture in the *Cotswolds on Sunday*. I think you're awfully brave.'

Chapter 38

It was haymaking time on the farm. Six hundred golden bales lay dotted on the yellow stubble, the result of a week's hard work. After an intensive effort to get the grass cut, dried and baled, it was time to heave the same bales back on to the trailer, ready to store them away for winter.

Fleur's arms ached just thinking about it. She was going to feel it in her muscles when she woke up tomorrow.

There was far less grass this year. The freakishly hot weather might be great for everyone's tans, but it wasn't good when you had to feed your livestock through the winter.

She wiped the sweat from the back of her neck. It was so hot she'd reluctantly swapped her normal polo shirt for a New Look vest top. The straps of the cheap garment felt worryingly flimsy.

Ben came up to her, Tinker and Bess following in his wake. He'd caught the sun in the past few days, making him even more ruddy-cheeked than normal.

'Tractor's revved up.'

For the first time she could remember, Robert Blackwater wasn't haymaking. It was clear he wasn't up to the work at the moment. He had no memory of the accident. She had fed him a story about falling off the quad bike. They both knew it wasn't true, especially as his pickup had mysteriously gone into the garage for repairs, but he hadn't challenged it.

Ben's eyes did another furtive swoop over Fleur's chest. She turned away and yanked the ineffectual straps up.

'Let's get going, then.'

An hour later they'd only gone down a few rows. Fleur was driving the tractor, while Ben hauled bales on to the trailer at the back. He was built for hard work, but it was clear he was struggling. As well as throwing them up, he had to then scramble up and stack them. It was too much for one man alone.

'This is ridiculous!' Fleur shouted above the roar of the engine.

'What?'

'I said.' Fleur cut the engine and the great machine shuddered to a stop. She stuck her head out the window. 'This is stupid, Ben. You're going to end up killing yourself at this rate.'

'I'm fine,' he gasped, sweat streaming down the sides of his face. 'Just give me a minute.'

'We need another person! You can't do this by yourself.'

Ben took a swig of water from his bottle. 'How about your dad?'

'I've told you, he's not feeling good,' Fleur snapped.

Ben kept quiet. She gazed out gloomily over the field, the bales lined up like rows of mini Weetabix . 'It's going to *be* bloody winter by the time we've finished this lot.'

There was a loud revving in the distance. They both turned round. A familiar red car was hammering along the track towards them. It screeched to a halt by the field and a tall figure in a lilac shirt climbed out.

'Making hay while the sun shines,' Beau Rainford drawled, sauntering over. 'What a good idea.'

Even though she was high up in the tractor, Beau still had the effect of making Fleur feel like he was looking down at her. 'How did you know we were up here?' she said, rather rudely.

'Your father. I dropped by the farmhouse,' Beau said smoothly, tucking his sunglasses away into his top pocket. 'He wasn't too pleased to see me, but at least he told me where you were. I told him we've become, ah, reacquainted. I hope you don't mind.'

She couldn't help but notice how Beau's eyes were a perfect match for the blue sky above. His hair was even the same colour as the cornfield. *Oh, stop it, Fleur,* she told herself furiously. She wasn't falling for his charms.

Beau looked at the bales on the trailer. 'Hard at work, I see.'

'Yes, mate, some of us have to work for a living,' Ben said.

Fleur stared at him. He was never normally like this! Ben looked derisively at Beau's leopard-print loafers. 'Fancy lending a hand? We're a bit short on man power.' He emphasized the word 'man'.

225

She saw a flash of challenge between them. 'I'm sure I could squeeze a few bales in,' Beau said coolly.

An hour later, Ben was looking distinctly sick. They'd picked up almost three times as many bales as when he'd been working alone. Beau was tossing them up on the trailer as if they weighed nothing, barely pausing for breath.

Both men had stripped to the waist and while Ben had a good physique in a chunky rugby-player sort of way, it paled into comparison beside Beau's. It was like watching a carthorse work alongside a pure thoroughbred.

Beau had the kind of body that belonged in an advert or on a film poster, not in one of her fields, walking in the wake of diesel fumes from her ten-year-old tractor. He was built like a panther, his powerful swimmer's shoulders tapering into a lean, narrow waist. Fleur watched, mesmerized, as he bent down for another bale, the movement flexing the muscles in his back. Ben, no slacker in the stamina department, was struggling to keep up.

Beau chucked another bale high in the air. His blue eyes caught Fleur's through the back window. She whipped round in the seat, cheeks burning. 'Are we ready to go?' she yelled.

A few seconds later his blond head appeared under her window. He wiped a streak of dust off his six-pack. 'I don't know about you, but I'm starving!'

Lunch was normally a non-event for Fleur. The days of sitting round the kitchen table while her mum prepared a home-cooked meal were long gone.

Nowadays it was a rather sweaty squashed roll of some kind grabbed on the run. Anything was preferable to going back to that sad, lonely house where her dad drifted round like a ghost.

With Beau things just seemed to happen. Burning off in the Mustang, he'd returned a short while later with a hamper. The contents made Fleur's eyes boggle. They included smoked wild salmon from the River Severn, poached quails' eggs, Cotswold cheeses and ginormous fat Blaisdon plums. There were even china plates, tucked away next to the snowy white napkins.

At least the shirt was back on. The thought of all that smooth brown flesh close up was too unnerving. Ben was watching them from his truck, balefully chewing on a hunk of bread and cheese. He'd refused Beau's invitation to join them.

Beau pulled out a bottle of champagne, a French label Fleur had never heard of. He set two glass flutes upright on the ground.

'What's this for?' she asked.

'Does there have to be a reason?' he said, expertly massaging the cork out. He shot her a look. 'How about us not being friends.'

It was clearly meant as a joke, but it just made Fleur even madder. 'You really have no idea, do you? You turn up here with champagne that probably costs more than it does to feed our animals for a week . . .' She dropped her head so he wouldn't see the hot angry tears that had sprung up.

'I didn't mean to upset you.' He appraised her with those cool blue eyes. 'Are things really that bad?'

'As if you care.' She didn't care if she sounded bitter. 'You've taken half the farm off us!'

A pheasant screeched somewhere nearby. He put the champagne bottle down on the grass. 'It was purely a business decision. I'm sorry if I've caused you any upset.'

He might have been putting it on, but he did look contrite. 'Yeah, well,' she said. 'Just think next time, before you try and buy up someone's farm, OK?'

'Message received loud and clear.' Beau grinned again. 'Are we going to drink this? Only it would be an awful extravagance to let it go to waste.'

Fleur had no idea picnics could be so heavenly. Beau took her on a gastronomic tour, introducing her to tapenade on wafer-thin Melba toast and Devon crab so fresh it was as if it had leapt out of the sea straight on to the plate. It was food for the soul. Fleur felt full afterwards in a way that had nothing to do with a straining waistband. The atmosphere felt surprisingly relaxed. Beau was lying on his back, one brown leg crossed over the other. His calves were athletic and shapely, covered with a fine dusting of downy blond hair.

'Thanks again, for helping my dad,' Fleur ventured. 'I would have dropped round a card or something but . . .' she trailed off. 'It felt a bit random.'

'I have the name of a very good rehab place,' he said lightly. 'Plenty of my friends have been there. Their alcohol-recovery programme has a very high success rate.'

'My dad is not an alcoholic,' she snapped.

'My old man was in and out of rehab the whole time I was growing up, Fleur. I know what it's like.'

'You have no idea what my life is like!'

'Well,' he said after a moment. 'The offer's there if you're ever interested.'

'Thanks,' she muttered. 'I doubt we could afford it, anyway.'

He picked up his glass. 'Bottoms up! Why *do* all farmers have such fat ones, anyway? Present company excluded, of course.'

'Ssh,' Fleur giggled, looking at Ben. He glowered and tapped his watch.

Sod work for the moment, she thought. The sun was on her arms and bare legs. The champagne had been tart and still danced on her tongue. Everything felt warm and deliciously swimmy. *I could get used to this.*

'Don't you have your own work to do, then?' she said cheekily.

There was no answer. She looked over. Beau was stretched out on the grass, glass lolling in his hand. He was fast asleep.

Chapter 39

On the positive side, John's heroics in saving Fleur Blackwater had made the Beeversham Big Charity Game Show front-page in the *Cotswolds on Sunday*. On the downside, the six accompanying pages had reported how people had been 'crazed on champagne' and 'passing out in their dozens'. Rather than a town pulling together, it had come across as a middle-class knees-up of bacchanalian standards. There were snipes from some quarters of the press about a 'hooray haven' out of touch with the real world. Pictures of the Powells looking intoxicatingly glamorous on all the celebrity websites didn't do much to help their cause.

But, as Catherine, who was well-versed in these things, pointed out, there really was no such thing as a bad press. If people hadn't known who they were before, they certainly did now. Donations and emails of support came pouring in, even if a large proportion were phone numbers for John. Ginny Chamberlain, who was in charge of all SNOW-related mail, had nearly had a heart attack when she'd opened an innocuous pink envelope addressed to John and found a photo of a lady of advanced years wearing nothing apart from her hearing aid and a big smile.

The press were billing it as the battle of 'Rural versus Retail'. Felix promptly called another meeting, at which he urged people to keep emailing and writing to the planning department. All they could do was pray that the council saw reason.

Catherine, feeling she had to do some exercise rather than mope round the house, had taken a walk up to St Cuthbert's on Saturday morning. Looking out over the fields, she'd been mortified to find herself weeping uncontrollably. A kindly Japanese couple had come over and given her a tissue. Mopping herself up, she had decided she was in dire need of some reassuring company.

The front door opened before she had a chance to knock. 'I saw you out of the window,' Felix said. Bonnie, the Chamberlains' black Labrador, was hovering by his legs.

'I'm not interrupting anything?'

'Not at all, I was just failing miserably at the *Telegraph* crossword. I'm afraid it's just me, Ginny's gone to visit her sister for the weekend.' He peered at her blotchy face. 'You all right?'

'Hay fever,' she lied.

'What a pain. Come on in.'

It wasn't a huge house, but the Hollies was cosy and welcoming. The Laura Ashley curtains were hand-made by Ginny, while the sunny kitchen had colourful touches of red gingham. Pictures of the Chamberlain children stood on the dresser amongst the Portmeirion china.

The back door was open on to the patio. The remnants of Felix's breakfast were on the table next to the discarded newspaper. His Panama hat was on the ground by his chair.

'Take a seat, I'll put a pot of fresh coffee on.'

Bonnie immediately came over and plonked herself by Catherine's feet. She gave the dog a pat and sat back. The smell of cut grass hung in the air. A bumblebee buzzed through Ginny's prize hollyhocks. It was so pretty that Catherine's dark mood lifted.

Felix came back out with the coffee. 'How's Beeversham's big hero?' he asked.

'Don't.' She groaned. 'It's like being married to George-bloody-Clooney. You know, someone actually asked for his autograph in Mr Patel's the other day.'

He laughed. 'I'm sure John is taking it with his customary good grace.' Felix stirred sugar into his coffee. 'I know what I was going to ask: has your reporter friend made any progress with Pear Tree Holdings?'

'I haven't heard back from him since a few days ago; it must be proving even harder than we thought.' Catherine caught sight of his face. 'Don't worry, he won't have given up just yet.'

Felix sighed. 'I don't want to appear the voice of gloom, but I fear your friend could be wasting his efforts.'

'Maybe.' She didn't want to dash his hopes just yet.

'How's the hay fever? I'm sure we've got some antihistamine in the bathroom cupboard. I can get one, if you like.'

'I'm feeling much better, but thank you.'

He was such a kind man, Catherine thought, as he gave her a smile. In a way, she'd come to see Felix as the father figure she'd never had.

After a pleasant hour chatting about everything from Beeversham gossip to the state of the government, she got up. 'I should leave you in peace and let you get back to your crossword.'

'Gosh, don't worry. You've been a very pleasant distraction.'

Walking back inside, she could see a picture in the corridor of Felix with Margaret Thatcher in the eighties. His hair was dark back then, and he was leaner and rather hunky. Catherine was struck by the similarity between him and Beau.

'That was at a fundraiser at Conbury Castle. We raised a couple of hundred thou that day.' He looked rueful. 'Lot easier to get donations in those days, when we weren't tainted by the whiff of corruption.'

He walked Catherine out. The scent from the climbing wisteria on the front of the house was heavenly. Both were blissfully unaware that the peace was about to be shattered.

Chapter 40

'Why won't they leave me alone?' Conrad sighed, as a second Sky helicopter swooped past. 'Isn't a man allowed privacy in his own home?'

Vanessa watched the aircraft whirr off down the hill. 'I don't think they're interested in us.'

'Oh.' His face fell. 'What the hell's going on, then?'

He'd just come inside, complaining about his sunbathing being spoiled by the constant stream of aircraft overhead. 'I'm going to put *Sky News* on,' Vanessa said.

Immediately she saw there were chaotic scenes on Beeversham High Street. The place was jammed with news trucks and press milling about. 'BEEVERSHAM MP ARRESTED AFTER DRUNKEN RAMPAGE' was the headline scrolling across the bottom of the screen. A reporter was doing a live broadcast from outside the mini market.

'The picturesque Cotswold town of Beeversham is in shock today after its MP, Jonty Fortescue-Wellington, went

on a drunken rampage in a House of Commons bar in the early hours. After drinking heavily all afternoon, witnesses say Mr Fortescue-Wellington became violent and attacked several Labour MPs in the infamous Strangers Bar, including delivering a roundhouse kick to the head of the MP for West Gilbey, Steven Dawdry. Mr Fortescue-Wellington was arrested at the scene, and released on bail this morning, charged with several acts of GBH and possession of Class A drugs.'

Another helicopter whirred overhead. The reporter continued her solemn broadcast. 'This latest scandal could have catastrophic consequences for the government. After the latest round of spending cuts, their popularity is at an historic low. The Cotswolds town of Beeversham and its surrounding area has always been seen as a Tory stronghold. If they lose their seat here it is feared it could start a chain reaction amongst other Conservative constituencies, spelling the end of the current government. The Prime Minister has yet to comment, but one thing is for sure. Big questions are being asked in Downing Street right now.'

'For a moment there I dared to think it was something exciting.' Conrad stalked back out to the garden, six foot plus of moisturized muscle in a pair of skimpy Prada bathing trunks.

Popping into town to get milk that afternoon, Catherine got caught in the crossfire. You could barely move along the street for the scrum of reporters. Tristan Jago was being interviewed by one of them outside Bar 47.

'This kind of behaviour is typical of our Conservative government!' he thundered. 'I've been predicting

Jonty Fortescue-Wellington's downfall for years. The man is a disgrace to politics.'

Catherine bumped into Mrs Patel, wrestling her way out of the mini market.

'This is utter madness!' Ursula cried. 'Dilip's just been asked by someone to recreate the roundhouse kick!'

'Has anyone seen Jonty?' Catherine shouted. The press were clustered round his house further down the street. Chamberlains & Co. had a 'Closed' sign up and the blinds were pulled down. The rest of the old duffers at Beeversham's Conservative Association headquarters had locked themselves away and were refusing to talk to anyone.

Mrs Patel shook her head helplessly. 'No idea!'

Someone grabbed Catherine's arm. 'It's Catherine Connor, author of the bestselling *Cathy: My Story*. Fancy seeing you here,' said a woman with over-plucked eyebrows and wearing a tight red suit.

'I live here,' Catherine said grimly, as a camera lens was shoved in her face.

'Julia Perkins from ITN! Can you give me a few words? You must all be in shock at your MP's antics.'

'It was rather a surprise,' Catherine answered tactfully.

'First Ye Olde Worlde and now this! Beeversham must feel like a town under siege right now. Do you? Do you feel under siege right now?'

The cameraman moved closer. The reporter's nose quivered expectantly. Everyone held their breath.

Catherine gazed down the camera, hideously aware she was being beamed into millions of people's living rooms. Her mind went blank.

'Uh well, you know the old saying. When the chips are down it's time to make ketchup.'

Things got even worse. The next day it was all over the news how Jonty had been secretly filmed being wined and dined by a big-scale property developer in return for various favours. Fresh debate started about whether he was behind Pear Tree Holdings. Would he really have the gall to shit on his own doorstep like that? Meanwhile, in London an effigy of the PM was unceremoniously burnt outside Number 10 by a group of angry campaigners.

Calls for Jonty to stand down gained momentum. There were stories of him being whisked out under cover of darkness to rehab in France. Someone even started a rumour he'd gone to America for reconstructive plastic surgery. Jonty had become a national hate figure; an emblem for everything that was wrong with the ruling party. Overnight, Beeversham changed from a market town fighting a big theme park to the most famous place in Britain.

As the hours ticked by there was still no announcement of Jonty's resignation. The media became increasingly desperate. People were pounced on for a quote as soon as they set foot outdoors. CNN wheeled in a martial-arts expert to recreate the now infamous roundhouse kick. #chips and #ketchupgate trended worldwide on Twitter.

At 3 p.m. BBC Gloucestershire's harried female reporter threw herself in front of Beau Rainford's passing Mustang. 'Beau! Do you think Beeversham will be forced to call a by-election?'

Beau, in a white T-shirt with a V-neck that only just reached his navel, lifted up his Ray-Bans. 'I've as much of a clue as you, sweetheart. I had no idea Jonty swung both ways.' He roared off, giving her the biggest line of the day.

Chapter 41

Vanessa stirred restlessly on her sunlounger. Normally she could stand any kind of heat, but the air felt unrelentingly hot and still. All around, the walls of the huge garden seemed be closing in. *A metaphor for my life*, she thought despairingly.

It was madness to try and sneak out to see Dylan with the hoo-ha going on. A gaggle of paps had congregated at the end of the drive, hoping for a quote from Beeversham's celebrity couple. Conrad, moaning incessantly about press intrusion, had already been out twice that day on errands, something he'd never done before. He'd taken the bronze open-top Mercedes, not as show-stopping as the Porsche or the Bentley, but a perfect match for the new glossy hues in his hair.

Vanessa's iPhone beeped with an email alert. It was her stylist again, asking her to get in touch about her Silver Box dress. She had narrowed it down to a choice of six, including a Stella McCartney . . . *'That I know you're going to LOVE. Can you call me back, darling? I hope you're OK.'*

The fact that such big designers were clamouring to dress her was a huge compliment. Normally, Vanessa would have been back and forth from London in a whirl of dress fittings and accessory meetings. For the National Television Awards last year she'd had her yellow diamonds from Garrard picked out for months. But for some reason, she couldn't get excited this time. It felt like being forced to attend her own birthday party, one she didn't want to be at.

She put the phone down and lay back. The garden felt empty without Dylan. She wondered what he was doing. Thinking about her, as well? Vanessa imagined him topless as he worked at the camp, his sinewy brown back gleaming in the sun.

A trickle of sweat snaked its way down her chest, disappearing into the golden canyon of cleavage. Heat began to grow between her legs. She put her hand on her lower belly and stroked it, contemplating.

The house was cool and quiet. She padded up the stairs in her bikini, her bare feet sinking into the soft carpet. Once in her bedroom she pulled the white blinds down. Just in case.

She lay on the king-sized bed and looked down at her nearly naked body. She tried to imagine it as Dylan saw it. Closing her eyes, she slipped one hand inside the front of her Missoni bikini bottoms.

Her fingers brushed the soft, neat line of her Brazilian. She had always been very self-conscious about masturbation before, but Dylan had such an arousing effect on her that she was desperate for the release. She started to touch herself, hesitantly at first and then more fluidly and confidently.

'Aah,' she moaned. She felt so swollen it was almost painful, yet in a completely delicious way. She started to work harder and faster, pressing urgently against her clitoris. Then she came, arching her back as the glorious spasms ebbed through her body. All too quickly it was over. Exhausted and euphoric, she flopped back on the silk pillows.

'That was an Oscar-winning performance,' drawled a voice from the doorway.

She leapt up like a startled rabbit. Conrad was leaning against the door frame with a predatory smile as he filmed her on his iPhone.

'What the hell are you doing?' she shrieked, grabbing an embroidered cushion to shield herself. 'Stop it!'

'Nice to see you enjoying yourself for a change, instead of lying there like you're about to be embalmed.' Mercifully he stopped, coming over to sit on the edge of the bed.

She tried to snatch the phone off him. 'Give that to me!'

He held it away from her. 'Can't a husband film his own wife?' His other hand began to move up her inner thigh. She tried not to flinch. 'Do I still make you horny, Vanessa? Do you still want me?'

'Yes,' she whispered.

His fingers started to probe her, like a doctor carrying out an examination. 'Good,' he said briskly, taking her wetness as his own achievement. 'I'm going downstairs.'

She lay on the bed, trembling. The truth was that suddenly, she was frightened of her own husband.

Chapter 42

The next day brought the inevitable news. Jonty was resigning as MP for Beeversham and as a member of the Conservative Party. The Labour and Lib Dem leaders were in their element, gleefully coming together on that evening's BBC *Question Time* to denounce Jonty as: 'the blackened heart of a corrupt government'. The political bloggers were even less charitable. The by-election, in which candidates of the local political parties would campaign against each other to win Jonty's seat, would now take place in the next four weeks.

In the wake of the scandal Jonty had suffered a complete breakdown and been sent off somewhere obscure to dry out. It had been left up to Felix, as his constituency chairman, to hastily write Jonty's official resignation letter. It was read out in the House of Commons that afternoon.

'I deeply regret my actions and I remain a loyal supporter of our Conservative government.'

In the wake of Jonty-gate, circulation figures of the flailing *Cotswolds on Sunday* had leapt up for the first time in years. Their coverage was extensive and typically lurid, describing Jonty as 'a drug-addled drunk' who was 'wildly unpopular' amongst his constituents. People were lining up in their droves to have a pop. The *Mail on Sunday* had found an ex-good-time girl now running a hedgehog sanctuary in Hastings, who claimed Jonty had spent most of the 1980s putting Class As up his nose and condoms through on his expenses. He had been skirting a very fine line for years and everyone wanted to get the boot in.

Sid Sykes was interviewed for the six o'clock news, in a vast, chintzy living room at home, a fairy tale drawing of Ye Olde Worlde framed on the wall behind him.

'I'm in total shock,' he said, looking quite the opposite. 'Jonty Fortescue-Wellington has let the people of this country down.'

'Does this affect your plans for Ye Olde Worlde, Mr Sykes?' the reporter asked.

'Quite the opposite! Fortescue-Wellington was meant to bring these poor people jobs, stability, more opportunities in the district. That's what I'm doing with Ye Olde Worlde. I feel so angry about what these poor people are going through, I'd like to take the opportunity to offer anyone living within the theme park area fifty per cent off the entrance fee.' Sykes leered into the camera. 'I guess you could say I'm the Minister for Fun.'

A car pulled up in the yard. Fleur looked up, from where she'd been glued to the kitchen TV. She was astonished to see it was Beau's old Mustang

She rushed out in a panic. 'What are you doing here?'

'Lovely to see you too,' he told her.

Fleur went pink. 'S-sorry. I meant, I wasn't expecting to see you.'

He was wearing a mint-green shirt, a white jumper knotted over his broad shoulders. Fleur had never known a man to wear so much pastel, but somehow on Beau it worked.

'Fancy coming to play at mine?' he asked.

'What do you mean?'

'Darling, you're not very good at this.' He sighed. 'I'm asking you over for dinner.'

Fleur looked down at her jeans, which had cow saliva all over them. 'Now?'

'Now or never.'

'I'm not dressed for it.'

'Go and get dressed, then.'

Fleur thought about the mountain of paperwork piling up, her drunk unhappy dad locked away in his study. She had an overwhelming urge to escape and have some fun for once.

'Give me five minutes.'

'I love a girl who can wash and blow.' Beau grinned wickedly. 'Sorry, wash and go.'

Upstairs Fleur quickly showered and brushed her teeth. She had to keep telling herself it wasn't a date. *This was Beau Rainford.* She wasn't falling for any of his smooth-talking crap.

Even so, there was a blotchy rash on her chest and a little pulse thudding in between her breasts. She scrabbled round in her ancient make-up bag and found the stump of a black eyeliner. She applied an uneven line, hands shaking with nerves and lack of practice.

It didn't take long to choose from her dismal collection of clothes. She went for a black shirt that didn't show too much cleavage and her best – make that only – pair of going-out jeans. There was a bottle of something on the dressing table and Fleur squirted it on her neck and wrists.

She looked in the mirror and her heart sank. Instead of an effortless beauty, a raccoon-eyed girl in a frumpy shirt looked back at her. In desperation, she pulled out the band from her ponytail, the luxuriant red hair tumbling over her shoulders. Thank God she'd washed it that morning. After running a brush through it, she pulled on a pair of semi-decent ballet pumps. It wasn't much, but it was all she had.

Beau was leaning against the car, texting. His eyes slid expertly over her. She blushed again and touched her hair self-consciously

'Four minutes forty,' he announced, looking at his watch. 'It takes Valentina twice as long just to reapply her lip gloss.'

'Is she, I mean, Valentina, going to be there?' Fleur asked politely.

He shook his head. 'Some catwalk thing in Paris.'

It sounded very glamorous. 'You didn't want to go?'

'Those things bore the hell out of me.' He slid the Ray-Bans back on. 'Come on, Cinderella, your carriage awaits.'

He drove like a maniac – a confident maniac who could handle corners at eighty miles an hour while carrying on a full conversation. By the time they'd screeched up outside Ridings, her eyes were watering madly and her hair was a mass of tangles. So much for trying to look cool.

'First impressions?' he asked.

They'd driven at such terrifying speed she hadn't had the chance to take it in. Staring up at the huge gleaming white box where her grandparents' old house used to be, she felt quite overcome.

'Let's start round the back,' he said more gently. 'I think you'll be surprised.'

Still upset, she followed him round the side of the house. This was a mistake, she shouldn't have come. A second later she stopped in her tracks.

Beau grinned. 'Not what you expecting?'

Fleur gazed at the extraordinary vision in front of her. Her grandparents' house was still there, except it had new windows and a much-needed new roof. It was connected to the modern part by a gleaming corridor of glass. She had to admit, the contrast of the original farmhouse and the new extension looked really cool.

'I only got rid of the bits that were beyond saving.'

She was lost for words. She couldn't believe her grandparents' house was still here, hidden behind the stark white facade.

'Come on then,' he told her. 'You can tell me what you think of the rest of it.'

When her grandparents had lived there, Colmwood Farm had been rather dark and chintzy. He had knocked through walls and opened the place up, exposing the beams and flooding the place with light.

'What do you think?' he asked.

'I think it's really cool,' she admitted. It was a completely different place, yet she felt instantly at home.

The modern side was huge and seamless, walls of white running into floors of polished marble. There were no skirting boards or lamp switches, or anything else you'd find in a normal house. A blown-up cover of Italian *Vogue* hung on one wall. Valentina, hair flying behind her, cheekbones soaring, stretched her elongated proportions into an exaggerated pose.

'V gave that to me.'

'She looks amazing.'

He shuddered. 'I always feel like her eyes are following me around.'

Another canvas hung in the corridor. A young brunette, pensive as she gazed past the camera. The blue eyes and full lips were unmistakable. 'My mother,' he told her.

'She's beautiful,' she said.

'She was, rather.'

'Do you miss her?'

He gave her a brief glance. 'I do, actually.'

'I miss my mum, too.'

'What happened?'

'Cancer. Five years ago.' She felt like she'd become an old woman in that time.

'I'm sorry,' he told her. 'You're never the same, are you?'

'No,' she said softly. 'You're really not.'

There was a brief flame of recognition between them. 'Right,' he said briskly. 'Let's get on with the tour.'

The futuristic kitchen was spotless, a sleek MacBook

open on the top of the central island. By contrast the living room in the old part of the house was simple and homely, with squashy white sofas, and magazines scattered across the coffee table.

They headed outside to the landscaped gardens and swimming pool. There was even a poolside bar and big, luxurious day-beds that made Fleur feel like she was at a posh hotel. A bright green thong hung off one of them. From the minuscule size it had to belong to Valentina.

'I was wondering where that had got to,' Beau said airily. 'My tan lines have been giving me hell.'

She giggled. He *was* quite funny.

The outbuildings that used to house the farm machinery were still there, but they had been spruced up. There was a new paved area outside, dotted with oversized plant pots.

'My latest venture,' he told her. 'We've converted them into recording studios.'

'Really?'

'You want a look?'

There were four studios, exactly like the ones she had seen in films.

'This is amazing! Do you ever get anyone famous?'

'Darling, we only get famous. They go mad for the prime Cotswold location.'

She resisted asking who, for fear of sounding like a saddo. Beau probably hung out with famous people all the time.

The helipad with its red H painted on the grass was in a nearby field. 'The helicopter's in for a service,' he told her.

'Yeah, mine too. It's a bugger.'

His eyes flashed amusedly. 'Do you think I'm showing off?'

'I don't know what to think,' she admitted.

Beau's office was a converted stable block, knocked through to create one massive space. His desk was glass and dominated the entire room. On the top was a small, framed picture of a sultry blonde woman.

'Lindsay St John,' he told her. 'One of the most fun people ever to grace the earth.'

'Who was she?' Fleur had a closer look. The woman was definitely on the mature side, but there was no mistaking the winning smile and mischievous dark eyes.

'An ex-girlfriend who taught me a lot about life.' He looked at the picture for a long moment. 'She's dead now.'

On the far wall was another blown-up cover, this time of *Time* magazine. A sandy-haired Doug Rainford, sprawled across the bonnet of a Ferrari in a pair of seventies-style bathing trunks. It was clear where Beau got his strutting good looks from. Fleur blushed. Doug wasn't just big in the talent department.

Beau stood behind his desk, rapidly working his way through a pile of glossy envelopes.

'Why don't these people move into the twentieth century and use email?' He opened another invite. 'Oh look, a weekend with the Henley-Bassets. She's fun, but he's a fucking bore. Atrocious nostril hair. There's no way I'm schlepping all the way up to East Yorkshire.'

The invite sailed into the bin. He continued to rip through the rest, verbally demolishing each one.

'Tamara Houseman's thirty-fifth at Maggie's. She certainly was the size of a house when I last saw her, grouse-massacring in Scotland. I hate the shooting season. Oh look, another gallery opening! If I have to listen to one more coked-up arsehole gushing on about how Caesar's latest African dunghill installation is a remarkable interpretation of the Third World's quest for enlightenment, I won't be held responsible for my actions.'

'What parties do you like?' she giggled.

'Any that aren't in this country. Who the hell is *this*? "The break-out star from TV's *Made in Chelsea*"?' He shuddered. 'God!'

'Have you ever met the Duchess of Cambridge?'

'A few times.'

She tried not to sound impressed. 'Is she nice?'

'If you like the Home Counties type. I prefer my girls with a bit more chutzpah.' Beau looked up, fixing her with his brilliant gaze.

She flushed and changed the subject. 'So, you have your own company?'

'Yup, we buy up old wrecks and do them up.'

'Like my farm?' Fleur challenged.

'No, not like your farm, as it happens. You've made yourself loud and clear.'

A strained silence followed. 'I didn't get you up here to try and talk you round,' he told her.

'Didn't you?' she asked boldly.

'Of course not!' He sounded irritated. 'Look, Fleur, I invited you round tonight in the hope of cementing us Not-Being-Friends, and to try and show you I'm not this complete bastard who bowled in and ripped your grandparents' house down. If you'd rather, I can take you home . . .'

'No! No.' She bit her lip, feeling ungrateful. 'I'm sorry.'

'It's fine,' he sighed. 'You've got every right to be suspicious, but I can assure you, I have no untoward intentions. Well, none that involve your farm.'

He gave her a smile, the easy charm back again. 'Shall we have dinner? I don't know about you, but I'm bloody starving.'

A fish pie was produced from somewhere and they ate on the terrace, a sweeping stretch with an uninterrupted vista across the valley. Bats swooped across the pink and orange sky, the last streaks of sunset filling the huge panes of glass. It was wonderful, as if the windows were glowing with light. Up close, Fleur could see how the house had been cleverly moulded to make stunning use of the landscape. There were breathtaking views from every window, the sharp corners and skylights framing the sky and greenness perfectly. She had lived in Beeversham all her life, yet it felt like she was seeing it all through new eyes. There was a depth of glamour that had never been there before.

'How the hell do you keep everything so clean?' she asked. 'I'd like to see this place in winter!'

Beau forked up a huge flake of salmon. 'I wouldn't know. I'm never here in winter.'

'Where do you go?'

'I'm thinking of Buenos Aires this year.'

Fleur, who'd never been further than Spain, thought it sounded impossibly glamorous.

They sat and worked their way through dinner. The fish pie was delicious, but she was too on edge to eat.

She reached for her wine again. The alcohol was going to her head.

'This is really nice,' she asked. 'What is it?'

'A Meursault,' he said, pronouncing it impeccably.

She stuck her nose in the glass. 'Smells like honey.'

'Spot on. We'll make a wine connoisseur of you yet.'

He looked over and grinned at her. Fleur's heart suddenly seemed to falter, before resuming in a rather wobbly manner. Suddenly she understood why so many women threw themselves at Beau, why she herself had been so desperate to get back in his good books earlier. When he looked at you like that, it was like being caught in a ray of sunlight.

'Beautiful night,' he remarked, looking up at the stars.

The wine loosened her natural reserve. 'Do you ever get lonely up here by yourself?'

'I'm rarely by myself up here.'

She'd walked into that one. 'So *is* Valentina your girlfriend?' she asked, determined to have an adult conversation.

'Well, she is a girl and we've certainly been friendly.' Beau surveyed her through his blue eyes. 'You are a funny little thing, aren't you?'

'What does that mean?'

'Don't get so defensive. It's a compliment.'

Fleur felt an unexpected glow. She looked out across the valley, to the golden rooftops of Beeversham.

'Do you think your brother might go for Jonty's job? He'd make a much better MP.'

Beau picked his glass up. 'I've got about as much idea as you have.'

She tried again. 'It must be hard, I mean being

252

brothers and not talking to each other, in a small town like this.'

He gave her an amused look. 'What's with all the questions?'

'I guess it's just nice to have a proper conversation with someone,' Fleur admitted.

'Me too,' he sighed. 'Valentina and I are definitely bigger on screwing than talking.'

He was trying to embarrass her again but she wasn't having it. 'How about Ginny?' Fleur persisted. 'Do you get on?'

Beau looked genuinely sad for a moment. 'Ah, Ginny's not allowed to speak to me. I'm *persona non grata* in my family.'

'Do you want to talk about it?'

'Nothing to say, really. I'd far rather hear what skeletons you've got in your family closet.'

'I haven't got any skeletons.'

'Tell me, anyway.'

She gave him a brief life story, leaving out the years since her mum had died and how her dad had gone to pieces. He listened in silence, his sharp eyes constantly roving round the terrace. Fleur wondered if she was boring him.

'Have you always wanted to go into the farm thing?' he asked.

'I actually wanted to be a trading standards officer. But then my mum died and my dad—' She stopped. 'I had a place at college but I gave it up to work on the farm.'

They looked out across the fields to where a lone light burnt at Blackwater Farm. She snuck a glance at Beau. His face was relaxed, unreadable. *Can I really trust you?* she thought.

A car horn blared from up the drive, making her start. Beau checked his watch. 'The Cavalry have arrived. Come and say hi.'

As they walked round to the front of the house, a souped-up Range Rover with blacked-out windows was pulling up. The sound of the bass horn reverberated through the glass. The back doors opened and four very familiar faces tumbled out.

'Oh my God, it really is The Cavalry!' she squeaked.

One of the hottest new bands in the UK, The Cavalry had arrived under the cover of darkness to record their much-anticipated second album. They greeted Beau like an old friend, giving him high fives. Fleur got a picture with them and they all gave her a hug, smelling of cigarette smoke and aftershave, before they were bundled down to the studio to start work.

'I'll never wash again.' She touched her cheek with wonder where Jonny Faro, the gorgeous lead singer, had kissed her.

Beau raised an amused eyebrow. 'So you *are* impressed sometimes.'

'What does that mean?'

'Nothing. Come on, let's get you home.'

Beau put on the stereo as they drove back towards Blackwater Farm. Fleur couldn't believe it as the opening strains of 'Total Eclipse of the Heart' blasted out of the speakers.

'Bonnie Tyler? You are kidding me. My mum used to love her!'

'Never underestimate an eighties power ballad,' Beau said gravely. 'Bonnie Tyler is a goddess.'

'This is comedy!' she hooted. 'I thought you'd be much more 50 Cent.'

'As a strident feminist I'm strongly opposed to the objectification of women.'

'Yeah, right. Wanting to sleep with loads of women doesn't make you a feminist!'

He laughed out loud. She grinned back, ridiculously pleased she'd made him laugh.

Bonnie's gravelly vocals filled the car, drowning out conversation. In the compact space of the car, Fleur realized how powerful Beau was, his shoulders almost touching hers, the long muscular thighs nestled under the steering wheel. She crossed her arms, trying to quieten her thumping heart.

All too soon the Mustang pulled up at the farmhouse. He left the engine running.

'Thanks for a nice evening,' she mumbled. 'I really enjoyed myself.'

'My pleasure.' In the dark, his grin was brilliant white. *Crocodile teeth*, she thought from nowhere. He leant across to open the passenger door for her, his arm brushing her right breast.

'Night then. Sweet dreams.'

'Night.' Fleur tried not to feel too disappointed. What had she been expecting?

'What perfume are you wearing, by the way?' he asked, as she was about to shut the door. 'I've been meaning to ask all evening.'

'Oh! Um, I think it's Stella McCartney,' she lied.

'It's very distinctive.'

She shut the door. He whirled the car round and zoomed out of the gates without a backward glance. She raced up to her bedroom to find the perfume he had liked so much. She stared at the bottle in horror.

She'd only sprayed on flea repellent meant for the dogs.

Chapter 43

As she had done every day for the past week, Catherine was in the living room slumped in front of the television. Empty chocolate bar wrappers were scattered on the sofa beside her. When her mobile went off she was in such a sugar slump it took a moment to locate it under a cushion.

'Hello?'

'This is Quentin Fellowes. Private secretary to the Prime Minister,' said the crisp male voice on the other end. 'I've got the PM on the other line.'

'Yeah, and I'm the Queen of Sheba,' snapped Catherine. 'So why don't you piss off?' She hung up.

Bloody crank callers! She was gloomily staring at the chocolate stain on her camisole top when the phone rang again.

'What now?' she howled. It was clearly some scam, a way to try and take her money. *Have it all,* she thought, pressing 'answer'.

'Catherine?' a voice asked.

'Can't you think of something a bit more original?'

she sighed. 'How about my credit card's about to spontaneously combust and you need my pin number? Or that I've won fifty million quid on the Bosnian lottery, and a helicopter's on its way to whisk me away to Sarajevo?'

'Sorry?'

She warmed to her theme. 'I may as well warn you, I'm a woman on the edge. My husband thinks I've gone completely mad and he's probably right. Do you know I've just sat here and troughed my way through a family-size bar of Dairy Milk. Didn't even touch the sides. And before that, a biscuit sandwich! I don't even have a sweet tooth!'

'What's a biscuit sandwich?'

'I just made it up. You get two biscuits, and stick them together with chocolate spread. Or anything else sweet, like honey or *dulce de leche*. Unfortunately we're all out, so I had to make do with cream cheese, which is why I went on to eat my own body weight in chocolate. And I've got half of it down my top, so now it looks like I'm sitting here with a bloody great skidmark.'

There was an amused snort at the other end. She sat up. 'Sorry, who is this? Why do you want to know about my biscuit sandwich?'

The deep voice spoke again. 'It's the Prime Minister.'

'Not this again! I just told your mate to do one.'

'Catherine, it really *is* me. Do you want me to send you a picture for verication?'

She sat bolt upright. Unless it was Rory Bremner on the other line doing a bloody good impression, those rich, caressing tones were unmistakable.

'Fuck a duck,' she gasped. 'It really is you!'

The Prime Minister gave a throaty chuckle. 'Sorry to let you down. The Bosnian scam sounded quite exciting.'

Catherine froze in shock. Their PM was something of a pin-up, even among rival parties. Young, dynamic and boyishly handsome; she'd only just been watching him on *BBC Breakfast* that morning.

'Am I interrupting anything?' he asked.

She switched off *The Jeremy Kyle Show*. 'Nothing that can't wait.'

There was a pause.

'How are you these days?' he asked, as if they were old friends. 'It's been quite a while since I saw you at the "Women In Media" lunch.'

'I know, it seems like ages ago.'

'I took on board what you said about the donkeys, by the way.'

She cringed. Fired up on several glasses of cheap Downing Street white wine, she'd ended up ranting at him about how 'fucking braying' donkey sanctuaries got more funding than domestic violence charities. The memory still made her toes curl in horror.

'Sorry,' she said.

'Don't be. It was a valid point.'

She stared out of the living-room window. Was this conversation really happening?

'Catherine?'

'Sorry, missed that.'

'I was saying, I didn't realize you'd moved out to the Cotswolds. Until I saw you on the news.'

'Right.' Why the hell did he care where she'd moved to? Were they behind on council tax payments or something?

'Lovely part of the country. Even under the present circumstances.'

'You mean quiet and sleepy Beeversham becoming a Mecca for the angry and disillusioned?'

'What did you think of Jonty?' he asked suddenly.

She was a bit taken aback. 'You really want to know?'

'I do.'

'OK, I think he's a fat, lazy, unscrupulous toff who abused his position of privilege and not only let Beeversham down, but the entire political system.'

He sounded amused. 'Don't hold back.'

'You did ask.' She was starting to get impatient. 'Look, PM – I can call you that, can't I?'

'Of course.'

'I don't mean to be rude, but you haven't rung me for a slagging-off session about Jonty, have you?'

'You're absolutely right, Catherine. I haven't.'

There was another pause, this time longer. She frowned. What the hell was going on?

'How do you vote?' he asked.

'Labour. Always have.'

'How do you feel about running as the Conservative candidate in the Beeversham by-election?'

Catherine laughed out loud. 'Ha ha! And they say politicians don't have a sense of humour!'

'I'm serious.'

'Yeah, right, me too.'

'We need a new approach to our candidate. We have to move forward and modernize.'

'I agree with you there, but why aren't you ringing Felix Chamberlain about this? He'd be amazing.'

'I think you would make a better candidate.'

'This is a joke, isn't it?' Catherine said.

'Far from it.'

She slumped back on the sofa. 'I can't believe we're having this conversation!'

'Why are you so opposed to it?' he asked calmly.

'Where do I start? The Conservatives are anti-women, anti-anything outside the mainstream.' She started to get going. 'You demonize disadvantaged young people instead of helping them, you've got an appalling track record for equal pay in the workplace and, like every other government, you're still not doing enough for domestic violence charities.'

'Exactly why we need someone like you in the party. I know the image we've got, Catherine, and I'm trying hard to rectify it.'

'Go and rectify it, then! I don't know the first thing about politics!'

'You've got passion and that's enough.' He paused. 'What's your purpose in life, Catherine? Are you really happy living quietly out in the country?'

'Yes, thank you very much!'

'You told me that day that your mother's death has defined you, Catherine. That it was the most important thing in your life. How it inspired you to go on and change other people's lives.'

Shit, he was good. He'd remembered every word. 'Don't try and use my mother against me,' she said sharply.

'I'm sorry. I didn't mean it like that. But Catherine, think about it.' His voice became more urgent. 'If you win the seat back for us, you'll have a voice in parliament, a voice for all the disadvantaged and underprivileged out there. A voice for the average person on the street. You could pass laws with your name on them. Think about it: the Catherine Connor Domestic Violence Bill. *You* could help save women's lives.'

'I'm strangely flattered, but this is still a joke. I'd make the worst MP in the world.'

He wasn't giving up. 'Let me ask you something. When you're on your deathbed will you look inwards at yourself and say, "Yes, I made a difference"? "Yes, I was willing to stick my head above the parapet because I believed in what I was doing"?'

She gave a mirthless snort. 'I'm having trouble making sense of my own life, let alone anyone else's.'

'Why don't you just think about it?'

'I have and it's still a no. I don't mean to sound rude, but you're wasting your time. Now if you don't mind, I've got two back-to-back episodes of *60 Minute Makeover* waiting.'

John and Catherine were eating pasta alfresco on the patio. The sun was disappearing on the horizon. *Like my sanity*, Catherine thought.

The scrape of cutlery against china was excruciatingly loud. A night flight streaked across the sky, carrying passengers to a far-flung destination. Catherine desperately wished she were up there. Not sitting across from her husband in the garden with absolutely nothing to say to him.

'I had an interesting call from Jeff today,' he said.

'Oh, right?' Jeff Brownlee was John's old business partner. He had just started up his own company.

'He's found this site for sale in the Heredia region of

Costa Rica. Five hundred acres being earmarked for a hotel chain. Jeff wants to put a bid in for eco housing for the local communities. It would be a great thing to get involved in.'

She pushed her plate away. 'What do you think?'

'It depends.' He was watching her closely. 'What do you think? It would be a big project. I'd have to go away a lot.'

She shrugged. 'I don't mind.'

'Don't mind, or don't care?'

'You know what I mean, John. Of course I care.'

'Do you really?' he asked softly. 'Because I'm getting really seriously worried about you, sweetheart.'

'I don't know what you're talking about,' she said defensively.

'Cath.' He leant across the table. 'Something is going on with you. You don't want to do anything, even go running, you're just lying round the house eating junk food and watching crap telly. I feel like I'm walking on eggshells the whole time round you. Yet when I try and talk to you about it, you just clam up.'

She stared at her wine glass and desperately wished it wasn't empty. 'I don't know, John. I just feel *depressed*.'

He took her hands in his. 'Cath. You've got nothing to be depressed about.'

'I KNOW that!' she cried. 'Don't you think that makes me feel even worse?'

'I know you're disappointed about not being pregnant.'

'Oh God, can't you just leave the bloody pregnancy stuff alone! I'm sick of you going on about it.'

He released her hands and reached for his wine. 'Didn't you say you had something to tell me?'

She had been waiting for the right moment all evening. Sitting here now opposite her angry, confused husband, the Prime Minister's phone call seemed like a dream. In a petulant way she suddenly wanted to hug the incredible secret to herself. John wouldn't believe her anyway.

'Doesn't matter,' she muttered.

Chapter 44

The Smart Car had originally been bought as a run-around for Renata, but Conrad had banned her from getting behind the wheel again after she'd reversed into his Mercedes the first time she'd driven it. The vehicle had been gathering dust in the garage ever since. Paranoid about attracting attention in the Porsche she usually drove, Vanessa had taken to driving it to her trysts with Dylan.

She zoomed out of the gates of Tresco House that afternoon. She'd found a route through the back roads that only took six minutes, but as she got to the bottom of Pavilion Heights she saw a 'Road Closed' sign ahead. A lone workman with his yellow hat pushed back off his head stared at her blankly.

Vanessa cursed inwardly. The long route round was twenty minutes and she didn't have the luxury. She'd have to go down into town instead. Praying the hot weather would have kept people indoors, she whipped the Smart Car around and set off.

*

Catherine was in a world of her own as she drove down the High Street. She didn't notice the elderly man on the zebra crossing until the last minute. She jammed on her brakes, earning herself a disapproving wave of his walking stick.

He started at a snail's pace across the road. A rowdy group of political reporters were drinking outside Bar 47. One of them lifted up his T-shirt and showed the others his sunburnt beer belly.

Catherine pulled a face and looked back at the road. Mr Walking Stick was still doddering along. They'd be here all day at this rate.

He finally got to the other side. She put the MG into first and promptly stalled. There was an impatient toot behind her.

'All right all right,' she muttered. It was worse than driving in bloody London!

The car beeped immediately again, this time flashing its lights. 'Jesus, what is wrong with people!' Catherine cried.

To prove a point she took her time restarting the engine and drove five miles under the speed limit to the end of the High Street. The car was on her bumper the whole way. At the Black Bull pub she pulled over to let it past. A black and white Smart Car zoomed past before slamming on its brakes up ahead. She watched it reverse back up the road towards her. *Uh-oh.*

A familiar petite woman was behind the wheel. Catherine did a violent double-take. Was that Vanessa Powell in dark glasses and a Gucci headscarf?

'You did that deliberately!' the celebrity hissed.

'Did what?' Catherine said innocently.

Vanessa whipped off her Chanels. 'Held me up so the paparazzi could get a good shot! Are things that bad, that you've resorted to doing deals with the paps?'

Catherine laughed out loud. 'Get a life!'

'Stop ruining other people's!' Vanessa jabbed the glasses at her. 'You're the lowest of the low!'

'And you're a jumped-up twat!' Catherine yelled. 'Why don't you go and get your tits out and jump out of someone's birthday cake?'

Vanessa glared at her. 'I could sue your arse for that.' With that she floored the Smart Car and screeched off.

Catherine rested her forehead on the dashboard and groaned. Of all the people to have road rage with! And what the hell was Vanessa Powell doing in a bloody *Smart* Car?

She stared down the empty road for a moment, before picking up her phone from the passenger seat. She re-read the Prime Minister's text message.

'I haven't given up on you yet, Catherine. Call me back, we need to talk.'

Dylan and Vanessa made love under the canopy of trees. Afterwards she lay wrapped in his arms. 'I should go,' she said reluctantly. 'Conrad will be back from London soon.'

He hugged her tighter. 'Don't go just yet.'

She rested her head back on his chest, and heard the slow, rhythmic thud of his heart. She trailed her hand down the concave belly and caressed his sunkissed hips. Everything about him was warm and alive. Everything about her husband was cold and reptilian.

'You make me feel safe,' she said.

'I want you to be safe.' He paused. 'Leave Conrad.'

She sat up. 'What?'

Dylan's eyes had a curious moving quality to them, like liquid mercury. 'I mean it. Leave Conrad. I'll look after you.'

She gazed into his kind, lovely face and looked round the woodland camp where she'd spent the happiest times of her life. 'Oh, Dylan.' She burst into tears.

'Oh God, please don't cry.' He wiped her cheeks. 'It's not that bad an idea, is it?'

'It's a lovely idea,' she sobbed. 'That's what makes it so hard.' Vanessa started crying even harder. 'I have so much responsibility.'

'I know.' He pressed his face into her hair. 'Ssh. It's all right.'

'I l-love you,' she whispered.

'I love you, too,' he said softly.

She flung her arms round him, clinging on for dear life. How was it possible to feel desperately happy and yet so wretched?

Chapter 45

The announcement was finally made: the Beever-sham by-election campaign was starting on 1 August and would run for four weeks. The Conservatives were remaining tight-lipped about their candidate, but press speculation was swinging between the Conservative Association chairman Felix Chamberlain and Alexander Farthing, MP for Driffield and one of the Tory party's rising stars.

Tristan Jago had practically announced himself as the Labour candidate while Jonty's roundhouse kick was still hanging in the air. The town was plastered with election posters of him sitting on a set of cottage steps cuddling a Mallard duck, long legs stretched out to full advantage. His slogan 'I'm Cotswolds and I Care' was simple but effective. It was widely assumed he'd walk the by-election.

Buff Nail Bar was a symphony in pink, from the cerise wallpaper and blush ceiling to the neon chandelier that dangled down like one of Pat Butcher's earrings.

Black and white framed photos of Marilyn Monroe and James Dean provided a bit of light relief, while Mel's young technicians carried on the colour scheme with their glossy lips and shiny, rosy cheeks. It was hard to know if they'd been chosen to match the decor or the other way round.

Mel greeted Catherine with a hug and a glass of Pinot. 'It's gone mental down here. Mike had a night stop in Beirut last week, said it was nothing in comparison to this place.'

Catherine giggled. 'Oh, Mel. It's good to see you.'

Mel guided her to a manicure station and started to take her polish off. 'I heard about your run-in with Vanessa Powell. Amanda said you practically came to fisticuffs on the High Street.'

'Amanda's exaggerating as usual.'

'Did you really tell Vanessa to get her tits out?'

'Pretty much.'

Mel cracked up laughing.

'Don't,' Catherine groaned. She needed distracting from the horror; at least it hadn't ended up on the *Mail Online*. 'Tell me the latest gossip round town instead?'

'Apart from you abusing our resident celebrity?' Mel rubbed at a tricky bit on Catherine's thumbnail. 'Lynette Tudor's been driving round in a new convertible Peugeot. She's like the cat who's got the cream. We all think she's got a new man.'

'Good for her. Do you know who it is?'

'No idea, but he's got to be worth a few bob.' Mel massaged cream into Catherine's hand. 'Amanda and Olympia are on another diet: the Cambridge one this

270

time. And Henry's been made to get a back wax. He came in the other day for some aloe vera, he was in all sorts of trouble.'

'Poor bloke!'

'Amanda's totally got his balls pinned to the Aga. Ooh, and apparently there was an amazing punch-up amongst the journos outside Bar 47. Vincent caught one of them buying Talia Tudor drinks – she'd made out she was twenty-one and was working for *3AM*. Vincent chucked the whole lot out, and two blokes from the *Daily Star* ended up rolling round in the gutter.'

Catherine began to feel better about her spat with Vanessa. One of Mel's girls came over with two more wines. 'Anything else, Mel?'

'Put the new Bruno Mars album on, will you, babe? All this house music is making my head hurt.'

'Have you seen Felix or Ginny?' Catherine asked.

'Not a squeak. I haven't seen Felix in his office for days, and Dilip said Ginny hasn't even been in for her *Cotswolds Life* this week, which is very unusual. They must be keeping a low profile with all the drama going on.' Mel squinted critically at a cuticle. 'I'm thinking of offering a "Politics Pedicure" with the different parties' colours for the by-election. May as well cash in.'

As Catherine left the salon feeling slightly woozy after yet another glass of wine she bumped into someone standing on the pavement.

'Sorry, I wasn't . . .' Her words fell away.

'Hello, Catherine,' the Prime Minister said.

Her mouth opened and shut again. 'What. Are. You. Doing. Here?'

'Seeing as you wouldn't return my calls I decided to come down here in person,' he said amiably.

'You've come all the way out here to see me?'

The PM glanced at the TAG on his wrist. 'I've got a Cabinet meeting at three and there's a pack of journalists circling up the road. Can we drive and talk?'

Drive? Where the hell was he taking her?

The black Jaguar glided out of Beeversham, Catherine and the PM sitting either end of the back seat, separated by a leather armrest. Aside from the discreet Range Rover following behind containing the Prime Minister's security advisers, they could have been any well-heeled Cotswolders out for an afternoon drive.

She couldn't stop sneaking amazed glances at him. The PM stared ahead, cool and collected in a sharp navy suit. By the cut of the lapel she hazarded a guess it was Armani. 'Are you sure you're not kidnapping me?' she joked nervously.

The PM looked amused. 'Perfectly.'

The air conditioning was cool to the point of chilly. An empty Pret A Manger sandwich box was tucked into the seat pocket in front. Proof the Prime Minister was a human being after all.

His iPhone went off. He had 'Piano Riff', the same ringtone as her. It was getting more surreal by the moment.

'Excuse me,' he said. He listened intently. 'No, I'm not budging. We need more time on the euro.'

'Trouble at the office?' she asked when he came off.

He gave her a boyish grin. 'Isn't there always?'

Green fields raced by. She still had no idea why she

was there. She glanced at him, tapping away on his phone with long, elegant fingers. He wore a thin gold wedding band.

'How's the family?' she asked.

'Good, thank you. Sam's madly into aeroplanes, and Maddie's just decided she wants to be a tube driver.'

'How old is Maddie?'

'Three.'

'She sounds over-qualified for the job.'

He laughed. 'I think you're probably right.'

The drive continued more comfortably. 'I suppose you're about to try and convince me to run again,' Catherine said.

'I'm doing nothing of the sort,' he replied mildly.

'So where the bloody hell are we going?'

'You'll see.'

Chapter 46

There had been several wild scenarios running through Catherine's head, but she had never imagined this hot, cramped house with the windows shut despite the heat of the day. The owner was a tiny, greying woman called Linda Giachetti. She'd shown no surprise when she'd opened the door to them, as if they were expected.

Linda was in the kitchen making them a cup of tea that Catherine really didn't want. She and the PM were in the tiny living room, squeezed into two over-stuffed armchairs either side of the gas fire. Even with his privileged London gloss, the PM looked remarkably at home in the chintzy surroundings. Then again, he was an expert at that sort of thing.

The room was filled with the usual sort of knick-knacks and ornaments. Five framed photos were arranged neatly on the mantelpiece. There was one large one of a baby, and several others, including one of a little girl in a school uniform and another of a young woman, dressed up in a cat costume laughing into the camera. Even with the age differences, Catherine could tell by the dimples and the sparkly green eyes that they were all of the same person.

Linda came back in and handed the Prime Minister a mug with the Royal Lifeboat logo. Catherine's had a faded floral pattern. Linda's own mug was put down on the floor still on the tray, already forgotten.

Catherine recognized the haunted tiredness on Linda's face as typical of somebody who had gone through a huge amount of grief. She thought about Linda's surname again. Giachetti. Where had she heard it before?

'How are you, Linda?' the Prime Minister asked caringly.

Linda gave the ghost of a smile. 'I got a beautiful card from your wife last week.'

'My wife is a patron of one of the charities Linda works for,' the PM explained to Catherine. 'They've become friends.'

'She's a lovely woman,' Linda said. 'Her support has made such a difference.'

'What's your charity?' Catherine asked, but she already knew the answer.

Linda glanced briefly at the photographs on the mantelpiece. '"Behind Closed Doors", or "BCD". It's a domestic violence charity.'

'Have you heard of it, Catherine?' the PM enquired innocently.

'Yes, I've heard of it.' Catherine smiled at Linda, but inside she was seething. How dare he put her in this situation!

He ignored her death stare. 'BCD is a cause very

close to Linda's heart, for obvious reasons. You may remember the name Debbi Giachetti.'

Of course, it was all coming back now. Debbi Giachetti had been brutally murdered by her common-law husband, while attempting to protect their two young children. Stabbed through the heart with a kitchen knife, she'd died at the scene. The trial had been all over the news. Her husband had eventually been sent down with a twenty-year sentence.

'I'm sorry for your loss,' Catherine said inadequately.

Linda Giachetti gave her an unhappy smile. The PM cleared his throat. 'I thought you two would have a lot in common.'

There was a long strained silence. The feeling of clutter and memories was overwhelming in that boxy living room. Catherine stared out of the window, desperately wishing she were anywhere but here. She had absolutely no idea what to say to the poor woman.

'It never leaves you, does it?' Linda Giachetti said suddenly.

'I'm sorry?'

'The guilt.' Linda smiled again, but this time it was emphatic. 'The guilt that you couldn't save them.'

Catherine was suddenly transported back to that terrible night at the top of the stairs, all those years ago. A terrified fifteen-year-old, cowering in her bedroom. Her mother's cries as the brutish Ray Barnard squeezed the life out of her. Her mum's helpless face as she stared across the landing at her daughter, pleading.

Cathy. Help me. I can't breathe!

Catherine had saved her mum from Ray Barnard that night, but it hadn't been enough. In the end, he had still destroyed her. After years of being told she was a worthless piece of scum, that her life was worth nothing, Annie Fincham had come to believe it.

Catherine was horrified to find herself welling up. 'Me and Debbi were so close,' Linda continued. 'I still didn't see how bad it had got. She put on a brave face, she didn't want to worry me.'

Catherine thought about her mum explaining away the black eyes and sprained wrists. *Your mam was just being clumsy again, pet.*

'I should have done something. I *knew*. I tried to convince myself everything was all right because I couldn't bear what was happening.' Catherine's voice caught. 'I let Mam down.'

'You can't blame yourself, Catherine,' Linda said gently. 'Your mum, my Debbi, they were trying to protect us. No matter what we think, they thought they were doing the right thing.'

'Doesn't make it any bloody easier.' Catherine sniffed.

Linda took Catherine's hands into her own worn ones. 'I'd rather have had them for a short time than not at all. Do you know what I mean?'

'Yes.' It sounded trite but Catherine did know.

At the front door Linda gave Catherine a hug. 'You should come down to the charity one day,' she told Catherine. 'They do wonderful work there.'

'I'd like that very much.'

For the most part the PM had been sitting there quietly, but now he gently cleared his throat. 'There are still thousands of women out there, too frightened to speak out. "Behind Closed Doors" do what they can, but they're desperate for more funding, more people on board. Catherine, these women need our help.'

Catherine didn't say a word as they drove off.

'I didn't mean to upset you,' the PM said.

'Well, you did.' Catherine had wanted to let rip at him in there, but now all she could see was the sweet, smiling face of Debbi Giachatti. She blew her nose with the tissue he handed her.

He pulled an A4 sheet out of his briefcase. 'This is for you.'

'What is it?'

'Statistics about domestic violence charities.'

'I know the statistics. You don't do enough for them.'

'I can't do it all by myself, Catherine. If you became an MP, you could campaign for new laws. What better way to honour your mum's memory?'

'That's a cheap trick,' she warned him.

He fixed her with big brown eyes. 'Catherine,' he said honestly. 'I wouldn't pursue this if I really didn't think there was a chance. I want to change the world and make it a better place. And I know that's what you want, too.'

'I hate what you lot stand for!'

He brought his fist down on the armrest. 'Help me bloody change it, then!'

The passion in his voice surprised Catherine. 'You don't give up, do you?' she said.

'So you'll think about it?'

'I'll think about it, but that's it. No promises.'

'Of course not.' His eyes sparkled.

Oh God, Catherine thought. What was she getting herself into?

Chapter 47

'What's this in aid of?'

Fleur looked at her dad. 'What?'

'Eating outside,' Robert Blackwater said. 'You've gone all Mediterranean on me.'

'I haven't.' She smiled. 'I just thought it made a nice change from the kitchen. It's such beautiful weather.'

A ploughman's on the old picnic table in the garden wasn't exactly the French Riviera, but the view was still breathtaking. The valley swelled and dipped like a rolling sea, crested on the top with bottle-green woodland. The sun bobbed on the horizon, taking its time to slide out of the day.

Fleur's dad chewed reflectively on a piece of cheese. 'I suppose this is to butter me up.'

'What do you mean?'

'You taking up with Beau Rainford.'

She eyed her dad. Did he really not remember the car crash? As with everything else, the events of that night had been swept under the carpet. Fleur didn't know if her dad had really been out of it, or he was just embarrassed.

'Beau's OK, Dad.'

'You've changed your tune.'

'I'm not saying we're like best friends or anything.'

'Be careful, Fleur. I've met men like Beau before. They're always after something.' He gave her a meaningful look.

'Dad, we are not having this conversation! I told you, we're just friends!'

Fleur sat out in the garden after dinner, but her good mood had been spoiled. Her dad's words ran through her head. *I've met men like Beau before. They're always after something*. Did Beau see her as some sort of novelty conquest? She had a sudden image of him in bed with Valentina, their perfect bodies coiled round each other. She bet Valentina's boobs never rolled into her armpits when she lay down.

'What are you looking so miserable about?' a voice suddenly asked.

She nearly fell off her chair. Beau was standing in the shadows at the side of the house. 'I did knock but no one answered.' He grinned. 'I took a punt you weren't out clubbing.'

Even in faded jeans and a white T-shirt, he radiated devastating glamour. Fleur was horribly conscious she hadn't washed her hair for days.

He jangled his car keys. 'Fancy a drive?'

'Bit late to be going out, isn't it?' Robert Blackwater was standing at the back door.

Beau walked up and held his hand out. 'Evening, Robert.'

For an excruciating moment Fleur thought her dad wasn't going to take it. He shook Beau's hand briefly.

'I just dropped round to see Fleur,' Beau said.

'So I see.' Robert Blackwater was already slurring slightly. 'Got designs on my daughter, have you?'

'Dad!'

Beau smiled easily. 'Fleur and I are just friends. I hope I haven't caused any upset by coming round.'

She jumped up. 'You haven't. Let's go, shall we?'

'I'm sorry about that,' she said as they drove away. 'My dad, he's just a bit protective.'

'It's cool, don't worry.' Beau glanced at her. 'I mean it, Fleur. Your dad's just looking out for you. I'd be the same.'

She gazed out of the window. *The same about what?* she wondered.

Ten minutes later the Mustang was bumping along a grassy track. 'I know this place!' Fleur exclaimed. 'Cooper's Croft.'

'Best sunset in the county.'

'I haven't been here for years. Wow.'

The ruins of the old crofter's cottage still nestled amongst the wild grass. Just as she remembered, there was a little opening through the hedge. It led to a ledge jutting out over the valley.

The starry sky had darkened into a million tiny fireflies, hovering above them. The shape of the land reminded Fleur of the voluptuous body of a woman:

the plunge of valley like a cleavage; the high, round rumps of hills. She had sex on the brain. She grew hot again as an image of Beau and Valentina together flashed into her mind again.

'I used to come up here when I was a boy,' Beau said. 'It was about the only place where I couldn't be accused of causing trouble.'

They sat down on a grassy ledge. Beau's elbow brushed Fleur's. Her heart started to gather pace.

He stretched out his legs in front of him. She looked at the stripy espadrilles and bare brown ankles. 'What is it with all you posh boys and no socks?'

'I don't know; we like showing off our thoroughbred ankles. What is it with you farming girls, anyway?'

'What about us?'

He gazed straight at her. 'Why do you never wear clothes that show off your cracking figures?'

She suddenly found it hard to breathe. Failing to think of a witty reposte, she stared at the landscape.

An owl hooted overhead, making her jump violently.

'Relax, sweetheart,' he said gently. 'I'm not going to eat you.'

Her heart was fluttering wildly, like a trapped bird; there was no way he couldn't not hear it.

'I called my dad the other day,' he said conversationally. 'First time in months.'

She blinked, mometarily wrong-footed by the swerve in conversation. 'Oh. Was he pleased to hear from you?'

'He had no idea who I was. He's got stage six Alzheimer's.'

'Oh. I'm sorry.'

'Don't be. It's not your fault.'

'Were you close to him?' she asked. 'I mean, before he got ill.'

Beau chucked a twig down the hill. 'I went to boarding school at the age of seven. I never really got to know him.'

'Seven sounds so young.'

'It wasn't the greatest moment of my life,' he said dryly. 'I cried every night for a week, convinced they'd come back and get me. Of course, that soon went.'

Fleur imagined a tiny, blond moppet of a boy sobbing into his pillow. Her heart ached. Her upbringing might not have been glamorous, but she'd had love and stability.

'Tell me about your mum,' she said. 'What was she like?'

'Good fun. We were as thick as thieves. I think that's one of the reasons I got packed off to school; my dad didn't like having to compete for her attention.'

'Did you see Felix much?' It was easy to forget they were even brothers.

'No,' Beau said shortly. 'He was off doing his own thing by then, and I only came home for the holidays.' He changed the subject. 'How about your mum, were you close?'

'Really close. It sounds so cheesy, but she really did light up the room when she walked in. She was great for my dad.'

He tugged softly on the end of her ponytail. 'Is that where the red hair comes from?

'N-no,' Fleur stuttered. 'That's my dad's side of the family.'

Every follicle on her head tingled. Her heart had started to thud again painfully. 'I-I'm not going have sex with you,' she blurted.

He almost looked pained. 'Is that all you think I'm after? Oh, come here.' Cupping his hand round the back of her head, he pulled her in and kissed her.

His lips were astonishingly gentle. Fleur inhaled intoxicating smells of citrus aftershave and washing powder and started kissing him back. *Any second now I'll wake up to real life.*

When he pulled away, it was like she'd been dropped from a cloud back down to earth.

'W-what's going on with you and Valentina?' she stammered.

'Nothing. It's over.' He touched her cheek. 'God, Fleur. What *is* it about you?'

Bending his head, he kissed her again, making her forget all about Valentina.

Chapter 48

It was barely two weeks since Catherine had been round to the Hollies, but it felt like a lifetime ago. Felix greeted her on the doorstep with a wry smile.

'I've been expecting you.'

Ginny was coming down the stairs behind him. 'Hello, darling. Felix said you were coming over.'

She looked rather pale and washed out, dark circles ringing her eyes. 'Poor Ginny's had a nasty stomach bug,' Felix explained.

'You poor thing,' Catherine said. 'Are you feeling better?'

'I am, thank you. The upside is I've lost a few much-needed pounds.' Ginny's smile seemed forced. 'I'm going to take Bonnie out for her walk. Felix, there's a fresh pot on in the kitchen.'

'Is Ginny really all right?' Catherine asked in the study.

He glanced up from pouring the coffee. 'Yes, why do you ask?'

'She didn't seem herself. It's nothing I've done, is it?'

286

Catherine was only half-joking. She was still relatively new to the friendship game.

'Heavens no! She's under the weather. Poor darling is so full of get-up-and-go usually; this bug has really hit her for six.' He held up a plate piled high with biscuits. 'Homemade shortbread?'

'So,' Catherine said a moment later. 'I guess you know about my surprise visitor.'

'I was aware, yes.'

She put her cup down on the windowsill. 'Felix, I feel really bad about all this.'

He fixed her with his blue eyes. 'Do you? Why?'

'You should be running for MP, Felix, not me. I know sod all about politics.'

'Catherine, I've been in this business a long time. One thing I've learnt is that it's about personalities and not politics. And apparently the PM thinks you've got the personality to go all the way!'

He put his cup down and sat back. 'Let's put our party differences aside for the moment, Catherine. What do you believe in?'

She thought. 'A fair and free society. Equal rights for women, safety in the home. Young kids with a shit start in life given a chance instead of being demonized.'

'I want those things as well.'

She chose her words carefully. 'Present company excluded, but the Conservatives still come across as a bunch of over-privileged, Eton old boys. How can they be trusted to run the country, when the majority have no idea how the rest of us live?'

'Contrary to what you might think, we aren't all the intolerable old toffs you imagine. Many of us are born with a silver spoon in our mouths, but there's a lot that haven't. I've always been in the camp that believes it's our duty to look after others. As the great Harold Macmillan once said, it is a necessary price we have to pay for our privilege.' His eyes twinkled. 'It's easy to sit round at dinner parties criticizing others, but how do you know what's really going on unless you're out there doing something yourself?'

She caught the gentle rebuke. 'You're saying I'm just an armchair critic,' she said.

'It's healthy to have strong opinions,' he said mildly.

'This whole situation is so absurd, Felix! I don't know what to do.'

'What do you think of the PM?' he asked.

'He's like a dog with a bloody bone.'

His eyes twinkled again. 'Rather reminds me of someone else I know. Young, tenacious, idealistic.'

'Do you really think I could do it?'

For a moment his face was unreadable. Was he covering up his misgivings?

'I believe we're all capable of anything, providing we put our minds to it. But you have to want to do it, Catherine. I'll run your election campaign for you, but make no mistake, it's a bear fight out there. You'll be pulled apart and humiliated, your private life will be up for grabs. You'll spend hundreds of hours going from house to house to people who don't know who you are and don't care. Trust in politics is at an all-time low. It will have to be a strong man – or woman – who puts themselves out there.'

'You make it sound horrific,' Catherine joked.

He looked serious. 'Believe me, it can be.'

'Why put yourself through all that for something that isn't going to change anyway?'

'If we don't try, then who will?'

She thought about the gap-toothed smile of a young Debbi Giachetti, and the wretched face of her mother Linda. Catherine thought about her own mother, dying alone in her prison cell.

The words were out before she realized. 'OK, I'll do it.'

Chapter 49

Her mother called out as Vanessa crept into the house after another ecstatic hour with Dylan. 'Is that you, Vanessa?'

'Yes, Mother.' She hovered at the bedroom door. 'I didn't want to wake you.'

'I was awake anyway. Come in.'

Vanessa pushed the door open. The curtains were drawn, the heavy velvet fabric concertinaing on the floor. The familiar scent of lavender perfumed the air.

It was a big room, a beautiful one, and yet it felt strangely impersonal, like a suite in a five-star hotel. The only touches of humanity were the framed photos Dominique always kept on her bedside table. Her own wedding day and her daughter's.

Dominique was lying on the vast bed. She looked so small amongst the realms of satin and over-stuffed cushions. Vanessa felt a pang. She'd been neglecting her.

'Where have you been?' her mother asked.

'Just out for a drive.'

'Another one?'

'They help clear my mind,' Vanessa lied. 'I tell you what, it's better than any therapy!'

Her mother didn't smile. 'Sit down for a minute.'

'I really need a shower.' Vanessa was conscious of smelling of sex. 'I'm so hot.'

'Sit down.' Dominique's voice brooked no discussion. Reluctantly, Vanessa perched on the end of the bed.

'Are you all right?' her mother said.

Vanessa plucked at an imaginary crease on the duvet. 'Of course I am. Why do you ask?'

'Are you and Conrad having problems?'

'Why?' Vanessa said carefully. 'What would you say if we were?'

'I would say that you're going through a rough patch, and that all marriages have them.'

'Even you and Daddy?'

'Even me and your father.' Dominique allowed herself the ghost of a smile. 'I know how you have him on this pedestal.'

Vanessa gazed at her parents' wedding photo. 'Conrad's not kind like Daddy, though, is he?'

'Conrad is . . . *different* from your father. He has an artistic temperament. You have to understand it.'

No, Vanessa thought. *He's just an outright bastard.*

'Look at the wonderful life you've built together,' her mother told her. 'You'd be a fool to throw it away.'

Vanessa recognized the warning. 'What if I'm not happy?'

'There are different kinds of happy. We've built up a family again. You're lucky to have a husband.'

Dominque put a bejewelled hand on top of Vanessa's. It felt suffocatingly heavy. 'Promise me you won't do anything stupid.'

'Of course,' Vanessa said emptily. 'I promise.'

Vanessa walked back to her room to have a shower. How could she be screaming so loudly inside yet nobody could hear her?

Conrad was at the bedroom window, staring out. 'Marty wants us to do *OK!* the week of the Silver Box. Of course, normally I don't like doing these things, but these are exceptional circumstances.'

'I'm not sure it's a good idea,' Vanessa said desperately.

'I thought you'd be all over it for the exposure for Brand Powell.'

'I just feel uncomfortable talking about our personal life.'

He gave an incredulous snort of laughter. 'You? The woman who'd have sold our bottled farts for money in the past?'

Vanessa crossed her arms with more resolve than she'd felt in weeks. 'Sorry, Conrad, I'm not doing it.'

'Why's that, sweetheart?' His voice became dangerously soft. 'You do love me still, don't you? My fans are desperate for a peek into our dream marriage.'

'Of course I love you,' Vanessa made herself say. 'I just don't feel the need to shout it to the rest of the world.'

'You've changed your tune.'

'People change, Conrad.'

'You're right, they do.' He walked over to her and

moved his face to an inch from hers. 'I never imagined I'd catch my uptight wife playing with herself.'

She flinched. 'The awful thing with these films . . .' he continued '. . . is that they can end up in the wrong hands. Just imagine if I left my phone somewhere and the press got hold of it!'

She went cold. 'You wouldn't.'

'Oh, sweetheart, I would never do it on purpose.' His smile was reptilian. 'But you know how forgetful I am sometimes.'

'You bastard,' she said through gritted teeth. 'I can't believe you're blackmailing me!'

'Darling, how could you even say such a thing?' He gave her cheek a lingering kiss. 'This is the most important week of my career. And nothing is going to fucking spoil it.'

Chapter 50

John came out of the shower to find his wife sitting cross-legged on the bed.

'Can we talk?' she asked.

'That sounds ominous.' He walked over to the wardrobe and opened it. 'What do you want to talk about?'

'I had a visitor this week.' Catherine's palms started to sweat. Why was she so terrified of telling her own husband?

He selected a pair of jeans and began to pull them on. 'Who?'

'The Prime Minister.'

'Is there a good punchline to this?'

'John, I'm being serious. The Prime Minister came to see me this week.'

He straightened up. 'Are you being serious?'

'Yes! Deadly.'

John blinked. 'And he came to see you because?'

'Because, because . . .' Catherine desperately fumbled for the words. 'He wants me to run as the Conservative candidate for the Beeversham by-election.'

He stared at her for a good five seconds. 'You?'

'I know it sounds completely crazy.'

'Sorry, Cath, let's rewind a bit. How long have you known about this?'

'Well, he phoned me last week but I didn't take it seriously at the time . . .'

'Last *week*. You didn't think to mention it to me?'

'We've had so much else going on,' she said lamely. 'And I wanted to make sure before I made my mind up.'

'About what?'

She swallowed. 'I've said yes. John, I'm running as the Conservative candidate.'

She braced herself, but he just stood there. The calmness was more frightening than any yelling.

'John,' she begged. 'Say something!'

'What do you want me to say?'

'Look, I know I should have discussed it with you earlier. I'm sorry.'

'Damn right you should!' he exploded. 'Cath, I can't believe you've agreed to something as big as this without even talking to me about it!'

'I thought you might try and talk me out of it,' she said weakly.

'I wonder why! Jesus! Have you gone totally insane?'

'Is it really that inconceivable?' she shot back. 'They do let women into politics these days, you know! To be honest, I'm just grateful that someone still thinks I'm capable of doing something.'

'What the hell does *that* mean?' He collected himself visibly. 'Cath. Look, I understand how flattering it must be to have the Prime Minister of the country singling you out for special attention.'

'Don't patronize me,' she said tightly.

'Can't you see they're just using you? This is the last thing you need. The stress of this campaign will be huge, even if you win. What if you get ill again?'

'I can't go round wrapped in bloody cotton wool for the rest of my life!'

He faced her, towering and furious. 'Don't you think that before you take on the world's problems, we should sort out our own first?'

'I don't know what you mean,' she said defensively.

'Cath, you're not well! I'm not talking about physically.'

'Oh, great! So you're saying I'm a lunatic now?'

'Of course not! All I'm saying is that I'm really trying here.'

'It's not all about you, you know! Not all of us bounce out of bed every day knowing exactly where we're going in life.'

'Why do you always go on the attack and blame me? Why can't you just say how you feel?'

'I DON'T KNOW HOW I FEEL!' she screamed.

Outside the wind rustled through the hanging wisteria. Catherine felt her eyes bubble up.

'I know it's a shock. But it's something I feel I have to do. It's given me a purpose for the first time in a long while.'

The look he gave her made her heart split into two. 'Please, John,' she begged. 'I can't do this without you. Don't make me choose.'

'I'd never ask you to choose, Cath,' he said tiredly. 'You should be able to come to the right decision by yourself.'

'Thank you,' she said quietly.

'I take it Felix knows about this?'

'Yes,' she said.

He ran a hand over his face. 'What now?'

'We've got two weeks to prepare until the by-election. I've got some woman from Conservative HQ in London to coach me in political PR. She's called Victoria Henley-Coddington.'

'Of course she is.'

'Couldn't make it up, could you?'

The tension between them thawed a millimetre. 'Jesus, Cath,' he said. 'You know how to spring things on me.'

'I'm sorry. I really am.' Catherine smiled tentatively. 'Are we still friends?'

'Ask me in three weeks, when the campaign's over.'

He selected a shirt off the hanger and put it on. She desperately wanted him to come over and put his arms round her, but he walked towards the door.

'Are you sure this isn't about something else?' He stopped suddenly.

'What do you mean?'

'Throwing yourself into this,' he said. 'To get away from us.'

She hesitated for a second too long. In that time, something cataclysmic shifted between them. 'Of course not!' she exclaimed. 'Don't be silly.'

He walked out without a backward glance. She was left hugging the pillow in terror. *Oh shit. What have I done?*

Chapter 51

Things were not going well in the Blackwater house. The accounts were down again. Fleur had hoped the barbecue weather would have helped, but the supermarkets were buying so much less meat these days. To make matters worse the government had just announced another rise in the price of diesel; at this rate Fleur wouldn't even be able to get her animals to market. That was without even thinking about the Land Rover's MOT, or the fact that Fleur's quad bike was on its last wheels . . .

She sat in the kitchen surrounded by mountains of unpaid bills. The bank manager's deadline to start paying their loan was looming. No matter what she did, it wouldn't be enough. *We're going under . . .*

It took several seconds to realize her mobile was ringing. She snatched it up off the table. 'Hello?' she sobbed.

For a moment she thought it was someone playing silly buggers, then a distinctive voice swam into her ear. 'Fleur?'

She sat up. 'Beau?'

'Who else?'

It was a really bad line. She wiped her eyes. 'Where are you?'

'Montenegro. What are you doing tomorrow night?'

'I'm not sure yet, why?' As if she had plans.

Static crackled into her ear. 'You're . . . party with me. I'll arrange . . . get picked up.'

'A party? Where?'

'Christ, this reception is shit. Can you hear me?'

'Yes!' she shouted. 'Where's the party?'

'The Serpentine Gallery. Be ready for six.'

The Serpentine Gallery in London? Fleur blinked, all thoughts of financial ruin forgotten. 'Wait! What do I wear?'

But the line had already gone dead.

Fleur had been in a state all day. Googling the Serpentine Gallery summer party, she'd realized what a massive deal it was. How was she going to fit in with the likes of Cheryl Cole and Alexa Chung? She'd been on the verge of ringing Beau half a dozen times to cancel. A desperate rummage through her wardrobe had produced a floral shift dress from Oasis that was at least five years old. It was also too tight across the bust and had a stain on the front but it was the best – make that the *only* – thing Fleur had.

Clueless about what to do with her hair, Fleur had rung every salon in the area to get an appointment. The only place available at such short notice was Julie's, the one her gran used to go to. Trying to ignore the dated hairstyles on the walls, Fleur had given the hairdresser a photo of Keira Knightley looking elegant in a chignon. Two hours later, after an alarming amount of backcombing, she had emerged looking like Marge from *The Simpsons* and full of fresh despair. Even the dogs had whimpered when they'd seen her.

Her face was so flushed she hadn't bothered with blusher. She'd circled her eyes in an amateur fashion with her stump of black eyeliner. The dress had felt horribly short when she'd put it on: she was sure she'd grown since she'd last worn it. The only heels she owned were a pair of clumpy black court shoes. Not possessing a clutch bag, she had rooted round and found a dusty one that had belonged to her mum.

By five past six she was circling the kitchen table nervously. Was a taxi picking her up? Or did Beau have his own chauffeur? She strained her ears for the sound of a vehicle. A ghastly thought struck her. What if it was all a horrible wind-up and she'd been stood up?

Her dad came in, sober for once. 'What do you think?' she asked hopefully.

'Looks like you're going to a wedding.'

'Is that a good or a bad thing?'

'Not sure.' He gazed at her hair. 'What time are you being picked up?'

'Six.'

'He's late.'

'I know that, Dad!' she said hysterically. 'Will you give me a break?'

Tinker and Bess had been lying in the porch, listless in the heat. Suddenly they pricked their ears up and whined. A few seconds later Fleur heard a humming in the distance, like a giant wasp buzzing across the fields. It was a sound she'd heard many times before, but never this close.

'What the hell is that?' For the first time in weeks, Robert was roused out of his stupor. Following him out to the back garden, Fleur was greeted by a scene straight out of an action film. A hundred metres from the house a red helicopter was hovering in the air. It started to descend into a nearby field, sending nearby trees into a flapping frenzy.

Robert Blackwater was taciturn at the best of times, but his face was a picture. 'That's your lift?' he said.

Chapter 52

Catherine was on the High Street when Beau's helicopter buzzed overhead. As it swooped off into the distance she heard her name being called. The Patels were sitting in the open window of Bar 47, along with Mel and Mike and Amanda Belcher.

'You were in a world of your own!' Mr Patel called. 'Come and join us.'

Catherine hesitated. The last thing she felt like doing was socializing at that moment.

'Oh, come in!' Amanda cried. 'We haven't had a good chinwag in ages.'

The hot topic was who was running as the Conservative candidate. 'We just assumed it would be Felix,' Mrs Patel mused. 'It's very strange.'

'Henry bumped into him last night, and Felix was very top secret about it,' Amanda told them. 'Said all would be announced shortly!'

'Probably going to parachute someone in from another Conservative constituency,' Mike Cooper-Stanley said.

'Whoever it is, they're in for a shock,' Mrs Patel said. 'After Jonty, people round here are baying for Tory blood.'

Catherine started to feel distinctly sick. 'I'm sure it's not that bad.'

'They'd better be clued up on Ye Olde Worlde.' Mr Patel stirred his flat white darkly. 'I hear there were lots of men in high visibility jackets up at Blaize Castle the other day, measuring up.'

A sporty black Peugeot drove past with the roof down. Rap music was blaring out, shattering the peaceful morning. It was Lynette and Talia Tudor, both in matching dark glasses. Mother and daughter wrestled over the stereo. Talia shouted something and slumped back in the passenger seat.

'Talia's making the most of Mummy's new sports car.' Mel smiled. 'Any clue as to Lynette's new bloke yet?'

'None.' Amanda sounded disappointed. 'But she's just had all the rotting windows in her cottage replaced. I bet he paid for that.'

'I should bloody hope so,' Mel declared. 'Lynette deserves someone who will look after her.'

Amanda's eyes were elsewhere, trained on the mop-haired, sinewy figure padding along on the other side of the street. 'The delectable Dylan! You don't see him in town very often.'

'He is very good-looking,' Mel conceded. 'In that lean, David Beckham kind of way.'

'Apparently he's practically mute,' Amanda breathed. 'And runs round the countryside, foraging for food.'

Mr Patel went to object, but Amanda was in full

flow. 'They say he's descended from a family of famous Romany gypsies. One look in those silver eyes and you're either cursed or spellbound!'

'How do you know all this?' Mrs Patel asked.

'Because I've seen him, Ursula! Up close!'

'Where?'

Amanda looked faintly embarrassed. 'In the fruit and veg aisle at Waitrose. But he didn't even use a bag or anything, just carried it all out in his hands!'

'On that note . . .' said Mike Cooper-Stanley.

Chapter 53

Fleur gazed at the bewildering array of instruments in front of her and wondered if she was dreaming.

'Can you hear me?' a deep voice said into her earphones. Brad, Beau's pilot, was lantern-jawed with a moustache like Magnum P. I. He even had the tinted aviator sunglasses.

She nodded and watched Brad pull up on the controls. The noise of the rotor blades was deafening. As if by magic the aircraft rose up again. Within moments, her dad was a tiny figure waving from the ground.

Blackwater Farm was soon left behind. They swooped up high across the valley.

Brad spoke into her ear again. 'Are you all right?'

'Yes!' she said, giving him the thumbs-up.

He grinned and went back to flying the aircraft. Getting over the shock of being picked up in a helicopter, she started to enjoy the experience. It was a perfect summer's evening; the skies soared endlessly above them. She pressed her face against the window, seeing the toy houses and blue rectangles of swimming pools below. Everything was so small and neat. It reminded her of the Mobil farm set she and her sister were given one year for Christmas.

The helicopter carried on towards London, Brad giving her a running commentary as they went. From the Cotswolds they flew over the beautiful Oxfordshire town of Henley. She saw the boats nestling on the glittering River Thames and imagined Beau in his white blazer at the regatta. They headed east, passing Windsor Castle on the way. Fleur could just about make out the flag flying at full mast, before her attention was on the huge passenger jets taking off above them out of Heathrow.

Green fields gave way to urban sprawl as they hit the traffic-snarled M25, before swooping down the river towards Central London. Richmond Park opened up on their right, the herds of deer like tiny brown insects. The next moment she was looking down at the million-pound houses fronting the Thames. Was this really happening?

Hugging the river, they flew across south west London, high above the glass waterfront apartments. She heard Brad speak in her ear to an unknown person, and the aircraft started to descend. For a terrifying moment she thought he was going to land on one of the apartment blocks, before she saw a small concrete pad on the jetty below them. The blades lowered gently as the helicopter settled down. They were back in the real world again.

Brad pulled his earphones off and turned to her. 'Beats travelling by the M4.'

Fleur was met by a chauffeur with a black Mercedes.

She sat back on the cool leather seats and took in the capital. It was hard to believe that ten minutes earlier she'd been up in the sky. The car drove through the elegant streets of Fulham and Chelsea, beautiful people packed on to pavement cafés and bars. They drove down the King's Road and past a sprawling council estate, completely at odds with its more genteel neighbours. In the narrow lanes of Knightsbridge Lamborghinis sat bumper-to-bumper with red buses. *Where have I been all my life?* Fleur marvelled, as they drove right past the entrance of Harrods. The glamour and buzz were incredible.

A few minutes later Hyde Park appeared on the left. Their car joined the line of Bentleys and black cabs turning off. As they headed down the road towards the Serpentine Gallery she started to feel sick.

The Mercedes pulled up behind a huge black Bentley. 'This is about as near as we're going to get,' the chauffeur said. 'Are you all right to walk the last part?'

She watched Simon and Yasmin Le Bon get out of the car in front. He looked dapper in a black suit, his wife coltishly beautiful in a pale-green dress.

'I can't go,' she said in terror. 'Don't make me go!'

The chauffeur, who was in his fifties and reassuringly like someone's dad, gave her a smile. 'You should see them on the way home, lolling all over the back seat with a McDonald's and no shoes on.'

'Really?'

'Really. It's just a party like any other.' He handed her an oblong ticket. 'Here's your pass to get in. Mr Rainford will meet you inside.'

He got out to open the passenger door for her. She

started to follow the stream of people walking towards the entrance, pretending to know where she was going. Unused to wearing heels, she nearly went over on her ankle twice. A tall, beautiful creature swept past her, gliding effortlessly on five-inch stilettos.

Get me out of here, Fleur thought frantically. At that moment she'd have done anything to be back in the farmhouse kitchen, in her stinky old work clothes with the dogs.

Except there was no turning back now. Following a tiny blonde woman who looked very much like Geri Halliwell, she walked up to the park gate. A huge bank of photographers was lined up outside, taking pictures of a pair of stunning blonde girls.

'Cara! Give us another smile, darling. Poppy – look this way. Lovely!'

The photographers took no interest in Fleur. She gave her ticket to the smartly dressed woman on the gate. She half expected it to be handed right back, but the woman smiled.

'Come on through. Have a fantastic evening.'

A big 1930s-style pavilion lay directly in front of her. She had no idea where to go, so she followed the stream of guests walking round the side of the building. The scene that greeted her was like nothing she'd seen in her whole life.

It was like walking on to a Hollywood movie set. The beautiful and famous stood amongst the landscaped gardens, shoulder to shoulder. She spotted Pierce Brosnan talking to a surprisingly short Kevin Spacey. Over in the corner Cheryl Cole, ravishing in a backless dress, stood clutching a glass of champagne as she chatted to fellow Girls Aloud band-mate Nicola Roberts.

The Serpentine lake shimmered seductively in the distance. The view of the royal park was unbelievable: miles of impossibly green, perfect grass stretching out like a kingdom. A giant-sized chess set, with real people dressed up as the pieces, was being played by a stylish couple, giggling as they instructed their knights to move.

The *pièce de résistance* was a huge mirrored canopy that stretched over the revellers like a big, shiny, expensive puddle. Waiting staff moved through the crowd seamlessly, topping up glasses and refreshing cocktails.

Fleur couldn't see Beau anywhere. She tried his phone, but it went straight to voicemail. Where was he? Someone handed her a drink and she gulped it back without knowing what it was.

'Cheska, darling!' Two stick-thin women wearing diamonds the size of eggs effusively air-kissed in front of her.

'You look amazing,' one said. 'Where have you been?'

'Kenya.' She pronounced it: 'Keen-ya.' The first woman linked skinny tanned arms with her companion. 'How are you, darling? Is Rollo here?'

They drifted off into the crowd. Fleur checked her phone again, Beau still hadn't called. She started to get a horrible feeling in the pit of her stomach.

With no one to talk to, she concentrated on people-watching. Even though almost everyone was undeniably beautiful, there was something curiously identikit about the crowd. The faces and smiles were a little too frozen, jutting clavicles favoured over any kind of bust. She was gawping at a one-time famous model who'd had far too much plastic surgery when two men walked past, deep in conversation. 'They say he paid two billion for the Alexis deal,' one said.

'Two billion?' snorted the other. 'They're talking out of their arses.'

She gazed open-mouthed after them. Two billion? She couldn't get her head round that kind of money. *I don't belong here*, she thought again, panic-struck. Where the bloody hell was Beau?

Leaving the garden, she went inside the gallery and wasted a few minutes walking through the different rooms. She stopped at a huge photograph of a Tibetan man floating upside down in a sea of orange fabric.

'Fabulous interpretation of the uprising, isn't it?' the woman next to her drawled.

'Fabulous,' she spluttered. 'Can you tell me where the toilets are?'

Hoping to find respite, or at least a cubicle to go and hide in, she pushed the door to the Ladies open. Three women stood in a row at the mirrors, preening at their reflections. They were all tall and skinny, the middle one wearing a sheer column dress that left little to the imagination. Fleur looked into the glass and her blood ran cold. She turned to make a run for it, but Valentina's eyes had fixed on her.

'Don't I know you?'

'Don't think so,' Fleur mumbled.

Valentina swung round, her dark eyes flashing maliciously. 'Sorry, I didn't recognize you without all the cow gunk.'

Valentina's friends had the same predatory, beautiful faces. They circled Fleur like a pack of malevolent giraffes.

'Who *is* this, V?' the blonde one said.

'No one,' Valentina said nastily. 'On the serving staff tonight, are we?' she enquired.

'I was invited,' Fleur said stiffly.

'You? Invited?' Valentina's right eyebrow shot up. 'Who would invite you?'

Fleur clutched her mum's bag protectively across her chest. 'Beau did, actually.'

The three women exchanged looks. 'That's bullshit,' Valentina snapped. 'If Beau was going to invite anyone, it would be me.'

'Has he, then?' Fleur asked boldly.

The supermodel's eyes narrowed. 'I don't know what kind of charity ticket you're on, but someone's playing a big joke. Beau didn't invite you. Why would he, when he's not even coming himself?'

A horrible unease started to creep through Fleur. 'What do you mean?'

Valentina's smile was triumphant. 'He's away on business, darling. I'm surprised you didn't know if you're *such* good friends.' She gave Fleur a sneering once-over. 'Didn't you read the dress code? Night-gowns are like, so twenty years ago.'

'And ugly shoes,' her blonde friend added.

Fleur started to burn up. She flinched as the brunette girl raised her hand.

'Is that for real?' She touched Fleur's hair. 'Oh my God, it doesn't move!'

Valentina smirked. 'I had no idea they were doing auditions tonight for the lead role in *Hairspray*!'

The three of them fell about, honking with laughter. Fleur looked past them into the mirror and saw how short and frumpy she looked with her with hideous helmet hair.

Eyes streaming, she fled down the corridor towards the exit, not caring who saw her. This was the worst night of her life. How could Beau do this to her? 'You bastard,' she sobbed. 'I trusted you!'

She was crying so hard she ran slap bang into someone just inside the gallery entrance.

'Take it easy,' a voice said. 'Where's the fire?'

'I'm sorry,' she sobbed. 'I was just leaving.'

'Why on earth would you do that? You've only just got here.'

She gazed up through a mist of tears. Beau was standing there, wearing a light-blue suit that made him look more tanned and blond than ever.

'What on earth's the matter?' he asked, guiding her into a corner.

'W-where have you been?' she heaved.

'A work thing came up, I'm sorry. What's happened?'

She sucked up a noseful of snot. 'I j-j-just had a r-run-in with Valentina. She was really horrible to me.'

'Valentina's horrible to everyone, don't take it personally.'

'She said I was a mess, and she's right,' Fleur gulped. 'It's really nice of you to invite me, but I don't fit in here.'

'Of course you do.' He produced a hanky. 'Most people here have red noses from all the coke they do, anyway.'

312

'It's not a joke. I can't go out there again, Beau, I can't,' she pleaded. 'Please don't make me.'

Beau looked out at the party thoughtfully. 'I have a plan.'

Chapter 54

'More champagne, madam?'

'Yes, please.' Vanessa let the waiter give her a refill.

'Sir?'

'No,' Conrad said rudely.

The waiter moved on. Vanessa lifted her glass.

'Don't get pissed and embarrass us, we're here to work,' Conrad told her.

She glared at him. 'As if I would.'

A handsome silver-haired man came up to them. It was Les Goodman, head of ITV1. Conrad snapped into charm mode.

'Les!' he exclaimed, pumping the man's hand.

'Conrad,' Les replied. He kissed Vanessa on both cheeks. 'You look wonderful. Chanel, isn't it?'

'I'm impressed!'

'My wife is Chanel-obsessed.' Les smiled. 'How are my star presenters doing?'

'Wonderful!' Vanessa gushed. 'I can't tell you how excited we are.'

As Conrad started to hog the conversation, Vanessa

took the chance to observe the party. It was so strange how she'd once loved these things: the intoxicating mix of the rich and the powerful. She used to look round and think she'd made it. Now she saw it for the sham it was. All these awful people who pretended they were your best friend one minute and cut you dead the next. They were like sharks with their dead eyes and big white teeth. How could she ever have wanted to be part of it?

'Vanessa, darling!' A TV presenter Vanessa knew vaguely rushed up. She'd lost a terrific amount of weight since the last time Vanessa had seen her, the Temperley dress hanging off her starved frame.

They air-kissed extravagantly. 'My God, how amazing you're doing Silver Box.' The woman nudged Vanessa with a sharp elbow. 'I can tell you, it's set the cat amongst the pigeons, but I said to everyone: "Vanessa is a complete professional. I just know she'll pull it off."'

She flashed a cosy, artificial smile. 'Who are you wearing?'

'I haven't decided yet.'

'Oh, come on. You can tell me.'

'Really, I haven't decided yet.'

The woman's eyes were already flickering over Vanessa's shoulder. 'Oh, there's Les! Les, darling!' She practically pushed Vanessa out of the way to get to him. 'Les! How are you?'

Vanessa felt her mobile start buzzing in her evening bag. It was a local Beeversham number she didn't recognize. She rushed off to stand under a tree. 'Hello?'

'Vanessa?'

'Dylan?' she said frantically. 'Where are you calling from?'

'A phone box. I know it's dangerous, but I had to speak to you.'

'Oh, darling.' Just the sound of his voice made her feel a million times better.

'Where are you?' he asked.

She watched her husband slap Les on the back and roar with laughter. 'At an awful party.'

'I miss you. Every day without you feels like a week.'

'Me too.' *Oh God, it was so hard.* Vanessa blinked away the tears.

'Hey, you OK?' he asked.

'Yes,' she said.

'When can I see you?'

'Soon,' she promised. 'I've got to go.'

'OK. I love you.'

'I love you too,' she whispered.

Les had a big smile on his face when Vanessa returned. 'Conrad's just been telling me about *OK!* I love the idea!'

Chapter 55

The Gucci store on Sloane Street was the most intimidating place Fleur had ever been in. A vast glass-fronted space with items of clothing laid out beautifully, it felt more like an art installation than a clothes shop.

Ivanka, the ice-blonde Amazonian assistant behind the till, had broken out in a huge smile when she'd seen Beau walk in. He'd told Fleur the two of them were old friends. Judging by the adoring way Ivanka was looking at Beau, Fleur thought they might have been a lot more than that.

'We need at least to drag Fleur into this decade,' he told Ivanka. 'Something that shows off her figure.'

Ivanka cast an expert eye over Fleur. 'You're a size eight, right?'

'I guess so.'

'And a big chest!' Ivanka smiled. 'You're a lucky girl.'

Fleur wanted to die, especially when Beau grinned like a Cheshire cat.

'Take a seat,' Ivanka told them. 'I'll get some pieces. You want champagne?'

Beau threw himself down on an armchair. 'You read my mind. Thank you, darling.'

Ivanka disappeared in a waft of something musky.

'You get champagne?' a gobsmacked Fleur asked him.

'It's the only way to shop.' He was already back on his phone.

'I'm not sure how much money I've got on me.'

'Don't worry. It's all part of the service.'

She perched on the other chair, trying to look as if she frequented these sorts of places all the time. Ivanka reappeared with two fizzing flutes. She handed one to Fleur. 'You enjoy this, I'll get to work.'

'Ivanka is a maestro when it comes to styling,' Beau told Fleur. 'She'll have you shipshape in no time.'

He went back to whoever he was texting. Fleur gazed at a glittery scrap of material hanging off a rail. Ominously, she couldn't see any price tags.

Ivanka was back within five minutes with a selection of dresses laid across her arm. 'We'll just experiment until we get it right,' she told Fleur.

'I feel like Julia Roberts in *Pretty Woman*!' Fleur joked nervously.

Ivanka's eyes widened. 'Wasn't she a prostitute?'

There was a snort of laughter from behind them.

In the changing room Ivanka helped her on with the first dress. It was long and black, heavily boned round the corset. She looked at her bare shoulders and décolletage. She would never show off this much flesh normally.

'Redheads are huge on the catwalk this season,' Ivanka told her.

'Come on, then,' Beau called.

Fleur shuffled out of the changing room feeling hideously self-conscious.

'Oh look, it's the Scottish Widow.' He tipped the last of the champagne down his throat.

'You're right,' Ivanka agreed. 'Far too serious.'

'Nice freckles, though.' Beau's blue eyes gleamed. 'Do you have them everywhere?'

Fleur fled back into the cubicle. The next one was a wraparound dress in a geometric print. Beau glanced up from his phone. 'Perfect! If we were about to go to the annual Rotary Club dinner.'

Fleur was starting to feel like one of her cattle at market. The third dress was so short it was practically gynaecological. Ivanka had to shove her out on to the shop floor.

Beau looked up again. 'That's more like it.'

'No way,' Fleur spluttered, fleeing back into the changing room.

She was beginning to lose hope, until Ivanka held up the last dress. Bottle-green and above the knee, it had a high neckline and cute capped sleeves. Simple, but so stylish.

'Stunning,' Ivanka declared. 'Now for accessories.'

She came back with a pair of beautifully delicate strappy heels and a gold clutch bag. The shoes felt as soft as clouds, adding a good four inches to Fleur's five-foot-four frame. After fastening a gold cuff bracelet on Fleur's wrist and fitting on dangly gold earrings, Ivanka stood back to study her protégée. 'Now I'm happy.'

Fleur gazed at herself in the mirror. She couldn't

believe the radiant, leggy person looking back was really her. The dress skimmed her narrow waist and hips, the fabric emphasizing her bust just the right amount. The vivid colour brought out the rich tones of her hair and complemented her pale skin.

'Hold on,' Ivanka said, taking some make-up out of a box by the mirror. She wiped away Fleur's amateurish eyeliner, and deftly shadowed and mascaraed her eyes until they were huge and dewy.

Ivanka whipped a lipstick out of her pants pocket. Fleur baulked when she saw how red it was.

Ignoring her protests, Ivanka dabbed it on. Fleur gazed at her mouth. It looked so big and shiny and sexual. 'I'm really not sure,' she said.

Before she could wipe it off, Ivanka took her by the hand and led her back out. 'I think we've done it,' she told Beau.

He had been staring out the window, but now his blue gaze swept over Fleur. 'I knew you had a pair of legs under there somewhere.'

The unashamed way his eyes were lingering on them made her flush even more. 'I'm not sure I can walk in these heels,' she said.

He stood up. 'You'd better practise, then, while I go and pay.'

'I can't let you pay for this!'

He ignored her. 'Ivanka, darling, can you throw in a bikini as well?'

Fleur was perplexed. 'What do I need a bikini for?'

'When you go in my pool, of course.'

'How about this?' Ivanka held up two scraps of black material.

'No way!' Fleur spluttered.

'Yes way,' Beau said. 'Let's get a move on; we've got a re-entrance to make.'

Ivanka was at the till ringing things through. Fleur caught sight of the price of the bracelet and nearly had a heart attack. Three hundred and seventy quid! She couldn't bear to think about how much the dress was.

'What shall I do with the other dress?' Ivanka asked.

'Burn it and put the poor thing out of its misery. Otherwise, it will make somebody a wonderful Halloween costume.'

'I'll hold on to it in case you change your mind,' Ivanka told Fleur.

Beau kissed Ivanka on both cheeks. '*Ciao, bella.* Thank you for coming to our rescue.'

He sauntered out, back on the phone.

'Thank you,' Fleur told Ivanka. 'You've been really nice to me.'

'Incredible, isn't it?'

'What is?' Fleur asked.

Ivanka smiled wistfully after Beau. 'The way he looks at you. It makes you feel like you're standing in the sun.'

She turned back to Fleur. 'Enjoy your time with him.' The look of pity was clear.

Chapter 56

Fleur tugged on the hem of her dress, wishing she'd invested in some fake tan. Despite the car's air conditioning she could feel a line of sweat trickling down her back. It was very distracting having Beau sprawled out next to her, his long limbs taking up half the seat. The swell of hard thigh under his suit trousers was making her tummy turn over.

He'd been his usual flippant self so far, and she had been starting to wonder if their kiss had ever happened. But since they'd got back in the cab, there had been a weird electricity between them. It was the speculative way he eyed her, with new interest. Dressed in a designer dress, jewels at her ears and on her wrists, she felt like his equal for the first time.

The car pulled up at red traffic lights. Two leggy blondes sauntered past, both with tiny chihuahuas on leads. She glanced at Beau, but it was impossible to tell under the Ray-Bans where he was looking.

He yawned as the car pulled off. 'I could sleep for a week.'

'Late night?' She immediately wished she hadn't asked.

He smiled enigmatically. 'You could say that.'

This time they were whisked through a private entrance, no questions asked. Fleur started to feel sick again. What if Valentina and her cronies were still there? Her python-skin heels were perilously high. *Oh God, please don't let me fall over in front of them.*

'You OK?' he asked.

She nodded, unable to speak.

'You look gorgeous, sweetheart,' he said softly. 'Relax.'

Next moment she'd got her feet in a tangle and nearly went flying. Beau caught her. It was like running into steel. Fleur went all wobbly again.

'Baby steps,' he told her. 'I've got you.'

They walked round the side of the gallery. The music got louder, echoing the drumming of Fleur's heart. On the outskirts of the garden, Beau stopped. 'I've been wanting to do this all night.'

He pulled the combs out of Fleur's hair and ran his fingers through it, raking out the lacquer. 'At last. The spirit of Great-Aunty Muriel has been laid to rest. I don't know why you don't wear your hair down more often, it's really very sexy.'

'Gets in the way,' Fleur mumbled. Her scalp felt on fire from his touch, tingling, dripping down her body like melting candle wax.

He put his arm round her. 'Let's show them what you're made of.'

*

323

Before, Fleur had been an invisible wallflower. Now she met artists and aristocrats, sheikhs and celebrities. She air-kissed television presenters and chatted with a famous singer about how wonderful it was to have no rain this year. Everyone wanted to know who was the tiny Titian-haired girl in Gucci hanging off Beau Rainford's arm.

'Love your dress!' gushed one woman. 'I'm going to get one put on hold first thing.'

'You look very familiar, darling!' said another anorexic crow in black. 'Do you work in fashion?'

'Fleur throws around straw bales for a living,' Beau said, guiding her away.

She was completely star-struck when Beau paused to kiss the Prime Minister's wife, elegant in floor-length navy. The two chatted away like old friends for ten minutes.

'We were at Cambridge together,' he told Fleur as they walked off. 'She was a very naughty girl in her youth.'

She got excited when she spotted Vanessa and Conrad Powell with a group of men. Vanessa was as beautiful as ever, but Fleur thought she seemed a bit sad and distant, standing apart from the others.

'All this arse-licking is boring the, well, arse off me,' Beau said. 'Let's take a breather.' He steered her over to the oyster bar.

'Aren't you enjoying yourself?' she asked. Everyone was clamouring to talk to him, especially the women, but Beau treated the majority with mild disinterest or open disdain.

'It's just the same old crap. Who's-doing-who-with-how-much, everyone gushing over everyone else and stabbing them in the back the second they walk away.' Beau saw her fallen face. 'But I am having a good time, darling. Are you?'

Fleur was too high on life and champagne to stay down for long. 'Fan-bloody-tastic!'

A tall, chunky man in a black tuxedo and jeans came up. 'Bro, I was wondering where you'd got to.'

The two men bumped fists. The man looked at Fleur. 'You've been hiding this one away, Beau. Who is she?'

The Ronseal tan and weak chin looked familiar. She realized it was Spencer, the awful friend Beau had brought round that night when he'd tried to buy the farmhouse.

'You've met before, this is my neighbour Fleur Black-wood. Fleur, this is Spencer Churchill.'

'Hello,' she said stiffly.

Spencer didn't bother hiding his astonishment. 'Crikey. No wellies this time?'

'They're in the car,' she replied sarcastically. She didn't like the sly look he was giving Beau, as if there was some secret between them she didn't know about.

'Well, I'll leave you two to it,' Spencer said. 'Mate, there's an after party at Raffles we're going on to if you fancy it,' he told Beau. 'Antonia's going.'

'We'll probably head home.'

'No worries. Laters, bro.' Bumping fists with Beau again he swaggered off.

'Do you really like him?' Fleur asked. *And who the hell was Antonia?*

'Spence is all right once you get to know him. We boarded together all the way through school.' He drained his glass. 'Do you fancy meeting Elle Macpherson?'

Orange skies merged into inky blue as Fleur drank champagne and met more fascinating people. Everyone was interested in who she was, what she had to say. Tonight, she was one of them. For a few hours, she could forget her problems and pretend.

It was getting on for eleven and she had been talking to a charming, silver-haired banker who apparently owned half of Chelsea.

His hand slid around her waist. 'You really are very sexy,' he murmured. 'I've got a suite at the Dorchester we can go and fuck in.'

She felt herself being whipped out of his grasp. Beau flashed a charming, cold smile.

'Hello, Evan,' he said, putting his arm round Fleur. 'How's that gorgeous wife of yours?'

'That guy has slept with half of London,' he told her as they walked off. 'I wouldn't recommend it.'

Fleur really was quite drunk by now. 'Pot calling kettle,' she quipped.

He cocked his head to one side. 'Sorry?'

The renowned DJ Rev, fresh back from a set in Hamburg, had been providing the music until now. Rumours were circulating that some special guests were about to make an appearance. The crowd was buzzing about who they could be.

'I heard it's Coldplay,' Fleur overheard someone say.

'That would make sense, Gwyneth's here,' her companion replied.

All the champagne was playing havoc with Fleur's

bladder. 'I have to go to the loo. Will you be all right by yourself?'

He looked amused. 'I think I'll survive, don't worry.'

Fleur dreaded running into Valentina and her cronies again, but thankfully the Ladies was empty. When she came back Beau was talking to a short, round little man in a flamboyant paisley jacket.

'Ah, there you are. Fleur, I'd like you to meet a very good friend of mine, Prince Karim of Brunei.'

A prince? Aside from the serious bling round his neck he looked very normal. Not that she was sure what princes were meant to look like.

'How do you do, Fleur?' The prince's accent was pure Eton.

The music stopped and DJ Rev's cockney tones came through the microphone. 'Evening, ladies and gents. I hope we're all having a good time tonight.'

Fleur took the opportunity to grab another flute of champagne off a passing waiter.

'Careful,' Beau told her. 'You're lethal enough on those heels as it is.'

'I'll just have to rely on you to catch me, then,' she said flirtily. He raised a quizzical eyebrow. DJ Rev started stirring the crowd up.

'Now listen, people! I know rumours have been flying about our special guests tonight. Coldplay, Mick and the boys, someone's even mooted the resurrection of Michael Jackson.'

The crowd cheered. 'Michael, I love you!' a woman cried.

'RIP, Michael, you legend.' DJ Rev bowed up to the sky. 'I'm happy to tell you however, that the next act is very much alive and kicking. Ladies and gents, put your hands together for The Cavalry!'

A corner of the garden that had been out of bounds all night suddenly lit up like a fireworks show. The Cavalry appeared, framed in a white stage that was meant to look like a photo frame. For the next thirty minutes they played all their hits, including a world premiere of their new single. The jaded crowd went wild, Fleur included. She'd never seen or heard anything so incredible.

Afterwards the band came over to see Beau and they all hugged Fleur, increasing her cachet amongst the other partygoers. Jonny Faro, the lead singer, sporting a new tattoo and an amazing quiff, put his arm round her.

'What did you think of the set?'

She couldn't believe he was asking her. 'You were amazing!'

The lead singer grinned. 'Right answer. Make sure you talk to our manager and get tickets for our next gig.'

For the thousandth time that night, she had to ask herself if this was really happening.

As The Cavalry were led off to speak to the press, Beau came back over to get her. 'Having fun?' he asked.

'It's been the most incredible night of my life,' she said. 'I don't want it to end!'

A furious voice cut across the chatter. 'So this is where you are. If I wasn't such a fucking hot property, Beau, I'd think you were avoiding me.'

Fleur went cold. Valentina had materialized in front of them like an avenging demon.

Chapter 57

Valentina's eyes were hostile and black. One of her wings of eyeliner had smudged, giving her the appearance of a sinister clown.

Beau didn't miss a beat. 'V, darling. How are you?'

'As if you care!' she hissed. 'I thought you were busy. Why did you lie to me?'

'I didn't lie to anyone.'

Valentina swayed on the spot. 'I demand an explanation!'

Conversations screeched to a halt around them. This was a stand-off people didn't want to miss.

Beau eyed Valentina coolly. 'I wasn't planning on coming. It was a last-minute thing.'

'You still had time to invite *her.*' Valentina glared at Fleur. 'What, you're buying her a new wardrobe now? Making her into one of your little Beau clones?'

He checked his Rolex. 'We should get going,' he told Fleur.

'You can't be serious,' Valentina said. 'You're screwing that over me?'

'Shut it, V.' His voice was pure ice. 'Shall we?' he asked Fleur. 'This party has suddenly become very boring.'

Valentina put a hand on his arm. 'Beau,' she pleaded. 'Why you do this to me?'

Her accent had suddenly become a lot stronger. Fleur watched, transfixed, as a thin red line of blood trickled out of Valentina's right nostril.

'Baby, I love you. Please come back.'

Beau gazed into the supermodel's eyes. 'The only thing you love are your Class As. If you carry on this way, your lovely looks aren't going to last long.' He shook Valentina's hand off him. 'Let's be honest, sweetheart, you've not got much else going for you.'

Her face collapsed like a soufflé. 'You bastard!' Bursting into tears, she fled, leaving a trail of open-mouthed onlookers in her wake.

Fleur stood there in shock. She actually felt *sorry* for Valentina.

'I have no intention of becoming the latest "Bystander" gossip,' Beau told her. 'Let's get out of here.'

Fleur was very quiet on the journey out of London.

'What's up with you?' Beau asked. They were in his Mustang, Beau flagrantly breaking speed limits as they hammered towards the M40. He'd obviously not drunk much, like Fleur.

'Did you have to talk to her that way?' she asked.

'Who?'

'Valentina. You really humiliated her.'

He raised an eyebrow. 'I didn't have you down as a fan.'

'I'm not.' She looked out of the window. 'I just thought you could have handled it better.'

Fleur heard him sigh. 'Valentina's big enough to look after herself. I only told her the truth. If she doesn't get a handle on her drugs consumption, her modelling career is going down the pan. She's pissed off enough people already.'

'Wow,' she said softly. 'I wouldn't want to be one of your enemies.'

They continued back towards Beeversham. Beau put an album on that she didn't recognize and turned it up, loud. She sat beside him, feeling drunk and confused. He hadn't touched her all night, but she was sure there was chemistry. The image she suddenly had of Beau's big, bronzed body pressing down on hers made her stomach lurch.

The car zoomed through a deserted Beeversham and up into the valley. She glanced at his face again, but his eyes were still fixed ahead on the road.

The entrance gates for Ridings were coming up. She was crushed with disappointment as the car drove past. He was going to take her straight home, but she didn't want that. She wanted him to take her in his arms and have his way with her . . .

'Stop the car!' she cried. 'Stop now!'

The Mustang screeched to a halt in the middle of the road. 'What the hell?' Beau exclaimed. 'Are you OK?'

She lunged clumsily at him. 'Take me back to yours and make love to me!'

'Woah!' He held Fleur back with iron wrists.

'Don't you want me?' she asked breathlessly.

'Sweetheart.' Very gently, he placed her hands back in her lap.

'But isn't this what you want?' she stammered. 'The clothes, the helicopter, I thought that was you seducing me.'

'Fleur. Jesus.' He ran a hand through his hair. 'I just thought you needed a nice night out.'

'You felt sorry for me?' she said in horror.

'Of course not!'

Mortified, she shrank against the window. 'Take me home please,' she said tightly.

The rest of the journey passed in excruciating silence. Fleur couldn't even look at him. She had the door open before the car had even stopped.

'Thank you for a nice evening,' she said stiffly.

'Fleur, wait,' he said, but she was already sprinting across the yard towards the house.

Chapter 58

Catherine's masterclass in political PR was not a great success. Victoria Henley-Coddington from Conservative Party Central Campaign Headquarters rocked up at the Crescent in an ancient old Saab. Refusing offers of drink and food, she'd chain-smoked out of the patio door whilst laying down the law.

'You're one of us now,' she told Catherine. 'The press are out to destroy you, no matter what. Your worst nightmare is being misquoted; don't even take a breath without having a tape recorder on you. It's the best defence against them that you have.'

'You make it sound like I'm going into battle,' Catherine joked.

Victoria didn't smile. 'What else do you think this is?'

They moved on to something called 'opposition research'.

'It's basically a nice way of describing the dirt people can dig up about you, yah?' Victoria said. 'Of course, we're at an advantage in that everyone knows your past, but are there any more skeletons lurking in your closet?'

'I don't think so,' Catherine said, desperately thinking. Parking tickets didn't count, did they?

'You kiss goodbye to any dignity or privacy when you enter politics,' Victoria barked. 'What you love, who you hate, how you take your coffee, where you shop, even what position you have sex in the morning; it's all up for grabs.' She plucked at a split fingernail for the tenth time in as many minutes. 'You think you can handle that, Catherine, yah?'

Catherine gulped. 'Yah. I mean, yeah.'

Her trepidation increased when she phoned Nadia Cohen that evening, the straight-talking Tory MP for West Icklesford. It was hard to hear Nadia over the crying in the background.

'I've had to miss parents' evening for the third time this year. My kids' teachers are on the verge of calling social services.' She broke off to screech at someone. 'No, Theo! The RED one!'

'Sorry about that,' she said, coming back on the phone. 'Where were we?'

'Your workload.' Catherine was starting to feel dizzy.

'Yup, it's full-on. I'm on call twenty-four seven and my constituents are pretty demanding.' Nadia laughed. 'Westminster is like a holiday camp in comparison!'

Catherine didn't say anything.

'You married?' Nadia asked.

'Er, yes.'

'Uh-oh, that won't last long! Most don't.'

'I'm hoping mine will,' Catherine said weakly.

'That's what I said, ha ha! Mind you, it's not as if I miss it. I haven't got time to go to the loo these days, let alone have a love life.'

That won't last long. Nadia's words were chiming through Catherine's head as she climbed up the steps of Beeversham's Conservative Association the next morning. Pausing at the top, Catherine had a strong desire to flee to Bar 47 and seek solace in a large glass of wine. There was no such escape. Taking a deep breath, she went in.

The entrance hall had a faded grandeur and the musty air of a place not used very often. A large board was on one wall, tacked up with old election posters and memos from as far back as 2003. On the other wall was a grim portrait of a stern man in black with white whiskers. His expression was thunderous, as if to say, *You've got no right to be here.*

There were no signs of life around the place. She was getting out her phone to call Felix when a door opened at the end of the corridor and he stuck his head out. 'Ah, there you are, Catherine.'

'Hi, Felix. Sorry if I'm late.'

'Not at all, we're early.' He came to guide her back down the corridor. 'How are you feeling?'

'Pretty nervous,' she confessed.

'Nothing to be nervous about,' he reassured. 'Come in, everyone's looking forward to meeting you.'

His smile was slightly strained. Her nerves went into overdrive.

The meeting room had the same stale air as the entrance, fused with the woody scent of cigar smoke.

Catherine looked at the group of men sitting round the leather-topped table.

'Gentlemen, I have the great pleasure of introducing Catherine Connor,' Felix told them.

'Hello, everyone,' she said brightly. Two of the faces were vaguely familiar, but it was common knowledge that most members of Beeversham's Conservative Association liked to spend more time on the golf course than anywhere else.

Felix gestured to the stiff, upright man on his right. 'This is Charles Knatchbull, our long-standing secretary and one-time RAF wing commander.'

'Three Squadron,' Charles boomed, crushing Catherine's hand in his grip. He had the kind of whiskers not seen since Lord Cardigan had led the Charge of the Light Brigade at the Battle of Balaclava.

'And this is Aubrey Taunton-Brown, our very efficient treasurer.'

Aubrey was younger than the others, the pink Pringle sweater clashing horribly with his ginger comb-over. 'Delighted,' he said silkily. 'I was wondering when we'd be meeting the great saviour of the Conservative Party.'

She looked at his small eyes and mean mouth and knew instantly they'd be enemies.

Felix pulled out a chair for her before carrying on with the introductions. 'Our deputy chairman is recovering from a stroke, so this is pretty much it. Aside from our legion of gallant helpers, of course. Some of them are coming down to meet you here afterwards.'

Charles Knatchbull was staring at her as if she'd just fallen off a passing spacecraft. 'You really are a woman?'

'Last time I looked in the mirror,' she said dryly.

'As you know, I'm electing Catherine to run as our candidate,' Felix said. 'We've got two weeks to get her ready and nail our campaign. The PM has pledged us his support, and will be following with close interest.'

'Extraordinary,' Aubrey Taunton-Brown murmured.

Felix shot him a look. 'Of course, Catherine can count on our full support here.'

'Our full support,' Aubrey said. 'I'm extremely keen to hear your policies.'

This was her chance to win them over. She cleared her throat. 'Obviously I'll be going big on planning laws and Ye Olde Worlde.'

'As will everyone,' Aubrey told her. 'You can't risk getting stuck on a single issue.'

'That's a fair point,' she said. 'I know the Conservatives are big on stuff like law and order, but I want to appeal to a wider spectrum. I guess you already know my history with domestic violence charities.'

From the looks she was getting she might as well have been talking in Mandarin. 'I also want to go big on youth unemployment,' she said, ploughing on. 'I don't know if you've heard of Soirée Sponsors, the charity I started up for kids in inner cities.'

'I can't imagine you'll find many of those ASBO hoodies round here.' Aubrey smiled nastily at her.

'Young people can be unemployed anywhere,' she smiled back. 'Then there're the issues facing women in the workplace. Under this current government the pay gap between the sexes is nearly 20 per cent and men still dominate at boardroom level. It's crazy we're putting up with such sexism in this day and age.' We also need to introduce more flexi-hours, decent maternity packages and affordable childcare.'

'Oh God.' Charles groaned. 'We've got ourselves a bloody feminist.'

'What's wrong with that?' she asked nicely.

'You'll be chuntering on about women's rights the whole time! What about the rights of us men?'

Felix stepped in. 'I think what Catherine is trying to say is that as well as promoting our core policies she's keen to expand on certain areas of society that, historically, we haven't had the strongest rapport with. Isn't that right, Catherine?'

She gave him a relieved smile.

'You'll be laughed out of town,' Aubrey sniffed. 'People don't care about that kind of stuff round here. You need to be hot on council tax and inheritance tax; the farmers will expect you to know the price of a tonne of wheat. Not whether some yobbo is rewarded for throwing a brick through someone else's window.'

'I think that's a little unfair,' she said icily.

Aubrey examined a polished fingernail. 'Not to me.'

'I thought that went very well,' Felix said afterwards.

'It was a disaster,' Catherine wailed. 'Aubrey hates me.' *He's a disgusting chauvanistic dinosaur*, she wanted to add.

'Aubrey just takes a bit of time to come round. He was big chums with Jonty, believes things should be done a certain way.' Felix looked doubtful. 'Although to be honest with you, I'm not sure he's capable of accepting a female candidate.'

She sighed. 'Remind me again. What the hell am I doing here?'

'Don't give up at the first hurdle,' he told her. 'Now come along. There're some people I want you to meet.'

Catherine followed him through another door into a long, rather gloomy office. There was a dusty computer in the corner and piles of paperwork everywhere.

'Catherine, this is Clive and Kitty Anderson.'

Neither of them could have been more than five foot tall. Despite the heat of the day, they were both wearing matching windbreakers and round Harry Potter-style glasses. They could have been anything between thirty and seventy; it was impossible to tell.

'Delighted to meet you,' Clive squeaked.

Kitty shook her hand enthusiastically. 'I loved *Cathy: My Story*. I cried all the way through.'

Clive nodded. 'Kept me up past half past nine every night for a week.'

'Clive and Kitty will be your eyes and ears,' Felix told Catherine. 'I'll be keeping the home fires burning, but the campaigners are the ones who are with you every day, when you're out tramping the streets. They're up at five a.m. with you, and out until eleven p.m., even later sometimes. They're an integral part of your team.'

'We love a by-election!' Clive piped up.

'For the council elections we delivered over twenty thousand leaflets!' Kitty said.

'Hand-delivered,' Clive said proudly.

Catherine looked at this funny bespectacled pair who barely reached her shoulder. After the horror of Audrey and co., her saviours had come in the most unlikely of forms.

339

Chapter 59

Fleur was still utterly mortified. Her botched seduction of Beau was on a torturous loop in her mind. He had tried ringing a few times, but she hadn't picked up. How could she have misjudged the situation so badly? *I offered myself on a plate to Beau Rainford and he didn't want me.* Fleur froze with horror every time she thought about it. She never wanted to see him ever again.

A black mood hung over the house. Robert Blackwater had shut himself away in his study and wouldn't even come out for meals, let alone to help her with the farm. She was at the end of her tether. Briefly, she'd pondered ringing Felix, but he had enough going on with the election. She didn't feel like she could go to her sister – Claire had her own life. And Fleur was still too proud to accept Beau's offer of rehab, especially now. Besides, she knew there was no way her dad would ever go along with it.

I'm at the helm of a sinking ship, she thought desperately. The rocks – the repercussions if they didn't meet the bank-loan deadline – were looming in the distance.

The clock told her it was dinner time. She wandered listlessly over to the fridge. A tub of Flora and some dehydrated cheddar looked back at her. She didn't have much of an appetite, anyway.

A bat swooped across the window. She looked up, the dogs were quiet tonight. Normally she'd hear them snuffling round, and pulling at their chains.

Oh shit. Had she remembered to put their chains on? She was losing it. She shut the fridge and rushed outside.

'Dogs?' She whistled. 'Tinker? Bess?'

Tinker came trotting out of one of the sheds. 'There you are, boy,' she said. 'Where's your sister?'

The dog sat on its haunches as if to say, *Don't ask me.*

The track outside the yard was empty. 'Bollocks,' she muttered. Bess was a terror when it came to going off.

She spent five minutes whistling fruitlessly, and was just starting to envisage an all-night search party when a black shape came rustling through the field.

'There you are!' she said in relief as Bess gambolled over. 'Where have you been?'

There was something hanging round the dog's neck. She bent down to get a proper look. Someone had tied a purple ribbon there. Even weirder, there was a little silver barrel hanging off her collar. Bess had to know whoever had put it on; she was funny about people going near her head.

She examined the barrel. There was a piece of white paper inside with a handwritten message.

Seeing as you don't want to see me, I've gone through the dogs instead. We need to talk. Dinner at mine. Beau.

Astonished, she looked round, but he was nowhere

to be seen. How the hell had he done this? She glanced down at the note again.

We need to talk. It sounded ominous. No kiss at the end, either.

She was setting herself up for another fall, but the desire to see Beau, even just one last time, was overwhelming.

Racing back inside, she headed for the shower.

Ridings was lit up like a lighthouse when Fleur drove up thirty minutes later. An unfamiliar Golf was parked round the side. Her heart sank. She couldn't handle any more of Beau's stuck-up friends.

She rang the doorbell and stepped back. Her heartbeat was slow and painful. The dress she'd chosen to wear was an insane choice. She should have worn something smarter.

After what seemed like an age the door opened and Beau stood before her, taller and more handsome than ever. He was obviously fresh out of the shower, damp blond hair slicked back off the fine planes of his face. He was wearing a simple grey T-shirt and chino shorts, his elegant brown feet bare. Her stomach did a slow somersault.

'Hello, you,' he said.

'Hi. I brought this.' She held up the bottle of Blossom Hill.

'Thank you, darling.' He took it off her and kissed her on the cheek. She caught a waft of body heat and citrus aftershave and felt her stomach flip over again.

He gave her his lovely smile. 'It's good to see you, Fleur.'

*

He took her straight out to the pool, where the table had been laid for two. She sat down and watched as he went over to the bar to mix her a drink. A beautiful sunset glowed overhead.

'Have we got company?' she called.

He came back with two clear cocktails and handed her one. 'No, why do you ask?'

'I saw a Golf outside.'

'Ah, that's Sergio's car. He's my chef.'

'We've got a chef cooking us dinner?'

He flopped down in the chair opposite. 'Well, you are a very special guest.'

She was becoming more confused by the second. Was this meant to be a nice send-off? She took an overly large sip of her drink and started coughing.

'Careful,' Beau said. 'I like my martinis strong.'

She surreptiously wiped her eyes. 'How did you know I'd come?'

'Of course you were going to come. I told Bess not to take no for an answer.'

'She's wary of strangers, I'm surprised you got near her.'

'My methods are simple but effective. Fillet steak.'

Fleur gave an appalled giggle. 'You fed my dog fillet steak?'

'The very best. Be warned, she's had a taste of the high life now.'

'You can pay for it when she won't eat anything else.'

Beau grinned. 'Deal.'

A man in chef's whites was walking up the side of the pool towards them. Beau sat up. 'Ah, the first course is served.'

It was moules marinière, followed by the biggest, fattest langoustines she had ever seen, swimming in garlic butter. Beau produced a bottle of white wine that danced on her tongue, and slipped down her throat like a silken waterfall.

The food was sublime and the wine even better, but she was still on edge. Why was she here? He had made it clear he wasn't interested in her, yet here she was being wined and dined. *He's letting me down gently*, Fleur thought miserably. Was she really that much of a sympathy case?

He was telling her about his chef. 'Sergio's from the Amalfi Coast. He's an absolute maestro. I stole him from some friends of mine. They weren't very happy.'

'Do all rich people have a chef?' she asked.

'I don't know, Fleur. You tell me.'

'I'm not the one born with a silver spoon in my mouth.'

He rolled his eyes. 'Of course, Beau Rainford, the spoilt little prince. Never had to want for anything.'

His answer intrigued her. 'Aren't you?' she asked. 'You don't exactly do much to dispel the rumours.'

He looked momentarily devilish again. 'Oh, I've lived up to most of the others, don't worry.'

Why didn't Beau care if people thought badly of him? 'Don't you want people to know who you really are?' she asked.

'Not really.' In the fading half-light his eyes were navy. 'Who do you think I am?'

'I don't think you're as bad as you make out,' she said carefully.

The night seemed to hold its breath. Even the gentle

breeze had stopped blowing. She could hear the slosh-ing of her heart alongside the gentle *slap, slap* of water against the pool edge.

'I'm sorry you got upset the other night,' he told her. 'I didn't mean it to end like that.' He gave a wry smile. 'I mean, I do know how I'd have liked it to have ended. You probably won't believe me when I say this, but I have too much respect for you.'

It was the answer she was least expecting. 'But . . .' She trailed off. 'I thought you just felt sorry for me.'

'God, Fleur,' he said quietly. 'Will you stop putting yourself down?'

He got up and came to sit right beside her. 'Listen here, OK? I think you're funny and adorable and brave and prickly.' He smoothed a strand of hair off her face, holding it between his fingers. 'And I love this. I love the way you stand up for yourself, yet you still blush a hundred times a minute.'

'I do not!' she protested, blushing violently.

'Fleur, look at me.' He tipped her chin up and made her look at him. 'I don't feel sorry for you. I admire you. It's a hell of a task to run that farm. I know how diffi-cult your life is.'

'I'm OK,' she mumbled.

'You keep saying that, sweetheart,' he said gently. 'But every time I look at you, I just want to gather you up in my arms and look after you.'

Unexpected tears sprang into her eyes.

'Oh Christ, I didn't mean to upset you,' he said.

'It's fine.' She blinked the tears away. 'It's not that often that people get where I'm coming from.'

'I mean it,' he told her. 'You're a hell of a girl.'

345

Her hands started to tremble. She put her glass down.

'Oh, sweetheart, what are we going to do?' he said soulfully. 'All I know is that I want to tell you things I've never told anyone before. You have the most extraordinary effect on me. I feel like a schoolboy around you.'

'Take me to bed,' she whispered.

'Are you sure? I don't want to pressure you into anything.'

'I've never been more sure of anything in my life.'

He leant in and planted the softest kiss on her lips. 'We can take this as slow as you like. You don't have to do anything you don't want.'

She found herself melting into him, insubstantial against Beau's powerful body. Fleur knew then that he was capable of loving and hurting her in equal measure.

Beau's bedroom was white, minimal, an entire wall taken up by one window. The moon had come out, bathing the room in luminous light.

She stood in the doorway clutching his hand. 'Don't be frightened,' he told her.

He led her over to the bed and laid her down with infinite care. As he lay down beside her and started kissing her, Fleur felt like her whole body had come alive. Their kissing got harder and frantic. He rolled on top of her, pinning her to the bed. She could feel his erection pressing into her body.

A moment later he pulled away, panting slightly.

'Have I done something wrong?' she asked anxiously.

'Quite the opposite.' He blinked and shook his head. 'Let's try again, shall we?'

He started kissing her again more slowly. 'Do you have these freckles everywhere?' Beau murmured, planting a line of heavenly kisses along Fleur's collarbone.

'N-not everywhere.' Her nipples had whipped up into hard peaks, the throbbing now a drumming between her legs.

When he tried to take her dress off Fleur froze. 'It's OK, we don't have to do anything you don't want to,' he told her.

'It's not that.' She looked away miserably.

Beau pushed himself up so his forearms were either side of her. 'What is it, then?'

'I'm s-shy.' She stuttered horribly on the last word. 'A-about my body.'

'Sweetheart, you have nothing to be shy about. You have a fantastic body. In fact, I'm banning you from ever wearing another piece of shapeless clothing again.'

'I hate my boobs,' she said miserably.

'What?' He looked down at them. 'Your boobs are amazing.'

'No they're not. They're too big.'

'Let me be the judge of that.' He started to tug her dress gently over her head.

'This matronly bra isn't doing them any favours,' he said, sliding a hand round her back to undo the clasp. He pulled the bra off and her boobs fell out, full and heavy. He pushed them up in his hands, the spare flesh pooling through his fingers. 'You're beautiful and they're beautiful. You have nothing to worry about.'

He started fingering a rosy pink nipple between long tanned fingers. It grew even stiffer.

'God, you're gorgeous,' he said.

As he sat back to pull off his T-shirt, Fleur had the weirdest sensation: as if she was a spectator looking in, watching it happen to somebody else. Was Beau really straddled above her, body hard and magnificent, beautiful face full of intent?

Tentatively she reached up and ran a hand across the corrugated-iron stomach. He moved deftly out of his chino shorts, revealing long, muscular thighs. There was a definite swell of penis in the tight white pants. She had a moment of panic. It looked *really* big.

He lay back next to her and put a warm hand on her quivering belly.

'Relax, sweetheart.'

He started to kiss her again, tongue pushing into her mouth, teeth tugging on her lower lip. They kissed and kissed until Fleur wasn't sure where she started and he ended. She desperately wanted him to touch her. Finally, just as she was about to spontaneously combust, his hand slid down her stomach into her knickers.

'Christ, you're soaking.'

'Oh!' she breathed as Beau's fingers slid down on her clitoris and started to rub gently. It was the most amazing thing she'd ever experienced.

Next her knickers were pulled off and thrown off into the darkness.

'Don't stop!' she panted, when he eventually looked up from between her legs.

'I have no intention of stopping.' Reaching up to the bedside table, he opened the drawer. Fleur saw the metallic flash of a condom packet. Her stomach rolled over.

He wriggled out of his pants and his cock sprang out. It was so big Fleur gave an involuntary giggle.

He raised an amused eyebrow. 'Is something funny?'

'I-I'm sorry. I always laugh when I'm nervous.'

He silenced her with his mouth, and she had the disturbingly erotic sensation of tasting herself for the first time. Sweet, yet musky. Like freshly cut hay, she randomly thought.

His energy had changed into something hungry and expectant. He nudged her legs apart with his knee. 'Oh, Fleur,' he said into her ear. 'You've no idea how much I want this.'

She was pinned under his weight. She couldn't move. The tip of his penis was pressing into her. Any moment now.

'I'm a virgin,' she whispered. It was so quiet she didn't know if he'd heard.

He sat up like a shot. 'What?'

'T-this is my first time.'

'Sweetheart, you should have said something.' He looked stunned.

'I-I didn't want to put you off,' she said miserably. 'All the women you've slept with must have been amazing in bed.'

'Don't be so silly.' He shook his head. 'You've never had a boyfriend?'

'I did sort of, but I never went all the way with him.' She wanted to cry; she'd ruined everything! 'I'm sorry.'

'What the hell are you sorry about?'

'For being a virgin.'

'Oh, Fleur.' He half laughed. 'I'm sorry for coming on too strong,' he told her, stroking her cheek.

'You didn't!' She clung on to him. 'Please, I really want this.'

He gazed into her eyes for what seemed the longest time. 'You sure?'

'I'm sure.'

'OK. I'll take it nice and slow.' Repositioning himself, very slowly, he pushed himself in her. As a sharp pain shot through her, she gave an involuntary gasp.

He looked worried. 'Am I hurting you?'

'Yes, but in a nice way.'

'How about if I do this?' He moved out and in again, super-gently.

'That's lovely.' It was still painful, but in the most exquisite way. He started rocking back and forward, getting her used to him.

It took a few minutes to find their rhythm. He was a patient, tender instructor who took things at her speed. 'How about that? Is that nice?' he asked constantly. 'Wrap your legs round my back, sweetheart, you'll feel it deeper then. Is that too much? Wow, you feel amazing. This is incredible, angel.'

'It is?' She couldn't believe she was having amazing sex!

'You have no idea. Hold on, I want to see you on top.'

Next moment, she was sitting astride him. He smiled at her; taut and tanned against the white sheets. He took hold of her hips, rocking her back and forth. 'Does this feel good?'

'Amazing!' The momentum started to build up

again. She started grinding against him, chasing the hot, tight, exciting feeling.

'Don't stop, sweetheart.' He gripped her by the hips, driving her on him.

'Oh God!' Fleur cried, as the most amazing feeling burst through her body. Exhilarated, she flopped down on his chest. The world had changed. *She* had changed.

Beau looked delighted. 'You were spectacular, sweetheart.'

'But you haven't had yours yet.'

He kissed her again. 'Don't worry, we've only just started.'

Chapter 60

It had been agreed that it would be best to hold off announcing Catherine's name until the last minute, giving her much-needed time to prepare. Meanwhile, debate raged about who would run. For the first time ever in that part of England, anti-Tory feeling was at a high. People were fed up with the government, fed up with Jonty, and fed up with the country going to the dogs. Catherine got the feeling that any articles about the Conservative candidate being thrown to the wolves were being skilfully whisked out of her way.

Charles Knatchbull was still treating her as if she was a member of an alien race, but the worst was Aubrey Taunton-Brown. Anti-modern, anti-change, he was a vile snob of a man who'd made it clear he thought Catherine had no place running in the election. Just as bad was his horrific wife, Viola. A scrawny cordon-bleu chef, she came by the Conservative Association HQ to give Aubrey his vitamin tablets and drop snide comments about how women shouldn't be Members of Parliament.

Thank God for Felix. Placatory, diplomatic, stepping in to calm Catherine down when she was on the verge of losing it. The only thing they had disagreed on was the campaign's official slogan. She wanted something fresh and modern. He had told her she couldn't run the risk of alienating people. They'd finally decided on the rather unimaginative 'Vote Connor', but as he had said, at least it did what it said on the tin.

As her campaign manager, Felix was the man in charge. He was the one drumming up funds from party donors, deciding which areas she'd be canvassing and the local 'meet and greets' she'd go to. He was also in charge of fielding all press enquiries and liaising with the national Conservative Party. If central government announced a new policy, or something controversial like cutting welfare, Catherine would be expected to know which line to take. From being a complete amateur, she was now supposed to be an expert on the political system.

Aside from Tristan Jago, three other candidates had already been announced. The Lib Dems were putting forward Helen Singh, a rising young star in the party. There were also two independents running: a pagan witch called Esme Santura who was campaigning to get an astrologer appointed in central government, and William 'Bill' Fairclough, a retired colonel who had a manic eye twitch and an even more manic desire to bring back capital punishment. It was still widely assumed that Tristan, super-hot on local issues, had it in the bag.

If Catherine had let herself think about it, she would have died of terror. Instead she threw herself into the job, making Kitty and Clive give her geography tests on every town, village and hamlet in the constituency. She memorized the names of influential farmers, shopkeepers, WI members; people who could win or lose the campaign for her. It was exhausting and overwhelming but she was beginning to feel alive. It was inspiring being part of a team again who wanted to bring about change.

On the downside, she had barely seen her husband. Away at the crack of dawn, not returning until late, they were like two ships that passed in the night. Dinner, if they had it together, was on laps in front of the television, because all the surfaces were taken up with paperwork as she frantically tried to cram every policy and piece of legislation that had been implemented in the last twenty years.

They were being civil to each other, but their relationship lacked the intimate familiarity of before. Catherine knew she'd messed up, but her pride wouldn't let her explain to John that she'd wanted to prove that she could do something by herself. He was clearly still angry she'd gone behind his back. Both were obstinate and strong-willed and neither was willing to back down.

'So what's he like, then?'

Catherine looked at her husband across the table. 'Who?'

'Your new mate the Prime Minister.'

She forked up a mouthful of pasta. 'You can see what he's like on television.'

'I meant in person. You've spent quite a lot of time on the phone to him.'

'No, I haven't.' She felt herself becoming defensive. 'What does that even mean, anyway?'

'It means nothing, Cath. Unless it should?'

'For God's sake!' She laughed awkwardly. 'What are you insinuating? He's a happily married man!'

He gave her one of those hard looks that she seemed to be increasingly on the end of, and went back to eating his dinner. 'I had my meeting in London with Jeff.'

'Shit, sorry. I completely forgot! How did it go?'

'Good. Jeff won the bid.' He put his fork down. 'He wants me to go out to Costa Rica with him and take a look.'

'Oh, right,' she said neutrally. 'Are you going to go?'

He gave a shrug. 'I'm thinking about it.'

'It might be worth it, seeing as I'm going to be tied up for a while.'

They exchanged a polite smile across the table. *This is all wrong*, she thought.

She put down her fork. 'Do you actually have any faith I might win?'

'I think you're capable of anything, Cath,' he said carefully. 'What I'm worried about is that these people are using you. I don't think you're strong enough to deal with something like this at the moment.'

'I am used to dealing with people. I edited a major magazine in case you'd forgotten.'

'Of course I haven't forgotten.'

He was still speaking in that slow tone, as if she were a small child. 'God, John! Why do you always make me feel so useless?'

'Jesus, why do you take everything the wrong way?

You're not yourself, you haven't been for a long time, as I think even you would agree. Now, the hopes of the nation are being put on your shoulders. I'm just asking you to think, really think about what you're doing. I'm worried about you.' He paused. 'I'm worried about us.'

'Do you think I've made the wrong decision?'

'Yes, I do,' he said bluntly. 'I think you need to concentrate on you, Cath, not this hare-brained idea of being the saviour of Beeversham. Go and see someone, get better, and then go out and do whatever you want. I'll back you all the way.'

Catherine, exhausted, stressed, terrified he was right, went on the attack again. 'Why can't you just be happy for me? I'm sick of the way you always treat me like a victim. You've always treated me like a victim, John. Does it make you feel better about yourself or something?'

She knew instantly she'd gone too far.

His chair went flying as he got up. 'That is the most fucking insulting thing you could ever say to me.'

'I didn't mean it, I'm sorry.'

'Jesus Christ, Cath.' He walked out in disgust.

She was left at the table, tears streaming down her face. Why was she jeopardizing the most important thing in her life?

The following day came the shock announcement that Catherine Connor, ex-magazine editor and bestselling author of *Cathy: My Story*, was running as the Conservative candidate in Beeversham's by-election. 'We're extremely pleased to have Catherine running for us,' Felix said in the official statement. The Prime Minister's endorsement was even more resounding. 'She's a bright star, a face for the future, and a huge asset to the Conservative Party,' he told the assorted press outside Downing Street. 'There's only one thing left to say: vote Connor!'

Chapter 61

'Have you seen this?'

Vanessa looked up from her BlackBerry. Her husband was in the corner of the room getting a foot rub from the make-up artist. He shook the front page of the *Daily Telegraph* at her. The headline was about Catherine Connor running as the surprise candidate for the Beeversham by-election. There was also a box-out on Catherine's career and the Crimson Killer case.

Actually, Vanessa wasn't that surprised. Catherine had always been fanatically campaigning for one issue or the other when she'd edited *Soirée*. The woman just loved being in the thick of it.

'What's her manifesto going to be?' Conrad continued. 'Picking off the entire constituency one by one? God, they must be desperate!' He flashed a smile at the young make-up artist. 'Careful, sweetheart, I've got sensitive arches. Ballet dancer's feet, I've been told.'

Their *OK!* 'at home' shoot was actually taking place at an oligarch's mansion in south-west London. The house was full of people. As well as the journalist, there was the picture editor, the art director, the fashion editor, the fashion editor's assistant, the photographer and the photographer's assistant. Outside caterers had been brought in to provide lunch; they didn't want to mess up the spotless kitchen.

The Powells had brought their entourage: Vanessa's hair and make-up person, Marty, Tamzin and their PR guru Simon Ferrari, who was conducting the couple's four-week press campaign before the Silver Box Awards.

Tamzin came in with a Starbucks tray. 'Coffees are here.' She handed Vanessa an Americano and took the other cup over to Conrad.

'Skinny decaf dry cappuccino with sugar-free hazelnut syrup?' he said, without looking up from his BlackBerry.

'Yes, Conrad.'

He stuck his hand out. 'No organic cinnamon dusting?'

'No, Conrad.'

Vanessa gave Tamzin a sympathetic smile. She was a sweet girl. Not for the first time, she thought how lucky they were to have her as their PA.

The kitchen shoot was first. Vanessa went off to get changed. The fashion editor pulled out a pair of white jeans and a turquoise silk vest. 'I thought we could try these. With the wedge espadrilles. It's very summery and "kitcheny".'

'"Kitcheny"?' Vanessa repeated.

'Yes, you know, "kitcheny".' The woman looked a bit panicked. 'The whole domestic goddess thing.'

'Fine,' Vanessa sighed. 'Let's go for kitcheny.'

Conrad's hair and make-up took so long they were late getting started. Terry Johnston, the fabulously flamboyant photographer, soon got them going.

'Conrad, look into Vanessa's eyes! If you can both hold the knife. Conrad, put your hand over Vanessa's like that – perfect! Now give me your best smiles. Gorgeous!'

Next up was the two of them lovingly reading copies of *OK!* in the opulent living room. Vanessa changed into knee-length Missoni, while Conrad was in a seductively unbuttoned shirt and Italian loafers, Ralph Lauren jeans rolled up just enough to show off his fine ankles. Sukie, fragrant and fluffy after a special fifty-pound trim and blow-dry, was brought in to sit on Vanessa's lap.

Vanessa's make-up artist reapplied another layer of lip gloss. 'And that's for you, darling,' she said, touching Sukie's button nose with her powder brush. 'Can't have you looking all shiny.'

Terry started snapping again. 'Conrad, if you stare at the page, and Vanessa, giggle, as if you're pointing something out. Beautiful!'

A restless Sukie shoved her nose in Conrad's crotch. 'Conrad, pick Sukie up,' Terry said. 'Perfect! Adorable!'

'You breathe on me, mutt, and you're history,' Conrad beamed through gritted teeth.

The dining room was next, with the couple lounging languorously in evening wear at a table to sit thirty. Afterwards they went to change into matching bathrobes for the bedroom scene. Though she normally had an iron stamina for shoots, Vanessa's head was starting to throb. It was a relief when Terry called a wrap and they stopped for lunch.

Marty found Vanessa wandering barefoot round the end of the garden, Sukie in her arms. 'They want to start the interview,' he said.

'OK. Just give me a minute.'

Marty glanced at her. 'You all right, kid?'

Vanessa had spent the last ten minutes sobbing quietly into her dog's fur. 'Just a bit of hay fever,' she lied.

'I'll get Tamzin to go out and get something for you.' Marty put his arm round Vanessa. 'Come on.'

They did the interview in the living room, Vanessa and Conrad on opposite ends of the sofa. The journalist was perched awkwardly on a pouffe in front of them.

'You must be so excited about presenting the Silver Box Awards!'

'Oh, extremely excited,' Conrad gushed. 'To host an evening amongst one's peers, it's a tremendous honour.'

'Conrad, obviously you had a very successful four years on the long-running soap *The Saviours*.'

'Four and a half,' he interrupted with a smile.

'Sorry, I meant four and a half.' The journalist looked at her notes. 'Was it a massive disappointment getting dropped from *Mice and Men*?'

Conrad's smile faltered. 'Obviously it wasn't ideal, but it happens to all the greats. Martin Sheen, Gary Oldman, Billy Bob. The director's prerogative is an occupational hazard.'

'Are you hoping Silver Box will resurrect your career?'

He looked pained. 'It's not as though it needs

resurrecting. In fact I was reading an extremely exciting script on the journey in.'

Conrad had spent the entire car journey on the fashion website Mr Porter. 'Yeah, right!' Vanessa scoffed without thinking.

They both looked at her strangely. 'Sorry,' she said. 'I mean, Conrad has been sent some amazing scripts recently. It's a credit to him what an incredible actor he is.'

'Incredible,' the journalist echoed. 'Vanessa and Conrad, you've been happily married for seven years now, and you've built up a multi-million-pound business together. What's your secret to your successful relationship?'

'There's only one secret,' Conrad said, gazing fondly at his wife. 'Love.'

It was gone seven o'clock by the time they got back to Tresco House. The electronic gates swung open to let the Bentley pull in.

Conrad had barely said two words the whole journey. He was out of the car in a flash, disappearing into the house.

Vanessa lifted Sukie out and put her down. The dog raced off after a passing butterfly.

'Thanks, Billy. You can go now.'

The chauffeur nodded. 'Thanks, Mrs Powell.'

She went in and dragged herself upstairs, stopping to look at herself caught in the mirror on the landing. *All I want is Dylan*, she thought, looking at her huge unhappy eyes and defeated shoulders. *I'm trapped in a life I don't want.*

Conrad was standing by the bedroom window as she walked in. Vanessa went over to the dressing table to take her earrings out. 'I thought you were in your study.'

'Can I ask why you did that?' He was gazing outside, watching as if there were something of great interest out there.

She sat down. 'Did what?'

It happened so quickly she had no time to react. He sprang over and grabbed her by the wrists. 'I said, why did you fucking do that to me?'

'What? Conrad, you're hurting me!' She struggled helplessly. 'I don't know what you mean!'

'Yes you do! Embarrassing me like that in front of that journalist. Humiliating me!'

She looked into her husband's ice-cold eyes and became seriously frightened. 'Conrad, I didn't mean it. I know you're frustrated about not getting good scripts at the moment.'

'Do you? What the fuck do you know? How can you know what it's like for me, a *talented* actor, to be associated with any of this shit? I know what people are saying: "Oh, Conrad Powell will put his name to a loo roll if they pay him enough."'

His nails were digging into her. She began to cry. 'Conrad, please.'

'You of all people should support me,' he hissed.

'I do support you!' she wept.

'You've got a funny way of showing it.' His breath was rank, a mixture of the all-protein diet and dark malevolence. 'I'm sick of being married to a miserable cow who shows me fuck-all attention. What is it, darling? Do you prefer girls? Boys? Ladyboys? We can get whoever in if it turns you on.'

She was wearing the most exquisite Erdem dress. She heard the material rip as he yanked it up. 'Conrad! No!'

'You're my wife.' He forced her face down on the bed. 'I'll do what I fucking like.'

It was over in less than a minute. Zipping himself up, he walked out and left her frozen on the bed.

Chapter 62

1 August

Catherine had spent most of the night staring at the ceiling. By 5 a.m. she gave up, sliding out of bed so as not to wake John, who was breathing peacefully beside her.

The first smears of dawn were breaking over the hills. She curled up in the window seat and looked out. A ginger cat slunk across the back lawn, disappearing into the foliage. She gazed after the animal, envying its freedom. In a few hours' time the Beeversham by-election would kick off. For the next three weeks, she wouldn't be able to call her life her own. She would be eating, sleeping, breathing the campaign. In the still, peaceful dawn it was hard to believe such madness lay ahead.

The *Today* programme was on the radio as she walked into the kitchen. *'The campaigning for the hotly anticipated Beeversham by-election starts today . . .'*

Catherine went over and turned it off. She could throw up at any moment.

John was still in his dressing gown, dark chest hair poking out of the top. He came over and handed her a coffee.

'Thank you,' she said. His eyes were distant and devoid of their normal warmth. He was making an effort for her big day, but she knew he was still furious with her.

'How are you feeling?' he asked.

'Pretty sick,' she confessed.

'You need to eat something before you go.'

'John, I just told you I was feeling sick!'

The front doorbell went. She fled the kitchen to answer it. It was a delivery boy clutching a mountain of helium balloons. She read the accompanying card and felt a momentary lift. *Good luck, babe! You've got our vote already. Mel and Mike. Xx.'*

John came down the corridor. 'Someone having a party?'

'More like my funeral.'

Her stomach was churning like a cement mixer. She smoothed down the new navy dress she'd bought online from COS. Chic, but not too expensive. 'How do I look?'

'Good, Cath.'

They eyeballed each other through the balloons. 'Well, then!' she said with a heartiness she didn't feel. 'I'd better get going.'

He put a dry kiss on her cheek. 'Go get 'em.'

*

366

The press were out in force, and Catherine got ambushed on the High Street. Everyone wanted the same questions answered: how nervous was she and was she worried about the legacy of Jonty? 'Dead man's shoes' was how one reporter helpfully put it. By the time Catherine got to Tory HQ fifteen minutes later, she was ready to be sick in her handbag.

Kitty and Clive were waiting expectantly, along with half a dozen leaflet droppers Catherine had nicknamed the 'Blue Rosettes'. She was strangely touched to see them all wearing 'Vote Connor' T-shirts. It was no surprise that Aubrey and co. weren't there, but God bless him, Felix was calm and collected in chinos and an Oxford-blue shirt. 'Sleep well?'

'I slept, if that's what you mean.'

'First-day nerves. You'll be fine once you're out there.' His eyes drifted down to Catherine's Gucci heels. 'Goodness, look at those!'

'We did wonder about them,' Kitty said. 'I've got a spare pair of Crocs in my bag if you want.'

'Don't worry, I can climb mountains in these.'

They left the building armed with 'Vote Connor' leaflets, suncream and bottles of water. The first week of the campaign was to be spent canvassing target areas and meeting as many people as possible. As Catherine was a newcomer, it was vital they got her name out there.

They were going to start on Blackbird Rise, a long road snaking around the southern end of the town. The most densely populated part of Beeversham, it was perfect for hitting up lots of houses.

Catherine's gang turned off the High Street and stopped dead. The road was a sea of red. Posters of

Tristan Jago cuddling the sodding duck were in every house window. An 'I'm Cotswolds and I Care' placard was sticking out of someone's front garden. Tristan might as well have just cocked his leg against every door in the street to mark his territory.

'Rats,' one of the Rosettes muttered. 'They've beaten us to it.'

The man himself was striding towards them, a red rosette the size of a cabbage on his lapel. A photographer was running to keep up in his wake.

'Morning!' Tristan cried. 'Early bird catches the worm and all that.'

'Can we get a picture of the two of you together?' the photographer asked.

Tristan put an arm round Catherine and beamed into the camera. 'May I take this opportunity to wish you all the luck,' he told her. 'We've never had such a novice run before; it must be very daunting for you!'

The rest of Tristan's gang had arrived. They and the Blue Rosettes were facing off in a not entirely friendly fashion. 'Come on, Tristan,' one of them sniffed. 'We've got Cotswold FM at nine a.m.'

'Why aren't I on Cotswolds FM?' Catherine asked Clive as they walked off.

'Let's not run before we can walk,' he told her.

A harassed woman opened the first door, a crying child attached to her leg.

'Hello, I'd like to introduce myself,' Catherine said. 'I'm Catherine Connor, Conservative candidate for Beeversham and . . .'

'I don't do politics.' The woman shut the door in Catherine's face.

The living-room curtains were still drawn in the next house. After knocking for a good minute they were about to give up when the door opened, to reveal a yawning man with long dreadlocks. It immediately became apparent he slept in little more than the tribal tattoos covering 80 per cent of his body. The Blue Rosettes averted their eyes discreetly, as if they'd seen it all before.

'Morning!' Catherine said, desperately trying not to look at the huge piercing hanging out of the man's appendage. 'I'm Catherine Connor, Conservative candidate for Beeversham. I'm passionate about providing a good service, especially in regard to youth unemployment, domestic violence and equal opportunities for women in the workplace.'

The man tugged at his crotch. 'Where do you stand on legalizing weed?'

'Oh.' She blinked. 'Well.' She thought desperately on her feet. 'There is a legitimate debate as to whether we should change our laws. Some critics consider them too draconian.'

There was a collective intake of breath behind her. 'I'll look into it,' she promised the man, handing him a leaflet.

'We can't condone drugs!' Kitty squeaked, once the door had shut. 'We're not the Lib Dems!'

Next door Catherine repeated her spiel. An old man in a Pringle jumper with a West Highland terrier tucked under his arm eyed her suspiciously. 'What about Ye Olde Worlde? You don't care about that, then?'

She was so nervous she'd forgotten to mention the

most important thing. 'Of course!' she said. 'That as well.'

'Poppycock,' the old man said and shut the door in her face.

By lunchtime they'd only covered a fraction of the surrounding streets. People either weren't in, or pretended not to be. Of the ones that did open the door, Catherine now knew more about their haemorrhoids and spastic colons than could ever be healthy. There was no sign of the press; apparently they'd flocked to see Esme Santura the pagan witch conduct a Wicca circle by the church.

Under the unrelenting heat, she began to flag. Worried she wasn't going to make it through the afternoon, Clive and Kitty dragged her in for an emergency foot rub at Buff Nail Bar.

'Jesus.' Mel stared at Catherine's heel. 'You've got a blister the size of Puerto Banus.'

'I wish I was in Puerto Banus, Mel, I'm making a complete pig's ear of it.'

Kitty sprayed her with some Rescue Remedy. Catherine picked up her phone. There was a text from John.

'*Still alive?*'

'*Barely,*' she typed back.

In the afternoon it went from bad to worse. Catherine was single-handedly blamed for the pension crisis, starving orphans in Africa and the downfall of the NHS. Her saving grace was Olde Worlde, but she drew a blank on the rest. No one was interested in her pledges. Domestic violence was a dirty word. Stressed mothers didn't have the time to talk about whether they were getting a fair deal at work. Stay-at-home workers were just irritated that she had interrupted them. All the pensioners wanted to talk about was dog shit, why so-and-so down the road had got planning permission for *their* extension, and whether capital punishment was coming back. Forget green and pleasant lands; she had no idea the Jam and Jerusalem contingent were quite so bloodthirsty.

At eight o'clock, after nearly twelve hours of canvassing, they headed back to Tory HQ. Demoralized and defeated, Catherine shuffled in wearing Kitty's bright green Crocs. To her relief Felix was waiting there with a reassuring smile. She wasn't quite so pleased to see Aubrey Taunton-Brown.

'How did it go?' Aubrey asked smoothly. 'We caught you on the news.'

He gave her a look. Catherine had gone over on her ankle and mouthed the word 'shit' whilst being interviewed live by BBC Gloucestershire.

'Marvellous,' she said sarcastically. 'Hitler would have got a warmer reception.'

She and Felix went next door for a debrief. 'Don't look so glum,' he told her. 'These things happen.'

He didn't look very convinced. Catherine sank down despondently in a chair. 'Maybe Aubrey's right, Felix. People don't care about the same things I do.' She sighed. 'Maybe I'm the one who's out of touch.'

'You just have to win them over. People worry about their leisure centre closing, or bus routes being cancelled so they can't get to see a loved one in hospital. It's local issues every time.'

'But I care about the bigger issues!' she protested. 'That's why I'm running.'

'These are big issues to the people round here. You have to start at the grass roots, Catherine. Get it right there and the rest will follow.'

The Prime Minister had made it all sound so easy. Catherine was again struck by the niggling doubt that her husband was right. *I'm the sacrificial lamb*, she thought glumly. Only this slaughter was going to last another three weeks.

Chapter 63

Fleur found Beau stretched out by the pool. He was oiled and hard in a minuscule pair of black bathing trunks.

'Hello, you.' He got up to kiss her, his hands moving round to cup her bottom. 'Are you wearing knickers?'

'Of course I am!'

'Mmm. You won't be for much longer.'

The flames started fanning between her legs again. She was disappointed when he released her.

'What can I get you to drink?'

'Whatever you're having.'

'Mojito it is, then. Take a seat, angel.'

He came back over with the drinks and sat down next to her on the sofa. 'There you go.' His eyes held hers. 'To us.'

'To us,' she mumbled into her glass.

His face softened. 'It's good to see you, Fleur. I haven't been able to stop thinking about you.'

She glowed with happiness. 'Me neither.'

They smiled at each other. He put his drink down

and dropped a kiss on her shoulder. 'Come on. Let's go for a dip.'

'Now?'

'Right now.'

He strode over to the pool and executed a perfect dive, popping up like a muscular blond seal moments later. 'What are you waiting for?'

'Um,' she said, panicking. 'I'm not wearing a swimming costume.'

He wriggled under the water and waved his black bathing trunks in the air. 'Neither am I now.'

'Someone might come round!' she protested.

'Stop being so bloody English!' he roared.

With great reluctance, Fleur stood up and started to take off her shorts. His eyes gleamed. 'And the rest.'

Her T-shirt was next. 'We're really going to have to get you some new underwear,' Beau told her, as she stood in her bra and knickers. 'I'm sure they stopped making knickers like that after the Second World War.'

After that, it took some cajoling to get the offensive garments off. Fleur stood in her naked glory, feeling horribly exposed. 'Come on then, what are you waiting for?' Beau yelled.

It was now or never. She took off like Usain Bolt and skidded on a puddle at the water's edge. In slow motion her legs flew up in front of her and she landed on her back in the pool, making the most colossal splash.

Beau was killing himself laughing as he rescued her. 'I've never seen Tom Daley perform that manoeuvre. Are you all right?'

Water was cascading out of her nose. So much for being sexy. She clutched on to his shoulders until she got her breath back. Her boobs were bobbing merrily between them. 'Your tits look fantastic,' he told her. 'Have you ever thought about having sex in a pool?'

His body was like a big slippery eel wrapping around her. 'No,' she gasped as he pushed her against the wall.

This time they came together, Fleur wrapped round him like an orgasmic monkey. 'You're getting very good at this,' he groaned.

She felt ecstatic. 'I've got a very good teacher.'

They stayed locked together, Beau cradling her in his arms. The sun was on her back and shoulders, the water like a warm bath. She laid her face against his smooth chest and tried to remember a time she'd felt so happy.

'I've got to go and make a phone call,' he murmured. 'Do you mind?'

'Of course not.'

He put her down with a smile. 'Stay out here and enjoy the sun, I'll be back soon.'

Hauling himself out, he strolled off towards the house, naked as the day he was born. She marvelled at his wide back and taut buttocks like a pair of beach-balls, and marvelled at the fact she'd just had sex with him.

Half an hour later Beau hadn't reappeared. Wrapping the towel from his sunbed round herself, Fleur decided to go and find him.

There were no signs of life in the house, but she heard the murmur of voices in the kitchen. Did he have visitors? She crept along the corridor, ready to duck into the downstairs loo if someone came out.

The door was only open a crack, but it was enough to see Beau – now in a vest and chinos – and the blonde woman standing by the counter. There was something about their close proximity that made Fleur feel uncomfortable. The woman looked familiar, attractive in a slightly faded way. Fleur suddenly recognized her: it was Lynette Tudor, who owned the gift shop. That was weird. What was she doing here?

Clearing her throat, she pushed the door open. 'Hi.'

Beau turned round. 'Sweetheart. I was about to come and see if you'd drowned. Have you met Lynette? She does a bit of housekeeping for me.'

Lynette gave Fleur the briefest of smiles. 'I should get going,' she told Beau.

'Sure. I won't be a minute, angel,' he told Fleur.

She gazed round the kitchen dully. It didn't look like it had just been cleaned.

Beau was back within a minute. 'Sorry about that. Lynette dropped by to pick up her wages.'

'I didn't know you knew her.'

He went over to the fridge and opened it. 'I just told you; she cleans for me sometimes.' He came over with two beers and handed one to Fleur. 'Let's take these upstairs.'

Chapter 64

The Powells were in London, doing a script read-through for the Silver Box Awards. The setting was a boardroom at London Television Centre, overlooking the South Bank. They'd been looked after wonderfully, but Conrad still wasn't happy.

'I'm not sure it has enough pizzazz,' he said.

'It's great, Conrad,' the executive producer told him.

'Perfect,' the producer agreed.

The director checked her notes. 'We're running over as it is.'

'Les loves my ideas,' Conrad sniffed. 'As the controller of ITV, I think he knows what he's talking about.'

There were subtle eye-rolls all round. Conrad's incessant tweaking was starting to drive them all mad. Anyone would think he was delivering a presidential speech, not reading out the nominations between awards.

'What do you think, Vanessa?' the executive producer asked. 'It's slightly more geared towards Conrad at the moment, are you happy with that?'

'Yes, I really don't mind.'

The ITV people exchanged another look. They'd been warned Vanessa was a perfectionist, but she'd spent most of the meeting staring out of the window.

I don't blame her, the director thought. If Conrad was her husband she wouldn't want to be there either.

In the afternoon the Powells went on *The Scott Mills Show* at Broadcasting House. Their PR, Simon Ferrari, was rather concerned afterwards.

'Are you all right, Vanessa?' he asked her. She'd called Scott 'Steve' twice on air and had to be asked three times what she was wearing to the awards.

Conrad shot her a cold look. He'd been in a foul mood after being asked if he thought Colin Firth would win Best Actor.

Vanessa stared blindly ahead. Under the YSL sunglasses, her eyes were full of tears.

Mercifully her husband was staying in London for the night. After they'd dropped him off, she was like a zombie on the journey back home. She didn't even realize they'd reached the front door of Tresco House.

'Mrs Powell?'

'Oh.' Vanessa reached for her handbag. 'Thank you, Billy.'

For the first time ever, Billy took her hand as she got out. 'Are you all right, Mrs Powell?'

She looked into the concerned face of her loyal chauffeur.

'I'm fine, Billy, just a bit tired. Would you mind taking my mother's lilies into the house?'

Unable to face going in, Vanessa went straight into the garage and started up the Smart Car. It was a huge risk going out with the amount of press swarming round, but she was at breaking point.

At the end of the drive she nearly collided with a green estate car. Three people wearing blue rosettes looked back at her.

'Er, Vanessa?'

She gazed at the woman in the passenger seat. Catherine Connor gave an apologetic smile. 'Hi, I just wanted to . . .'

'Fuck off!' Vanessa shrieked. 'Haven't you done enough damage?'

She screeched off. When she got near enough, she left the keys in the ignition and ran sobbing through Foxgloves Woods and out into the field beyond. She hadn't even got halfway across when Dylan came racing out of the thicket. 'Eddie was whining,' he told her, as she collapsed into his arms. 'Vanessa. My God. What the hell has happened?'

Before she could stop herself, Vanessa found herself telling him everything – Conrad filming her, his threats, the rape. When she'd finished telling him, her sweet, gentle Dylan was shaking with fury.

'That bastard. I'm going round there.'

His eyes were wild, face taut with anger. She had never seen him look like that.

'He's not there, and anyway, you mustn't, Dylan!' she pleaded. 'It will only make things worse.'

'I want to kill him.' He put his arms round her. 'I want to kill him for what he's done to you.'

'I'm OK,' she sobbed. 'Don't worry.'

'You're not OK. I'll go and get Sukie and your things

from the house. We'll go to the police station together. He can't get away with this.'

It was all happening too quickly. 'I can't just walk out.'

'Yes, you can! What if there's a next time?'

'There won't be. I've got my mother and Renata around. Please, Dylan, just trust me. I have to do the awards. The minute they're over, I'm leaving him.'

'Forget the awards! Forget the press, or whatever else it is you're worried about. Your safety is more important.'

'We signed a contract, there would be huge repercussions. I can't just ride off into the sunset with you.'

His eyes burnt unnaturally bright. 'Promise me you'll leave the house, then. You can come here, or stay in a hotel or anything you want. I just want you to get away from him.' His voice broke. 'I can't stand what he's done to you.'

Somehow his anguish gave Vanessa strength. Knowing he loved her so much made her feel like she could cope with anything.

'It will all be over soon,' she said. 'Then we can be together.'

An unspoken fear hung between them, as palpable as a storm cloud. What was Conrad capable of before then?

Chapter 65

As Catherine dragged her head off the pillow early that morning, she felt like a cast member from *The Living Dead*. Her feet were in shreds, her throat hurt and her face was bright red from forgetting to put on suncream. At least it matched her knuckles, which were red raw from knocking on doors that never opened.

Catherine's popularity was showing no signs of improving. Derided for being a metropolitan feminist, she'd been stonewalled by the formidable 'Turnip Taliban' electorates of the Cotswolds. Tristan Jago was streaking ahead in the opinion polls. His tactic was basic but effective: slagging off the government and siding with Joe Public. He'd got 42 per cent of the votes in the latest YouGov poll, while the Lib Dem Helen Singh had come in next on 28 per cent. The two independents, Colonel Bill Fairclough and Esme Santura, were next. Catherine had trailed in last with a humiliating 6 per cent. She couldn't believe she was being beaten by a *witch*.

Dragging on her dressing gown, she went down to

the kitchen. John was making a pot of coffee. Sunrise Radio, their local station, was on in the background.

'I hope that's extra strong,' she said, flopping down at the table. 'I'm barely capable of stringing a sentence together.'

He handed her a mug. 'More of the same today?'

'Yes, if you mean being somewhere on the social spectrum between Rose West and a puppy drowner.'

He gave an unexpected snort. Seeing his old, familiar grin was like watching the sun come out after weeks of rain.

They looked at each other and began to laugh. 'What the hell have I got myself into?' she groaned. 'I just want to stay here with you and pull the curtains shut.'

'Do it, Cath!' he urged.

'You know I can't,' she sighed.

A moment later Tristan Jago's voice seeped into the room.

'We're extremely pleased with how things have gone so far.'

'It's six-thirty in the morning!' Catherine howled. 'Does the man not bloody sleep?'

'What do you think of the Conservative candidate, ex-Soirée editor Catherine Connor?' the Sunrise Radio DJ asked.

'Here we go,' Catherine muttered.

'I think we have to ask, what are Catherine Connor's real motives for running?' Tristan asked. *'The woman is desperate to claw her way back into the limelight, by whatever means are possible. Unfortunately, she's been allowed to use the Beeversham by-election to do it.'*

'Motherfucker!' Catherine yelled. 'You lying, lanky streak of piss!'

Tristan was just getting warmed up. *'The whole thing's a joke. What the good people of Beeversham need is a local person who cares about local issues . . .'*

'Like you, Tristan?' the DJ asked.

'*Exactly like me. Instead of some over-the-hill magazine editor who's written a tawdry tell-all book to get more exposure. Vote Catherine Connor? I'd say more like "Champagne Charlotte"!*'

John looked at his wife. 'Cath, don't.'

'He's not bloody getting away with this!' she said, furiously dialling 118. 'Hello? I'd like the number for Sunrise Radio. Urgently, please!'

Beeversham was slowly starting to wake up. People moved round their kitchens buttering toast and putting on pots of coffee. The upbeat pop songs of Sunrise Radio were a popular choice to start the day. As Gerry and the Pacemakers faded out the DJ came back on.

'*Today we've got Tristan Jago in the studio, Labour candidate in the Beeversham by-election. I'm also joined on the line by Catherine Connor, the Conservative candidate. Can you hear me, Catherine?*'

'Loud and clear.'

'*What do you think of Tristan Jago's claims that you're a "Champagne Charlotte"?*'

'It's an absolute load of sh . . . I mean, rubbish.'

Tristan Jago cut in. '*The only part of politics Catherine cares about is hobnobbing it in Westminster. This is her ticket back to London, to carry on with her champagne lifestyle!*'

'I don't believe this!'

'You deny you've ever drunk champagne?' the DJ interrupted.

'Of course not, but—'

'There we go!' Tristan cried. 'If you like posh drink and fancy clothes vote for "Champagne Charlotte". Her predecessor, Jonty Fortescue-Wellington, liked his bubbles, and look where it got him!'

'Charlotte, I mean, Catherine, how do you respond to that?' the DJ asked.

'Tristan is making scurrilous claims for which he has absolutely no evidence. I care about the people of Beeversham, that's why I'm running!'

'Oh?' Tristan Jago enquired. 'Perhaps you can tell us how many unemployed people there are in the constituency? Seeing as that's so important to you.'

'Well, um, I haven't got the exact figures on me at the moment.'

'That's because you don't know them! She doesn't care about the people of this constituency! It's one of the reasons the Tories have got this country into such a mess in the first place!'

'We're going to have to stop it there,' the DJ said. 'Next up, "Devil Woman" by Cliff Richard!'

Chapter 66

Beau dropped in to Blackwater Farm later that morning to find Fleur in the kitchen sobbing over another unpayable bill.

'Sweetheart.' He gathered her up in his arms. 'I can't bear to see you like this. Let me pay it.'

'We're a business, not a charity,' she wept.

He looked serious. 'Are things really that bad?'

She knew she shouldn't speak about their financial worries, but the burden was overwhelming. 'The b-bank are calling in a loan at the end of the month and we haven't got the money, and we're going to lose everything.' She dissolved into fresh tears, leaving snot all over Beau's Oxford blue shirt.

'Don't worry,' he told her. 'Things will work out.'

'How can they?' she sobbed. 'We're about to go bankrupt!'

'Let me talk to the bank. I'm sure we can sort something out.'

'No, Beau. I won't let you do it.'

'Angel, let me help. How much do you need?'

Fleur wiped her face and sat up. 'You've already done enough for me. This is our problem. I'll sort something out.'

He looked at her for a moment. 'If you're sure. In the meantime I'm taking you out for lunch.' He stopped her protest. 'No ifs, no buts. Go upstairs and get changed.'

She took a long, hot shower and changed into fresh clothes. As she came back downstairs, she heard voices coming from the garden. Beau must be out there with her dad! Panicking at the thought of the state her dad might be in, Fleur rushed outside to be greeted by a scene of contented harmony. Her dad and Beau were at the picnic table, looking out at the view. In the bright sunlight, and next to Beau's flawless beauty, Robert Blackwater looked even sicklier.

Fleur was in shock. 'What's going on here?'

'I was hardly going to make Beau wait in the yard, was I?' her dad said.

It wasn't exactly friendly, but it was a definite improvement on last time. 'Now let's take you out for lunch,' Beau said. 'That's if it's OK with you, Robert.'

He gave a shrug. 'She's hardly going to listen if I say no, is she?'

They drove back to Ridings, Beau's free hand resting on Fleur's knee.

'What's with the vibe between you and my dad?'

'What do you mean?'

'I don't know.' She looked at his elegant profile. 'What did you say to him?'

'What do you mean?'

'My dad doesn't like many people. Especially if they're dating his daughter.'

'Maybe I talked him round. I'm not a complete monster.'

Each time they made love Fleur got more confident. This time she went on top, boobs proud and free. They came together, Fleur collapsing on Beau's chest exhausted but replete.

'Did you see Felix on the lunchtime news today?' she said, after a long while.

'What land and glory shit has he been spouting off about now?'

She pushed herself up on one elbow and traced a finger around his bellybutton. 'He's really helped me and dad out, you know.'

'Has he now?'

'Why don't you two get along?'

He stared up at the ceiling. 'Felix and I are very different.'

'That's an understatement!'

'Yes, awful irresponsible Beau and dear responsible Felix. I suppose you would say that.'

'What does that mean?'

'Nothing.' He shot her a sideways look. 'God, Fleur, we aren't the first siblings to have fallen out. Just because we're blood relatives doesn't mean we're going to be the best of friends.'

'But why move back to Beeversham if you hate your brother?' she persisted. 'A family that doesn't speak is better than no family at all, isn't it?'

'Can we talk about something else? Funnily enough,

my brother isn't one of my favourite post-coital subjects.'

She could sense she was steering into dangerous waters, but Fleur had more questions. 'What about Lynette?'

'What about Lynette?'

She swallowed. 'Is she just your housekeeper?'

'What else would she be?'

She hesitated. 'Have you ever been lovers?'

His eyes darkened. 'No,' he said curtly. 'I told you. Lynette needs the spare cash and I need a cleaner.'

'I-I don't mind sharing you.'

He sat up and rolled off the bed. 'Don't be so bloody stupid,' he snapped.

'I'm sorry,' she said in dismay. 'I just wanted to know.'

'Well, now you do.' He started to put his pants back on. 'I'm going to get a drink. Getting the Spanish Inquisition off someone just after I've slept with them always gives me a headache.'

'Beau.'

He turned his back on her and stalked out. Fleur was left on the bed, horror-struck at what had just happened.

She'd forgotten how awful it was to be on the sharp end of Beau's tongue. How he could cut you down in an instant and leave you feeling worthless. Even when they'd had their feud, he had only been casually arrogant towards her. He certainly hadn't displayed the cold anger she'd just seen.

Fleur gazed miserably through the open bedroom door. He'd been such a player; had she really expected him to give it all up? *How many are there, apart from me?*

she thought. *Lynette?* She didn't know what he got up to on his business trips. How could she ever know?

She felt physically sick. How could she have just degraded herself like that? This thing with him had made her lose sight of herself. She had her self-respect. *I won't put up with it*, she thought. *I'll go down right now and tell him.*

There was the sudden sound of footsteps on the landing, and he burst back in the room. 'Sweetheart. I didn't mean to snap. I'm just tired, it's been a busy few days.'

She was completely wrong-footed by his change in mood. 'I didn't mean to make you angry,' she told him.

'I know,' he said, covering her face in little kisses. 'Will you forgive me? I just feel like I kicked a puppy or something.'

She gazed into the deep-blue eyes and her resolve melted. Beau had her exactly where he wanted her.

'Of course,' she said, thinking of the cruel way he had humiliated Valentina at the Serpentine party. *Is that what he'll do when he gets tired of me?*

Chapter 67

Wasting no time in capitalizing on his radio triumph over Catherine, Tristan hired a man in a giant champagne outfit to follow her round town. The last thing she needed on a constituent's doorstep, hearing how the NHS had killed their husband, was sodding Champagne Man in the background making glugging noises, but she refused to rise. In an interview with BBC Gloucestershire that afternoon, she was the model of calm.

'To be honest, it's what I've come to expect from Labour. I'm more worried about the fact that Tristan is thinking up silly pranks, rather than concentrating on the job in hand.'

Felix had been impressed. 'We'll make a politician of you yet.'

The day had been particularly busy. They'd been out canvassing all morning, and in the afternoon, she had visited several schools in the area, and an old people's home where the majority of the residents either stared vacantly into space or were asleep through her entire talk. 'The truth is, it's a waste of time,' the head nurse told her afterwards. 'You're better off just autographing my copy of *Cathy: My Story*.'

It was getting late by the time John turned up at Tory HQ to pick her up. He found Catherine online, scrolling through the *Cotswold Journal*.

'How's it going?'

'Brilliant. How can Tristan Jago have been at three fetes today and a charity luncheon? Does the man have a doppelgänger or something?'

'Have you forgotten about dinner?' he asked. He was flying to Costa Rica in the morning. He'd booked it without telling her. Catherine was sure he'd done it to give her a taste of her own medicine.

'Of course not,' she said distractedly. 'We've still got time, haven't we?'

'It's nearly nine.'

'Shit, is it?' Catherine looked at Kitty and Clive, who were stuffing leaflets into envelopes in the corner. 'Guys, do you mind if I shoot off?'

Kitty, who'd been staring at John ever since he'd walked in, dragged her eyes away. 'Of course not, have a lovely dinner.'

Vincent was all over them in Bar 47, which was just as well, as Catherine and John didn't have much to say to each other.

'So, all packed?' she asked again.

'All packed.'

'Got your passport?'

'Yes, Cath, I've got my passport.'

'You must be really excited!' she said, trying to sound enthusiastic. 'I'll make sure I'm back at midday tomorrow, to see you off.'

'I'm only going for a couple of weeks, Cath. You don't have to.'

'Of course I do!' she joked. 'I haven't gone down *that* far in your estimation, have I?'

He picked up his glass of wine. 'Are you sure you'll be all right on your own?'

'I'm a grown woman,' she sighed. 'I hope so.'

The meal passed with the sound of scraping cutlery and polite comments about the food. In bed that night he reached for her, but Catherine, tired, on edge, helpless to stop her marriage disintegrating, made her excuses. They went to sleep on either side of the bed, a pillow-width between them but worlds apart.

The next morning Catherine was back canvassing in the town square. She stood by the war memorial, trying to palm off leaflets on the shoppers and tourists wandering past.

'Hi! I'm Catherine Connor, Conservative candidate for Beeversham,' she said to one man. 'Can I take a moment to tell you my election manifesto?'

'Not really, love. My parking ticket runs out in a minute.'

Catherine gazed at the leaflets clogging the bin, where people had chucked them away without a second thought. God, this was depressing.

The heat shimmered above the cobbles. The square was starting to feel like a gladiatorial sandpit, with Catherine as the underdog. At half past eleven Kitty came up with another bottle of water for her.

'Bloody quiet today.' Catherine sighed gloomily, looking across the deserted High Street.

'It's the weather,' Kitty said. 'Most people are probably in their gardens.'

'I don't blame them.' Catherine checked her watch. She should head back soon.

'Where did you say John was going again?'

'Costa Rica.'

'Gosh, how lovely. Clive and I always go to the Peak District.'

Catherine smiled at this funny little woman, with her frizzy halo of hair and bright blue Crocs. 'Are you two ever apart?'

'We've only spent one night apart since we got married,' Kitty said proudly. 'And that was when I had to go into hospital for an operation and they wouldn't let him stay. He was back by six the next morning.'

They seemed completely devoted to each other. *I could probably learn a thing or two from them*, Catherine thought.

'John seems lovely,' Kitty said.

Catherine watched a woman strap her child into the back seat of their car. 'You want to know something, Kitty? I think he's too good for me.'

She looked shocked. 'Nonsense! You make a lovely couple. And he adores you.'

Catherine looked at her. 'You think?'

'Oh yes. You can tell by the way he looks at you.'

'I adore him too.' Catherine sighed. 'It's just that sometimes, I don't know how to show it.'

'Why don't you get John a going-away present?' Kitty suggested.

'You think?'

'It doesn't have to be anything expensive, just something little to remind him of you.' She gave her a smile.

'Thanks, Kitty,' Catherine said gratefully.

Butterflies was one of those shops devoted to random kitsch that was no use to anyone. A sign saying 'Hand Over the Chocolate and Nobody Gets Hurt!' was hanging in the front door, while the window display was a mishmash of cheap handbags, plastic jewellery and garish china cupcakes. Catherine picked up a hideous woodland ornament. How could Lynette make a living out of selling such tat?

The shop was empty. A door banged out the back somewhere. She heard voices, a man's and a woman's, low and intense. The woman laughed, then it all went quiet again. Was Lynette back there with her mystery man? Footsteps started down the corridor, accompanied by a soft whistling. It seemed like Catherine was about to find out.

She didn't know who looked more surprised. 'Hello there,' said Beau Rainford, striding round the counter. He cast his eyes over the shop. 'I hear the "gentleman ball-scratchers" are popular,' he told her.

'Thanks,' she said. 'I'll bear that in mind.'

He was wearing a snow-white polo shirt that hugged his spectacular torso. 'Good luck with your campaign, by the way.' His blue eyes gave Catherine the once-over. 'Legs like those will always get my vote.'

Flashing her a grin, he stepped out to the street.

Lynette came scurrying through a moment later. She saw Catherine and looked like a rabbit caught in the headlights. 'Oh! Have you been here long?'

'No, I just came in,' she lied. 'I'm in a bit of a hurry, I'm looking for a little present for John.'

'How about Batman cufflinks? Perfect for the man in your life.'

'I'm not sure John's that kind of man.'

'Or a battery-controlled helicopter? Hours of fun in the garden!'

Panicking, Catherine settled for a lucky toadstool snow globe. It was five to twelve by the time she hared out, straight into the crew from BBC Gloucester.

'There you are, Catherine!' the reporter said. 'Could we get a few words on the controversial badger-culling plan for the lunchtime bulletin?'

'Actually, I've got to be somewhere.'

'Look, there's Esme Santura! Let's get a piece on camera from you both.'

The pagan witch was floating dreamily up the High Street, flowers trailing from her raven hair.

'Good afternoon,' she said breathily.

'Esme, I'd like to ask you and Catherine a few questions about both your campaigns,' the reporter said.

'Of course.' Esme turned to Catherine. 'What star-sign are you?'

'Erm, Sagittarius.'

Esme's smile faded. 'Oh.'

The reporter looked excited. 'Esme, you're saying that's a bad thing?'

Five minutes later, after Esme had banged on about Catherine's ominous planetary alliances, she managed to escape. Haring past a pack of astonished journalists on the pavement, she belted back towards the Crescent.

'John!' she panted, scrabbling for her front-door key. 'Sorry I'm late!'

The hallway was empty. There was a note on the sideboard. *'Couldn't wait any longer. Will call you from the airport.'*

Chapter 68

Driving over to Beau's that evening Fleur pulled over and burst into tears by the side of the road. All those generations of Blackwaters, all the blood and sweat they had poured into the land over the years, had amounted to nothing. They were going to lose the farm.

She found Beau by the pool scrolling through his iPad.

'Hello, you,' he said. 'I was just catching up on my horoscope.'

'What did it say?'

'It's warning me off feisty redheads who know how to operate heavy machinery and have a great rack.'

He got up and kissed her. 'Are you all right?'

'Hay fever,' she said, rubbing at her red eyes.

He frowned, but didn't say anything. 'What can I get you to drink?'

'I thought I might go for a swim first.' The water looked wonderfully inviting. Fleur just wanted to submerge herself in it and block out her thoughts.

She went inside to get changed. Beau had been his

normal charming self since the bedroom episode but all the same, it was playing on her mind. But what was the alternative? Challenge him and risk being left out in the cold again? His wrong side was not a nice place to be, as she had discovered. She was back in the sunlight again – and that was all that mattered.

You're weak, she told herself furiously.

There was the sound of movement in the kitchen when she came back down. 'Ta da!' She bounded in wearing the Gucci bikini. 'What do you think?'

Spencer looked up from the fridge, a bottle of beer in his hand.

Fleur stopped dead. 'I didn't know you were here.'

'Well, you do now.' His eyes roamed horribly over her near-naked body. 'Nice bikini.'

At that moment Beau walked in through the other door. 'Angel, you look fantastic! Scrubs up all right, doesn't she?' he asked Spencer.

He looked lasciviously at her chest. 'Yes, mate.'

'Spence is going to stay the night,' Beau told her. 'You don't mind, do you?'

'I just drove up from London,' Spencer said. 'Seriously heavy night.'

Fleur joined them by the pool, where there was already a bottle of Moët on the go. Beau looked at her shirtdress. 'I thought you were going for a swim?'

'I changed my mind,' she said. 'I'll go another time.'

'Come and sit by me.' He put his arm round her as she sat down. 'Spence and I were just having a catch-up.'

Spencer smiled at her in that horrible, sly way of his. 'Farm going well?'

'Yes, thank you,' she replied stiffly.

He turned to Beau. 'I bumped into Valentina at the Groucho the other night. She asked after you.'

'Oh?' Beau said. 'Do send her my best.'

Tinie Tempah's latest track started blasting out on someone's mobile. Spencer jumped up. 'Mate!' he said to someone, walking off down the side of the pool.

Fleur turned to Beau. 'Has Valentina been in contact with you?'

'Of course not. Why would she?'

'Did you know Spencer was coming?'

'No. Turning up unannounced is just his thing.' He raised an eyebrow. 'You don't like him, do you?'

'He just seems a bit sneaky. Like there's some private joke I'm not in on.'

He leant across and kissed her on the mouth. 'I know he's a bit much sometimes, but give him a chance.'

Unfortunately Spencer was extremely hard to give a chance to. An unappealing mix of arrogance and not being very bright, he barely spoke to Fleur all evening, hanging off Beau's every word instead. It was only when Beau had gone to get another bottle of champagne that he gave her his full attention.

'So, are you and Beau serious?'

'You'd have to ask him,' she said defensively.

'You're not his usual type.'

She knew she shouldn't rise. 'What's his usual type?'

He gave a smirk. 'Oh, you know.'

Mercifully Beau came back at that point. 'I'm just going to the toilet,' Fleur said, leaving before she ducked Spencer's fat head in the pool.

Fuming, she hung round the house for a while,

putting off going back out. When she did both men were deep in conversation.

'You're putting in the groundwork with this one,' she heard Spencer say. 'I hope it's worth it.'

Fleur could only see the back of Beau's blond head. 'It is, don't worry.'

Spencer saw her then and shut up. 'Fleur!' he said, just a little too loudly. 'How's it going?'

Beau jumped up. 'I was wondering where you'd got to. Sit down.' He made a big fuss of her, plumping up the cushions and refilling Fleur's drink. 'We should think about ordering some food soon. How does curry sound?'

Chapter 69

It had been four days since John had left. He hadn't been convinced by Catherine's excuse for not being there to see him off, and they'd parted via the telephone on even worse terms. Due to the time difference and her crazy schedule, they'd only had a few brief conversations since. A cowardly part of her was relieved. If they didn't speak, she didn't have to face up to the fact that her marriage was falling apart.

It was a dispirited atmosphere that Monday at Tory HQ. The day before, the *Cotswolds on Sunday* had run a disastrous piece on Catherine. Instead of focusing on her policies, the reporter had conjured up lurid tales of the Crimson Killer case. 'Catherine Connor is a woman on the run from her past,' he'd written. 'Considering her blood-soaked history, it's little surprise she's entered the cut-throat world of local politics.'

'It's not ideal,' Felix admitted. 'You'll have to go out today and work extra hard to win them over.'

'Why don't you start wearing mini-skirts?' Charles Knatchbull boomed.

'Charles,' Felix reprimanded mildly.

'What? Worked for Angela Fairbottom in the 87 election. By Jove, she had a pair of pins on her!'

'Thanks, Charles, but I'm not quite desperate enough to start taking my clothes off yet,' Catherine snapped.

A cloying scent of Lily of the Valley entered the room. 'Not interrupting, am I?'

Catherine rolled her eyes. This was all she needed. Viola Taunton-Brown, in pearls and a check Aquascutum two-piece.

'Morning, boys.' Viola ignored Catherine. 'How are we all?'

Felix's mobile went off. 'Morning, Viola. Would you excuse me while I take this?'

He left the room. Viola turned to Catherine. 'I hear you were condoning underage sex the other day!' She gave her husband a scandalized look. 'Patricia Hornwell told me, she heard it from Pamela Linley, who saw Catherine campaigning in the market square.'

'I wasn't condoning underage sex, Viola. I was asked a perfectly legitimate question about making the morning-after pill free over the counter.'

'The morning after what?' Charles bellowed.

'That contraceptive pill,' Viola told him. 'For girls who sleep around. Really, the moral compass of the younger generation these days.'

'Would you prefer unwanted pregnancies, then?' Catherine enquired icily.

Viola looked at her nastily. 'Whatever does your husband make of you, running all over the countryside delivering your pornographic manifesto?'

'I really wouldn't know,' Catherine snapped. 'He's in Costa Rica.'

'He's gone away? During your *campaign*? It must make you wonder if he really approves of what you're doing!'

It scored a direct hit. 'Why don't you fuck off,' Catherine shouted. 'And stick that beak in someone else's business?'

Viola gasped. 'Of all the . . .'

'What on earth is going on?' Felix was standing in the doorway.

'She started it!' Catherine howled.

'I most certainly did not!'

'Felix, Catherine has just abused my wife! I demand an apology!'

'Really!' Viola was purple. 'I've never heard such language in all my life!'

'STOP IT, ALL OF YOU!'

Everyone turned round in shock. 'Thank you,' he said more evenly. 'I've just had some news. The Prime Minister is coming to Beeversham tomorrow.'

They all gaped at him. 'Tomorrow?' Catherine echoed.

'I'm hosting my bridge lunch,' Viola fretted.

'I'm sure we'll survive without you,' Catherine said acidly, earning herself another look from Aubrey.

'It's action stations from now on,' Felix told them. 'The PM's ETA is ten o'clock tomorrow. He's got a morning of photo ops, starting at Blaize Castle, then he's got a meet-and-greet round town. Catherine, we need to work out your new schedule. I suggest we all stop squabbling and use our time to plan tomorrow.'

*

Catherine found Felix in the office afterwards, looking out of the window. 'I'm sorry,' she said. 'I was out of order.'

He gave her a rueful smile. 'Tensions are running high.' He went back to the window. She followed his gaze. The ruins of Blaize Castle huddled on the hill like an old man who knew his time was up.

'Think I might go and stretch my legs, and then we'll get on with planning tomorrow.'

Giving her a brief smile, he picked up his Panama hat and walked out. She was left cursing her insensitivity. Felix must be worried sick about the outcome of the council meeting on Ye Olde Worlde the following week.

She watched his solitary figure walk off down the street. She thought about how Ginny wasn't herself at the moment, and the phone calls Felix kept going off to make in private. Maybe she and John weren't the only ones having problems. No matter how happy people seemed, you never knew what really went on behind closed doors.

Chapter 70

The hype for the Silver Box Awards had started. Vanessa and Conrad were back and forth from London in a whirl of dress-fittings, interviews and rehearsals. Moaning about all the time they were spending on the M40, Conrad had booked a permanent room at the Dorchester.

It was a blessed relief. Vanessa could no longer stand to be in the same room as him. Mercifully he hadn't touched her since forcing himself on her. The thought of ever being intimate with him again made her feel sick. The nights they were together were a ritual of face-masks and eye creams, his feet resting on a pillow under the duvet to stave off fluid retention. She would lie awake listening to her husband making that irritating 'pop' sound in his sleep and dream of the day she could finally be rid of him. She was just thinking this when she became aware that Conrad had asked her a question.

*

'I mean, do they want to suck all the integrity out of me?'

'They only want to take one "and" out, Conrad,' Vanessa said. 'It's hardly going to make a difference.'

The Powells were at the renowned Wolseley restaurant on Piccadilly, having lunch with Marty. Conrad's 'artistic vision' was starting to send them all crazy.

He stabbed at a scallop. 'That "and" – my clueless darling of a fuckwit – is essential for providing that moment of drama. Not that I'd expect you to understand; you haven't got one creative bone in that ridiculously over-ripe body of yours.'

Vanessa jumped up. Rushing through the opulent dining room, she ran down the stairs to the toilets. Heading straight for the nearest cubicle, she sank down on the seat.

I hate him. I hate him. I hate him. She wasn't sure if she could keep the pretence up for much longer.

The door opened and she was surprised to hear two male voices. There was the sound of zips being undone and liquid splashing against ceramic. It suddenly dawned on her that they weren't the ones in the wrong place. She'd come into the Gents. *I'm losing my mind*, she thought.

One of the men spoke. 'Did you see Conrad Powell on the way in?' Vanessa held her breath.

'Yeah, smug bastard. ITV1 are pulling their hair out; apparently he's being a fucking nightmare.'

'Tell me something I didn't know. You know he's, like, their fifth choice to present the Silver Box Awards? The organizers have had a nightmare this year with

406

people's filming schedules. I heard Hugh Grant and Benedict Cumberbatch both turned it down.'

'Really? Vanessa Powell is pretty hot, though.' *Zip.* 'I'd give her one.'

'Someone needs to, while her husband is busy cock-sucking his way round the industry.'

'Christ, he's deluded. We wouldn't touch him at the Beeb, and Sky think he's a talentless cunt as well. He can't even act on the packet for Valiant Hair Colour For Men.'

The other man laughed. 'Not the big comeback he's hoping for, then.'

That evening Dominique walked into Vanessa's dressing room to find her emptying her jewellery tray. 'What are you doing?' she said curiously.

'I'm having a clear-out,' Vanessa lied. 'I've been thinking of auctioning some of my things off.'

Her mother peered at the dressing table. 'The De Beers drops? Are you sure?'

Vanessa swiftly closed the leather case. She'd been stockpiling valuables to go in her deposit box at Coutts. When she told Conrad she was leaving him for Dylan he would try and screw her for everything.

Dominique stood in the doorway. 'What's going on?'

'Nothing.'

'You're lying to me.'

Vanessa got up slowly. 'If you really want to know, I'm leaving Conrad.'

There was a long pause. 'Don't be so ridiculous,' Dominique said. 'Put your jewellery back in the safe and come downstairs.'

'Do you hear what I'm saying, Mother? I'm leaving Conrad!'

'And I just said you're being ridiculous,' Dominique hissed. 'Now *put the jewellery back.*'

Vanessa gazed at the woman who'd given birth to her. The woman who should love her unconditionally, no matter what she did. Vanessa had told her she was leaving her husband, and still Dominique did nothing.

'Why have you always hated me so much?'

'I don't hate you. How can you say such a thing?'

Vanessa scrutinized her mother's face. The once-vibrant complexion had gradually been deadened by Botox, and a permanent look of displeasure had settled around the lipsticked mouth. She was no longer beautiful, Vanessa realized.

'You may think I'm hard on you, but it's only because I love you,' Dominique told her.

'Bullshit! You're incapable of love.'

'My life is difficult! You have no idea what you're talking about!'

'My life is difficult too, Mother! Not that you've ever taken the trouble to notice!' Vanessa stormed over to her dressing table. 'I'm leaving Conrad, and there is nothing you can do about it!'

'I forbid you! I'm going downstairs right now to tell him.'

Vanessa turned round. 'I will never, ever speak to you again,' she said softly. 'You're either with me, or against me. It's your decision.'

Chapter 71

The Prime Minister arrived in Beeversham with his beautiful wife on his arm and a fleet of security cars. First stop was a photo-shoot up at Blaize Castle, where the PM's wife's yellow Christopher Kane dress perfectly complemented the surrounding fields of oilseed rape. The Prime Minister expertly batted away questions about Ye Olde Worlde. 'I'm here to see the beautiful town of Beeversham,' he told BBC South West charmingly. 'And lend my support to Catherine.'

Next up was a local school, and then tea and cake with a mother and children's group. The PM's wife enchanted the kids by getting down on the floor to play, while the PM enchanted the mothers with his caring bedside manner and soft brown eyes.

Their charisma started to melt even the hardened anti-capitalists. By the time the fleet of cars hit the High Street, huge crowds of people had gathered. Everyone wanted to see if the PM's wife really was so beautiful in the flesh and if the PM was as dashing as everyone said.

*

Catherine was waiting outside the entrance to Tory HQ. The brief had been short and sweet. The PM would turn up and make a brief speech, before going inside with Catherine. Then there would be a thirty-second turnaround and then out the back door, back to London.

Except that the Prime Minister's wife, who was so wonderfully friendly and stylish, insisted on walking up the last part of the High Street to meet some local shopowners. She bought an angel mobile for her daughter from Butterflies and gave all her loose change to the *Big Issue* seller outside the Co-op. By the time the crowd arrived at Tory HQ, the woman was one step away from becoming the new patron saint of Beeversham.

Catherine was feeling sicker by the second. Felix was on hand to reassure her. 'Take your lead from the PM, he's done thousands of these.'

The cameras started flashing. The discreet security men began moving the crowd back. The PM and his wife were strolling along as if they had all the time in the world. He was tall and handsome in a petrol-blue suit, his wife bending down to take flowers from the little children.

'Catherine, hello!' he exclaimed. 'Wonderful to see you.'

'Hello, PM, I mean Prime Minister.'

He grasped Catherine's hand and allowed the pop of cameras to go off. 'We've had a wonderful morning.'

'We have indeed.' The PM's wife smiled. Close up, she had the most amazing porcelain skin.

Sky News put a microphone in the PM's face. 'Any words of advice for Catherine?'

'Catherine doesn't need my advice, she's doing an admirable job.'

'What about the fact she's a complete unknown?'

'Catherine Connor is a brilliant contender for the job,' the PM replied seamlessly. 'I have every belief she can win this by-election. She's passionate, determined and knows what the people of Beeversham want.'

Champagne Man was pushing his way through to the front. Victoria Henley-Coddington exchanged looks with security. The PM waved goodbye, and the whole group was rushed into the front reception.

'We need the PM's car back round like, now, people,' Victoria announced.

The PM's wife turned to a star-struck Kitty. 'Could you show me where the loo is? I'm dying for a wee.'

Everyone was bustling round with a job to do, apart from the PM and Catherine. She suddenly felt very shy and unsure of herself.

'Catherine, you're doing a wonderful job,' he told her.

She gave him a quizzical smile. 'You sure?'

'Oh yes. You held your own on cleaning up politics in the ITN interview. You think on your feet, which is good.'

'You mean bullshit my way out of it when I need to?'

The PM's eyes twinkled. 'An essential trait for any politician.'

*

Everyone poured into the town hall on Wednesday evening for the last Ye Olde Worlde meeting. Photographers were assembled outside, while indoors journalists lined the front row. With the decision on Beeversham's fate a mere week away, the theme park was big news again.

The PM's goodwill mission had worked wonders. For once Catherine wasn't being universally treated like a master criminal.

She found Ginny in the kitchen opening another carton of orange juice. 'Hiya,' Catherine said from the doorway.

Ginny's expression faltered when she saw who it was. 'Oh, hello, darling.' She picked up the jug. 'I'd better take this orange juice out.'

'Ginny, is something wrong?'

'Of course not! Why do you think that?' The protestation was just a little too loud.

Catherine gave a rueful smile. 'I haven't seen you for ages, and you haven't returned any of my texts.' The dark circles were still there under Ginny's eyes. 'You don't seem yourself at the moment.'

'I've just been really busy.'

Catherine decided to play her wild card. 'You're not mad at me because I'm running instead of Felix in the election?'

Ginny looked stricken. 'Of course not!' She glanced through the door. 'If you'll excuse me, I should get back.'

As Ginny passed, she stopped and planted a kiss on Catherine's cheek. 'You're doing a wonderful thing,' she whispered fervently. 'I'm so very proud.'

Catherine was left completely confused. *What had that been about?*

It was past 11 p.m. by the time Catherine walked up the Crescent. The house was dark and quiet. She looked up at the big, empty windows and didn't want to go in. It felt too scarily like her old life: a big, expensive space devoid of love and laughter.

Her mobile started ringing. She got it out of her bag. It was John again. She wanted to speak to him so badly, but she couldn't bear hearing the disappointment in his voice and realize how much she'd fucked up. She stared at the small glowing screen.

Answer it, she willed herself. *Just bloody answer it . . .*

After the tenth ring it cut off. She waited hopefully for a voicemail bleep, but the phone stayed silent. 'Shit!' Catherine wailed tearfully. 'What is *wrong* with you?'

She suddenly desperately wanted someone to talk to. She couldn't go to Ginny, especially after today. Catherine's thoughts turned to Mel. Mel's cheery company was just what she needed. She remembered Mel mentioning Mike was away; Mel would probably appreciate the company. The thought of companionship and a glass of something made Catherine feel happy for the first time that day.

All the lights were off at the Cooper-Stanleys' house. Disappointed, Catherine started down the path. As she got to the end she heard the front door open and Mel appeared on the doorstep in a leopard-print dressing gown.

Mel was talking to someone inside. Catherine watched in disbelief as a familiar lanky figure appeared

413

behind Mel. Tristan Jago pulled her into a passionate embrace, holding his briefcase in the other hand.

Panicking, Catherine dived behind next-door's conifer. She heard the murmur of voices and Mel laugh softly. A moment later Tristan walked down the path, passing her by mere inches. She held her breath, convinced she was about to be discovered, but Tristan strolled off down the close and disappeared into the night.

Everything fell quiet again, but she stayed where she was. Tristan and *Mel*? Catherine couldn't get her head round it. Did everyone have a secret in this town?

Chapter 72

The Powells were back in London. Conrad had insisted on an acoustics test at the Royal Albert Hall so Vanessa, the executive producer, producer, director and a bemused cleaner were watching from the wings as he strode round the stage testing his voice.

'Lord, Conrad does know he's going to be miked up?' the producer muttered. It earnt him a nudge from the director, but Vanessa barely heard. She was in a world of her own.

All week she'd been making surreptitious arrangements, transferring assets, freezing bank accounts, looking into nearby houses she could rent. The meeting with her lawyer had been sobering: they would lose out to the tune of millions by reneging on contracts and losing endorsements. Vanessa had come out and been sick in the loo, and then promptly phoned a legendary PR who was an expert in damage limitation. When Conrad came for her, she'd be ready.

*

And he'd come earlier than Vanessa had expected. When she stopped by the Dorchester on her way home she found Tamzin on her knees in Conrad's suite giving him a blow job.

'Is this why you've been spending so much time away?' she'd yelled after their PA had fled in tears.

'I needed stress relief from somewhere,' Conrad hissed back. 'It's not like you're giving me any.'

'You're a despicable human being!'

'I'm also your loving husband.' He advanced towards her dangerously. 'If you breathe a word of this, your little home video is going viral.'

Chapter 73

With less than a week until election day, campaigning had stepped up to a whole new level. So had the smear tactics, as the parties tried to bring down their rivals by any means possible. An unfortunate photo of the Lib Dem Helen Singh smoking a bong at university had been published in the previous day's *Sun*. Esme Santura's real name had been revealed as Elaine Scroggins. The *Guardian* had got hold of a picture of Major Bill Fairclough smoking a cigar with a member of the BNP. The major hadn't helped his cause by saying the BNP guy had been a jolly nice chap and all serial burglars should face the death penalty.

Catherine had got off relatively lightly. Everyone knew her past. In the face of the colourful new accusations, her 'Champagne Charlotte' moniker was seen as a bit old hat. Annoyingly, Tristan Jago was managing to stay squeaky clean as well. The hard-working social worker seemed dedicated to his cause, a pillar of the local community.

It was extremely frustrating as Catherine knew

exactly which member of the community Tristan had been showing his pillar to. But what could she do? Mel was a good friend. She had to stick a smile on and suck it up.

Besides, there was a sense things were starting to change. The PM's visit had altered everything. Catherine was now third in the MORI polls, behind Tristan and the bong-smoking Helen Singh. The press was starting to describe her as a late contender, a possible masterstroke for the beleaguered government. Perhaps, they were saying, the PM's wild card would pay off.

Catherine's campaigning became even more zealous. Desperate not to spend any time at home where the empty rooms reminded her of John's absence, she passed every waking hour tramping the streets. Even Clive and Kitty were expressing concern she was pushing herself too much, but Catherine did what she'd always done and threw herself into work. She knew her marriage was in real trouble. But every minute she kept busy meant she didn't have to face up to what was happening.

Catherine was dead on her feet by the time they got back to the High Street that evening. She could see Ursula Patel behind the counter at Soraya closing up for the day. Telling the others she'd see them back at base, Catherine knocked on the door. Mrs Patel looked up and smiled. 'It's open,' she called. 'Come in!'

The boutique was a wonderful relief from the hot dusty day. 'My dear, you look exhausted.' Mrs Patel gestured to the velvet armchair in front of the counter. 'Take a seat.'

Catherine sank down gratefully. 'How are you? Please tell me something that doesn't involve the case against wind farms or someone's wall falling down.'

Mrs Patel gave a regretful smile. 'Rather worried, if you really want to know. This council meeting is hanging over our heads like a black cloud. Dilip's getting up four times a night with the stress.'

'He's not the only one. We just have to cross our fingers and hope for the best.'

'Anyway, to what honour do I owe this visit?' Mrs Patel smiled. 'You're a very important and busy person these days.'

'In fact, I do want something. Or to buy something. I need a new dress for election day.'

'Of course. Why don't you sit there and I'll pull you out a few things?'

In the end Catherine settled on a silk belted Diane Von Furstenberg in peacock blue. Despite her protestations Mrs Patel insisted on giving her a generous discount.

She handed the bag over. 'Have you heard from John?'

'A few times.'

Ursula Patel observed her across the counter. 'My dear, is everything all right?'

'Not really.' Catherine felt her lip wobbling, and burst into tears.

The blinds were swiftly pulled down and the door locked. Mrs Patel handed her a box of tissues and let her have a good old cry.

'I'm sorry,' Catherine sniffed. 'I'm just so tired.'

'Of course you are,' Mrs Patel said soothingly. 'This must be a very emotional time for you. All this pressure and stress, and with John being away.'

'I've driven him away,' Catherine said, bursting into fresh floods of tears.

'There, there. I'm quite sure that you didn't.'

'We haven't been getting on.'

'I did think something was up. Oh, my dear.'

Catherine exhaled shakily. 'It's all such a mess. You know, with my career I've always been so sure of my instincts. I could communicate what I wanted in an instant. It's completely different with my marriage. John sees me as this problem to fix, but I don't know what makes me happy.'

'You have to keep talking,' Mrs Patel said firmly. 'Communication is the most important thing in a marriage. Even if it's something you don't want to hear.'

'Do you and Dilip ever argue?'

'Of course we do. Especially when he leaves his cotton earbuds by the side of the sink!' Mrs Patel smiled. 'I'm sure I have habits that annoy him as well.'

Catherine looked at this tall, graceful woman whose husband was three inches shorter than her and walked around in socks and sandals all year. 'How do you make it work? Because I could really do with the advice right now.'

Mrs Patel looked thoughtful. 'You need common ground. Dilip and I agree on how to raise Pritti, and the importance of family. Respect is important, as is being kind to each other.' Mrs Patel smiled. 'Dilip can drive me crazy, but he's always made me laugh. You have to have fun together.'

'I can't remember the last time John and I had fun together,' Catherine said sadly.

'Talk to him. Look into your heart, Catherine, and find what's troubling you.'

'Do you think I should wait until he gets home?'

'I think you should do it sooner.' Mrs Patel looked serious. 'Be careful. You don't want to get to the point where you can't get him back again.'

Catherine got home and headed straight for the loo. Ursula was right, they hadn't been communicating. Or rather John had, and she – irrational, defensive, stubborn – had pushed him away.

Her behaviour had been reprehensible. Catherine only hoped he'd forgive her. And suddenly, a huge piece of the jigsaw fell into place. The mood swings and low-level nausea she'd put down to nerves. The permanently full bladder and inexplicable craving for McCoy's ridged steak crisps . . .

She still had some spare pregnancy tests in the bathroom cabinet. She got one out and re-read the now familiar instructions.

She was still staring at the words 'Pregnant 3+' when her mobile started ringing out in the hallway. She knew instinctively it was John.

The phone was lost in the depths of her handbag. 'Fuck's sake! Where are you?' Catherine whipped it out just as John's number cut off before her. *Missed call.*

'I'm here!' she cried, frantically redialling. 'I didn't miss you!' A second later: *'You've reached the voicemail of* . . .' John was leaving her a message.

Her voicemail beeped with a message a few minutes

later. *'You have one new message,'* the automated voice intoned. *'Message received today at ten twenty-two p.m.'*

'Bloody get on with it!' she shouted. Her heart swelled as she heard the familiar Geordie burr.

'Hi, Cath. I was hoping you'd pick up, but you're probably out campaigning. I hope it's going OK, we're in a pretty remote place but I've been getting BBC News *when I can. I saw you with the Prime Minister the other day. You looked great.'*

There was a long, horrible pause. *'Cath, sweetheart, we're in a load of trouble here.'*

She felt her heart detach and roll down to the bottom of her stomach.

'This is the world's worst timing. But I can't keep pretending. I owe you the truth about how I feel.

'The truth is, Cath, I'm not sure we have a future together.' His voice sounded broken. *'You've only ever been the one for me, Cath. I've waited my whole life for you. But now I'm starting to wonder if it was just a romantic notion, an ideal I had of us being together.'*

Catherine's legs dissolved underneath her. She slid down the wall.

'All I've ever wanted to do is love you and look after you. You're an amazing woman, Cath, and I've been so proud to call you my wife. Your independence is one of the things I've loved most about you, but now I realize you've been trying to tell me something. I can't seem to make you happy, Cath. It's like I suffocate you, and that's a bloody horrible way to feel. I'm starting to wonder if I made you feel like that all the way along.'

The line crackled, muffling John's voice. Or was he crying? *'I used to think loving someone was enough to make it work. Now I'm not so sure. I can't be with someone who doesn't want to be with me. We're both too good to live our lives like this.*

'*I can't believe I'm saying this into a voicemail. Then again,*' a wry note entered his voice. '*It's the only time I've been able to tell you how I'm feeling without it descending into an argument.*' There was another burst of static. '*I'm going off on a trip by myself for a few days. I don't know if there will be any phone reception. I'll let you know when I'm back. Thinking of you always, good luck on Thursday.*' The call ended abruptly.

Catherine was shaking so much she dropped the phone twice. 'John!' she cried. 'You've got it all wrong. Please, please pick up.'

It was too late. It went through to voicemail. He'd already turned his phone off.

She put her face on the cold floor and howled.

Chapter 74

Fleur drove into the yard that night and immediately sensed something was wrong. The house was too still. Jumping off her quad bike, she raced inside.

'Dad?'

The dogs hung back at the door, unwilling to come in. Fleur saw the gun cartridges scattered on the kitchen table.

'Dad!'

She raced down the corridor. 'Dad!' She tried the study door but it was locked. 'Are you in there?'

No answer. She was sweating with fright. *No, no, no.*

'Dad!' She started beating on the door with her fists. 'Let me in!'

She jumped as it was suddenly wrenched open. Her father stood there, eyes puffy and bloodshot.

'What the hell is going on?' he growled.

'I could bloody ask you the same thing!' she cried. 'Why do you always lock yourself in?'

The table was strewn with old photographs of her mother. Embarrassed at what she'd stumbled in on, angry, inordinately relieved, she went for her dad.

'Why are there spent gun cartridges on the kitchen table?'

'I've been out, shooting rabbits. What are you yelling for?'

She was close to tears. 'I came in and thought . . .'

Her dad stared at her. 'What did you think?'

She bit her lip, holding back. 'So this is what you come in here to do? Look at pictures of Mum?'

He went back to his armchair. The way he walked reminded Fleur of the tired, stiff way her grandfather had moved round before he had died.

'Now you know,' Robert said. 'The sad secret of a sad old man.'

'It's not sad!' Fleur said tearfully. 'Why don't you talk to me about Mum?'

He picked up his glass. She looked back at the desk. There were other photos laid out alongside the ones of her mother. Fleur picked up one of her granddad as a young man. It must have been harvest time; he was standing stiffly in one of the fields holding a pitchfork.

She glanced over the other black and white photographs. The way the farm's history was all laid out like this; it seemed so final.

Her dad picked up his glass. 'It's all right, lass. You've got Beau now. Maybe I was wrong about him after all.'

'What do you mean I've got Beau? I've still got you, haven't I? Dad?' she said. 'We've still got each other, haven't we?'

Her dad wasn't listening. 'I won't be a burden to you for much longer. Then you can have your life back again.'

'Dad,' Fleur said in a tiny voice. 'You're scaring me.'

'Don't be scared,' he said distantly. 'Everything will be all right.'

Fleur went over and knelt down by him. 'Please tell me you're not about to do anything stupid. We'll get through this somehow.'

That night, she hid his shotgun.

Chapter 75

Two things dominated the papers the following morning: the Beeversham by-election and the Ye Olde Worlde meeting. The *Sunday Times* ran a headline about the fate of the government being in Catherine's hands. The *Sunday Telegraph* went with it being crunchtime for the future of rural England, asking: 'Will it be concrete car parks or fields of dreams?' Catherine, skimming the papers at 7 a.m. after barely sleeping, had run upstairs to be sick.

She felt utterly helpless. She'd called John obsessively all night, waking up fully dressed at 5 a.m. on the bed, still clutching her phone. Clive and Kitty had taken one look at her and asked if they should call a doctor. Numb, Catherine had gone on to autopilot. She went back out, smiling, cajoling, and talking people round. On the inside she was an empty shell.

Desperate to keep busy, she insisted on knocking on twice as many doors when they went out. By one o'clock, after she'd nearly fainted on someone's doorstep, Kitty and Clive had persuaded her to take a break. Unable to bear the concerned looks, Catherine had asked to borrow Clive's Volvo.

Without thinking she'd found herself driving up to Blaize Castle. The view, as ever, was heart-stopping. She looked out over the swaying fields and wondered what John was looking out on at that precise moment. Was he consumed with wretched misery and thinking about her, the way she was about him?

This place had always brought her happiness, but now it seemed so bleak. How could she stay here without John in her life? She wasn't being melodramatic. Her husband saw things in black and white. Once he made his mind up about something, there was no going back. Maybe he was right. Maybe she had always kept him at arm's length, and, little by little, year by year, even he had been worn down. 'Oh, my darling,' she sobbed. 'I'm so scared I've lost you!'

'Are you sure you don't mind?' Vanessa asked Dylan for the umpteenth time.

'She'll be fine,' he reassured her. 'Look, her and Eddie are best mates already.'

They looked over to where a delighted Sukie was rolling in the long grass with Eddie. She'd hared round like a mad thing when they'd first got here, excitedly seeking out all the new sights and smells. Her pristine white coat was already strewn with leaves.

It was one less thing to worry about. The little dog had been getting so anxious with the strained atmosphere in the house, but Vanessa hadn't been able to put her precious Sukie into kennels, no matter how luxurious.

She knew her dog would be happy and well cared for with Dylan.

She put her arms round his waist. 'I wish I could stay here as well.'

'Stay. Let me take care of you.'

'I just have to get through this week.' She pressed her face against his T-shirt and breathed his familiar fresh-air scent in.

'The next time I see you we'll be together properly,' Vanessa murmured.

He held her so tight she thought she would break. 'That's all I've ever wanted,' he told her.

Catherine was driving back into Beeversham when she saw a familiar Smart Car by the side of the road. The wheezing sounds coming from the engine did not sound healthy.

She pulled up beside the window to see a hysterical Vanessa Powell behind the wheel. She shot Catherine a murderous look.

Two paparazzi motorbikes were zooming down the track out of Foxglove Woods.

'OH, FUCKING START!' Vanessa screamed.

Catherine had no idea why she was so desperate to get away, but the woman was in a complete state. 'Get in,' she shouted.

Vanessa looked across at her. 'What?'

'I said, get in! Unless you want those paps to catch you!'

She could see Vanessa wrestling inwardly, before she grabbed her Birkin handbag and jumped out. She threw herself in the passenger door, almost sliding off Kitty's bead seat-covering. 'Drive, drive, drive!'

Sensing a kill, the bikes weren't giving up easily. The Volvo roared down Beeversham High Street at twice the normal speed limit. Several people did a double-take but decided it simply couldn't be the Conservative candidate Catherine Connor at the steering wheel because, at this stage in the campaign, such flagrant law-breaking would be suicidal.

Vanessa had her head jammed in the footwell.

'Where do you want me to go?' Catherine asked.

'Just get rid of them!' came the muffled cry.

The W reg Volvo was no match for the powerful Yamahas, but Catherine had always driven on the fast side, and she knew the lanes around Beeversham. Zooming through the outskirts, she took a sharp right and floored the car down a little turn-off. Moments later the powerful engines of the bikes roared past.

The car came to a stop under an ancient oak. 'You can come out now,' Catherine said.

Vanessa stayed where she was.

'I said, you can—'

'I heard you!' Vanessa said crossly. As she sat up, Catherine was shocked at the state of her. Vanessa's eyes were red, and her hair was everywhere. Her Chanel sunglasses hung comically off the end of her nose. She glared at Catherine.

Don't mention it, Catherine thought. *It's not like I've got other things to do.*

The two women sat there in silence for a while.

'I'm having an affair,' Vanessa suddenly announced. 'With a man called Dylan Goldhawk.'

Catherine tried not to show her surprise. 'Dylan, the guy who lives behind Foxglove Woods?'

Vanessa nodded. 'The bikes were waiting nearby when I got back to the car. I was scared they'd put two and two together and go and find him.'

Catherine didn't know what to say, so she kept quiet. She noticed how slight Vanessa's wrists were. They looked too fragile to hold the weight of her Cartier watch.

'I suppose this is your big exclusive,' Vanessa said bitterly. '"VANESSA POWELL'S SHOCK AFFAIR." You'll probably have me jumping naked out of a cake somewhere.'

Catherine sighed. 'Vanessa, what you do in your personal life is no concern of mine.'

'You've changed your tune.'

'Are you ever going to get over this? I apologized at the time. It was a bad call and you ended up being well compensated.' *And building your career off it,* Catherine wanted to add.

'That makes it all right, does it? It was a horrible experience to have to go through. It's not just the celebrity who gets hurt when you print these things, you know.'

Catherine felt deeply chastised. 'I'm sorry I made you feel like that.'

'Yes, well. Maybe you should think next time,' Vanessa retorted. 'Just because someone's in the public eye doesn't stop them being human.'

Catherine glanced across at her adversary with new-found respect. 'So what now?' she asked. 'Do you want me to drop you home?'

'I hate my husband!' Vanessa burst out passionately. 'He's a total bastard!'

Catherine was about to add that she agreed but she could see it was no time for jokey remarks. 'I'm leaving him,' Vanessa said. 'Right after the Silver Box Awards.'

'Oh,' Catherine said inadequately.

Vanessa gripped on to the Birkin in her lap. 'Catherine, I'm scared.'

It touched Catherine that Vanessa had used her name. 'What are you scared about?' she asked gently.

'Breaking up Brand Powell. The repercussions. All the bad press. I've worked so hard to get here, and now I'm about to throw it all away.' Vanessa's eyes welled up. 'The dreadful headlines my mother will have to read. Conrad will try and portray me as a home-wrecker, I know it.'

'A few bad headlines aren't the end of the world,' Catherine told her. 'And I should know. You just have to be true to yourself.'

Vanessa turned to fix Catherine with her famous caramel gaze. 'You really think so?'

'I do. Vanessa, you've built yourself back up before. You can do it again. The public will side with you once they find out what an arsehole Conrad is.' Catherine looked at the celebrity closely. 'Is Dylan worth it?'

'Oh yes,' she said fervently. 'He's a wonderful, kind man who loves me for me. Not what I've got. I feel like he's the only person in the world who's ever understood me. When we're apart it's like a piece of me is missing.'

Tears pricked the back of Catherine's throat. 'Then do it. Take it from me, life is nothing without the person you love.'

Chapter 76

It was fast becoming a two-horse race between Tristan and Catherine. She was second in the latest poll on 31 per cent compared to Tristan's 40 per cent. As the hours ticked by, the dirty tricks intensified. A pro-Tory street had woken up that morning to find the 'Vote Connor' placards in their front gardens had been mysteriously replaced overnight with Tristan's placards. Meanwhile, Esme Santura was going round pulling the Lib Dem leaflets out of people's letterboxes (the party was notorious for never posting their leaflets through properly), and replacing them with horoscope sheets promising great things if she got voted in.

That lunchtime Catherine found herself at a local primary school. It was the long-serving local dinner lady's retirement party, and in campaigning terms, electoral gold dust. Catherine had done herself no favours by turning up late and interrupting an emotional speech by the headmistress.

She was standing on the sidelines, trying desperately to keep down a piece of shortbread when Tristan sprang up, jaunty in red skinny jeans and a paisley shirt. 'You're looking rather peaky,' he remarked. 'Pressure getting to you?'

'Piss off, Tristan,' she replied bleakly.

A local reporter sidled up between them. 'Catherine's catching you up in the polls,' he said to Tristan. 'You must be getting a bit worried?'

Tristan adopted a pompous expression. 'The only person who should be worried is Catherine, when I claim that seat on Thursday. It's about time someone with principles and a sense of honour represented the decent, hard-working people of this constituency.'

Catherine dragged herself away from a horrible daydream about being a single mum. 'So you're that decent, principled person?'

'As a matter of fact, I am.'

'So there're no skeletons in your closet? No night-time canvassing we should know about?'

Tristan's mega-watt smile dimmed slightly. 'I don't know what you mean.'

Catherine went in for the kill. 'Is Lavender Close on your hit list?'

She had him. Tristan went as white as a sheet. If Catherine exposed him for being a home-wrecker it would almost certainly scupper his chances of winning.

'Catherine?' the reporter pushed. 'Can you elaborate?'

For a brief moment Catherine imagined the glory on election day as she surged past Labour to win. Perhaps it would make her dreadful sacrifice the tiniest bit bearable.

'It was just a joke.' She watched the relief seep into Tristan's face.

'I did that for Mel, not you,' she hissed afterwards. 'Now get out of my way, I need the loo.'

It seemed the pressure was getting to everyone. Later on in the day Catherine and Felix had their first ever argument.

'I've scheduled another visit to the old people's home,' he told her.

'Is that a good idea? They didn't even know I was there last time; even the head nurse said so.'

He walked off across the office. 'No, you need to do it.'

Tired, distraught, unable to confide in anyone, Catherine lost the plot. 'I'm not doing it!' she yelled. 'Anyone with half a brain can see it's a waste of time!'

Felix whirled round, his blue eyes icy. 'You'll do what I bloody tell you to do!' He jabbed his finger at her. 'I'm in charge of this campaign, not you!'

She watched in shock as he stormed out.

Chapter 77

It was twenty-four hours until the council meeting. When Fleur went into Mr Patel's she found him behind the counter staring into space.

'Hello, Fleur,' he said gloomily. 'I'm just trying to imagine what it will be like when my family are destitute and homeless.'

'I'm sure it will be OK, Mr Patel.'

'Maybe,' he sighed. 'And how about you? How is your father?'

The stock response. 'We're great, thanks.'

'What can I get you?' Mr Patel asked.

'Just the bread, please.' Fleur gazed at the pile of *OK!* magazines on the counter. The Powells were on the front cover, Vanessa curled up in Conrad's arms in a loving embrace. 'The only award I care about is being best husband,' was the cover line.

'You want a copy, my dear?' Mr Patel asked. 'How people can waffle on about themselves for fourteen pages is beyond me.'

The invitation to go into Vanessa and Conrad's

glamorous world was a brief respite from her own life. Fleur went back to the farm and spent an indulgent hour poring over the interview and photographs. They looked totally in love with each other, and Vanessa was so beautiful. Some people really did have it all.

The magazine only provided a brief distraction. Beau had been off the radar for twenty-four hours. He hadn't responded to any of Fleur's texts. Her bad feeling was growing by the hour. By 9 p.m., when she still hadn't heard anything, Fleur could stand it no longer. She was going to drive over and see if he was there.

Ridings was lit up like a lighthouse, Beau's Mustang parked out the front. She wasn't sure if she was relieved or gutted.

Instead of knocking on the front door, Fleur went round the side instead. *Am I trying to catch him out?* she thought. She found him in the kitchen, alone, taking the head off a bottle of beer.

'Angel.' He looked surprised. 'I didn't know you were coming over.'

'You didn't get my texts?' She smiled quizzically.

'Yes, sorry. I just haven't had a chance to answer them.'

How long did it take to reply to a text? For the first time she noticed that his flawless beauty had been knocked around the edges. There was stubble on his chin, violet circles under the dazzling blue eyes.

It only made her want him even more.

'Do you want to go to bed?' She slid her arms round his neck. Just the smell of him made her glow between the legs.

She tried to kiss him, but he pulled back. 'I've got

a ton of work to get through. I've got a couple of big meetings in London in the next two days.'

She felt like she'd been sucker-punched. 'OK,' she said, trying not to show her upset.

'You don't mind, do you?'

'No,' she lied. 'So you're not going to the county council meeting?'

'I've got bigger fish to fry.' Beau glanced at the clock, distracted, already in another place. 'I'll see you out.'

Oh God. He was trying to get rid of her. 'D-don't worry, I'll see myself out.'

'Don't be silly.' Beau draped his arm round her, steering her towards the front door. She couldn't believe it was happening. He was bored of her already.

At the front door, he gave her a perfunctory kiss. 'I'll be in touch, angel.'

His eyes strayed over her shoulder. Was he expecting someone? Fleur gazed into his perfect, fathomless face and realized that she'd never really had him at all.

Chapter 78

Barely awake, in the half-light, for a blissful moment Catherine thought John was lying next to her in bed. She opened her eyes and was confronted by the empty right-hand side.

Utterly wretched, she hugged her gently rounded stomach. She knew John would love and protect any child she brought into the world. It was the thought of him not loving *her* anymore that Catherine was terrified of. She'd been calling him non-stop without any success. Each time Catherine heard the automated voicemail, she had panicked and hung up. She'd heard it in his voice. He'd given up on her.

Catherine reached out and touched the cool pillow. She felt desolate at the thought of never going to sleep at night again with his arms around her. She'd thrown away everything. She'd thrown away their future.

She started to sob gently into the pillow.

Vanessa stood on the bedroom terrace in her dressing gown, watching two rabbits scamper round the back lawn. The garden was swathed in an early morning mist. It was an oddly peaceful scene, considering the drama that lay ahead.

'Who's opened the window?' Conrad moaned.

'Go back to sleep,' Vanessa said. 'It's still early.'

There was a moment of silence then: 'It's five fucking a.m.! Do you want me to have under-eye bags that show up in all their HD glory?'

Vanessa looked at the bed. Conrad was stretched out like a corpse, his eye-mask still on. What a despicable human being. How could she ever have loved him?

The rabbits were still gambolling round, the bigger one springing joyfully after the smaller. It made Vanessa think of Sukie and Eddie. The animals stopped their capers, noses twitching. Vanessa looked for whatever predator they'd heard, then gasped. Dylan was standing in the far corner of the garden, looking up at her with his gorgeous lopsided smile.

'What are you doing here?' she mouthed ecstatically.

Dylan put his finger to his lips. He bent down and picked something up. Vanessa's heart swelled when she saw Sukie in his arms. The dog had a new spotty green neckerchief.

Sukie spotted her mistress and her tail started beating frantically. It was all Vanessa could do to stop herself climbing down the balcony and running over to join them.

They grinned idiotically at each other. There was no need for words. Dylan had known to come when she needed him the most.

*

Fleur was woken by the sound of pigeons cooing outside her bedroom window. She turned over in the narrow bed and immediately checked her phone. Her heart sank; she'd been hoping Beau had texted her in the night.

Fleur looked round the room, at the cracked washbasin and oppressive dark furniture. Had it always been this scruffy and tired-looking? Her depression intensified. Now she'd tasted real luxury it all seemed so much worse.

Getting up, she went over to the window. Ridings was just visible in the morning mist, a white castle on the dewy landscape. Already it felt like a gilded tower she had no way of getting back into. She imagined Beau stretched out in bed, naked body against the white sheets. Was he even alone? Was Lynette Tudor with him, or some other leggy beauty who'd been waiting on the sidelines?

Her stomach clenched with misery. *You knew this was coming*, she told herself. *Beau's too beautiful for you to have all to yourself.*

Close to tears, she gripped the flaking windowsill. The lights had been turned out in her life once again.

Chapter 79

A coach had been put on to take people from the High Street to County Hall. When Catherine got down there that morning she had to fight her way through hordes of press.

'Quick word, Catherine,' *Sky News* asked. 'You're nearly neck and neck with Tristan Jago in the latest YouGov poll. Do you think you can overtake him?'

She stared at the man. 'What?'

'You're only three per cent behind! You're in with a serious chance of winning.'

Catherine shook her head. She was incapable of speech right now.

Everyone was there: the Belchers, Lynette and Talia Tudor, the Patel family, the Cooper-Stanleys, even TV presenter Gideon Armstrong. Vincent had taken the morning off from Bar 47 and was looking very Italian in a silk black shirt as he smoked furiously by the war memorial. Even the Taunton-Browns had deigned to honour everyone with their presence. Aubrey and

Viola stood apart from the crowd, clearly miffed at having to stand with hoi polloi.

The Blue Rosettes were swarming about; campaigning had been put on hold for the morning. Catherine saw Felix coming out of the mini market and went over.

'Felix.'

He had two bottles of water in his hand. 'Have you heard about the latest YouGov?'

'I can't believe it.'

'Tremendous work, very well done.'

'I'm sorry about yesterday,' she said. 'I shouldn't have flown at you like that.'

'I'm sorry too,' he told her. 'Nerves are running high this week, we're all feeling it.'

She gave a strangled laugh. 'Don't I know it.'

He had an odd expression on his face. She wondered if her eyes were still puffy, or if she looked as rough as she felt. If Felix asked about John, Catherine knew she'd burst into tears again.

He glanced over her shoulder. 'I'd better get back to Ginny.'

She turned round, to see Ginny standing outside Soraya with Mrs Patel. Catherine was dismayed by her appearance. Her normally rosy face was drawn and haggard and the gingham smock top she was wearing was hanging off her.

'Ginny's not well, is she?' Catherine said quietly. 'Felix, if there's anything I can do . . .'

He touched her arm and stepped out into the road.

*

County Hall had never seen scenes like it. Sky's Kay Burley was reporting from the top steps, while camera crews swarmed through the crowds, hoping to collar a familiar or famous face.

Catherine sat in the back of the stifling hot Volvo and tried to compose herself. All she wanted was to flee home and climb into bed, but for now she had to put her personal problems aside. People were depending on her.

John's absence felt palpable as she approached the scrum. Another reporter pounced on her as soon as she got near.

'What does this mean for Beeversham if Ye Olde Worlde goes ahead?'

She mumbled something about having faith in the county council, but then the press surged forward, granting her a reprieve. Sid Sykes had arrived with his posse of minders. The rural campaigners held their banners aloft and started jeering.

'Sid! Mr Sykes!' There was a lot of jostling and pushing and several bystanders got caught in the mêlée. Suddenly Sykes and Felix found themselves face to face. It was an electrifying moment: the chief campaigner against Ye Olde Worlde and his adversary.

Everyone held their breath. The assorted press waited for a reaction. Sykes's mouth spread into a smug smile. 'Morning, Felix.'

A second seemed to last an age. Felix gave a curt smile and turned on his heel. Disappointed, the press pushed after him, but he was already propelling himself towards the entrance.

Chapter 80

The Blue Rosettes formed a protective circle round Catherine, knowing something was wrong. Mel grabbed her arm as they all filed in.

'Babes, you look terrible. Are you OK?'

She shook her head.

'Is it John?'

'I can't talk about it,' she whispered.

Mel put her hand on Catherine's arm. 'Deep breaths, you're OK.'

Tristan Jago was walking towards them. There was a camera crew nearby and Catherine waited for him to pounce, but he put his head down and rushed past.

'Tristan told me you know about us,' Mel said quietly. 'Thank you for not saying anything.'

'Mel, it's really none of my business.'

She kept her hand on Catherine's arm. 'I love Mike very much. I know it might sound strange, but it works for us.' Mel looked over and smiled at her husband. 'He was married to someone else when we met. I knew what I was getting myself into.'

'Honestly, Mel, as if I'm someone to judge other people's marriages.'

'Are things really that bad?'

Catherine welled up again. Mel squeezed her arm. 'I'm here if you want to talk, babe.'

'Thanks, but I think it's a bit too late for talking.'

The car park outside County Hall was rammed, so Fleur had to use a side street to park. By the time she hared in, the meeting was about to start. Hundreds of people looked down at her. To her relief she spotted Ginny Chamberlain in the public gallery, with a spare seat next to her.

'Oh hello, Fleur dear. What a surprise to see you here.'

Ginny was dressed in her normal bright clothes, but Fleur was shocked by her appearance. She had always been round and reassuringly mother-like, but now she looked like she'd halved in size. Fleur wondered if she was ill. *Not Ginny*, she prayed. Ginny was one of the lovely people in life.

Even with the air conditioning up full blast it was uncomfortably warm. People were fanning themselves, a mixture of heat and nerves. The press had taken up the entire first row. Fleur saw Catherine Connor sitting upright, looking very poised in a khaki shirtdress. Directly across the room was a man Fleur recognized as Sid Sykes, talking intently to a younger man in a grey suit beside him.

The thirty-nine members of the county council sat at their desks in the middle of the room, looking awfully serious. The leader of the council was at the front of the chamber, next to the mayor. The latter reminded Fleur of a fat robin in his red robes.

A clock chimed outside. The chatter in the room died away. The leader of the council addressed the room.

'Good morning, everyone and thank you for coming. First off, apologies from one of our councillors, who is unable to attend due to ill-health.' He glanced at the clock again. 'We're here to discuss the amended proposals by Sykes Holdings, for the Ye Olde Worlde development on the site of Blaize Castle in Beeversham. The original plans were advised for amendment by this council on the fourth of July this year, after the planning officer raised three areas of concern.'

Heads round the chamber nodded furiously.

'I understand emotions have been running high on this particular case,' the leader continued. 'The council is sensitive to the difference of opinion on both sides. I would now like to take the unusual step of inviting Felix Chamberlain to say a few words.'

Felix stood up from his seat. 'Ladies and gentlemen.'

Fleur noticed how much Ginny's hands were shaking. Sensing Fleur's gaze, she tugged her sleeves down, but not before Fleur saw the large black bruise on her left wrist.

'This is a life-changing day for Beeversham,' Felix told the packed court. 'We are a friendly town, a hardworking town, who welcome newcomers as warmly as we welcome our own. We are bound together by a sense of community, our heritage and a love for the countryside. If Ye Olde Worlde gets the go-ahead, it will destroy everything that this town stands for. I urge you, members of the council, to consider the history of our market town, as well as the future of all who live there. Thank you.'

It was short, but to the point. Felix sat down again. A thin sheen of sweat had formed on his brow. Fleur watched Sykes's face. He could have been listening to the football results, he seemed so unconcerned.

The leader of the council turned to Team Sykes. 'Now I'd like to invite Damien Sykes, spokesman for Sykes Holdings.'

Damien may have looked like a Sicilian gangster, but his voice was pure public school.

'I would like to read a statement on behalf of my father, Mr Sidney Sykes. "As a conscientious member of society and happily married father of four . . ."'

'Here we go,' groaned one of the reporters.

'"Ye Olde Worlde has always been about much more than financial gain for me."' This time there were actual snorts from the press pack, earning themselves a disapproving look from the mayor.

'"I firmly believe that from my position of privilege, I can create a world, a happy, carefree world where the British people can forget about their problems and learn to love life again."'

Even some of the council rolled their eyes at that one, but Damien wasn't finished yet. '"Aside from the fun factor, Ye Olde Worlde will create hundreds of much-needed new jobs. I'm willing to dig into my pockets, and invest in the future of the people of the Gloucestershire. Let's build a bigger, better England together."'

'What a load of rubbish!' Amanda Belcher bristled in her seat. 'As if Sykes is doing all this out of the good-ness of his heart!'

448

'Quiet, please!' the leader called crossly. He looked down at his notes again.

'Here in front of me are the revised proposals of Sykes Holdings. The planning officer has been through them in full. I will now read those proposals out.'

'Point one: the concern of environmental blight. Sykes Holdings have promised significant landscaping and remedial work to ensure the development is in keeping with the surrounding area.'

All that could be heard was the gentle humming of the air conditioning. A car exhaust backfired outside in the street.

'Point two: insufficient transport structure. Sykes Holdings have promised a new roundabout and traffic-light system on the congested road out of Beeversham, which residents can make use of, as well as visitors to the park. In time they would also propose a Beeversham bypass.'

'Oh great, let's carve up even more of the country-side,' someone shouted.

'Not to mention taking away passing trade from the town centre,' cried Mr Patel.

The leader started to look irritated. Mrs Patel laid a placatory hand on her husband's thigh.

'The third concern was the inappropriate scale of the development to Beeversham and the surrounding area. Again, Sykes Holdings propose to landscape accordingly.'

'As if a topiary hedge is going to hide a bloody great theme park!' someone else yelled.

People dared to exchange hopeful looks. The leader of the council spoke again.

'Sykes Holdings have also proposed one more amendment. As well as the Ye Olde Worlde theme park, they've put in plans to build a thousand affordable homes on the site, to address the current shortage of housing across Gloucestershire.'

Sharp gasps echoed around the room. Ginny Chamberlain went so pale Fleur thought she was going to faint. The journalists started conferring excitedly.

A babble of voices rose up. 'You can't do that!' someone shouted. 'It's a bloody outrage!'

'Quiet!' the leader of the council said crossly. 'I think we've heard enough. It's time to vote.'

He looked faintly embarrassed. 'Unfortunately, our new electronic voting system has crashed, so we'll have to do it the old-fashioned way.'

He stood up. 'Ladies and gentlemen of the council, can I have a show of hands voting against Ye Olde Worlde?'

The female councillor nearest Catherine put her hand up straight away. Catherine smiled at her gratefully.

One by one, the hands went up. Everyone started frantically counting.

'Nineteen against,' the leader declared. 'And now, all those in favour.'

More hands started to go up. Ten, twelve, fifteen, sixteen. When it got to nineteen Catherine felt sick. They were going to get it.

'I'm sorry, but I'm going to have to abstain,' the remaining female councillor said. 'Moral reasons.'

It was nineteen either way. Stalemate. There was one person left to vote. All eyes were on the leader of the county council. *Come on,* Catherine willed him. *See sense and put us all out of our misery.*

The atmosphere was electric. The leader raised his hand aloft like a gladiator. *Live. Or die.*

'I vote,' he paused, 'in favour of Ye Olde Worlde.'

There was a moment of utter shock and then Mrs Patel burst into tears. 'How could they?' she cried out.

People were either stunned or very emotional. No one could believe it.

'Order, order!' the leader of the council shouted. 'The result is as follows: twenty votes to nineteen in favour of Ye Olde Worlde. I now declare the motion passed. Planning permission for the development is granted!'

Sid Sykes jumped up and smoothed his tie down. He shook hands with the man on his left, before clapping his son Damien on the back. Smug didn't even start to describe it. They filed out, protected by burly minders.

Catherine watched them go. A very real anger started to bubble up. This wasn't about a desire to improve society; it was a greedy, ruthless man's pursuit to line his pockets. How could such an injustice be allowed to happen?

The leader of the council also made a sharp exit, followed by most of his colleagues. Felix just sat there, gazing into space. People went to approach him, but seeing the expression on his face, backed away again. It was like intruding on the grief of a man who'd just lost everything.

Chapter 81

The producer's voice sounded in Vanessa's ear. 'Conrad, we need a little more expression.'

'I am giving you bloody expression,' he hissed. 'It's called nuance!'

The crew exchanged looks. No one dared bring up the subject of Conrad's frozen face. He'd turned up at the dress rehearsal at the Royal Albert Hall looking like a cross between Sharon Osbourne and the Bride of Wildenstein.

'I told you not to have Botox so close to the ceremony,' Vanessa said.

She got a malevolent look in return. 'What do you know, you wrinkled old hag!'

One of the cameramen was reading a discarded copy of that week's OK! He looked at the couple, then back at the magazine again.

'I've had enough of this. I'm an artist, not a performing seal!' Conrad pulled out his earpiece and stalked off the stage.

Vanessa was left standing up there by herself.

'Conrad's just got a headache,' she said apologetically.

'He's giving *me* a fucking headache,' the producer sighed.

Thank God they'd been given separate dressing rooms; it was bad enough sharing a stage with him. Vanessa sank down in a chair and put her head in her hands. Her iPhone started ringing. It was the Beeversham phone box she'd come to know so well. She snatched it up joyfully.

'Where are you?' Dylan asked her.

'The Royal Albert Hall.'

'How are you feeling?'

'Totally sick. Oh, Dylan, I don't know if I can do it.'

'You can do it,' he said. 'I'll be there watching you.'

'Wait, hold on a minute. You're not coming here?'

'You won't even know I'm there.' He sounded resolute. 'I'm not letting you do this by yourself. Don't worry, I won't do anything stupid. And don't worry about the dogs; Renata is minding them.'

Vanessa couldn't even imagine how that arrangement had happened. 'You're crazy,' she said happily.

There was a knock on the door. 'Mrs Powell? We're ready to start again.'

'I have to go,' she told him.

'I love you. You can do this, Vanessa. It's just one more day.'

'I hope you're right,' she whispered. Tomorrow was the biggest night of her life, let alone her career.

A runner was leaning against the wall as she walked back out. The girl looked up from her iPhone. 'Holy shit. Ye Olde Worlde got the go-ahead!'

*

453

The show had to go on. When Catherine went out campaigning that afternoon, she was met by anger and fear. Everyone was furious Ye Olde Worlde had got permission. No one wanted it. No one understood why it had happened.

In the very worst of times, the best things could happen as well. For once Catherine was united with her constituents on a common goal.

'It's a disgrace,' she was quoted on the local news that evening. 'The people of Beeversham won't go down without a fight. I want to take this all the way to parliament and see what they have to say about it.'

That evening people met in Bar 47. There seemed little else to do than have a drink and be with friends. Catherine arrived at ten o'clock, well after all the others. A solemn atmosphere met her. Everyone sat round looking shell-shocked. They had the stunned faces of people who'd just survived a near-fatal rocket attack.

No one knew where the Chamberlains were. They'd left straight after the verdict in their car and hadn't been seen since.

At least Catherine had been wrenched out of her own misery for the time being. Felix was still her campaign manager. To go AWOL at such an important moment . . . He must have been hit even harder than they'd thought.

'Have you heard from John?' Mr Patel asked Catherine, receiving a sharp jab in the ribs from his wife.

'We can still appeal to the council,' Mel said hopefully.

'Won't make any difference,' Mr Patel said gloomily. 'We've been tossed to the wolves and no one cares.'

Chapter 82

One of the ewes had got wedged under the hedge. Fleur had a hell of a job to pull it out. By the time she did, both were stinking and exhausted. The ewe's lamb stood a short way back, watching anxiously. After checking the mother's legs, Fleur patted the animal on the back. 'Nothing wrong with you, off you go.'

She watched mother and baby reunite, the ewe rubbing her face against her offspring's neck. She thought wistfully that it must be nice to have someone to depend on like that.

For the umpteenth time that morning, she looked across at the high ridge of Blaize Castle. Ye Olde Worlde was approaching, seemingly unstoppable after yesterday's verdict. She tried to imagine a huge Disney castle looming down on the town. The idea was horrific.

When she had broken the news to her dad he'd seemed strangely unmoved. In fact, he'd seemed almost happy. Resigned, like he'd given up. She had been left seriously worried her dad might be about to do something foolish. For the first time, she had contemplated staging some sort of intervention.

It was ironic, seeing as her own life was tumbling down like a pack of cards. She looked across the fields to Ridings for the thousandth time. She'd heard the whirr of the helicopter late last night, so she knew Beau was back. She'd broken her resolve at 2 a.m. and sent him a text, but there had been no reply.

An unpleasant sheep smell wafted off her, adding to her despair. It reminded her of the time when Beau had found her in the field covered in cow mucus. She'd hated him so much back then. If only she'd known then how things would turn out.

Suddenly, something stirred inside her. Something she hadn't felt for a long time. Determination. How dare Beau swan in and pursue her, then drop her like some used toy? She wasn't going to stand for it, and she wasn't going to be messed around, either. *I'm going over there now and telling him.* If that was it between them, she was going to come out with her dignity intact.

There was a green Golf parked outside when Fleur pulled up. Fleur found Sergio, Beau's personal chef, in the kitchen, whisking up egg whites.

'Hi, Sergio. Is Beau around?'

'Sorry, Miss Fleur. He's gone out for the day.'

Fleur looked at the pile of ingredients on the side. 'Cooking for someone?'

Sergio looked a bit uncomfortable. 'Mr Rainford just said he had someone special coming to dinner.'

A heaviness settled in the pit of Fleur's stomach. 'Well, I won't keep you. Oh, and Sergio?' She paused at the door. 'Can you not mention to Mr Rainford I was here?'

Outside in the hot sun, she started shivering. How could Beau have just replaced her like that?

As she walked in, she could see that his office was empty, the fully stocked wine fridge humming away in the corner. An unopened Fortnum & Mason picnic hamper was on the floor by the desk. Fleur's anger flared up. What woman was he intending on sharing that with?

God, you're an idiot. You let him wine and dine you like all the rest.

She crossed the room and went behind his desk. She was entering dangerous territory and she knew it. She clicked on the computer mouse, her eyes flickering back and forth from the door. The screen came up immediately. She clicked again on Outlook. She expected Beau to have a password, but his inbox immediately came up, for all to see.

Valentina's name was at the top. Her stomach heaved. Heart in mouth, Fleur opened it.

'*Baby, I miss U so much. I'm straight now, I promise. I've been going 2 rehab and I'm feeling really positive about the future. UR right; I did need 2 get clean. Can't we work this out? Candice is having her party on the fifteenth, I would love U 2 to come with me. Call me, text me, email me. Anytime. I miss U. V xxxx*'

Fleur didn't know how to feel about that one. At least he hadn't been sleeping with Valentina behind her back. He hadn't replied yet either, although that didn't mean he wasn't going to.

The next few emails looked disappointingly normal,

including one from Spencer titled 'Boys' Ski Trip'. There was also one from someone called Francesca B. Fleur clicked on it, and got an eyeful of Beau in a hot tub, with his arm round a topless ravishing blonde.

'Found this the other day and it brought back memories! Hope all's good, darling. See you at Goodwood next month? F xx.'

Fleur closed it promptly, feeling sick. It took a moment for her to focus on the next one. It was from an Anthony Protheroe at something called Beauchamp & Associates.

'Beau. Re: Blackwater Farm.

The funds are in. Do you want me to go ahead and transfer?

Ant.'

She gazed at the screen in confusion. Who was Anthony Protheroe? What was he talking about, funds for the farm?

Her hands had started to shake violently. Fleur moved the mouse on to the 'Sent' items. There had been a response from Beau at 11.44 that morning.

'Ant,

Great, go ahead. The deeds should be with you later.'

Fleur fell back as if the desk was contaminated. Beau had never been interested in her. He'd seduced her to get to the farm.

She was hit by another sucker punch, as vicious as the first. How could her dad have gone behind her back and done this?

Fleur collapsed in the chair. She couldn't breathe. Her head swam as her heart tried to pump blood round her shocked body. The colossal betrayal was literally overwhelming her.

Her eyes fell on a photo lying on the desk. The incongruousness snapped her back into the present. It was a picture of Talia, Lynette Tudor's daughter, sulkily ravishing in her school picture. Fleur frowned, distracted for a moment. Why would Beau have a picture of Talia Tudor on his desk?

She stared at it. Suddenly everything began to fall into place. The penetrating blue eyes, the sublime bone-structure. The arrogant tilt of Talia's chin. It was unmistakable. Beau was Talia's father.

For the second time that day, Fleur's world caved in.

Her father was in the kitchen eating a piece of bread and cheese.

'Dad.' Fleur's voice was unnaturally calm. 'Have you sold the farm to Beau?'

Her father stopped chewing. He put his knife down slowly.

Fleur started to pray. *Please, please, tell me there's been some kind of mix-up. Please, Dad.*

Robert eyed his daughter carefully. 'How did you find out?'

'Is it true?' she shouted.

'Yes,' he said simply.

'How could you?' she whispered. 'How could you betray me like this?'

Robert started to get up. 'Lass, listen. Fleur, wait!'

But Fleur was already running.

Chapter 83

Vanessa emerged from her hotel suite. Her stylist and make-up artist gasped.

'You look stunning,' her make-up artist cooed, rushing over to add a last touch of highlighter to Vanessa's cheekbones. 'I adore the new you.'

The dress, by famed British designer Bibi Brown, was far edgier than Vanessa would normally go for. Her cleavage was covered up for once, the green-gold fabric plunging deep off one honey-brown shoulder instead. With all the stress, Vanessa had lost weight. It had accentuated her collarbones and tiny waist, giving her a leaner, more feline look. Two hundred thousand pounds of diamonds dripped from her wrist and ears.

While her stylist fussed round with the hem of her dress, Vanessa stared at herself in the full-length mirror. By this time tomorrow she would have left her husband and Brand Powell would be over. Her stomach turned over. It wouldn't take Conrad long to drag her through the press as a scheming adulteress.

It was 5.45 p.m. It would be a thirty-minute drive

to the Royal Albert Hall in this traffic. Then it would be the red-carpet run; posing for the cameras and being interviewed. The awards kicked off at 8 p.m. An estimated six million people would be tuning in.

Vanessa's stomach lurched again. She shut her eyes and tried to imagine herself back with Dylan at the camp, lying in his arms on the grass. It was her safe, happy place, and it made her feel a fraction better.

Her mother came out of the adjoining guest suite looking regal, in Oscar de la Renta. Vanessa turned back to the mirror to fix her earrings and avoid looking at her.

'You look beautiful, Vanessa.'

'Thank you,' she said tonelessly. 'So do you.'

The two women had been avoiding each other as much as possible at home, exchanging brief polite pleasantries. Vanessa had expected her mother to side with Conrad, but Dominique had kept to herself and barely come out of her bedroom.

'Vanessa?'

She turned round, and was shocked to see her mother's heavily made-up eyes brimming with tears.

'Mother, what's wrong?'

'I'm sorry for not being a mother to you.' Dominique sat down heavily in a chair. 'I'm sorry for everything. The truth is, I've been jealous of you and Conrad, still having each other.' She started to weep. 'How awful, to be jealous of your own daughter.'

Vanessa went over and knelt down beside her. 'What's brought this on?'

Dominique's hands were twisting in her lap. 'I know I've always been hard on you. I just wanted you to

461

make something of your life, and not be like me.'

'You did make something of your life. You had a wonderful marriage.'

'Your father was the only one who ever understood me. I never felt like I fitted any place in the world until I met him.' She started to cry again. 'I miss him dreadfully.'

There was a shout from next door. 'Vanessa! Get your arse into gear. We need to go.'

Vanessa's own eyes filled up. 'I miss him, too,' she told her mother. 'But we've still got each other.'

'Are you still leaving Conrad?'

'Yes. Tonight, after the awards. Don't look frightened. I'm going to take care of you. You have to trust me.'

'VANESSA!' Conrad roared. 'What the fuck are you doing in there?'

Dominique gazed at her daughter through huge eyes. 'I trust you.'

Vanessa reached for a tissue and dabbed her mother's face. 'I'll always be here for you. OK?'

The door flew open and Conrad burst in, lean and menacing in his new dinner jacket. He glared at the two women. '*So* sorry to interrupt your little chat, but when you've got a moment, our car's here.'

They headed out into the rush-hour traffic, tailed by paparazzi motorbikes. It was a balmy evening in the capital, street cafés and bars packed with people. The well-heeled passers-by barely gave a second look to the gleaming Bentley swooping down Sloane Avenue like a presidential car. They were well used to such sights in that part of London.

The temperature outside was still at twenty degrees. Inside the car it was considerably colder. Conrad had instructed Billy to turn the air conditioning up to full blast so he wouldn't arrive at the Albert Hall looking flushed.

Vanessa was shivering violently, although she couldn't tell if it was from pure terror and nerves. 'Conrad, can we turn the AC down a bit?'

'Shut up,' he said, staring out of the window.

The traffic came to a halt again. A pap bike pulled up beside Vanessa and started snapping through the tinted windows. Gritting her teeth, she gave the man a smile.

'Oh, come on.' Conrad crossed his arms impatiently. 'We haven't got all day.'

'We've got lots of time, don't worry.'

'Oh, I'm sorry! I didn't realize you'd become director of London traffic.'

She felt Billy's eyes on her in the rear-view mirror. A white-hot rage started to build up inside her.

They pulled up at the traffic lights on to Kensington Road. She looked at her husband's profile, the cruel dark eyes and petulant mouth. What a disgusting human being he was.

'Conrad?'

He was staring at his fingernails. 'What?'

She took a deep breath. 'I'm leaving you.'

'What are you talking about?' he said irritably. 'We travel in the same car, don't we? If you want your own car, get your own fucking driver.'

He wasn't listening. 'I said, I'm leaving you,' she said, louder. 'I want out of this marriage.'

He turned to her, almost looking amused. 'You want what?'

'I want a divorce, Conrad!' she cried. 'I was going to wait until after the show, but I can't do it. I can't pretend any longer.'

He gave a snort of laughter. 'Oh, that is funny.'

'I'm serious. I'm leaving you, and there's nothing you can do about it!'

She watched him digest the information. 'You want to leave *me*? I made us, darling, and don't forget it.'

'*I* made us,' she said furiously. 'I'm the one who put in the hard work, negotiated the contracts, smoothed things over when you upset everyone! I'm the one who made Brand Powell!'

The Botox made it hard to gauge Conrad's reaction. It only made him even more dangerous, an unknown quantity.

'You're a talentless bitch, Vanessa, who's used her tits and arse to make her fortune.'

'And you can't act for toffee,' she shot back. 'They only hired you tonight because Hugh Grant couldn't do it!'

His eyes narrowed. 'You lying bitch.'

'You want to know another truth?' she cried. 'I'm leaving you for someone else!'

She watched his mouth fall open. He held himself in such godly esteem it would never have occurred to him that she would find someone else.

The word shot out like a bullet. 'Who?'

She swallowed. 'Dylan, the gardener.'

A flashbulb went off outside Conrad's window. Out of habit he flashed a smile. 'You're leaving me for the fucking gardener?' he hissed. 'Are you insane?'

'No, I'm bloody miserable!' she yelled. 'I've wasted too many years putting up with you. I love Dylan, and he loves me.'

The Royal Albert Hall was just ahead. Hordes of excited fans were lined up outside.

Billy slowed down. 'Do you want me to pull over?'

'Keep going!' Conrad snarled. He whipped back to Vanessa. 'I'll fucking ruin you. How dare you do this to me?'

'Because you're the biggest bastard that ever walked this earth! Try what you want, Conrad, anything's better than being married to you!'

The car pulled up. People started screaming their names.

'You are not breaking up Brand Powell,' he said, enunciating every syllable.

'Oh yes I am! Then see where you are, Conrad! I want to be married for love, not money!'

'Get out of the car,' he snarled.

'No! This charade has gone on long enough!'

'I said, *get out of the fucking car!*'

His phone was on the seat beside him. Vanessa took the opportunity and lunged.

'What the hell are you doing? Give me that back,' Conrad ordered.

'No!' She shoved it in her clutch bag. 'I'm not letting you put that video of me out there!'

A face outside Conrad's window made Vanessa catch her breath. Dylan! He'd made it!

'Oh,' she breathed. Dylan looked at her, concern on his face. *Are you all right?*

465

Conrad followed her gaze. 'He's here?' he shrieked. 'You brought him here to humiliate me?'

Vanessa tried to open the door. Her husband wrenched her hand away. 'Let me go!' she cried.

'You're not going anywhere!' he snapped.

She pressed the window button and the glass slid down. 'I'm afraid I won't be presenting the awards tonight,' she cried. 'I'm divorcing my husband.'

'Shut up! Shut up!' Conrad roared, but it was too late. The assorted press gasped. There was a moment of stunned silence. A microphone was shoved through the window.

'Vanessa! Can you confirm you're leaving Conrad?'

The whole interior was ablaze with flashbulbs. She could barely see. Conrad was wild-eyed; the stunned expression of a man who'd just lost the dream. He lunged through the seats, landing on the chauffeur in a grotesque jumble.

'The fucking *gardener!*' He grabbed the wheel.

Vanessa watched in horror as the car aimed straight for Dylan.

Chapter 84

Six and a half million people tuned in to watch the Silver Box Awards. Six and a half million people watched a berserk Conrad Powell drive his Bentley into a crowd of onlookers, scattering them like dominoes. Ambulances quickly arrived on the scene. Conrad was led away in handcuffs. Stephen Fry gallantly stepped in and offered to host the occasion.

A hysterical Vanessa Powell was filmed crouching down in her gown, beside a young, dark-haired man who looked seriously injured. The ambulance had wailed off, lights flashing, towards Chelsea and Westminster Hospital.

In Beeversham half the journalists drafted in for election day rushed off to the gates of Tresco House instead. That evening when Catherine went out for the all-important final push, she found constituents glued to their television sets.

By 11 p.m., there was one street left to tick off. Blackbird Rise, the pro-Labour street, had been a thorn in Catherine's side ever since she'd started. Everyone had told her to leave well alone. She had just seen it as a challenge.

The woman who'd shut her door in Catherine's face that very first morning greeted her with a knowing smile. 'Hello. I suppose you've come to hassle me about turning out to vote tomorrow?'

'I'd prefer to use the word cajole,' Catherine said wearily.

A TV blared down the hall. Catherine could hear a crowd screaming and the screech of brakes. 'You know how it was,' the woman told her. 'I've always voted Labour, but you've ended up by impressing me. You tell it how it is, which makes a change from most of these politicians trying to cover their arses.'

Catherine felt ridiculously close to tears. 'Thank you.'

Kitty and Clive were waiting faithfully at the bottom of the street. 'Are you OK?' Clive asked.

'Not really.'

Kitty put her hand on Catherine's arm. 'Look,' she said gently. 'Look at the houses.'

She turned round. Once a sea of red posters, every second window now had a 'Vote Connor' poster up. She felt herself welling up again.

'I really think we can do this,' Kitty told her.

Kitty and Clive dropped Catherine back at Tory HQ. Aubrey and the others were long gone. 'Are you sure you're going to be all right by yourself?' Clive asked, for the umpteenth time.

'Honestly, I'm fine,' she lied. 'I've just got a few last-minute things to catch up on.'

Felix had turned up as usual that morning, but any relief Catherine might have felt at having her campaign manager back had swiftly disappeared. Clearly devastated by the Ye Olde Worlde decision, he'd been preoccupied and short-tempered all day. It had surprised her and made her nervous. She'd expected him to come back fighting, and be right behind her. Instead, he'd seemed to have given up at the last hurdle.

The office looked like they were preparing for a military advance: piles of polling cards stacked neatly alongside thousands of names and addresses. She knew she should run through everything a final time, but she couldn't face it. Instead she left the cluttered office and went down the corridor to the meeting room. Pulling out a chair, she sat down in the dark.

A beam of moonlight streamed in through the window, turning her hands a ghostly white. They were trembling, just as they had been since she'd listened to John's voicemail. Had it really only been six days ago? It felt like she'd lived a lifetime since.

It had become an exercise in futility, but she tried his mobile once more. She waited for her new best friend the voicemail woman to finish. *'Please leave your message after the beep.'*

'John. It's me. Again.' She stared at the wall, desperately thinking what to say.

'I'm so sorry for the way I've acted. I wish you'd come home and we could work it out.' A lump rose up in her voice. 'Things have been ruined and it's all my fault.

'I've had a lot of time to think, and you're right. I have been pushing you away. I've deliberately sabotaged our marriage. Our wonderful, beautiful, amazing marriage.

I think, deep down, I've always been scared I wasn't good enough. I think, deep down . . .' God, why couldn't she just say it? 'I was scared you'd leave me like my mum did. I guess I thought I might as well get in there first and make you go.'

Catherine choked out a laugh. 'See what a pathetic fuck-up you married? I know it's too late for us, John, but I want you to know I take full responsibility for what I've done. If you came back . . .' She stumbled over her words. 'I know I would never take you for granted again.

'I've got something else to tell you. I'm pregnant. I know I should tell you face to face but, well, I guess this is how we're communicating these days.' She took a deep breath. 'I've decided I'm keeping the baby. It's not a trick to try and keep you. I'll understand if there's no chance for us.'

Tears ran silently down her cheeks, pooling in cold streaks around her neck. 'I should go now. Leave you to digest the bombshell.' She felt her heart break in two. 'Wherever you are, I hope you're happy.'

Her phone went off a few minutes later. Catherine lifted her head from where she'd been sobbing on the table.

'John?'

It was a familiar Welsh accent instead. 'It's me. Gwyn.'

'Oh.' The disappointment was crushing. 'Gwyn, hi.'

'You sound terrible, is now a bad time?'

'Heavy cold.' Catherine wiped her eyes. 'What can I do for you?'

'Well.' He paused. 'Don't want to set the cat amongst

the pigeons the night before your big day, but I've found out who owns Pear Tree Holdings.'

Catherine sat up. 'Who?'

What Gwyn told her next made Catherine forget everything else, at least for the time being.

Ten more minutes later she was in her car, heading for Beau Rainford's.

Chapter 85

There had been two places sacred to Fleur growing up. One was Cooper's Croft and the other was in the little copse, high up on the outskirts of the farm. She and her sister had spent entire summer holidays there, stretched out, eating apples from the garden, or homemade cookies if they were lucky. It was their own private kingdom, in which real time had no meaning. It was only when her mother hoisted the red blanket up on the washing line that Fleur and her sister knew it was time to go home for tea.

It had been years since she'd been there, but the little corrugated iron shack was still there, as were the sisters' initials carved into a tree. After discovering her dad and Beau's treachery, it had been the first place she had thought of.

She lay on the grass, curled on her side. A swathe of stars was sprinkled across the sky. In another lifetime, she would have thought how pretty it was. She had no idea how long she'd been here, only that it was very late and that no one would have fed the animals. If her dad had any wits left about him, he would have called Ben in to do it.

She was still only wearing shorts and a vest, but she couldn't feel the cold. She couldn't feel anything. Shock and anger had given way to numbness. It was all starting to make sense now. Beau's interest in the farm, the loaded comments Spencer had made about 'laying the groundwork', that she'd assumed was him referring to another business deal. They'd been laughing at her the whole time: Beau's textbook seduction of the hick country girl. Fleur wanted to tear herself apart. When she thought about the things she'd let Beau do to her, how he'd made her feel.

Deep down, she knew she couldn't blame her dad. In his own misguided way he'd thought he was doing the right thing. He was ill. Did it really matter that they were losing the farm? It was going to be sold off anyway. What mattered was that Beau had wormed his way into their lives and struck when they were at their most vulnerable.

The same questions kept tormenting her. *How could one human being do that to another?* He'd pretended they had a connection, bonding with her over their dead mothers. *How could someone be so beautiful on the outside, and be so ruthless and calculating inside?* How could she have fallen for it?

'I loved you,' she whispered.

Catherine pulled up outside Ridings and sat behind the steering wheel, wondering what to do. There was a pile of manifesto leaflets on the back seat. She got a pen out of her bag. She started to compose a note, taking her time. It might be the most important thing she'd ever write in her life.

Vanessa sat on the plastic seat in the waiting room at A & E. She was still in her five-thousand-pound ballgown. Even the old drunk across from her had woken up to stare. News reports were playing endlessly on the hospital TV screens.

Thank God, it was looking as if the other injured onlookers had escaped with cuts and bruises. Conrad was in custody. The police wanted to talk to Vanessa, as did her mother and Marty and her lawyer, but she didn't want to see anyone. All she wanted to know was if Dylan was going to be OK.

A doctor approached. 'Mrs Powell?'

She jumped up. 'Is he going to be all right?'

Everyone around craned their ears. 'Please,' the doctor said quietly. 'Come with me.'

Chapter 86

The downstairs hall light was on as Catherine pulled up in front of the Hollies. She sat and composed herself for a moment, before unbuckling her seat belt and getting out.

She rang the doorbell and a figure appeared through the stained glass. Felix pulled the door open, looking surprised to see her. 'Is everything all right?'

'Sorry to disturb you so late. Can I come in?'

'Of course. I'm still up, anyway.' He led Catherine through. 'Can I get you a nightcap? I was just having a whisky myself.'

'No, thank you.' She sat down in the armchair. 'Is Ginny here?'

'No, she's at her sister's.' He frowned at her. 'You look awfully serious. Is it John? I did hear you two were having some trouble.'

'Felix, I'm not here about John,' she said quietly.

He sat down in the chair opposite her. 'Oh, right.'

'I found out something tonight that is going to have huge implications for this town and everyone in it.'

He looked concerned. 'What is it?'

'There's no easy way to say this, so I'm just going to come right out with it.'

'Dear girl, you're starting to worry me! Has something happened at the office?'

'I know you're the one behind Pear Tree Holdings.'

Felix's silver eyebrows shot up. 'I'm sorry?'

'I've received credible information tonight that you own Pear Tree Holdings, and have done so for a number of years.' Catherine looked him squarely in the eye. 'You've been in cahoots with Sid Sykes all along.'

'That's preposterous!'

'I wish it was. I also know that you fixed the county council verdict and paid off several of the key councillors. Ye Olde Worlde was always going to get the go-ahead, whatever we did to try and stop it.'

'Don't be so ridiculous!' he said angrily. 'Why would I do that? I'm the one who's against the bloody thing!'

There was a loud hammering on the front door. 'What the . . .' He got up. 'Who the hell's that?'

He left her alone in the room. She looked down at her hands; this time they were perfectly still. A moment later there was the sound of an altercation in the hallway and she heard Felix exclaim. Beau appeared in the study doorway, blond hair dishevelled. 'I just got your note,' he told her.

Felix pushed past his brother and went over to the window. 'I don't know what you two are trying to cook up against me,' he snapped. 'But it's not going to work.'

Catherine felt oddly detached, as if the whole thing was happening to someone else. 'I'm afraid it is. I've got all the evidence: how you've already put an offer in for a three-million-pound house in Belgravia, and another for a pile in Yorkshire. You're planning to sell up and leave, aren't you? You never had any intention of sticking around once the planning permission got through.'

A vein started to pulse in his throat.

Beau gave a low whistle. 'My God, Felix, you've got more balls than I thought. It takes some nerve to try and pull off a stunt like this.'

'What the hell would you know about nerve?' Felix spat at him. 'You've had everything handed to you on a bloody plate!'

'You were in control of everything,' Catherine said quietly. 'By being at the forefront, you ensured no one would suspect you.'

The once-twinkly eyes were flat and hard, like pebbles on a beach. 'Do you have any idea what it's been like all these years? *Do you?* A small-town solicitor, bogged down in the mundane pettiness of other people's lives?' His voice rose. 'Having to put up with the likes of Aubrey Taunton-Brown when I should be in parliament, alongside my contemporaries? I was destined to make decisions, not follow them!'

'You've got some God complex,' Beau told him.

'Shut up!' Felix snapped. He rounded on Catherine. 'And you! Breezing in here like you owned the place. Beeversham should have been my seat years ago.' He jabbed his chest. '*Mine.* I've dedicated my life to my party, and all they've done is use me.' He put on a horrible whiny voice. '"Oh, Felix will do it, he's a good old chap. You can dump anything on old Felix."'

'Why did you help me?' she asked quietly.

'I didn't have much bloody choice in the matter, did I? Not that I thought you had a hope of winning.'

'So the plan was to buy yourself a nice new life?' Beau asked. 'Slip out of here with no one any the wiser?'

'No one else was going to give it to me! And then *she* came along and I was nominated as her chief babysitter.' The look he gave Catherine made her blood run cold. 'Poking your nose in where it wasn't wanted.'

'And where did Ginny fit into all this?' Beau enquired coldly. 'Were you going to tell her, or just up and leave?'

Felix stared him out. 'Of course not, I was going to get a divorce.'

'Aren't you the big man,' Beau said softly. 'Actually, leaving Ginny is the one good thing you could ever do for her. You've made her life miserable enough through the years.'

'Why do you care so much about my wife? Do you have designs on her now?'

Beau's jaw tightened. 'Ginny is like a mother to me. And you can talk about putting it about, you disgusting hypocrite. At least I take care of my responsibilities.'

'Don't you dare talk to me like that! Show me some respect!'

'You have to earn respect,' Beau shot back. 'Clearly something you're incapable of achieving.'

Every ounce of warmth had gone from Felix's face. Catherine was mesmerized. There was nothing left of the person she had known.

'Christ,' Beau said casually. 'If you needed the money that badly, I would have given it to you.'

It hit the spot, just as intended. Felix came for Beau, roaring. Catherine only just got out of the way in time.

The age gap was too great. Beau was too quick and too strong. Grabbing Felix's wrists, he got him down on the floor in a headlock.

'Get your hands off me!' Felix screamed. 'How dare you!'

'You're a sad, fucked-up bully, who's terrorized his wife and kids for years.' Beau pushed his brother's face into the carpet, subduing him. 'For God's sake, man, have some dignity. It's over.'

All the fight went out of the older man and he crumpled on to the floor. 'I was meant to be *more* than this,' he moaned.

It was a pitiful sight to witness. Beau released him and got up.

'What are you going to do?' he asked Catherine.

'I'm going public with the story. First thing tomorrow.'

Felix moaned again. 'You can't.'

She glanced at the pathetic heap on the floor. It was hard to believe she'd ever looked up to him.

'People need to know the truth,' she said quietly.

'You do know it will cost you the election?' Beau told her. 'Tory chairman turns out to be major player in Ye Olde Worlde. It will ruin your chances of winning.'

'I know.' Taking one final look at Felix, she walked out.

Chapter 87

'I'm pretty sure it's not an exaggeration to call Felix a sociopath. He's always had a major chip on his shoulder.'

Catherine and Beau were at her kitchen table, a bottle of red wine between them. They had stayed long enough to watch Felix hastily pack a suitcase and disappear into the night. It was hard to feel any sympathy for him.

'From the few things Ginny's said over the years, he's very like his own dad,' Beau continued. 'Apparently Trevor Chamberlain was a model citizen on the outside, but a real bully at home. He thought he was too good for Beeversham and clearly passed that on to Felix. The fact that he ended up back here after university and never left must have pissed him off deeply. He already harboured a deep resentment against my mother for leaving, but the truth was, that bastard Trevor Chamberlain abused her nearly every day of her life. Unfortunately, history went on to repeat itself.'

Catherine was shocked. 'Felix beat Ginny up?'

Beau's expression was stony. 'I think it was mainly verbal, not that that makes it any better. How fat Ginny was, how useless and unglamorous she was compared to everyone else's wives.'

Catherine couldn't bear to think about what Ginny had been through. 'Poor, poor Ginny.' What a savage irony: that she had been campaigning against domestic violence, and it had been happening right under her nose.

'I tried to get her to leave him so many times.' Beau sighed. 'In the end he'd alienated her from everyone: me, their old friends, her sister. His own children can't stand him. Will, their son, had a massive fight with Felix a few years back and swore he'd never set foot in the family home again.'

'But how could Felix keep it secret? Why did no one suspect anything?'

'He was very good at keeping his public and private faces separate. A few people may have guessed what was going on over the years, but they probably didn't want to interfere. Ginny would never have said anything herself. Felix had ground her down.'

'I still can't believe it,' Catherine said. 'Ginny hasn't been herself for a while, but I thought . . .' She stopped. 'I thought she was ill.'

'Things have been worse lately,' Beau admitted. 'I thought it was just because he was resentful of you running in the by-election, but now we know he had other stuff on his mind.'

'I feel terrible I've made things worse.'

'If it hadn't been you, it would have been someone else. Felix is a very jealous, bitter man. He's obsessed with money and power because he's never really had it. Truth is, he was probably never good enough to be a big politician. He had the delusions of grandeur, but no conviction.'

'I thought you were the one behind Ye Olde Worlde,' she confessed. 'Felix hoodwinked us all.'

Beau shrugged. 'I could have let people know what my brother was like, but Ginny always begged me not to. This place is her life. So I kept my mouth shut.'

'You're very close to Ginny.'

'I adore her,' he said simply. 'I was a lonely, grieving kid after my mum died. My father had gone back to America, and Ginny was the only one who was there for me. As much as she could be, anyway. Felix always hated me. You heard how I was the one who "got lucky".' He smiled thinly. 'If I'd ever been asked to choose between money and family, I know what my answer would have been.'

'Is that why you moved back here?'

'It was a big reason. I knew things were getting worse. I thought I could keep an eye on Felix and be there for Ginny. And in a funny way, this town is home to me. Or it was, anyway.'

'Will Ginny come back?'

'I'm not sure yet, she's safe at her sister's.' He sighed again. 'The irony is, things had got so bad, I'd convinced her to see a divorce lawyer. That's where I've been this week. I guess she hasn't got a choice now.'

Catherine didn't press for more details about Felix's philandering. Her brain couldn't cope with any more revelations.

'What about you?' Beau asked. 'What are you going to do without your campaign manager?'

'I doubt I'll have much of a campaign to run.'

'Well, you know you've got my vote if it helps.' He gave her a disarming grin.

'Thanks for tonight,' she said shakily. 'I don't know what I'd have done without you.'

He shook his head. 'I just feel sorry for Ginny.' He stood up. 'I'd better shoot. I've got a lot of work to get through.'

'At this hour? Must be important.'

'It is.' He paused. 'I've just signed a deal for a big piece of land round here.'

'You're not going to build another theme park, are you?'

'Ha, no. But it could be pretty risky, especially in the current climate.'

'Sounds intriguing.'

He sized her up through his cool blue eyes. 'Maybe.'

A mobile ringtone went off. 'Excuse me,' he told her, pulling an iPhone out of his back pocket.

'Hello? Hi, Robert. Yeah, sorry, I've been a bit tied up.' He frowned. 'No. Why?'

Beneath the tan, his face drained of colour. 'Don't move,' he ordered. 'I'm coming over.'

Chapter 88

Dawn broke over the London rooftops but Vanessa barely noticed. She'd been by Dylan's side all night. When she'd seen him lying motionless in the road outside the Royal Albert Hall, she'd feared the worst. At one point the doctors had said it was critical, but miraculously he'd started to improve. He'd been drifting in and out of consciousness ever since.

There was a bed shortage, so he had ended up in a mixed ward for the elderly. The air was tinged with the smell of antiseptic and a faint waft of urine, the gentle sound of monitors and an occasional rasping snore. Vanessa was still in her dress, although the cripplingly high heels had been kicked off long ago.

An old man wearing an oxygen mask in the bed opposite had been watching her with great interest for hours.

'Wish my wife made such an effort when she came in to see me.'

'I don't always look like this, trust me.'

'No? Shame. You look very pretty. Young girls these days don't know how to dress.'

'I'm not that young but thank you for the compliment.' Vanessa felt like she'd aged a thousand years in the past few hours.

She looked back at Dylan. His eyes were closed and the normally brown face was a sickly white. A huge plaster covered the right side of his forehead. There had been so much blood. Too much blood. Vanessa's stomach turned thinking about it.

Despite the time, a few patients were awake. 'Are you on the television?' the cockney lady on Vanessa's right asked.

'I was meant to be, last night.'

'I know you: you're that Vanessa Powell! My Angela has your perfume. She loves it, but it's a bit overpowering, if you ask me.'

Vanessa smiled. 'I know what you mean.'

'So what's going on there?' She nodded to Dylan. 'That's not your husband, is it?'

'No.' Vanessa turned to Dylan. 'This is the man I've left my husband for.'

'That's going to cause a bit of a ruckus, isn't it?'

'It already has.'

'Well, you can't pretend to be happy when you're not. I've had four of the buggers. Husbands, I mean.'

She had to be twenty stone and then some. 'I was quite the stunner back in my day. It's no use blushing, dear, we all end up losing it along the way.' She peered at Dylan again. 'He's quite a looker. Are you going to feel the same about him when he's old and saggy?'

'I don't care about that. I love his spirit more than anything.' Vanessa pushed a black curl off his face.

A breakfast tray rattled past in the corridor, distracting her. When she looked back Dylan's eyes were open and he was looking right at her.

'Dylan! Oh my God.'

'Vanessa.' His voice was cracked and barely audible. She poured a glass of water and held it to his mouth.

'How are you feeling? Does it hurt?'

'I've felt better.' He gazed at her. 'What time is it?'

'Early.' She stroked his hair. 'You've been asleep for hours.'

He lifted his hand to caress her face. 'How are you?'

'I've left Conrad,' she told him. 'He's been arrested.'

She watched him slowly absorb the information. 'Wow. How do you feel?'

'I haven't really thought about it,' she admitted. 'I've been so worried about you.'

He smiled, his gaze falling on her dress. 'You look pretty. Sorry you got my blood all over you.'

'It doesn't matter. Nothing matters as long as you're all right.'

He took her hand in his. 'So, this is it. This is us, I mean.'

'I guess it is.' She looked anxious. 'If you're sure?'

'Of course I'm sure. You're not having second thoughts, are you?'

'Of course not! I just feel terrible dragging you into all this.' The press were already camped outside the hospital. 'You didn't ask for all this attention and scrutiny. I don't want you to sacrifice your life for me.'

'Vanessa, my life is you.' He gave her his crooked

486

grin. 'If we get any bother from people, I'll set Eddie on them.'

They gazed into each other's eyes, utterly lost. 'For pete's sake,' the cockney lady said. 'Are you going to kiss her or what?'

Dylan smiled, and with some effort, lifted his head and kissed Vanessa passionately. Clapping erupted round the ward.

'Go on, my son!' the old man called. 'About time we had a bit of excitement round here!'

Chapter 89

The rustle of a nearby animal woke Fleur up. She opened her eyes, wondering why she was so cold and stiff. A second later it all came back to her. The devastation was crushing.

She sat up. Her back ached horribly from the hard ground, while goosebumps pimpled her arms and legs. She rubbed her limbs furiously, but it would be a long time before she ever felt warm again.

Blackwater Farm lay beneath her. She saw past the crumbling buildings, the sagging fencing, the rusty machinery that should have been replaced years ago. The farm was her heritage, her identity. It represented three hundred years of work by the Blackwater family.

Now Beau had taken it all away from her.

The last thing she wanted to do was go home and face her dad, but there was no use putting it off. She started the long walk down the hill, feeling as if she was going to her own funeral. After all, she was dead inside now.

She stopped halfway to take in the view, while it was

still hers. In the west the sun was rising above a salmon-pink sky. The still air held the promise of another hot day ahead. Beeversham had never looked so beautiful.

I'm so tired, she thought. *I'm so tired of keeping everything going.*

She just wanted to lie down and close her eyes for ever. There was no more fight left in her.

A frantic shout made her start. 'Fleur!'

Beau was standing behind her, breathing heavily. He looked terrible, black circles under his eyes and sweat patches staining the pale-blue shirt.

'I've been looking for you all night. Where the hell have you been?' He took a step forward.

'Stay away from me!' Fleur hissed. 'You're a lying piece of scum!'

An anguished look crossed Beau's face. Guilty conscience? It was too bloody late for that.

'Fleur, I know how it looks . . .'

'You wanted the farm all along!' She was so furious the words tumbled out on top of each other. 'You knew how much this place means to me! You *knew*. And you used me to get close to my dad, so you could buy it behind my back. My God. How can you sleep at night?'

He pulled something out of his back pocket. 'I want to show you something.'

She looked at the wad of papers he was holding. 'What are you talking about?'

'The deeds for the farm. I've just signed them.'

She actually laughed out loud. 'You've come all the way out here to rub my nose in it? You're even sicker than I thought.'

'Just look at them, will you?' he said urgently. 'OK,

you think I'm the biggest bastard ever to walk this earth, but will you just stop shouting and take a look?'

He walked over and shoved the papers into her hand. She glanced at them unwillingly, before studying the first page more closely. 'I don't understand. These deeds are in my name.'

'Of course they are. The farm belongs to you.'

'What the hell are you talking about?'

'I've bought your dad out. But only to keep it running as a farm. I've signed it all over to you.' He tried a tentative smile. 'You'll make a real success of it. I know you will.'

She was utterly confused. 'But you want to turn it into a spa! I heard you and Spencer plotting.'

He frowned. 'What are you talking about?'

'That night you and Spencer tried to buy it off me! You said you wanted to turn it into a spa and later, when Spencer turned up at yours, I heard him out by the pool. He said, he hoped it was all worth it and said about "putting in the groundwork" with me.'

'That's because I'd just told him I was in love with you!'

'Don't give me that!'

'Fleur, it's *true*.' He sighed. 'I know I've made a total pig's ear out of this. I knew you wouldn't let me help, because you're so goddamn proud. So I took matters into my own hands instead.'

'You and Dad went behind my back!'

'We did, and I'm sorry.' He looked exhausted. 'I thought I was doing the right thing. Look, I admit I *was* interested in turning the farm into a spa at first. But that was before I got to know you, Fleur, and realized what a special girl you are.'

'Yeah, right,' she retorted, but she was no longer shouting.

'Look, I'm not trying to give you some cod psychology, but I don't want to live my life like that any more.' His smile made Fleur's heart clench. 'For some unfathomable reason, you've made me want to be a better person.'

She wasn't letting him off just yet. 'You said farming was over.'

'I might have revised my opinion.' His eyes sparkled. 'I'm not letting you off that easily, though. We need to sit down and work out a proper business plan.'

She looked down at the deeds again. He was taking a huge risk. 'You did all this for me? Why?'

'Because I love you,' he said simply. His voice cracked. 'Please, angel. Will you just come here so I can kiss you?'

A second later she flew into his arms. 'Oh, thank you, thank you,' she wept, covering his face in wet kisses, 'I won't let you down.'

'I know you won't. Christ, you're freezing. Oh God, Fleur. I've been so worried.'

'Where have you been?' she cried. 'I thought you'd dumped me.'

'What? Never. I had to go away and take care of something. I'm an idiot, I should never have just taken off like that.'

'I know Talia Tudor is your daughter.'

She felt him go still. 'What?'

'I s-saw her school picture,' she said. 'In your study. You should have told me there was history between you and Lynette.'

'*Me* and Lynette?' Beau shook his head. 'You're right. I should have been upfront with you from the start.

'Talia is family,' he told her. 'But not in the way you think. Talia is my niece.'

Her mouth fell open. 'Your what? Then that makes . . .'

'Felix is her father.'

Fleur desperately tried to make sense of it all. 'Felix had an affair with Lynette? When he was with Ginny?'

'My brother's had numerous affairs,' Beau told her. 'Not that he's ever stuck around afterwards. I only found out about Lynette recently. I've been doing what I can to help her ever since.'

'But, but . . . I'm sure if you told Felix, he'd help.'

'He knows, Fleur.'

'Oh. Oh,' she said again. 'Does Ginny?'

'Yes. Talia doesn't know, though, and I think it's probably best kept that way.'

'I can't believe it,' she said. 'First the farm and now this.' She looked up at him again. 'I thought you'd ruined my life.'

'I probably still can, if you let me.' There was a vulnerability in his face Fleur had never seen before. It only served to make him even more beautiful.

'I thought I was happy by myself,' he told her. 'I never wanted to let anyone in. Until I met you.'

His eyes were scorching in their intensity. 'The more you push me away, the more I want to look after you. You've never been impressed by me, and yet all I want to do is impress you.'

492

He cupped her face. 'You provoke this ridiculous reaction in me. I want to skip in the streets and shout from the rooftops. I've never felt this way before.'

'M-me neither,' she stuttered.

'Let me look after you, Fleur. We can live together and make beautiful babies. OK, we don't have to have babies,' he added hurriedly. 'Don't cry, sweetheart.'

'I'm crying because I'm so happy,' she sobbed. 'I want to have beautiful babies with you. I love you so much, Beau.'

Chapter 90

Election day

Was it really only four weeks since Catherine's campaign had started? It was terrifying how much a person's life could change in such a short amount of time.

The bedroom was horribly quiet as she got dressed. The empty space on the right-hand side of the bed matched the size of the hole in her heart. She went through the motions: hair, make-up, fastening her Rolex. As she put in the diamond studs John had bought her for Christmas two years earlier, she nearly broke down all over again.

An early check showed that Twitter was full of people complaining about O2 crashing. Catherine checked her own phone and saw she had no signal. The timing could not be worse. Her spirits plummeted to new depths.

She could hear voices at the front of the house, members of the press wondering why they'd been summoned there for a 6 a.m. press conference.

The bile came from nowhere. Catherine rushed back into the bathroom and was violently sick.

It was a composed Catherine Connor who opened her door ten minutes later, holding a single sheet of paper. Aside from the slightly red eyes, which was expected from a candidate at the end of a campaign, she looked poised and confident.

The pack jostled forward. 'Catherine, what's going on?'

'I'd like to make a statement on behalf of Beeversham's Conservative Association, to the British public.'

She stared at the piece of paper. The words swam into each other. She looked back into the cameras.

'For those of you who don't know, I'm Catherine Connor, Conservative candidate in the Beeversham by-election. I'm sure you're aware of the plight that faces our town. On Wednesday, plans submitted by Sykes Holdings for Ye Olde Worlde theme park were granted planning permission by the county council.

'Sykes Holdings are building the development along with another company, Pear Tree Holdings, which owns the land. There has been much speculation about who owns that company. Last night I found out that Felix Chamberlain, chairman of Beeversham's Conservative Association, is the owner of Pear Tree Holdings.'

She paused and waited for the significance to sink in. 'What the hell?' said the woman from *Sky News*.

'I believe there has been a huge cover-up involving key individuals in both the building industry and Gloucestershire County Council. On behalf of Beeversham Conservative Association, I would like to extend our sincerest apologies. I was not privy to this information during my campaign, nor is Felix Chamberlain remaining as my campaign manager. I am still running today, but I strongly believe that this constituency should know the truth immediately.'

There, she'd done it. Laid out the facts. What people chose to do with them was out of her hands.

The assorted press had been listening, gobsmacked, but now the questions started coming thick and fast.

'Catherine, where is Felix now?'

'Catherine, surely this is going to ruin your chances of winning?'

'Catherine, how can you not have known something about this?'

She folded her paper in half. 'At this time, I have nothing more to say.'

It was a political shit-storm, of apocalyptic levels. The Prime Minister was on the landline as soon as Catherine shut her front door.

'When did you find out this?' he asked.

'Last night.'

'Didn't you think it might be a good idea to run this past us first?' He sounded furious. 'You do know you've killed your chances of winning now?'

'I told you I'd make a rubbish MP! I'm not asking people to vote for me when they don't know the facts. Sorry if I've put integrity before your precious government, but that's just the way I tick!'

'Catherine. Listen . . .'

'Excuse me,' she said icily. 'But I've got an election to be getting on with.' She hung up on the Prime Minister of the country.

The news was across the Internet in minutes. Catherine had to struggle through a crowd of paparazzi to get through the front doors of Tory HQ. Inside, she was met by stunned faces. Even Aubrey Taunton-Brown and Charles Knatchbull had turned out at this unearthly hour. No one could believe what Felix had done.

Several of the Blue Rosettes were in tears. 'He seemed like such a nice man,' snuffled one woman.

Someone had to take charge now Felix was gone. 'I'm sure some of you don't agree with what I did,' she said, avoiding Aubrey's eye. 'Felix was a friend of mine, too. But we owe the people the truth. If I have any chance of winning left, I want to come in with people knowing the real me. It's going to be tough out there today. I'll understand if you don't want to do it, but I'm going out regardless. If any of you do want to join me . . .' she smiled wryly '. . . I'd really bloody appreciate the support.'

One by one, every single Blue Rosette put up their hands. Catherine felt close to tears again.

Aubrey sniffed. 'I suppose I'll have to take care of things here.'

The polling stations opened at 7 a.m., in local schools and village halls across the constituency. Catherine should have been concentrating on getting people out of their houses to go and vote. Instead she found herself facing a barrage of hostility.

'Don't tell me you didn't know something,' one householder told Catherine through the door chain. 'Now bugger off before I set the chihuahua on you.'

Tristan Jago wasted no time cashing in on this gift from heaven. 'It just goes to show they're the same old lying Tories,' he told *BBC Breakfast*. 'Corrupt, conniving and money-obsessed!'

At one house someone threw a cup of coffee at them. Kitty came away from another house in tears when the family Labrador was ordered to attack her. Bruised and stunned, they all took refuge in a café. No one could look Catherine in the eye. *Oh shit*, she thought. *What have I done?*

Fortified by coffee, they took to the streets again. The Ye Olde Worlde controversy had prompted an unusually high turn-out for a by-election. People were voting in their droves. Catherine watched miserably as another Labour pool car drove past, ferrying people to the polling station. The driver gave her a smug wave.

Tristan, buoyant in a new grey suit and reeking of sandalwood, intercepted Catherine at a T-junction.

'A moment, if you don't mind.' He pulled her away from everyone else. Catherine wrenched her arm back.

'If you want to rub my nose in it, don't bother.'

'What *are* you up to?' he asked her.

She looked at him. 'I don't know what you mean.'

'On the face of things, you've wrecked your campaign, but now I'm not so sure.' His eyes were quizzical behind the trendy glasses. 'Is this a game change to get the sympathy vote?'

'I've got one word to say to you,' she snapped. 'Mel.' She watched him go pale. There was no way she'd ever betray Mel, but he didn't know that. *My God*, she thought. *I've turned into one of them.*

As the hours ticked past, the scale of the fallout

became clear. The political pundits had Tristan down as the odds-on favourite. By sheer determination and grovelling Catherine had managed to talk round a few voters, but it wasn't enough. Something huge would have to happen to swing the voting in her favour. And Catherine could think of nothing that would be big enough.

There was an enormous press presence outside the gates of Tresco House. Billy put his foot down and scattered them in their wake. Dylan was hidden under a blanket on the back seat. Vanessa sat beside him, ignoring the bangs on the window. She was wearing no make-up and her hair was scraped back in a greasy ponytail.

Conrad was still in custody. He was facing seven counts of attempted murder and dangerous driving. The chances were he'd be put away for a very long time.

They'd driven back in a rented Mercedes. 'Does it hurt?' Vanessa asked, as she helped Dylan out.

'Not too much.' He gave her a smile and her world lit up. All the stress, all the legal battles in the coming months, it was all worth it.

Eddie and Sukie came rushing into the entrance hall to greet them. The wolfhound went mad when he saw his owner, covering Dylan's face and hands with frantic licks.

'Vanessa.'

She looked up from hugging Sukie. Her mother had come through from the corridor. Renata was at her shoulder. They'd obviously been waiting.

'Hello, Mother.'

Dominique was staring at Dylan. His hospital stay had only heightened the contrast between his black hair and white pallor, intensifying his wild beauty.

'Mother, this is Dylan Goldhawk. Dylan, my mother, Dominique.'

'Hello.' Dylan offered her his hand.

Ignoring it, Dominique looked at her daughter. 'This is him? This is the man you left Conrad for?'

'We've been through this,' Vanessa said quietly. 'I was miserable long before I met Dylan.' She smiled at him. 'He makes me so happy, Mother.'

Dominique looked at them, and then shook her head. 'Not that you're going to listen to me, anyway.' She walked off, back down the hall.

'She'll just take a bit of winning over,' Vanessa told Dylan. *And if she can't be won round, she can lump it.*

Renata was far more welcoming. 'Poor man! Come with me and I make you hot food.'

She glanced back at Vanessa as she led Dylan off.

'You do right. Much more handsome than Conrad!'

Vanessa smiled and headed upstairs. There was one more thing she had to do.

Back on the High Street, Catherine was on the verge of collapse. Another Labour pool car crammed with voters zoomed past. She checked her watch: four hours to go until the polls shut. *I don't know if I can do this. Oh John, my life is empty without you.*

'Catherine?' It was yet another reporter. 'Surely you must feel like giving up the ghost? This isn't a town that's happy with either you or the Conservative government, is it?'

A familiar Bentley pulled up. The reporter was still talking, but Catherine wasn't listening. She watched a stunningly natural Vanessa Powell climb out, clad in a pair of tight white jeans. Catherine's jaw almost bounced off the pavement. Stretched across Vanessa's famous assets was a 'Vote Connor' T-shirt.

The press pack surged forward. 'Vanessa! Are you pressing charges against Conrad?'

'Are you divorcing?'

'Who's Dylan Goldhawk?'

Vanessa flashed them a killer smile. 'Excuse me, guys, but I'm just here to support my friend Catherine.' She walked across, kissing Catherine on both cheeks. 'Congratulations for running a great campaign, we're all so proud of you.'

You little beauty, Catherine thought. She garbled something as Vanessa turned back to the cameras.

'If you're in a fix, Catherine Connor is the girl to come to your rescue. She's a passionate and dedicated campaigner and I've no doubt she'll make a fine MP.' She took Catherine's hand and held it aloft. 'So vote Connor!'

There was nothing like a celebrity in the middle of a scandal to hot up a campaign. Vanessa was arguably the most famous woman in Britain, the tragic heroine caught in a glamorous love triangle. She could have turned out to endorse Saddam Hussein and won him votes.

It gave Catherine the impetus she needed. Doors stopped being shut in her face. It had become a race against time: the polling stations closed at 10 p.m. on the dot. A lot of constituents had started tucking into their evening drinks and were unable to drive. Desperate not to let votes slip through their fingers, the Blue Rosettes set up a constant shuttle service in and out of the town. Aubrey Taunton-Brown was most put out at having to get his vintage Rolls-Royce out to ferry a gaggle of grannies in from the local nursing home.

By nine o'clock Catherine was dead on her feet. Taking a break from the madness outside, she went back to Tory HQ.

The O2 network was still down. 'Have I had any messages?' Catherine asked the Blue Rosette manning the phones.

'Thousands of press requests. And the Prime Minister called again.'

'Nothing . . .' Catherine bit her lip. 'There's been nothing from my husband?'

The woman looked apologetic. 'I'm afraid not.'

Catherine had been holding on to that last bit of hope that today, of all days, John would have tried to get in touch. She sank on to the floor in a heap.

'I can't do it! I'm so scared I've lost him.'

The door opened behind her. 'Oh, piss off!' she screamed. 'I'm not doing another bloody interview!'

'Catherine.'

She looked up through a mist of tears. Mel and Mike were standing there, along with the Patels, Lynette, Amanda and Henry, even the headmistress from St Gwendolyn's. Catherine blinked; was that really Talia Tudor, smiling ironically under an inch of fake tan?

'Come on, babe, get up,' Mel said gently. She and Mike lifted Catherine to her feet.

'What are you all doing here?' Catherine sobbed.

'We've come to help,' Ursula Patel said.

'Knock on doors,' Dilip said.

'I've made sure all the girls from WeightWatchers are going to go down and vote,' added Amanda Belcher.

Catherine started crying all over again. 'Thank you,' she wept. 'Oh, thank you so much.'

They walked the streets as an army, the troops turning out for their general. Gideon Armstrong turned up and enticed people out with the offer of audience tickets to watch his new series being filmed. Talia Tudor used her mobile to get on Twitter, urging all her friends to go and vote. Mel had the biggest success with her nipple-skimming nautical boob tube.

Catherine was exhausted to the point of no return. Mel and Mike had to practically prop her up on the last circuit of the streets. 'Babe, you need a break,' a worried Mel told her.

'I have to keep going.'

'You're about to drop dead!'

'Mel.' Mike touched his wife's arm.

'Mike, someone's got to say something. For God's sake, look at her.'

Her words faded away. Catherine turned to see what they were both looking at, and suddenly everything went perfectly still.

Was it really him? John, her John, standing on the other side of the road in his green check shirt, with his wonderful familiar smile?

She ran across, nearly getting flattened by a 4 x 4 in the process. 'John!' She flew into his arms. 'I'm so sorry!'

'You've got nothing to be sorry for.' He hugged her

fiercely, before pulling away. 'The baby . . . am I hurting you?'

'No,' she laughed. 'Of course not.'

He gazed at her. 'Is it really true?'

'I'm eight weeks and counting. I went to the doctor's yesterday. I mean, we need to have the three-month scan but . . .' She dared to smile. 'It's all looking good.'

'Oh, Cath.' He hugged her again. 'I can't believe we're having a baby! I'm so sorry I haven't been here for you both. I got the first flight back when I heard your message, and then I couldn't bloody get through to you.'

'It doesn't matter,' she sobbed. 'You're here now.'

He held her until her tears subsided. 'I thought I'd driven you away,' she told him.

John shook his head. 'I can't believe we let it get to this. I thought you didn't need me. How can I have been so bloody stupid?'

'I'm the stupid one. All you've ever done is fight for me.'

They fell into each other's arms again. 'I'm the one who owes you an apology,' John said. 'I know I can be an awkward bugger at times. I just want to protect you. And when you don't let me, I guess I get frustrated.'

'I don't mean to be ungrateful.'

'You're not.' John traced his hand down her cheek. 'I've been going about it all wrong. Protecting someone isn't trying to shield them from the world, it's about supporting and understanding them so they can be the person they want to be.'

'I can't stop crying,' she bawled. 'This is so embarrassing.'

'We're a right pair, aren't we?'

'Just as long as we are a pair,' she sobbed, from the depths of his chest.

'We are. We always were.' His own eyes filled with tears. 'I love you. I love our baby. I promise you, Cath, I will never, ever leave you again.'

'Oh John, I love you so much.'

He lifted her up and kissed her right out of her heels. A car drove past and beeped. John released his wife and grinned. 'Haven't we got some votes to get? Where's Felix?'

Catherine sighed. 'I guess you haven't heard.'

Chapter 91

The polling stations had closed. Catherine and the other candidates had done all they could. The official count was taking place at County Hall and was expected to go on well into the early hours.

When Catherine and John arrived at eleven o'clock the place was bustling. Teams of volunteers sat behind long trestle tables, methodically counting. The returning officer, the tall, whiskery man in charge of the proceedings, was striding round officiously, making sure everyone was doing their jobs. Each ballot box was opened and counted, and the contents stacked in bundles on a big central table. Tristan Jago's pile already resembled the leaning Tower of Pisa. Catherine's heart sank.

The upstairs balcony was crammed with press doing live broadcasts. It was an extraordinary night by anyone's standards, with several county councillors being investigated for misconduct. The returning officer was stoically avoiding reporters' questions. Felix had been such an integral part of the local politics scene. No one could yet believe what had happened.

The clock ticked on. Thousands more votes were counted. Conversations started to fall away as people stood on the sidelines, watching anxiously. Another box of votes was added to Tristan's pile. Catherine's depression intensified. They hadn't a hope in hell.

A ballot box from another village was brought over. 'Hold on,' Kitty said. 'They've always been pro us, I've got a good feeling.'

Sure enough, when the box was tipped out and counted, most of the voting were added to Catherine's pile.

'Forget Esme Santura,' she told Kitty. 'You want to predict a few more of those?'

It was incredible. More Conservative bundles started to stack up. By 3 a.m. her's and Tristan's piles were neck and neck. The Lib Dem Helen Singh had about half their number of votes, and, surprisingly so did the bloodthirsty Bill Fairclough. Esme Santura had the smallest pile, along with a used Euro Lottery scratch card someone had put in, the words 'Thanks for nothing' scrawled across it.

A palpable tension took hold of the room. Everyone was red-eyed and exhausted, running on nerves and sheer adrenalin.

'Whatever happens, Cath, you've done your best,' John told her. 'I'm so proud of you.'

It was clearly a close call between Catherine and Tristan. Tristan had been his usual smug self until about an hour earlier, but he had gradually fallen silent. He was standing with his gang on the other side of the room, all of them chewing their fingernails nervously.

Half an hour later all the ballot boxes had been counted. The returning officer cleared his throat. It was showtime.

Catherine was gripping John's hand so tightly she couldn't feel her fingers. She was holding on to Kitty with the other hand.

'Ladies and gentleman, the results for the Beeversham by-election are as follows,' announced the returning officer. 'The independent candidate Colonel Bill Fairclough, four thousand, three hundred and two. Esme Santura, also an independent, fifty-three votes.'

The pagan witch looked thrilled. 'Fifty-three, that's wonderful!'

'Wish I was so easily pleased,' Catherine muttered to her husband.

'Helen Singh from the Liberal Democrats, fourteen thousand, one hundred and twenty-seven votes.'

The young Lib Dem gave a stoic grin. The returning officer looked back at his sheet.

'The Conservative candidate Catherine Connor . . .'

She thought of all her friends back in Beeversham, of all the thousands of faces she'd met over the last month. She thought, too, of Linda Giachetti, mother of the murdered Debbi, and all the people like her that she'd promised to help.

'. . . Thirty-one thousand, four hundred and sixty-five.'

John squeezed Catherine's hand. 'Tristan's got more, I bloody know it,' she muttered.

The returning officer paused dramatically. Everyone held their breath.

'Tristan Jago, the Labour candidate, thirty-one thousand, four hundred and . . . *sixty-five.*'

The press balcony erupted. 'A bloody tie! That's never happened before!'

Tristan Jago's lot were heckling even before the commotion died down. 'Recount, recount!'

The returning officer sighed. 'OK, let's start again.'

Two nail-biting hours later, the count was in again. It was exactly the same.

No one seemed to know what to do. 'What happens now?' Catherine asked.

'I'm not sure,' Clive said. 'It's been close before, but no two candidates have ever got exactly the same number of votes. It's incredible!'

Tristan Jago was arguing loudly with the returning officer over one of Catherine's voting forms.

'That's a tick, not a cross! It's not a valid vote.'

'Stop holding your thumb over it,' the returning officer said wearily. 'That's definitely a cross.'

People milled around, looking uncertain. 'I can't go through this again,' Catherine wailed quietly.

Tristan started arguing with the returning officer again. The press swarmed amongst everyone, getting reactions. John pushed another microphone out of Catherine's face.

No one noticed a red-haired lady in a quilted waistcoat walking back to one of the empty ballot boxes. She peered inside and pulled something out. Her eyebrows went up. Rushing up to the returning officer, she dragged him away from a disgruntled Tristan Jago.

A moment later the returning officer shushed the

room. 'Er, it seems we have overlooked a remaining vote. And, as all the boxes were sealed when they came in, it has to be counted as legitimate.'

There were sharp intakes of breath. Tristan Jago went a funny sage colour. John had to physically prop Catherine up.

The returning officer triple-checked, just to be certain. There was no way he was ballsing this one up. 'The vote is for . . . the Conservative candidate Catherine Connor.'

Pandemonium erupted. Clive started hyperventilating. Catherine rushed over. She had to see for herself. It was a postal vote. She took one look at the name and burst into tears.

'It's from Ginny.'

Chapter 92

Two weeks later

It had been officially recorded as the hottest summer since 1935. Even by mid-September it was still unseasonably warm, and there was actually relief at the prospect of moving into a cooler autumn.

Three things were dominating the press: a new fuel crisis, the recently elected MP Catherine Connor and her first few weeks in Westminster (she'd already had a stand-up row with a backbencher at Prime Minister's Questions) and last but not least, the scandalous downfall of Conrad Powell. He was now on remand at Wandsworth Prison, awaiting trial. The press were salivating at the tale of the cruel husband, his beautiful wife and her star-crossed lover. Ironically, there was already talk of film rights.

Beeversham had become the most talked-about place in the country, yet as the villagers mingled on the lawns at Beau's house that day, the scene was one of relaxed conviviality.

For most of them, it was their first visit to Ridings. No one could believe what a beautiful restoration job had been done, or what a gracious host Beau was. Affable, blue eyes twinkling, he moved amongst his guests with easy conversation and an ever-full bottle of champagne. Mr Patel, who only ever had half a lager on Christmas Day, was already becoming very jolly.

The change in Fleur Blackwater was equally incredible. Beeversham's new coupling had surprised everyone, but as soon as they saw the pair together it all made sense. Beau was so sweetly protective of Fleur, constantly fussing over her, playing with her hair as they talked, asking her if she wanted anything. She had blossomed before everyone's eyes, and looked beautiful in a sunflower-yellow dress that danced against her red tresses and brought out her amber eyes, but it was Fleur's new radiance that everyone commented on. Finally, she was being allowed to be a girl again.

It was 4 p.m. by the time Catherine screeched up in her MG. The last two weeks had been completely manic. She'd spent most of the morning haggling for a computer and printer for the tiny office in Westminster she was sharing with two other MPs. So much for the glamour.

She got out of her car, marvelling at Ridings' clean precise lines framed against the empty sky. The building was a work of art.

A young waitress was waiting at the entrance to the garden. 'Champagne, madam?'

'Can I have an orange juice, please?'

Her mobile went off. It was the Prime Minister again. Pressing 'End' she chucked it in her bag and went to find her husband.

John was by the pool, talking to the Cooper-Stanleys. Mel looked like a sexy flamingo in an electric-pink peplum dress that barely skimmed her bottom.

'Have you been inside yet, babe?' she asked Catherine. 'It's amazing. I'm going to have to redesign our whole house!'

Mike groaned. 'We've only just had a refurb!'

Mel laughed and slid an arm round her husband's waist. She gave Catherine a warm wink. *Everything's all right.*

Amanda and Henry were together at the bar, watching the barman whip up a couple of Caipirinhas. On the other side of the pool an elegant Ursula Patel cooled her feet in the water. Lynette Tudor was happily talking to a handsome male waiter. Her daughter reclined on a sunbed behind her, wanton and carefree in a cutaway swimsuit. Olympia Belcher and Pritti Patel sat together on a sofa, enviously looking over at Talia's flat stomach.

'It's really good of Beau to put this on,' Mel said. 'It's just what we need to bring the village back together.'

What Felix had done had shocked everyone to the core. People felt like they were mourning the death of a person they'd once known. Mr Patel, who'd been friends with Felix for nearly thirty years, was still having difficulty coming to terms with the whole thing. Ginny was still at her sister's in Suffolk, but Beau was passing on all the messages of goodwill. Only time would tell if she'd come home.

The Chamberlains' house was all shut up, as was Chamberlains & Co. Catherine had heard on the Westminster grapevine that Felix was renting a place in London. She'd tried to imagine how he felt: no family, no friends, kicked out of his beloved Conservative Party and facing charges for dishonest dealings. She had struggled with her mixed feelings. It had been hard being a whistleblower, especially when he was such a good friend. But as she looked around her today, she knew she'd made the right decision.

Most importantly, Blaize Castle had been saved. Realizing he had a poisoned chalice on his hands, Sid Sykes had pulled out of the development. Felix still theoretically owned the land, but the National Trust had expressed interest in buying the site and turning it into a protected area.

Sykes had his own problems, anyway. A disgruntled out-of-work actor had sold his story to a Sunday newspaper, claiming he was still owed money by Damien Sykes for orchestrating the riot at County Hall. Catherine had taken one look at the man's jug ears and known she'd been right all along. Sykes Holdings would need all the hotshot lawyers they had to get them out of that one.

The champagne girl came round again. 'Just a tiny bit for me,' Catherine said, lifting her orange juice up.

'Babe, you're being very restrained,' Mel exclaimed. 'This champagne is seriously good.'

Catherine and John exchanged a grin. Mel clapped her hand over her mouth. 'You're not!'

'I am,' Catherine said. 'Ten weeks, to be precise. We had the scan last week.'

Mel leapt on her friend with a squeal. Mike pumped John's hand. 'Guys, congratulations! That's such fantastic news.'

'How long have you known?' Mel asked.

'About a month.' She squeezed John's hand. They were both still stunned with delight.

'Blimey!' Mike said. 'What are you going to do about your new job?'

Catherine looked at her husband. 'That's another phone call.' The poor PM probably thought she'd finished coming up with surprises.

The kitchen was a hive of activity as Fleur walked in. Sergio was putting the finishing touches to a platter of mini-rarebits made with Cotswold brie.

'You want me to take those out?' she asked.

'I'm not sure the hostess should stoop to such duties.'

'Don't be silly.' She smiled, hoisting the silver tray up.

Beau intercepted her coming out of the house. 'Sweetheart, let me take that. What are you doing?'

'I am capable, you know.' She laughed. 'I throw straw bales round for a living, remember?'

He nuzzled his face in her neck. 'Am I being too overprotective?' he murmured. 'I'm new to all this head-over-heels-in-love stuff.'

He bent his head to kiss her. They melted into each other for a moment. His hand moved on to her bottom. 'We could just nip upstairs.'

'No, we can't!' she laughed again. 'You're incorrigible.'

Out on the lawn Robert Blackwater was clutching

a Virgin Mary and talking to Mrs Patel. When Fleur had tentatively given her dad the literature about the rural rehab place in Somerset, Robert Blackwater had actually seemed relieved. One week in, he was looking better already.

'I'm so pleased Dad came,' Fleur said. 'He's doing OK, isn't he?'

'He's doing great,' Beau said. 'I meant what I said. I wish you'd let me pay for his rehab.'

'I told you, it's only a loan. We've taken enough of your money.' She looked over Beau's shoulder. 'Wow, look who's here.'

In a simple cream dress and looking uncharacteristically nervous, Vanessa Powell walked into the party. Her face was clear of the trademark glamour make-up, allowing her incredible skin to shine through.

She wasn't alone. Still slightly pale after his recent stint in hospital, Dylan's easy smile and demeanour suggested a man unperturbed at being splashed over the papers as Vanessa's 'exotic traveller lover'. Vanessa's mother was also with them, as was an incongruous old woman in a pink baseball cap and Minnie Mouse sweatshirt.

Vanessa came straight up to Beau and Fleur. 'Thank you so much for inviting us,' she said, with a dazzling smile. 'You have a beautiful home.'

'Now you've ditched that horrible husband you can come as often as you want.' Beau gave Vanessa two practised kisses on both cheeks. 'Glad you could make it.'

Vanessa was so pretty close up, like a tiny doll. Fleur was suddenly rather overawed.

'I love your dress,' the celebrity told her. 'Diane Von Furstenberg, isn't it?'

'Top Shop actually.' Fleur grinned at Beau. Vanessa Powell was complimenting Fleur on *her* dress!

The newcomers were a complete hit. Dylan was so easy to talk to and had such beautiful silver eyes everyone was enchanted. Vanessa's mother was rather aloof at first, but after Mrs Patel went over and asked where her kaftan was from, Dominique warmed up. Really, everyone said, she had the most beautiful smile. There was one sticky moment when the Powells' housekeeper tripped and nearly fell in the pool, but luckily Mike Cooper-Stanley was on hand to grab her.

The biggest surprise was Vanessa. Friendly and charming, she took her time to go round and speak to everyone. Mike Cooper-Stanley fell completely in love after a three-minute conversation with her about their favourite hotels in the Seychelles.

Catherine was at the bar when Vanessa caught up with her. 'I hear congratulations are in order.'

'They certainly are.'

'I'm really happy for you, Catherine. It's wonderful news.'

The pale shadows under Vanessa's eyes were the only hint of the stress she had to be going through at the moment. Both she and Dylan had been called to the trial of Conrad Powell as star witnesses. The press were ecstatic at the prospect of the three of them meeting across a courtroom.

'How are you?' Catherine asked.

The celebrity gave a small smile. 'What doesn't kill you and all that.'

Vanessa had not seen her husband since that fateful night. Marty had visited him in prison once. He hadn't said anything about it and Vanessa hadn't asked. She had expected to feel some sort of vindication, but all she felt was a deep sadness. Conrad's narcissism had been his ruin. What a waste of a life.

The sous chef manning the barbecue had been working hard. All the produce was local, and the beef and lamb had come from Blackwater Farm. People started to eye up the sumptuous burgers and steaks that were starting to appear.

Catherine took her plate over to where Amanda and Ursula Patel were sitting. She'd just taken an overly large mouthful of burger when Amanda gave a sharp intake of breath.

'What?' Catherine said, turning round. Beau was walking towards them, his arm round a pale, wan Ginny. She gazed at Catherine with huge, anxious eyes. The pair looked at each other. Catherine put her plate down and threw her arms round her friend.

'Oh, Ginny! It's so good to see you!'

'Beau insisted I came.' Ginny gave a small smile. 'I don't know what I would have done without him through all this.'

Catherine nodded. 'He's a good man.'

They were walking arm in arm round the perimeter of the garden. Ginny had been showered with hugs and kindness since she'd arrived.

'I wasn't sure if you'd want to speak to me,' Catherine admitted.

'Why on earth not?'

'Because I was the one who exposed Felix.'

'You did what you had to do.' Ginny squeezed Catherine's arm. 'My life was in ruins anyway.' She hesitated. 'I probably seem very weak to you.'

'Ginny, you don't at all. Never think that.'

'Maybe I'm old-fashioned, but I thought marriage was for life. And I did love him. Enough to turn a blind eye to his indiscretions, and to try and ignore the cruel things he said to me. I just put it down to frustration, and told myself that he would be the man he really was, once he'd got where he wanted to be. It was a terrible shock to find out Felix was behind Pear Tree Holdings. He always told me to keep out of his business affairs. He'd always said I was too stupid to understand.'

Once again Catherine marvelled at how she could have got someone so wrong.

'That's one of the reasons I was so scared to come back,' Ginny said. 'I was frightened people would think I'd been involved.'

Catherine patted her arm. 'No one ever thought that.'

Ginny gave her a grateful smile. They continued to walk in a companionable silence.

'So what happens now?' Catherine asked.

'Divorce is inevitable. We're communicating through our solicitors.'

'We're all here for you,' Catherine told her.

They stopped to look out over the valley. 'I am going

to come back,' Ginny said. 'Despite what's happened, I can't imagine living anywhere else. Beeversham is my home.'

'I'm so pleased to hear that.'

'I know it might sound strange,' Ginny said, 'but I want to get to know Lynette properly and try to help her. Felix put the fear of God into us both so much we were afraid even to speak in the street.'

'So you knew about Talia?'

Ginny nodded. 'Oh yes, all along. I've never really blamed Lynette. She was a vulnerable woman, and I know how charming Felix can be. The fact that he's always shirked his responsibility to Talia has been one of the hardest things to cope with. Family is so important, and Talia is such a beautiful young girl. I hope we can build up some kind of relationship, even if she never finds out the truth.'

'I think,' Catherine said gently, 'that you're a pretty amazing woman.'

For a moment Ginny looked like her old self. 'Felix has ruined my life for too long,' she said determinedly. 'I won't let him go on doing it.'

The sunset that night was later remembered as one of the most spectacular ever seen over Beeversham. Heavenly red skies were streaked with orange and purple. Underneath, the lights from the town twinkled like a thousand fireflies.

Up at Ridings, the atmosphere had become decidedly mellow. Vanessa and Dylan swayed gently in front of the soulful singer. Amanda and Henry were smooching on a sunlounger, prompting loud retches from a horrified

Olympia. Sukie and Eddie lay curled around each other on the grass.

Fleur found her dad and Beau talking intently in the kitchen.

'What are you two plotting this time?'

'Nothing you need to worry about,' Robert told her.

'Come on.' Beau took her hand. 'Let's go and say thank you to our guests for coming.'

The singer graciously stepped down to allow Beau and Fleur to step up on the platform. Beau slid his arm round Fleur's narrow shoulders and waited for the conversation to die down. Ginny and Lynette stopped chatting and turned round.

'Guys, it's been great to see so many of you today. I know it's been a slightly difficult day for some of us under the circumstances . . .' He gave Ginny a stoic grin '. . . but I hope you've all enjoyed yourselves.'

'Not half!' shouted a blotto Mr Patel.

Everyone laughed. Beau grinned and lifted his glass. 'I'd like to dedicate this night to new beginnings.'

'To new beginnings,' they all chorused.

'I have one final toast,' Beau continued. 'To the beautiful girl standing next to me.' He turned to Fleur. 'To Fleur Blackwater, my future wife.'

'I didn't know you were engaged!' cried a delighted Ginny.

'We're not yet.' Beau didn't take his eyes off Fleur's face. 'Would you do me the honour?'

Fleur went into shock. 'You're asking me to marry you?'

'Ask her properly!' Mrs Patel ordered.

Beau grinned, but Fleur could feel his hand trembling.

'I've loved you since the moment I first saw you covered in cow gunk,' he told her. 'My darling, gorgeous, spirited girl, will you do me the honour of becoming my wife?'

Mr Patel burst into tears. Fleur wasn't far behind.

'I will,' she sobbed, covering Beau's face in kisses. 'Oh yes, I will!'

Acknowledgements

A huge thank you to political supremo Toby Mason for his time and patience. Also to Caroline Maudlin, Nadine Dorries MP and Ghislain Pascal. I'd also like to thank Jess Morgan for her farming expertise, Dan Caunt for the cuisine, DS Helen Rance, Roamy Horton, Gill Linley, Cotswold tour guide Julian Linley and Katrina Kutchinsky. A massive thanks to the brilliant Transworld team: Cat Cobain, Sophie Wilson, Sarah Adams, Katy Loftus and Lucy Pinney. All mistakes are my own. The characters and plot are entirely fictional and bear no truth to real life!

Finally, eternal gratitude to my agent Amanda Preston. And to all my lovely readers out there.

Country Pursuits

JO CARNEGIE

The gorgeous women of Churchminster know exactly
what they want – a constant flow of champagne and the
love of a good man. But faced with the likes of beer-
guzzling farmer Angus, foul-tempered Sir Fraser and
conceited banker Sebastian, their attentions are drawn to
more *attractive* possibilities . . .

Meanwhile, when a part of their beloved village comes
under threat from a villainous property developer,
the villagers are united by a different kind of passion.
Can they raise enough money to save Churchminster?
Will Mick Jagger turn up to the charity ball?
Will good (sex) overcome bad?

**Introducing a glamorous and unforgettable cast,
Country Pursuits is Jo Carnegie's raunchy, rip-roaring,
gloriously romantic début.**

'Pacy, racy and enormous fun!'
TASMINA PERRY

'Carnegie gives Jilly Cooper a run for her money . . . A racy read
that'll have you snorting with laughter'
Glamour

Naked Truths

JO CARNEGIE

'Steamy, romantic and hiliarious'
TILLY BAGSHAWE

Newly-weds Caro and Benedict have swapped country life in
Churchminster for an exclusive London mews. It's blissful…
until Benedict's sister arrives, bringing with her a dangerous secret.

Fashionable **socialite Saffron** lives next door. She always thought
the countryside was boring, but when she's invited to Churchminster
she is shocked to learn just how *dirty* rural life can get.

Saffron's boss, **workaholic editor Catherine Connor**, is fighting
to save her ailing magazine. But her scandalous past threatens
to destroy everything, especially when rugged builder
John Milton strides into her life.

'Perfect for the plane or beach, I couldn't put it down!'
LORRAINE KELLY

Wild Things

JO CARNEGIE

Lights, camera, SCANDAL!

Meet the glamorous cast of Wild Things:

Sophia – the leading lady who gets what she wants.
And she wants

Jed – the village's gorgeous gardener, living with
devoted girlfriend

Camilla – sweet-natured and desperate for a baby,
unlike her sister

Calypso – fiercely ambitious, and unimpressed by the
penetrating gaze of

Rafe – dashing leading man, who quickly wins over
Calypso's grandmother

Clementine – whose only desire is for them all to go
away, so Churchminster can win 'Britain's Best Village'!

'Carnegie gives Jilly Cooper a run for her money'
Glamour

Horse Play

JO CARNEGIE

Churchminster village – picturesque, quaint, sleepy – OR NOT ...

A place where women know exactly what they want, and it's not cream tea with the vicar.

A place where anything can happen ... so be careful what you wish for.

And a place where the men had better behave ... because the ladies won't take it lying down (well, not unless they want to!)

'The new SATC (Sex and the Countryside)'
heat